A Stop in the Park

A Novel by

Peggy Panagopoulos Strack

Library of Congress Control Number: 2012906259
CreateSpace, North Charleston, SC

For My Family With Love,
Mom (Carol), Dad (Jim)
Cathy, Nick, John
Max, Greg
&
Keith

"Don't die with your music still inside you. Listen to your intuitive inner voice and find what passion stirs your soul."

- Wayne Dyer -

Margaret,
Thanks for being part of my beginning! enjoy!
Peggy

Chapter One

Michael Stolis glanced at his watch. His boss rambled on about growth figures and pulled out a stack of documents. This gathering was going to drag on for hours. He couldn't call Jamie and cancel their plans once again. So, Michael lied about having a phone conference with a money-spinning account, stuffed the packet of information into his briefcase, promised to review it over the weekend and hustled out of the conference room. The elevator was clogged with people, so he headed straight for the stairwell, ran down twelve flights, and emerged into the parking garage. When he reached his car, he took a deep breath. Hopefully, the traffic wouldn't be too bad.

What was he thinking? Of course the traffic would be bad on a Friday afternoon in DC. Three minutes into his commute, Michael slammed on the brakes of his BMW coupe then pounded the horn. The driver in front of him threw his hands up, turned and shouted some vulgarity. Michael clenched his fist then gave him the one finger salute. The asshole had plenty of time to make the green light but decided to take a nap in the middle of rush hour. Shaking his head, he glanced at the clock on the dash and groaned. It was nearly five, and he had dinner reservations at six. An invigorating shower was officially off the docket.

"Damn it," he shouted. His aggravation level was increasing, but yelling wasn't the answer to his predicament. If he came home fuming, his role as husband might be over for good. The warning had been given, the counseling had begun and the prescription for healing a crumbling marriage had been written.

Michael had anger management issues according to his psychologist and his wife, Jamie, strongly agreed. After their session on Monday, Dr. McCormack handed him a pamphlet delineating eight techniques that would help prevent outbursts. It was hard to believe that these simple tools would kill the agitation that ate away at his insides. Could a few sentences in a neatly folded brochure really abolish the stress of twelve-hour workdays and chaotic nights at home? Probably not, but right now they were all he had. He rapped his thigh as he tried to recall one of them. Oh yeah, if he acted nice, he would eventually become nice and before long it would be part of his persona. He cleared his throat, practiced smiling, glanced at the rearview mirror and rated it as almost genuine. It wasn't working. The knot that made a home in his stomach tightened.

Some time to unwind would help. He left the office early just to make that happen but not early enough to beat the traffic, and Michael hated traffic more than crowded bike paths and long lines. He released an audible laugh. Why then was he living in DC?

Michael wondered how he landed in this political pressure cooker as he waited at another red light. He had simply followed the instructions for a successful life that were hammered into him by his father—that included graduating from George Washington Law School seventeen years ago and becoming an attorney at prestigious firm. On top of that, Michael was married to a beautiful journalist, ran in marathons, owned a brownstone in Georgetown, and had two healthy daughters; yet he was miserable. Life had handed him a cup of cheer, but he didn't like the taste. *Too bad*, he mused. It was the only life he had, and he needed to make it work.

The congestion finally dissipated and Michael drove down the tree-lined brick street where his Federal-style home welcomed him. When the driveway came into view, he couldn't make himself pull in. Behind the front door, the TV would be blaring, the kids would be bickering and Jamie would be blasting her iPod in the kitchen. He just knew it. He let the car idle in front of the house and sat as still as a frozen tree branch, not sure what to do. If he went inside, he'd explode.

Michael rested his cheek in his palm as he thought about how this sanctuary used to quiet his hyperactive nerves. In the old days, he would wait hours before turning on the television or making a phone call, savoring the quiet. The sage and cream walls and cathedral ceilings calmed him. Before he knew it the frenzy from his work day would disappear.

Staring at his residence, Michael recalled the satisfaction he felt after signing the mortgage agreement. Although he had been having trouble finding the perfect house, this one murmured, "Buy me," whenever he passed it on the way to his studio apartment. At first he ignored the call because the seven-figure price tag and mega property taxes terrified him. One Sunday, out of curiosity, he stopped in during an open house, and his urge to buy it intensified. Built in the eighteenth century, it had been remodeled several times but still had many of its original features—bay windows, oval rooms and detailed crown molding—and it was one of the few houses in Georgetown that had a garage. He made a low-ball offer and was shocked when the sellers accepted it.

Upon his entrance, Michael would remove his suit jacket and hang it in the closet. He hated the sight of clothes strewn on the banister intruding on the richness of its cherry wood or casually draped on the art deco table that he was lucky enough to have found at an estate sale. A replica of *Fisherman's Cottage on the Cliffs at Varengeville*, his favorite Monet masterpiece, hung in the foyer, greeting him each evening. He would stare at it, imagining a man coming into his house after a day of triumphs and struggles at sea to this cabin of solace that was the centerpiece of the ocean landscape.

Jamie had insisted on removing the table and print when they married. She replaced his treasures with a shelf and a panel of hooks. When he objected, she complained that she needed to make her new residence more comfortable. He surrendered to this and other changes because he didn't want to agree to her suggestion that they search for a new home as a couple. In retrospect, they should have. Jamie's zest started to diminish once she moved in. She occasionally confessed that she still felt like the house belonged to him even after he added her name to the deed.

Now that they had two daughters, the days of finding peace in his castle were over. The entry was usually covered with an array of kid paraphernalia. The line of clutter continued from the ceramic tile of the main hall to the wood floors that ran through the remainder of the house. So instead of leaving the frenzied day behind him at the front door, the chaos continued in an endless twenty-four hour cycle.

A car horn beeped from behind jolting Michael out of his stupor. He still couldn't make himself pull into the driveway. All he needed was a few minutes of quiet, so he drove around the corner and parked on O Street. He sent Jamie a text message, saying he'd be home soon, then hopped out of his car. He unlatched the black iron fence that surrounded the backyard and hustled to the basement door.

Michael stepped inside the dingy space and pulled a string to turn on the ceiling light. His old guitar case welcomed him. A sense of calm flooded his insides. Like a boy who spotted a tire swing dangling from a tree near a river, this instrument summoned him to play. Michael folded his arms. What if someone heard him? He chuckled. The clamor of his household would drown out a herd of elephants parading through the street. No one would detect the humming of a guitar in this hideaway. So, he pulled it out of the case, sat with his back propped against the cold concrete wall, legs outstretched, and played and sang. After several minutes of plucking and strumming, his stress receded.

Michael didn't have the opportunity to visit his version of paradise often and oh how he savored the time spent in this dungeon making music. Once, he thought about bringing his guitar upstairs to play for his family, but it might ruin the pleasure, and he wasn't willing to take that risk. Megan and Emily would think it was a chore to turn off the TV just to listen to their father serenade them. And if he belted out songs in the bedroom, Jamie would complain that he was avoiding family obligations. So like a rare vacation, he came to this underground world only when he was in desperate need of rejuvenation.

A busy night lay ahead and Michael hoped the ten-minute break would be enough to prevent an outburst later on. He leaned forward. The thought of climbing up the stairs into reality caused the ogre who lived inside him to stir. "Damn it," he whispered.

What else could he do to make sure this outing with his family went smoothly? He committed a corporate sin and silenced his BlackBerry. Now the warden he called boss couldn't bother him. Michael gave himself two thumbs up for that brilliant idea.

As he placed the guitar back in its case, he tried to think of a way to proceed differently with the evening plans. Michael's inability to tolerate common earthly occurrences like excess noise, crowds, and waits was always at the root of his melt-downs, but he wasn't a wizard and couldn't make those annoyances disappear. He straightened the knot of his tie. It was a sunny late-summer day. Maybe it would be fun to stop at a park before the restaurant. That was it. He phoned Henry's Steakhouse and switched the reservation to seven thirty.

Michael popped up, pleased with his idea. He left the cellar, brushed off his suit with his hands, hopped back into his car, drove around the corner, and into the driveway. He climbed the front steps then took a deep breath before opening the door. A Barbie doll, sneakers, barrettes, a large pink ball and, of course, the blaring of the TV greeted him when he entered the hallway. As he was just about to shout, "Turn that damn thing off," he bit his tongue. It would not be a good way to start the weekend. Michael walked around the mess, put his briefcase in the closet and tightened his lips when Jamie shouted, "Glad you're home. We're going to be late."

He strolled into the kitchen, turned off the iPod dock and put on his well-rehearsed smile. "No we're not. I changed the reservations to seven thirty."

"Seven thirty? The girls need to eat before that."

Michael closed his eyes. He was committed to keeping his cool, but it was hard. There Jamie was rinsing out juice cans from the assortment of recyclables that covered half the quartz countertop. He felt like saying, "Expensive shelf for a garbage display, don't you think?" But he kept his sarcasm to himself. Instead he pleasantly replied, "They can have a little snack. I want to take a wake-up shower; then I thought we'd walk to the restaurant. What a great day, huh?"

Jamie rolled her eyes. "It's kind of far."

Where was that exuberant lady he married? Ten years ago, her eyes would have sparkled as she exclaimed, "Sounds like fun!" She had to be in there somewhere, but he had no idea how to start the search and rescue.

"Not really. The walk will be good for the kids and I need to stretch my legs. I had a long day of meetings." He sat on a stool at the center island and found himself admiring his wife. A pale yellow sundress had replaced her summer uniform of gym shorts and a T-shirt. She looked like the first day of summer. In spite of their many battles, he still loved her. But was love enough? She was so distant lately, and bitchy too. Even in counseling she was quiet or complaining, never coming up with solutions. It was up to him to revitalize this marriage. No time like the present to start.

"You look pretty. Yellow's your color."

She turned off the water, dried her hands on a towel and sat on the stool next to him. "Thanks, but I feel fat. This stupid diet isn't working."

"You always feel fat, but you look great. You're the all-American blue-eyed blonde."

She frowned. "You're just saying that."

He almost touched her wrist but didn't want to feel the rejection if she pulled away. "We've had this conversation about a thousand times, so let's try something different. I'll start over. You look pretty."

Jamie rolled her eyes.

"You're supposed to say, 'Thank you, and for a second I thought you were Adonis.'"

A whisper of a smile crept onto Jamie's face as she surveyed his features. "Adonis is sprouting gray hair and carrying eye bags."

"You missed your line."

"Let's get off the fat and old topic. Not a good way to start a Friday night."

"Agreed."

Jamie shifted in her seat. "I'm having second thoughts about bringing the kids to Henry's for dinner. It's way too fancy. They'd be much happier at Chuck E. Cheese."

Michael threw both hands up. "No way. Remember the last time we went there. My head screamed for three days."

"This is not about you. We're taking Emily out to celebrate finishing her first week of kindergarten."

"I can't do it. I'll explode in there with that giant rat running around—people yelling above those clanging video games."

Jamie sighed. "You don't get kids."

"Maybe not, but they're five and seven now and should be able to sit in a restaurant for an hour. If we walk, they'll be ready for rest and food by the time we get there."

"Your call, but we better move. Can your shower wait?"

"You bet." He grabbed two apples from the fruit bowl on the counter and went into the living room to give them to his daughters. Michael nodded once on the way. There had been a couple of opportunities for an argument to erupt during their conversation, but he stayed calm. Guitar therapy had worked. Then again, why did he care so much? Jamie had turned into a glum ice princess and he really didn't need her sour attitude after a long week. Maybe some time apart would be good. Then he saw the reason he could never let that happen: sprawled out on the living room floor were Megan and Emily.

"How are my little ladies? Time for our big night out."

No response.

He set the apples on the coffee table, picked up the remote control and shut the TV off.

"Dad, we were right in the middle of Dora," Megan whined.

"She'll be back. Where's my hug?"

Emily and Megan rose from their prone positions. He squatted, circled his arms around his girls and kissed their heads.

When he popped back up he said, "You both turned into princesses."

They smiled.

Emily looked adorable with her auburn curls cropped into a bob and a lavender dress garnished with tiny white flowers. Megan's long black hair was pulled into a ponytail and she wore aqua capris and a matching striped top. Michael just hoped their behavior this evening matched their sweet appearance.

He pointed to the apples. "Have a little snack. We're going to walk to the restaurant."

"Is it far?" Emily asked.

"No."

"How long will it take?" Megan asked.

"Not long. It'll be good to get outdoors for a little while."

They didn't respond by jumping up and down, but that was okay. Once they inhaled the fresh air, their enthusiasm would kick in.

Before leaving, Michael stepped into the bathroom, splashed warm water on his face and patted it dry with a towel. He would like nothing more than to strip out of his executive costume, take that long hot shower, throw on some shorts and a T-shirt, crack open a beer on the patio, and delve into the latest George R.R. Martin book he picked up a month ago— maybe munch on some peanuts and order a pizza. He looked at his raccoon eyes in the mirror. Jamie was right. The years were creeping in at an alarming rate, but there was nothing he could do about the tempo of his days. If their children adhered to the plan of good grades and acceptance into a top-notch college, he'd have to run at this pace for at least fifteen more years.

As he locked the front door, he thought about Dupont Circle, a park nestled in the center of four bustling streets. Maybe they'd stop in on their way to the restaurant. Michael used to go there to read when he attended law school, but now only rushed by as he raced from one point to another. It was a place where rich and poor, black and white, straight and gay, adult and child magically stepped out of their worlds and harmoniously gathered for music, games and respite. He glanced down at his family, who were waiting on the side- walk. Yes. Rest a little, enjoy the sights, and maybe—just maybe, he'd get in a game of blitz chess.

Chapter Two

Michael and his family strolled by Dupont Circle around six thirty. Rushing water from the two-tiered Samuel Francis Memorial Fountain cascaded into its white marble basin. It sounded like a babbling brook inviting people who passed to come in and leave the hustle of DC behind. A guitarist entertained a small crowd, a juggler tried his best to keep three oranges aloft, and at least fifty people relaxed on benches. He then spotted a magician performing tricks with a long, multicolored scarf.

He stopped walking. "Hey, do you want to see a magic show?"

"Where?" Megan asked.

Michael pointed to the performer. "Right there."

"Can we?" Emily asked excitedly.

"Do we have time?" Jamie said.

Michael looked at her sullen face, tapped his watch, and tried to mask his growing exasperation with a tight-lipped smile. "We have an hour until our reservation, and Henry's is only three blocks away."

Jamie shrugged, took Emily and Megan's hands, and trudged toward the magician.

Michael glanced at the stone game tables on the other side of the park. "While you guys enjoy the show, I think I'll see if anyone needs a chess partner."

Jamie shook her head and quietly said, "You had this whole thing planned, didn't you?"

"What do you mean?"

"Getting us here, so you could play chess."

He sighed. "It wasn't a manipulative ploy, but on the way over I did think about hanging out at the circle for a little while and playing some chess. Is that a crime?"

She waved him off. "Go on. Have your fun. We'll be over in fifteen minutes."

Michael's back stiffened as soon as Jamie's glare pierced him. Had it been fifteen minutes already? He didn't think so, but her eyes were telling him it was time to go. If he ignored the frigid invasion, maybe it would subside and melt away. Regardless, he was not going to let her visual assault influence his actions. It was the same look his father used to give him when he read a science fiction novel instead of a textbook. That man controlled his every move as a kid, and now his adult life was under surveillance. There was nothing wrong with what he was doing back then, and there was nothing wrong with taking a moment to play chess in the park. When he was ready to leave, he would walk over to Jamie, smile, and maybe say, "Thanks for letting me take a timeout from life in the fast lane." After ten years of dancing

12

in this marriage tango, he knew when to dip, turn, and twist most of the time—well, some of the time. Just like the game he was about to conquer, he could figure out the moves he needed to make.

His heartbeat quickened as he prepared for battle. Even the late-summer breeze didn't subdue the adrenaline rush. He had five minutes to wipe out his opponent's board, and the pressure made his hands quiver. Attack, think, take it, one more, retreat, he got me, go, just do it. In an instant, his king was robbed. Michael sprang to his feet and groaned as if someone had just ripped a Band-Aid off his skin. He looked at the clock, saw that there was time to spare, pounded his fist on the concrete table, and yelped, "Damn."

In the midst of his loser's convulsion, he glanced at his opponent. His eyebrows arched, and he wore an impish grin. Michael dropped his arms to his side, cleared his throat, and sat back down.

"That was entertaining," his foe said with a nod.

Michael rapped his fingers on the table. "It was a good game."

The man's eyes widened. "I meant you. Losing's not your thing?"

Michael shrugged. "Never cared much for it."

"Well, let's see what we can do about that. Time for one more?"

"You want to play me again?"

"Sure."

Michael was stunned. When it came to competition, most people ran away from him like they were being chased by a Rottweiler. He studied the man's wrinkles, which curled up along with his lips and eyes. Michael guessed he was in his late sixties. Someone that relaxed had to be retired.

After all, this wasn't a typical chess game. At Dupont Circle, blitz chess ruled. Each player had five minutes to defeat his adversary. Moves were rapid, and the enthusiasts who engaged in this mind sport reveled in the exhilaration. The pressure began when the clock signaled *Go* and escalated until a suicide move was made or time ran out. Blitz chess called for urgent fingers. This fellow hadn't heard. His hands glided over the board like a stone skipping over a placid pond, yet he won.

"Michael?" Jamie interrupted.

He squeezed the arch of his nose then looked at her. "We have time. I'm gonna play one more game."

She folded her arms.

The chess wizard looked at him, signaling that it was time for business. Michael nodded, hit the timer, and transferred the pieces around and off the board, but he lost again. His knuckles bent into a claw, and he almost gouged his thighs.

"A frosty mug of beer!"

The image of this treat popped into Michael's head, and his fingers never reached his legs. Why hadn't his counselor told him about this trick?

"That one always works," the man said, as he raised his pointer finger.

Michael's eyes widened, and the corners of his lips lifted. It felt good to truly smile. Sure he lost, but he was enjoying himself, and that was as rare as a solid night's sleep.

He had to figure out a way to get over here more often. The circle wasn't far from his house, but his calendar was so crammed, and recreational outings didn't exist on his priority list. The stone tables and benches were crowded with mostly men engaged in chess play, and Michael had a sudden urge to be part of this gang.

Now that he had been lured in by this chap, he didn't want to leave. Not only was the chess alluring, but he was curious about the man who challenged him, the man who was humiliating him. To Michael, most humans were similar to mosquitoes in July. If he wanted to get outdoors and enjoy the sunny warm days, he had to put up with these pests. This guy was different. He had a good feeling in his presence, and needed to find out why.

"How about I buy you a Coke and a bite for allowing me to play with one of the Dupont greats?" Michael offered, pointing to a nearby vendor.

"I'll take the Coke, but will pass on the bite. Got dinner plans."

"You do?" Michael responded, as he tapped his thumbs together. He had guessed his rival was among the DC down-and-out simply because that was the reputation earned by the Dupont Circle chess wizards. He remembered reading an article about it in the *Post*. The discreet entrepreneurs charged individuals for blitz chess lessons, game time, and interviews. Some even participated in tournaments, where they were often victorious. It was their way of earning the cash needed to survive in the world. The absence of dollar talk and refusal of free food told him that this particular player was in a league of his own.

The stranger wore a plaid button-down shirt that was tucked into relatively new blue jeans, with a belt keeping everything neatly in place. His cushioned, navy walking shoes were spotless and seemed to wrap his feet with comfort. Michael was envious of the man's tidy and relaxed style. Looking at this guy made him want to jump out of his silver-gray designer suit, stiff white shirt, and black leather shoes, which were causing his feet to sweat.

As he and his opponent rose from the table, Jamie began to move toward them. Michael faced her as soon as she took a step. Before she uttered a word, he said, "I'm going to grab a soda, and then we'll head on down for dinner."

Jamie's lower lip protruded.

"I'll only be a few minutes. Walk three times around the circle. Watch the juggler or whatever; then we'll roll."

He turned before he could see her reaction. She wouldn't try to stop him. Jamie saved her rants for home, and if she was still mad when they got there, he'd escape her wrath by hopping in the shower. When he got out, she'd be off chatting in cyberspace. After all, the counselor did tell them that they would still have rocky times, but things would slowly get better if they followed his advice. This would just be one of those rocky times, and he'd read that happy marriage pamphlet in the morning.

Michael caught up to his rival, who was already stationed at the vendor. The man turned and handed him a can of soda.

"Hey, loser always buys," Michael said.

The man chuckled. "You'll get another chance. By the way I'm Rufus Williams."

Michael momentarily grimaced then said, "Michael Stolis." After shaking hands, he started his investigation. "You're awesome at chess. Where'd you learn to play like that?"

"My granddad taught me when I was a boy. We'd spend hours in the evening or on the weekend glued to the board. Cold lemonade or hot chocolate right by our side, dependin' on the temperature. Many good times with chess, and they continue in this park with nice folks like you."

Michael felt like he had been jabbed in the gut. Tinkering the day away engaged in a game seemed strange to him, but so appealing. The vision of a boy and his grandfather huddled over a chessboard suddenly made him feel like he had been denied something special. Sure, he had played chess on teams, with timers and coaches pressuring him, but amenities like seasonal drinks and gentle laughs were never there. He wasn't sure why he sensed a heaviness behind his eyes but ignored the physical sensation and cleared the swelling from his throat.

"How much do you play?"

"Quite a bit. Come down to the circle in the late afternoon, and I usually end up on the bench with the board in front of me, and well…game time."

"Do you ever lose?"

"On occasion. The regulars here present quite a challenge."

Michael frowned. He was not among the challenging players being referred to. "What's your strategy?"

"Don't know."

"Oh come on. You have a strategy."

"No, I don't. Just look at the board and make the right move. Pretty simple."

"Man! Do you play in tournaments? I've read in the *Post* that the seasoned Dupont crew can really clean up at those events."

17

"Naw. Don't care much for tournaments. All that waiting around. Not much time for playing."

"But you'd win with your skills."

"Don't care about winning."

"You've got to care about winning. That's why you play."

"Nope. Winning just happens. I play for fun. My grand-dad and I would hoot and howl when the match was finally over. Never really mattered who won."

"Michael, we really have to go. The girls are hungry," Jamie interrupted.

After a few seconds of silence, Rufus looked at Jamie then back at Michael. "Out for dinner with your family? It sounds like you better move. Kids can get quite cranky when they're running on empty."

Michael contemplated the thought of his two daughters cranky at Henry's Steakhouse. He'd have a prime rib that could be cut with a spoon sitting in front of him with the whining of his children as background music. The all-too-familiar feeling of tension escalated in his body, causing his left eye to twitch. He checked his watch and walked over to Jamie.

"It's seven, and it'll only take us ten minutes to get there. We have plenty of time."

"Fine."

He rubbed his forehead. Why couldn't she find a way to amuse herself? Blowing off his agitation with a quick shiver, Michael chose to spend another five minutes chatting with this congenial man. He approached Rufus, who was walking toward the chess tables.

"You're back," Rufus said. "What about dinner?"

"Our reservation isn't until seven thirty, and the fresh air is good for the kids. We're going to Henry's to celebrate the completion of my younger daughter's first week of kindergarten," Michael said, immediately regretting his words. He couldn't imagine why this guy would care about his kid and her school.

"My my—kindergarten," Rufus said, as he shook his head. "I can still remember my first day—my mom walking me to school and leaving me in this strange place. I was so scared that she wouldn't come back, but of course she did. When I got home, she made my favorite grilled cheese sandwich and tomato soup lunch. Now how did your daughter do?"

Michael tilted his head. He got bored when people talked about their kids, but this man seemed sincerely interested. The chess whiz also recalled the grilled cheese sandwich and tomato soup that his mom made for him after his first day of school. Emily wouldn't remember this celebration dinner, which would cost a minimum of two hundred dollars, one week from now. "She did great, and thanks for asking," Michael answered.

As rushed as he felt, he could not force himself away from the conversation. Not only did he admire this man's chess skills, but his demeanor exuded serenity, and Michael wanted some of it. He gazed at him like a detective trying to solve a mystery. Rufus's skin was a mahogany shade of brown, and he had a short Afro that was a mixture of black and gray. He smiled and laughed often with sincerity, not like the people who wore those plastic grins and nodded at everything you said as if they were programmed robots. Michael wanted to ask him what his medication cocktail consisted of; he might seek the same prescription. As hard as it was to believe, it was evident that the chess wizard's effervescent character did not come from a bottle.

"You said you have dinner plans. Any place special?" Michael asked.

"Oh yeah! A deli called Sam's, in the Mount Pleasant area. Sam makes the best roast beef I've ever tasted. Now, that's not saying much because I don't dine out often, but Sam has a secret that keeps me coming back."

"I love roast beef!"

"Then you'd love Sam's. You see, I walk into his deli and tell him to slice me up his finest, and he knows exactly what I mean. He takes out—must be a ten-pound hunk of beef that's pink, not brown, not red, but pink all the way through. Don't know how he manages that. Then he puts it on his slicer and starts to carve me a delicacy of delicacies. When it gets to the half-pound mark, Sam takes my little bit of heaven and wraps it up in white paper; but no red leaks through, you see, because the beef is just the right pink. Then I pick myself up a loaf of rye bread that Sam's wife, Becky, bakes onsite. It's cut a little thicker than the kind you find at the grocery. I usually take one of Becky's specialties too—an extra big chocolate chip cookie, especially if they've just popped out of the oven."

Michael couldn't help but smile as he watched this man whose gestures and facial expressions matched the narration of his simple story.

"I order whatever salad Sam made that day and make sure that he hasn't forgotten the pickle. Say, 'Sam, you remembered the pickle?' And he says, 'When have I ever forgotten, Rufus, you old hound.' I reply, 'Just making sure.' Eating that sandwich without the pickle would be like eating a hot fudge sundae without the nuts—no way I'm gonna do that. I take my king's meal home, wrap up the cookie in foil, put it in the oven on warm so the chips stay in their slightly melted state, then I go to work on my sandwich. Now, you're in a hurry, otherwise I'd tell you how to create the most mouth-watering event you've ever experienced."

Michel squinted as he listened to this tale of a roast beef sandwich and licked his upper lip. "Who's in a hurry? Keep going."

"Are you sure?"

Michael glanced around the park and saw Jamie, Megan, and Emily tossing coins into the fountain. Michael pointed at them. "They're having fun."

Rufus shrugged. "I'll give you the short version, although people tell me I don't know the meaning of that word—*short*." He continued, "First I mix up some mayo, catsup, relish, horseradish, and a pinch of salt and pepper—maybe a shake of cayenne if I'm in the mood. Never measure, so it's always a bit different. I like that. Then I spread the dressing on the two slices of bread and let it soak in. I get a tomato—has to be from the farmer's market, just ripened—cut one slice, real thin: don't want it to take over the flavor of the roast beef. Next I get one piece of dark green lettuce and one piece of deli-fresh Swiss cheese—again very thin. I get a plate, put the bread on it, and begin the layering process. First goes the lettuce, then the tomato, then the star of the sandwich, the roast beef—slice by slice, the whole half pound. I cover it with the cheese, put the bread on top, and garnish with the salad and pickle. Get myself a tall glass of ice water, not a flavored drink as it would intrude on the taste of the food. I can't stand that. Cut the sandwich right down the middle and sit at my kitchen table, open wide, and think, my life is good."

Saliva crept onto the corners of Michael's mouth as he envisioned the culinary masterpiece. He swallowed hard. "Where's Sam's?"

"On New York Avenue, three blocks over from the zoo—been there for years."

"I'm gonna check it out," Michael said.

"Tell Sam that Rufus sent you, and he'll take care of you. Tell him I said, 'Don't forget the pickle.' It'll make him chuckle. Always good if you can make someone chuckle when the opportunity comes about."

"I'll do that," Michael said, as he pondered the idea of making someone chuckle.

Emily tugged at his suit jacket. "Come on, Daddy. I'm hungry."

"I really have to go," Michael said, as he patted Emily's head.

"Yes, you do. It's Michael Stolis, right?"

"Good memory. What's yours again?"

"Rufus. Rufus Williams. I hope to play chess with you soon, and I mean that. Now, you enjoy that special dinner with your family."

"Thanks. I'll look for you again and see if I can break your winning streak."

"Won't mind if you do, but I'm not giving it to you."

Michael nodded, knowing that he had just been hooked into more games.

He took Emily's hand and walked over to the fountain, where Jamie and Megan waited. He almost apologized for making them wait so long but decided against it because he really wasn't sorry. Dupont Circle was bursting with entertainment, and there was nothing wrong with hanging out for a little while. What was the hurry? Dash off to dinner, devour it so the girls don't become uninterested in the restaurant, then rush back home so everyone can take their places: Emily and Megan in front of the television; Jamie ogling the computer screen; and him upstairs in bed scanning fifteen hundred channels of digital cable, unsuccessfully seeking something of interest to watch until sleep set in. Ever since Jamie told him she was considering a trial separation, he'd been walking on eggshells, and he was tired of it.

Michael stuffed his hands in his pockets. He had trouble believing that a thirty-minute stop—well, maybe forty minutes—in Dupont Circle would make Jamie's mood curdle. She said she wanted to work on their marriage but sure wasn't acting like it. So instead of expressing regret, Michael surveyed Jamie's brooding face and took another deep breath.

Chapter Three

They arrived at the restaurant before Jamie had a chance to tell Michael to go to hell. She'd just love to do that. The circular driveway in front was bustling with cars, however, and she had to get her daughters safely to the entrance.

"Give me your hands," she said, then helped Megan and Emily maneuver their way through the people and traffic. Michael opened the door for them. As Jamie passed him, she winced.

Michael looked away.

She tried to release her aggravation by pulling on her hair ends, but it didn't do the trick. This night was for Emily, but Michael turned it into something he would enjoy. Now the girls were tired and irritable, and she'd have to do her best to salvage the remainder of the evening. Some prince her husband turned about to be—nothing like the men promised to her in the tales she read as a child.

Sulking was not an option right now, so Jamie did what she always had done. She tucked her disenchantment into that secret closet deep inside her and closed the door. She'd deal with it some other time. The only problem was her internal space was bulging and begging for an expansion. She thought about cleaning it out but feared what the cobwebs and their weaving spiders would do to her. Until she summoned up the courage for such risky exploration, she'd deal with the frustration by eating a chocolate bar after everyone went to bed, scanning her Facebook account to see if any new and interesting characters had invited her to be a friend, or maybe phone a comrade so they could commiserate about their tiresome partners. She had plenty of avoidance strategies that kept her life from collapsing. Tonight she'd choose Facebook. Her clothes were getting far too tight for candy, and she didn't want Michael to overhear a husband bitch session. That would really set him off. Maybe she'd be daring and take the cyber-chat she was having with that hunky tennis pro to a new level. He did create a private room just for her, and it was fun to go in and play. Why not live a little?

As they waited to be seated, Jamie peered at Michael, who stood a few feet from her. There he was, hands in his pockets, tapping his foot. He was the picture of neurotic, resembling a before scene in an advertisement for Xanax. Even that lush, dark hair against his Mediterranean skin could not melt the loathing. His classic good looks, false charm, and fat status had lured her in a long time ago, and she would not let that happen again. Her eyes felt heavy as she recalled the intense love she used to feel for him. What a hoax. Sure, they were in counseling and supposedly trying to work on things, but for her it was just another charade. She would like nothing more than to divorce that man. At this point, however, she didn't have a job and didn't want to be a part-time mom while her kids spent half their lives with Michael. Megan and Emily were not going to be shuttled between two homes, never knowing where they belonged. She'd grown up like that and hated it.

Suddenly Michael's gaze caught hers. She took one step back. Those thoroughbred eyes used to be so alert, so exhilarating, so intense. They once arrested her but were now sinking into a black lagoon. He had complained of fatigue, but this was the first time she really noticed it. Jamie wanted to feel compassion. A good wife would nurture her husband after a stressful workweek. Jamie clicked her nails. She really didn't know how to be a good wife. The only time she'd seen one was on the Brady Bunch, and yes, Carol Brady would have soothed her man. Guilt was sneaking in, so she shifted her focus to a woman already seated who was cutting her steak. From this angle, it looked delicious.

"Right this way," the host said.

Michael lightly touched Jamie's elbow as they moved through the restaurant. The feeling of his fingers on her skin made her flinch. He must have sensed her tension and dropped his hand. Smooth jazz and the chatter of people unwinding in anticipation of a night out filled her ears. The pleasant sounds helped her relax, and by the time they reached the table, she was actually humming along with the music. She had to perk up if only for Megan and Emily. Jamie also couldn't deny that Michael was at least trying to manage his temper, and as hard as it was, she should act civil toward him. Soon she'd tell him to take an entire weekend for himself. Go up to Bethany

Beach in Delaware and rest. The break would be good for both of them. With that, she blinked hard, smoothed out her dress, and decided to start the night over. By the time she sat down, she almost smiled.

"It's so beautiful here," Jamie said.

Michael's face brightened. "I knew you'd like it."

She grinned.

"And look at Megan," Michael said.

Megan shook out a red cloth napkin and delicately placed it on her lap. Emily immediately imitated her big sister.

"They look like miniature socialites," Jamie giggled.

A waiter, who looked like a lumberjack in a tux, set a cutting board displaying a golden loaf of Italian bread on the table. "Welcome. Are you ladies ready for a show?" he said, addressing Megan and Emily.

The girls nodded with open mouths.

The waiter shook a few drops of balsamic vinegar onto a plate of olive oil that was in the center of the table. He swirled it around, told Megan to break off a piece of the bread and dip it into the vinaigrette, then did the same for Emily.

After the girls thanked him, Emily said, "I don't even have to use a knife!"

"Not here," Michael said, breaking off a piece. He looked up at the waiter. "Can you bring two Sprites with cherries?"

"Anything to drink for the adults?"

"Just water for now," Jamie said.

"Me too." Michael steadied his gaze on Jamie. "See, they're doing fine in a real restaurant."

"I guess." She smiled at her daughters, who were tearing off pieces of bread and dipping them into the dressing as if it were a game.

28

Like an Italian chef, Michael lightly kissed his piece and said, "Magnifico!" before biting into it.

Maybe—stop. Michael was behaving right now, but a jockey doesn't snap his whip when the horse is performing perfectly. Jamie was certain his tongue would lash out if provoked—like a few weeks ago when they took the girls out for lunch and a movie at the mall. He didn't reprimand Emily for picking the cheese off her pizza slice, which surprised Jamie. Then he bought the girls ice cream sandwiches at the theater. For heaven's sake, Michael even rooted for Lightning in *Cars 2*, whispering, "Go...go...go." Before they went home, however, Jamie wanted to stop in a sporting goods store to buy a pedometer. The line was too long for Michael's three-minute-wait rule, and he started jiggling the keys in his pocket. When they finally reached the register, the clerk asked them to open a charge account so they could save fifteen percent. Michael abruptly said no. The woman then tried to sell them insurance for the device. Michael shouted, "I'm not buying insurance for a damn fifteen-dollar step counter." The clerk startled, and customers stared. Michael tried to convince Jamie that he had just spoken firmly, but she wasn't stupid. Jamie recognized shouting when she heard it.

The waiter returned with the sodas and set them on the table. Megan reached into her glass, plucked out a cherry, and popped it into her mouth. Emily imitated her big sister, but with more pizzazz. She swung the cheery around by the stem, tossed it in the air, and tried to catch it with her mouth. In the middle of the circus act, her elbow knocked over the drink, and it spilled on her dress. Emily cried, "My soda."

Jamie sprang up. "It's okay. We'll get you another one."

Emily cried louder, "My dress—it's wet."

Jamie glanced at Michael out of the corner of her eye. He was clutching a spoon.

Megan shook her finger at Emily. "You need to be more careful."

Jamie wished she could snap her fingers and disappear, but that was not an option. Time to step into her role as peacemaker. She took Emily's hand and signaled Megan to come along with her eyes.

"Stop crying, Emily, or no TV when you get home. It was just a little accident," Jamie said in her firm-mother voice.

"I'll try," Emily whimpered.

Jamie then directed her attention to Michael. "Go to the men's room and do some deep breathing."

"I'm fine."

Jamie leaned in. "Dr. McCormack said that you should take a small walk and breathe deeply when you're about to blow up."

"I'm fine, Jamie."

"No, you're not. You're choking that spoon."

Michael glanced at his fist, dropped the spoon, and turned away.

She faced the girls. "Let's go look at that aquarium up front, and Daddy will order you the best cheeseburgers ever. Then, if you're really good during dinner, maybe he'll get us a cab, so we don't have to walk home." She shot Michael her don't-you-dare-argue glare.

"Good idea," he wisely responded.

"Order me a Chardonnay and salmon for dinner. Make sure my salmon is grilled and that the salad dressing is fat free and on the side."

As she escorted her daughters to the fish tank, she couldn't help but hope that Michael really was learning to manage his anger. Except for some excess body tension, he did sail through this debacle with repose.

Michael gaped at his family as they departed. They just left him alone at a table for four. He picked up the spoon and rapped it on the table. He took one breath then shook his head. It wasn't working. He needed more than cleansing breaths to kill his agitation. That damn generic anger management program was a sham. He would bet a day as a couch potato that Dr. McCormack handed out the same pamphlet to every fool who walked into his office. The rapping of his spoon quickened. His teeth were clenched so tightly that it felt like they were wired together with steel. The waiter appeared at the table.

"Is everything all right?"

Michael dropped the spoon, laced his fingers together, and tried to fake a smile, but his lips wouldn't budge. He hissed, "Everything's fine. My daughter just spilled her soda."

The robust man bent over and furrowed his eyebrows. "No problem. I'll get her another." His concerned gaze deepened. "Are you okay?"

Michael held up his hand. "I'm fine."

"Can I get you sparkling spring water? A cold beer?"

"A cold beer sounds good. The darkest ale you have on tap."

The waiter straightened then took out his pen and pad. "Would you like to order now, so the children don't have to wait long when they return?"

Michael nodded and specified the menu items that would soon be delivered. After the waiter departed, Michael found himself thinking about the roast beef sandwich that the old chess whiz described. For some reason it distracted him from his angst. Too bad it wasn't on the menu here. Prime rib would have to suffice. His shoulders dropped. He had just dodged another outburst, thank God. He covered his mouth with his hands. What was wrong with him? Would he have to live like a hotdog sizzling on a grill for the rest of his life?

The waiter placed a chilled pint glass of beer in front of him. As he sipped it, he spotted Jamie at the aquarium several yards away. He wondered why she always had to alter her restaurant selections so that her meal contained the fewest calories possible. It had been so long since he heard her say, "I'll have a T-bone steak, baked potato with extra sour cream, and make sure to put lots of blue cheese dressing on my salad." She used to take such pleasure in occasional food splurges, and it was fun to eat with her. Now, she was obsessed with losing the fifteen pounds that never came off after Emily was born.

Except for the fact that being lighter might put her in a better mood, he couldn't have cared less about the outcome of her dieting battles. The extra weight was barely noticeable on the five feet six inches of her medium frame. He fixed his eyes on her shoulder-length blond hair that shone like a polished gold coin. Jamie was simply pretty. She had round cheeks that gave her a girlish appearance, and people were surprised to learn she was approaching her fortieth birthday. But it was her eyes that fascinated him most. They were a kaleidoscope of blue and gray that varied in hue along with her moods—one minute murky, the next austere, sometimes barren. It had been so long since he'd seen *vibrant*.

Michael knew his bad temper and perfectionism were mostly to blame for the abduction of her brighter side, but he had cohorts. Jamie's activities were more kid than adult. A smart woman like her needed stimulation, and she had to be bored with the monotony of her days. Although she denied it, Jamie never did completely recover from her screwed up childhood and needed to deal with some issues of her own. Plus, she was addicted to the Internet. The real Jamie was probably hiding inside her computer monitor. He had to talk to her about all of this. Maybe he'd take her out to dinner without the kids soon. Maybe that would help. He narrowed his eyes as he tried to remember the last time they went out on a date, but couldn't. His body went limp. No wonder their marriage was falling apart.

It wasn't just about going out for an occasional evening of play, however. Sharing space with another person was hard. As he took another sip of beer, he thought about his wife's casual nature. It was a trait that attracted him to her and, at the same time, drove him nuts. It didn't bother Jamie that the Sunday newspaper would lie on the living room floor for a week or that coffee mugs were placed in the same kitchen cabinet as water glasses. She was unsystematic with her living habits, and his lifestyle preference was in polar opposition. And she was so lenient with Megan and Emily. Michael grew up in boot camp. Although he didn't want to be as stern as his father, he did believe in discipline.

This thought was interrupted when his family approached the table—Jamie, his disillusioned wife, accompanied by their two daughters. Emily, strong-willed and spirited, had naturally rosy cheeks, which made her appear perpetually happy. Megan, his female counterpart, had deep brown eyes and olive skin. She was precocious and sensitive, which often made her seem aloof. As crazy as these females drove him, he didn't want to lose them to his fastidiousness. Divorce was so common, and although it would pinch, his salary could handle two households. The disruption this would cause in his life made him quiver. He had to keep trying. He was an expert at solving problems at work; he was sure he would find a way to combat the turmoil that had infected his domestic life.

Chapter Four

A breeze rustled the leaves on the oak trees that lined the sidewalk. Michael glanced up at the commotion as he and his family approached the cobblestone steps of home. He pulled the keys from his pocket and detected a tremor in his hand. The ogre inside him was stomping around, and Michael needed to dart to his bedroom before it lashed out.

The theoretical celebration never recuperated after the soda spill. Emily had complained that the cheeseburger was too big to fit in her mouth during dinner, and Megan whined when she realized she was going to miss *Phineas and Ferb* on TV. Jamie's body was at the restaurant, but her mind was nowhere near the place. When Michael turned on his BlackBerry, three text messages from his boss, Frank, screamed at him for leaving the office early. Michael couldn't wait to crawl into bed and end this day.

He was not fast enough. After opening the door, he reached to turn on the light and felt a sticky substance. As the hall became illuminated, he saw orange spots on the switch plate that splattered onto the wall. More remnants of childhood had been added to their home canvass making it look like an abstract piece of art that might be found in an obscure museum.

The girls ran by him and kicked off their shoes. Their soles banged against the wall and landed on the oriental runner, once bright and pristine, now dull and stained with the mark of careless treatment. They scurried to their stations in front of their amusement idol and began bickering about what to watch without so much as a nod to thank him for dinner.

Jamie casually placed her sweater on one hook and her pocketbook on the next. Ignoring him, she headed for the alcove to visit with her best friend, the computer.

Just like a distraught alcoholic finding a bottle of bourbon, this scene was the trigger that released Michael's nemesis.

"Jamie, what the hell is this?" he demanded, pointing to the orange splatter.

Jamie stopped and turned. She twirled her hair then pulled it behind one ear. He could tell she was trying to determine which one of her tricks she would use to stop him from attacking. The it's-no-big-deal act he surmised, as she tilted her head and wrinkled her nose.

She looked at the wall and laughed. "Those little spots? Must be from the popsicles the girls ate earlier. They obviously didn't wash their hands after they were finished. It's not a problem—very easy to clean." She headed toward the kitchen without looking back. Jamie returned to the crime scene with paper towels and a bottle of multipurpose cleaner. She then attempted to wipe away another one of his tantrums.

He watched her intently. His suit jacket was still on, his fists were clenched, and his eyes were in squint position. The monster had arrived, and he couldn't calm it down.

"What is wrong with you? Did you put your sticky orange hands all over the place?" he shouted.

She shot him one of her classic glares.

"Come on. Answer. Did you?"

Jamie hesitated and softly said, "No."

"Then why the hell are you cleaning it? Emily. Megan. Come here now—right now."

The girls ran in from the other room. Yelling always propelled them into action, and he wondered why this was the only thing that got them moving. He took the cleaning materials from Jamie, gave the paper towels to Emily and the solution to Megan.

"Now clean up the mess you made."

"For heaven's sake, Michael. Emily can hardly reach the light switch," Jamie said, defending the children again.

Just once he would like to see her come over to his side. "She did fine getting it there, so it shouldn't be a problem getting it off. Go get the stool from the bathroom, Megan, before we add permanent popsicle spots to this mess of a wall. Just look at it."

Megan immediately responded to his demand and returned from the downstairs bathroom with the stool. He watched with arms folded as his daughters removed the leftovers from their afternoon snack. It was amazing how rapidly they could work when pushed. Within a few minutes, they finished their chore and put the cleaning tools in the kitchen.

When they returned Jamie said, "Daddy's just tired. Go on up to the playroom, and I'll be there in a minute."

The girls ran up the stairs.

Michael faced Jamie, who looked at him like he had just killed a cat. He did not let her disdain disturb him. "Was that so hard? Honestly, you need to teach our kids how to take care of things, how to clean up after themselves. They do pretty good with a little instruction."

"What is wrong with you? There were a couple of popsicle drippings on a light switch left behind by a five-and seven-year-old that cleaned up in thirty seconds. I don't think it's worth a coronary, but be my guest. This is a home, not a museum. I won't have our daughters tiptoe around, fearful of every move they make because they're afraid of their anal father. Tonight when you get in the shower, make it ice cold. Maybe it will provide you with the chill you so desperately need."

She turned away before he could respond and marched up the stairs to reassure their daughters that they had done nothing wrong. Michael watched Jamie go, letting her think that she had the last word, although he had several comebacks up his sleeve. He was sick of this night, however, sick of his daughters, sick of his wife, sick of his messy house, sick of counseling, and sick with the thought of what his life had become. He removed his shoes, placed them neatly on the far shelf in the hall closet, and plodded up the stairs.

When he reached the top, Jamie's head poked out from the playroom. She coolly said, "Better get up early tomorrow if you want to get a run in. We have to be at the soccer field by ten."

"Whoopee," he whispered, as Jamie slipped back into the sounds of Cartoon Network and giggling girls.

Michael gazed at the closed door, leaned against the wall, and rubbed the back of his neck. Once again, he had managed to make the distance between himself and his family expand. His regret hangover would be arriving any minute. He went into the bathroom, swallowed a couple of Tylenol PMs, and turned on the shower.

Jamie kissed Megan on the cheek and pulled the tangerine comforter up to her neck. She stroked her daughter's hair and said, "I love you, muffin." She then went into Emily's room and did the same. When the good-night ritual was over, she pulled the sash of her pink cotton robe tightly around her waist and tiptoed into her bedroom. The TV was still on, but Michael was asleep. Stepping close to him, she listened to his breathing. It was definitely sleep breathing, so she was safe. She pulled her slipper socks over her feet, ambled down the stairs, poured herself a glass of Chardonnay, and approached the computer. She sat down, fired it up, and leaned back. Michael had proved tonight that he could not change. Jamie still wasn't ready for a divorce but certainly could use a separation—one that didn't take her too far from home. Rubbing her hands together, she said, "Let the games begin," then took a sip of wine.

When the machine was ready for action, she opened her Facebook page. She had a private message from Steve. "Hey, pretty girl. I'm waiting up for you."

Jamie gasped in delight. She liked hearing that she was pretty from him way more than she did from Michael. She tried to suppress a smile, but it didn't work. Before responding, she scanned Steve's wall. His five o'clock shadow and unkempt sandy brown hair seemed to invite her to take an adventurous walk in the woods with him. There were shots of him playing tennis, sitting at a bar, cuddling with his puppy, and sailing on a catamaran. She wished she could jump into the pictures and start a new life. Of course, Emily and Megan could come along, but that cad she married would be left behind. Jamie gazed at her fantasy man a little longer, hypnotized by his emerald eyes that danced with mischief and vigor.

She couldn't believe that he picked her out of all the women fishing for love on the cyberspace cruise. Of course, she touched up some of her visual posts with Photoshop, but not much. She shaved some hip fat and smoothed out the lines that were starting to creep around her eyes. The rest was real.

Jamie went back to her message, gulped her wine, and raised her eyebrows. She typed, "Can you come out and play?"

Within seconds she received a reply. "I wish you were ringing doorbell and not my iPad."

Jamie's eyes widened. This was so much fun.

Chapter Five

Michael stirred at 4:57, three minutes before his alarm went off. He never needed the beeping to jolt him out of slumber but had programmed his watch for a wakeup call just in case he overslept. His cheek had melded with the memory-foam pillow, but it was time to break the bond. Lounging was not an option this morning. He had to get a thirteen-mile run in before taking his daughters to soccer practice. The Philadelphia Marathon was two months away, and he didn't want to fall behind with his training schedule. He stretched, jumped up, and grabbed his athletic garb off the top of the dresser.

White nylon shorts slipped on easily over his lean muscular legs, but the wicking shirt tugged at the fullness of his black hair as he pulled it on. He was overdue for a haircut and would have to squeeze in an appointment next week. He stretched Cool Max socks over his feet, snapped a sweatband around his head, and scooted down the stairs, where his Saucony Pro Grids waited in the closet. He stretched his calf, hamstring, and quad muscles in the hall, but not nearly as much as running guides suggested. Elongating his legs in a static position was tedious, and he didn't have much patience for it. After his final ankle rotation, he was ready to roll.

As he dashed down Wisconsin Avenue toward the National Mall, the tension release began. Dawn had just surfaced, and the political city was still. All he could hear was the pounding of his soles on the pavement. The thumping was like a tranquilizer—just what he needed to work out his remorse after losing his temper again last night.

The White House greeted him as he slowed his pace to a jog on Pennsylvania Avenue. He wondered if the president had to bring his kids to soccer every Saturday from September through November. He doubted it. Just one of the perks of that job. Each week Michael tried to focus on the game but would be interrupted by the gushing of mothers and fathers as they pointed out how exceptional their children's athletic skills were, which led to the conversation about the mediocrity of the school curriculum. It just wasn't good enough for their little prodigies. "They're all just normal kids, right, Al?" he said as he saluted the Einstein Memorial on Constitution Avenue. The understanding face of this bronze statue obviously agreed with him, but the genius's weary eyes and arched brows seemed to say, "Accept what you can't change." Michael responded aloud, "Good advice, Doctor." Today he'd be polite at the field. He needed to earn some points with Jamie after last night and being a chatty dad might get him a few.

He pushed visions of the soccer scene out of his mind as he turned toward the Capitol. When he looked up, he noticed the roof of his office building. He shook his head. He began his time at this labor relations firm as a law intern. After receiving his LLD and passing the bar exam, he was immediately hired. By the time he was thirty, he earned six figures, and the pay raises steadily increased. Two years ago he had been appointed manager. Now he supervised eight lawyers and handled hundreds of cases annually. Although his job was stimulating, there were constant fires to put out, and his team always needed him to show them how to extinguish the flames. In fact, he thought about hanging a hose in all of their cubicles as a reminder that they had what it took to deal with any crisis.

Documents in need of major revision came to his desk for review, and he spent hours correcting these papers. Sugarcoating was not his forte, so critiques were blunt and sharp regarding his expectations for change. This made him an unpopular boss, and some of Michael's employees had submitted formal requests for a transfer away from his tyranny. Despite this, his job was not in jeopardy. The partners were always pleased with his ability to help clients develop constructive strategies for creating a positive workplace environment, and his cases were usually resolved through mediation. But like a nutritionist who had trouble convincing his family to eat healthy food, he couldn't motivate his own employees into peak performance.

Michael groaned when a twinge of pain shot through his right calf. He had a major spasm during his last marathon and had to hobble to the finish line. The promise he made to himself to stretch a bit more had faded, and he instantly recommitted to his resolution as he passed the US Supreme Court Building. The justices were rumored to work around the clock. Although Michael could easily devote fourteen hours a day to his job, he worked swiftly and efficiently, so he could leave the office by six.

When he got home, dinner would be ready, and he was at the kitchen table eating five minutes after walking through the door. It would have been nice to bask in some quiet before the supper bell rang, but this luxury was not an option. The girls were on a schedule and needed to eat by six thirty. When Emily and Megan were snug in their pajamas, he read to them. It was by far the best moment of his day. For twenty minutes he got to travel along with his daughters to imaginary worlds where talking animals and extraordinary heroes embarked on adventures. When they were tucked in for the night, he crashed in front of some TV news program, which lulled him to sleep.

He circled around the botanical gardens to run along the tidal basin of the Potomac River. It flowed next to him like an accepting friend, and Michael thanked the dark water with a nod. Jamie and he used to bike or walk along this path when they were dating and during the early years of their marriage. He smelled the sweet and rotten odor of the tributary and frowned as he took the water bottle from his fuel belt to quench his thirsty body. Their relationship had gone from being lovers to superficial friends to conflicting business partners. It was like a dilapidated building in need of major repair. He couldn't remember when they lost their desire for each other because at one time they had a passionate, fascinating sex life. Now, all that was left were quick obligatory encounters, which were about as frequent as holidays. By the spousal complaints Michael heard at the office and the flirting he witnessed, he concluded that a stale marriage was more the norm than the exception. Regardless, he wondered if he and

Jamie would ever have a hot night of love again. Even with counseling, it was highly unlikely.

His exercise routine increased as amorous encounters decreased and job demands swelled. Six mornings a week he would run or cycle through the summer, fall, winter, and spring. On bad weather days, he hit the gym. Sundays were reserved for golf outings with colleagues. His participation was essential. It not only provided him with connections to superiors, but often gave him inside information on issues that he might not be privy to while taking care of his unit's assignments during work hours.

Passing the reflecting pool, his mind was liberated as thoughts of his hectic life departed and the face of that amiable man who creamed him at chess the previous evening appeared. The guy was so serene. Michael would love to spend a day walking around in his shoes just to see what that felt like. What was his name? Whoever, never displayed a crease of tension on his face or a murmur of irritation—especially impressive for a game as adrenaline-producing as blitz chess. He was a chess master but didn't participate in tournaments, where he'd surely triumph.

Except for golf, Michael got satisfaction from taking his endeavors to a competitive level. He tracked his running and liked making gains with his time and speed. It made things more interesting. This man just liked to play chess regardless of the outcome.

Michael recalled something this fellow said. He liked making that deli owner chuckle. Michael certainly made people scowl, but chuckle? Megan and Emily giggled when he read them stories, but those were other people's words. Since he started trying harder to be more humane, he did catch the girls snickering at some of his spontaneous antics, but not often enough. Being silly a little more frequently might help his situation. As he turned onto N Street, he made that his goal for the day.

"Rufus," Michael murmured, pleased with himself for remembering. "That guy's name is Rufus."

He huffed up the stairs to his house, eyes glued to his sports watch. He clocked thirteen miles in 105 minutes, an 8.07 minutes-per-mile pace.

"Damn!" he exclaimed, as he walked into the hall.

"What's wrong?" Jamie shouted from the kitchen.

"I ran an eight and seven tenths mile, and I was hoping to be in the sevens."

"Do you think eight tenths of a second warrants a *damn?*" she asked, as she entered the foyer, munching on a handful of Fruit Loops, the opened box in her other hand.

"As a matter of fact, I do. Any objections?"

"None whatsoever. Better keep up your runner's pace, shower off that sweat, and get something to eat. We have to leave for soccer in an hour."

He sat on the third step of the staircase and untied his shoes. "Why so early? Practice isn't until ten."

"I see that you've blocked out soccer from your memory. About a mile before we get to the field, the traffic starts. If we get there early enough, we may beat some of it and will only have to crawl for a half hour or so. Then there's the parking. We should try to find something close enough so the girls aren't too pooped to play. Of course, we have to check in because it's the first day, so there will be lines and our daughters' teams could be practicing two or three fields apart."

Michael straightened up. "Why do we do this soccer thing, and why not just fix yourself a bowl of cereal?"

"Team sports are good for kids, and families should do stuff like soccer on Saturday; and I like my cereal fresh from the box. Now stop asking questions and move," Jamie ordered, as she approached him and poked his shoulder. "You're stinking up the house."

He gazed up at her. Her mouth was smiling, but her eyelids sagged.

"Sorry about last night. I blew it again, huh?" Michael said.

Jamie let out a long sigh. "We need to talk. Seriously talk."

"Let's go in the kitchen and have some coffee. We can be late."

"Come on, Daddy. We're going to soccer," Emily yelped, as she scampered down the stairs and threw her arms around his neck.

Michael swung her onto his lap. "You're on your way to the big leagues. We'll go in a little while, but I need to talk to Mom first."

"It's okay. We'll chat later," Jamie said.

"Are you sure?"

"We'll be too rushed now."

He nodded, stood, and placed his Sauconys in the closet. The day had begun.

Michael hopped into the minivan and glanced around. In the passenger seat, Jamie examined a map of the soccer field. She looked like she was studying for a test, and could have passed for a graduate student in her cargo shorts, polo shirt, and white Keds, with her hair tucked behind her ears.

Emily, in the middle seat, buckled her American Girl doll into place. Her curly red locks bounced, and her finger waggled, as she lectured this pretend playmate about car safety.

Megan, in the rear, ogled an electronic game that was blaring with pings and explosive bursts. Her eyes bulged as she gripped the device like a dollar bill on a windy day. If he didn't stop her, she'd surely have a seizure.

"Megan?"

No response.

"Megan," he shouted.

"Shhh," Jamie said.

"Megan's going to have a convulsion. Look at her."

Jamie turned and shook her head. She maneuvered her way to the back and snatched the gadget.

"Mom," Megan yelled.

"It's too loud for the car."

Megan folded her arms and pressed her lips together.

"Thanks," Michael said when Jamie plopped back into her seat.

"No problem."

He pulled out of the driveway, which was too narrow for a van of this size, and headed toward Arlington, where the mega sports field waited for thousands of children to trample on its turf.

Michael kept his eyes on the road and asked, "What's on for the rest of the day?"

Jamie shook the map once and replied, "As soon as we get home, I need to get the girls to Hop and Stomp for Kristen's birthday party and—"

"Who's Kristen?"

Jamie looked up and gaped at him like he was wearing a dunce hat. "You know who she is—the little girl next door."

"I forgot."

"You should try to remember our neighbors' names."

"I'll add it to my list of things to do."

"Anyway, you can get the yard work done while we're at the party; then we need to be at the Sharpes' for a barbecue at five. After that you're free."

He moaned. "The Sharpes? I hate the Sharpes. Why didn't you check with me first?"

"I did. On Monday, after work."

"Just wait twenty minutes after I get home before telling me stuff like that. You know I'm tired when I walk in the door."

"Whatever. We have to be there at five, and you don't hate them. *Hate* is a strong word."

He squirmed in his seat. The thought of spending four or five hours with those people gave him instant agitation. He had to get out of this gig. "I do hate them. Matt, with his boring monologues about his stock portfolio, and Matilda, with those skinny jeans that are so tight her belly hangs over the top and her boobs are always spilling out of her shirt. Who does she think is? One of those Pussycat Dolls?"

The more Michael thought about the impending evening, the more he dreaded it. He huffed, "There she'll be when we arrive: smile plastered on her face, hugging everyone. She'll be picking at the dip with her fingers then setting it out for us to eat. Honestly, she might as well just spit in it. I'm not going."

"It's too late to cancel, and I think you like the part where Matilda's boobs spill out."

"Trust me. I don't get any pleasure out of Matilda's un-obstructed boob display. She's gross. Just tell them I tripped over a soccer ball and sprained my ankle. And we should have that talk tonight after the kids settle in."

"We'll talk after we get home." Jamie slapped her knee. "Honestly, Michael, we have to go at this point, and you agreed to it even if you don't remember. I won't make you eat the dip—promise."

Jamie returned her attention to the map. She pulled out a pencil from her pocketbook and made asterisks with shaded routes from the parking lot to where they needed to check in and then to the uniform tent. Michael shook his head at the complexity of this child's game as he pulled into a donut shop drive-through.

"What are you doing?" Jamie asked.

"I need coffee bad."

Before he noticed the several cars in front of him, another vehicle pulled in from behind. He was trapped. It would be at least a ten-minute wait. He squeezed the steering wheel. "Damn it!"

"Don't swear in front of the girls."

"*Damn* isn't swearing, and anyway, they'll be exposed to all kinds of colorful language on the school bus. It's probably better that they hear it from us first." He looked at Jamie and offered a tight-lipped smile.

"*Damn* is swearing, and now we're going to be late," Jamie said.

"*Damn* is definitely the new *darn*, and we're not going to be that late. Besides, even if we are, I don't think it will hamper the girls' chances of getting full soccer scholarships to a division one college."

After twelve minutes of stop-and-go drive-through traffic, it was Michael's turn to order.

The voice from the speaker said, "We're featuring a new Colombian dark roast with five flavor options."

"Save me the special list. I want plain old coffee."

The voice kept going.

"It's a recording. You can't stop her," Jamie informed.

When the soundtrack was over, a real-time voice came through. "May I help you?"

"Two large coffees, one black and one with just a little cream, no sugar. And two apple juices."

"What?"

He leaned closer to the speaker and repeated the order.

"Did you say two sugars?"

"No sugar," he shouted.

"Drive around."

"Thanks for the coffee," Jamie said.

"Sure."

After five minutes, they reached the pick-up window. As Michael went to pay, the cashier asked in a munchkin-like voice, "Do you have one of our reward cards, Sir?"

"Yes," Jamie said, and pulled out a key chain with more than a dozen retail cards on it. She reached over and handed the bulky contraption to the teenage girl.

After the card was swiped, the perky cashier said, "You qualify for a free donut. What kind would you like?"

"Jelly," Megan and Emily yelled.

Michael could feel his voice rise with each syllable. "We're not getting donuts."

"But, Sir, you have to take the donut. It's already registered on the computer. If you don't take it now, you'll lose it."

Michael squinted and through clenched teeth said, "You can have the donut for your break. Just give me the drinks."

"Michael Stolis!" Jamie exclaimed.

He was in the doghouse, and it wasn't even eleven.

Jamie reached over him again and handed the cashier a twenty dollar bill. "We'll take two jelly donuts, and keep the change."

"Don't forget Samantha," Emily said.

"Make that three jelly donuts," Jamie said.

"Samantha's a doll, Jamie. We're buying a donut for a doll?"

Jamie waved her hand in the air. "Just go with it. Em thinks she's real."

He pinched the arch of his nose.

Michael took a sip of coffee as he drove away. "I'm going to say one thing. You just paid ten dollars for a supposedly free donut that our daughters do not need. That's exactly what marketers want you to do when they give out those reward cards."

"You think you're so smart? Look behind you. There isn't a line inside the store. You could have had your coffee in two minutes without a bag of donuts."

Michael looked straight ahead and continued driving.

"We're going to have to hurry," Jamie said, as Michael pulled the van into the parking lot. "We have a half hour to sign in, pick up the uniforms, and get the girls to their teams."

Michael pushed the button to open the electronic side doors. Megan and Emily jumped out. He sighed when Jamie said, "Oh no," and got out to see what was wrong. His daughters' faces and shirts were speckled with jelly and confectionery sugar. Jamie pulled out a baggie containing hand wipes from her bottomless shoulder bag and gave some to Michael.

"Here, you tackle Megan, and I'll take care of Emily."

Michael grabbed the wipes. "You had to get them jelly donuts." He squatted and began clearing the snack remnants off his older daughter.

In the middle of this process, Megan asked, "Why do I have to play soccer every year? I hate it."

Michael stopped cleaning, lifted her chin, and looked directly into her eyes. "You play soccer for the same reason I play golf. Everybody else does. It's become a life requirement, like learning to read. It doesn't matter if you like it or not." He gave his daughter his first real smile of the day then tweaked her nose. He showed her his thumb sticking between his fingers and said, "Now I got your nose, and I'm going to keep it in case I need an extra someday."

Megan burst out laughing. "Dad, give me back my nose."

He had made his daughter, not just chuckle, but laugh out loud; and what was the result? He laughed too. Michael placed his thumb on Megan's nose. "You get it back just 'cause I love you, little girl."

When he looked up, the first thing he saw was the astonished expression on Jamie's face. Normally Michael would have exploded at this point on a hectic morning. In fact, he surprised himself with his ability to diffuse the escalating tension. He shared a genuine smile with Jamie. She returned his gift with something he hadn't seen in a long time. A gleam illuminated her eyes, which magically brightened her face.

He didn't bother finishing the cleanup. It didn't seem to matter. Instead, he stood and clapped his hands. "Let's go kick some balls around."

With that, he and his family ran off to join the games.

That ten-second laugh was the highlight of his Saturday. A surge of warmth rushed through his body when his daughter giggled. It calmed him. This flash of serenity disappeared, however, as the schedule of the weekend surged forward. He endured the predicted soccer chatter that involved bragging about child accomplishments and summer vacations. Details were exchanged regarding house projects and the latest technology on the market. He tried to pay attention but failed miserably as his mind traveled to the vacant space where no one could bother him. The practice session was over in an hour, but it took about an hour and a half to walk back to the van, sit in traffic, and drive home. When he got there, the yard work waited for him.

Chapter Six

Although the Stolis's outdoor area was small, it did require meticulous grass trimming, shrub shaping and weeding. Jamie had created a garden so elaborate it could be featured in a home magazine. The French doors from the living room led to a brick patio that had an Azteca fire pit in the center. Four cedar planters stood in the corners and they each contained a yellow rose bush surrounded by a variety of green, pink and white perennials. Jamie occasionally tried to teach Michael the names of these plants, but he couldn't remember any of them. A winding patch of grass started where the terrace ended and led to a miniature hill that was full of colorful flowers and ornamental rocks.

The yard was captivating, but Michael hated the upkeep. Jamie spent so much time creating the garden masterpiece that he had offered to help with the maintenance. He had regretted it ever since. Trimming around the edges and crevices where the bricks were placed was tedious. He also had trouble maneuvering around the tiny lawn with a mower, so he used a weed whacker to cut the grass. By September the weekly chore was beyond old, and Michael found himself wishing for an early frost.

By the time he was finished with the exterior work, the girls had returned from the birthday celebration. When he went inside, Megan and Emily were watching TV while munching on candy from their party bags.

"Hey guys. Did you have fun?"

They nodded.

"Did you have cake and ice cream?"

They nodded.

Michael clicked off the TV.

"Dad!" they exclaimed.

"Sorry, but I need you to look at me and speak when I ask you questions. Mr. Swiss Cheese isn't going anywhere."

"He's a sponge, Dad," Megan said.

"Yeah, Dad. His name is SpongeBob," Emily said.

Michael shook his head. This was worse than he thought. His daughters were enthralled with a talking sponge. "Anyway, I don't want to be the bad guy, but give me your candy. You can save it for the movies tomorrow."

"Dad," they groaned.

"Seriously. SugarBob is in your teeth right now doing his best to make cavities. Go in the bathroom and brush; then you can watch your show."

"Is there a SugarBob too?" Emily asked.

"I certainly hope not. I'll wait here and you can show me your shiny smiles when you're through."

When they returned, he headed into the kitchen. He didn't want to get into another quarrel with Jamie, but he did need to discuss their daughters' diet with her.

"Why did you let the girls have candy on top of all the other junk they've had today?"

"Hello to you too," Jamie said as she peeled carrots over the sink.

"Jamie, come on. They need to eat better."

"I guess they're eating candy because it was given to them at a party," she said without looking up.

"Not a good answer. I'll review their diet for today." Michael pulled open a cabinet door and took out a cereal box. "Sweet morsels for breakfast and jelly donuts for snack. Cake and ice cream at the party, then candy for dessert. The Sharpes always bring out the brownies after dinner. We can count on that staple. Do you want me to tally up the sugar grams they will have accumulated in their body by tonight or should you?"

Jamie stopped peeling and turned around. "It's Saturday and there are a lot of special activities. If we don't let them eat their treats openly, they'll only sneak them later."

"They won't if we hide the candy and explain how bad it is for them. It's called good parenting, and what does Saturday have to do with anything? Is it the official fill-up-on-junk day? Our kids are becoming addicted to sugar and Em's got a protruding belly. They constantly sit around watching that damn TV, and you allow it. Let's start fostering healthier habits around here. Obesity and diabetes are epidemic in this country and I don't want them to catch the disease." Michael realized that he was ranting, so he paused and inhaled. "I'm glad to see you're getting them carrots to eat."

Jamie pointed the peeler at him and shook it with each word. "You tell them they can't have a brownie tonight. You take them to the next birthday party and say 'no cake.' You have no idea about anything. And these carrots are for the salad that I'm bringing to the Sharpes."

Michael threw his hands up. "I'm not going to argue. You know I'm right."

Jamie went back to peeling carrots.

He looked at her for a few seconds, shook his head and went upstairs to shower away the dirt from the garden and the queasy feeling in his stomach.

Jamie stood with her hands on the counter and her head bent over the sink. She breathed in and out for several seconds then turned and looked at the space where Michael had been. She picked up the peeler and threw it.

"I hate you, you son of a bitch."

Folding her arms, she walked to the window and looked outside. *How am I going to live with him forever? Forever!* She gazed up at the sky hoping to find an answer, but instead noticed a live hornets' nest that hung from the ridge on top of the window. *Oh dear, I'll have to get some spray and kill them before they sting somebody.*

She ambled to the refrigerator and added this item to her list. Stepping over the peeler, Jamie proceeded out of the kitchen and down the hallway. She stood at the bottom of the staircase, lifted her arm and placed her index finger and thumb together. "Pssss," she hissed as she pretended to spray the poison toward Michael. She wished it would be that easy to murder her marriage.

Jamie went into the living room where her daughters lay on the oriental carpet watching TV. Michael was right. They were in front of that screen way too much, but she didn't have the energy to intervene. A good mother would turn the TV off and invite the girls to play a game of Chutes and Ladders, but it was easy to let them escape to another planet, so she could do the same.

She walked over to her life center, the computer. She had created so many make-believe relationships here. Whether it was corresponding with people from her past or chatting with strangers, it provided her with comfort. Now she was having a cyber-fling with Steve. It was sick, but she couldn't help herself. It felt wonderful to be wanted. Michael usually didn't even say hello to her when he walked into a room. He had gotten better since she told him that she wanted to move into the spare room, but his attempts at communication seemed insincere. He complained more than discussed and was quick to blame her for "catastrophes" like leaving the TV on when no one was in the room. She wanted to run away, but for now the world inside that monitor was the best she could do.

Jamie wandered to the fireplace and looked at the photos elegantly placed on the mantle. They represented what appeared to be a happy family. She picked up their wedding picture and stared at it. The attractive couple was encased in a sterling silver frame, as if it would protect them from injury.

They met at a party and fell instantly in love. Two years later they married. Jamie thought Michael was the handsomest man she had ever laid eyes on. When he approached her, she just sat there like a fool not knowing what to say to make an impression. All she could think about was her racing heart and the problem she had with the simple act of breathing. It was like the prince from Cinderella had jumped off the page and magically appeared to carry her away.

She was twenty-seven at the time, working as reporter for a small Virginia newspaper and wasn't dating much. It had been a few years since her last real relationship with banker Bill, which was nice but forgettable. Jamie had made a pleasant life for herself with biweekly tennis matches, Friday night happy hours, killer kickboxing classes and plenty of friends. Although she wanted to meet someone special, she wasn't desperate when she met Michael.

Jamie sighed as she settled into the oak spindle rocking chair in the corner of the room still holding onto the photo. Tilting her head, she recalled how surprised and flattered she was when Michael hung around her most of the evening. He talked quite a bit, but she couldn't focus on anything he said. She was so consumed with the emotion swelling in her body. It was funny to think about that now. She placed one hand on her belly and closed her eyes. As hard as she tried, she couldn't summon up that Cinderella love feeling.

By the end of the night, he had asked for her phone number; he called a few days later, and that was the beginning of this life she now detested. How did she miss the warning signs, which were evident within the first six months of their courtship? She viewed his coldness as strength, his compulsions as discipline, his obsessions as passion and his cruelty as sharpness. They did have some fun. Bike rides, trips to the beach, exploring museums, watching movies, drinking too much wine and making love were all part of the package. Her lips parted as she recalled the passionate sex they once had. It made her heart twinge so she rocked the thought away.

After they were married and she moved into his house, her feelings toward him started to change. Michael was controlling, always insisting where things belonged and what was and wasn't important. She clicked her fingernails when she recalled how adamant he was about keeping that Monet print in the foyer along with that ugly art deco table. Those items could go anywhere, but a panel of hooks for hats, jackets and other stuff had to go in the hall. It was practical and alleviated the stiff character of this residence. She quickly realized that this wasn't her castle and suggested they search for a new home, but he told her to just redecorate. When she did, he complained.

Instead of recognizing her mistake early on, Jamie took the things she didn't like about him and threw them into an internal closet. It was easier than walking out on the only man she had ever loved. Plus, she was thirty when his irritability escalated. Her biological clock told her that if she didn't procreate with Michael, her dream of having children might never happen.

Their marriage tumbled farther when Megan was born and crashed soon after Emily's arrival. Jamie left her job because it would be too complicated to try and manage two careers, daycare, childhood illnesses and activities, as well as provide a loving and nurturing home for the girls. Jamie agreed to take on the primary child-raising responsibilities. Michael earned six times what she did, so it made perfect sense. It wasn't all about money however. Jamie welcomed the break from the newspaper and was thrilled with her new role as mother. She could return to her job anytime, but days with her precious babies would never come back.

Crossing her legs, she dropped the photo onto her lap. Reality set in when the demands of parenting were recognized. She was often tired and crabby from too little sleep, too little stimulation and too little support. She felt dumpy because of her weight gain but couldn't muster up the discipline to shed the extra pounds. Michael became even more short-tempered as pressure from work increased. He received a major promotion when Emily was three. With it came a lot more money and a lot more misery. Jamie could tell the switch from attorney to manager would not help mitigate her husband's perfectionism. At first, he came home, sat at the dinner table, and complained endlessly about his useless staff. This went on for months until she told him that she was sick to death of his grumbling. Now, they generally sat around the table eating quietly while Michael gazed into space.

After giving the picture of their union one last glance, Jamie stood and placed it face down on the back side of the mantle. A peanut butter cup would quell her—well, her depression. She had to be honest with herself. What she was experiencing was deeper than sadness, but what could she do? She secretly tried Zoloft a couple of years ago, but it turned her into a zombie. She only took the little pills for a few weeks before deciding she preferred distress to sedation. Then she remembered how chocolate soothed her when she she was a child.

While she waited in the checkout line at the grocery store the next day, Jamie scrutinized the candy display. She chose a Hershey's bar and peanut butter cups. After a secret taste test at home, she decided that peanut butter cups were her favorite and the indulgence instantly lifted her mood. These gloom busters were now an essential part of her diet. Sure, they were making her fat, but fat was easier to worry about than a bad marriage.

Jamie went into the kitchen, opened the refrigerator door and pulled out the vegetable bin. In between the leafy lettuce and spinach was her medicine of choice. It was the ideal hiding place for her delight. No one ever ventured to this abandoned spot. She took the candy wrapper off, revealing chocolate that covered sweet peanut butter. First she inhaled its decadent scent then she took a bite. *Mmm, tastes better than Zoloft too.*

She devoured her happy snack, grabbed two more, went back into the living room and clicked on the computer. A message from Steve waited for her. When she opened it, her jaw dropped.

"Hey baby. When can we meet?"

"Shit." She had no idea what to write, but something made her type, "Friday morning works."

"Awesome. I'll see you at the Hilton coffee shop at nine thirty. The one on Connecticut Avenue. Wear something pretty."

"Shit." She started to type, "Why not Starbucks?" Whoever heard of meeting for coffee at a hotel? Steve didn't care about coffee. He wanted sex. Someone actually wanted to have sex with her. She got to the s in *Starbucks* and stopped. Instead she wrote, "Can't wait!" After all, her life was as dull as a boiled ham sandwich. This little tryst just might be the delicious treat she craved.

If Steve suggested they move breakfast to one of the rooms upstairs, she'd just tell him no. It wouldn't be problem. He couldn't drag her by the hair through the lobby and push her into an elevator. She was simply meeting a friend who she met on the Internet in a public place.

Shrugging, she jumped up. Jamie saw her daughters napping on the floor. What had she just done?

Her own mother went on a man binge when she divorced Jamie's father. She was eight years old at the time and hated seeing all of those strangers coming in and out of their apartment. Megan and Emily would not endure what she did while growing up; traveling between houses, meeting new people her parents dated, sitting through her mother's wedding to that awful gambler, never feeling like she belonged anywhere.

"Jamie," Michael called from the top of the stairs.

"Yeah?"

"Are we out of toothpaste?"

"I'll bring up a tube from the downstairs bathroom."

Chapter Seven

Michael had heard a rumor that Sunday was a day of rest but didn't believe it. Even as a boy, he had to rise with the roosters, so he could attend church, help his father with chores, and prepare for school the next day. Now that he was a man, the activities had changed, but the buzz of the so-called holy day remained the same.

He woke up at his usual time, 4:57, and reached for his watch on the nightstand to shut off the alarm. Rolling over, he stared at Jamie. She had made it to bed, but he wasn't sure when. She didn't speak to him all the way home from the Sharpes' the previous night, except to tell him how disrespectful he had been. It wasn't that he said anything rude. He just didn't say very much. As hard as he tried, he had nothing to add to the mundane conversation that dominated the evening. So what if he yawned a few times. They were bores, and he was tired. His reaction had been absolutely out of his control, just like sneezing in an old, dusty room. As much as he wanted his marriage to work, he'd have to put his foot down and tell Jamie no more activities with the Sharpes. If she wanted to socialize with Matilda, that was up to her; but he wasn't going to spend time with those jerks anymore.

He got out of bed and went into the bathroom to take what was becoming his favorite activity—a shower. Tee time was at eight, and he needed to get to the golf course early to practice his swing. Maybe he wouldn't come in with the highest score if he warmed up a little. Looking into the mirror above the sink, he shifted his mouth from neutral into a frown. Who are you kidding?

Although he was amused by these golf outings when he first started working, his enthusiasm for the sport diminished with each passing season. His scorecard had not made the same progress as his career, and he now dreaded the Sunday morning ritual of smacking little white balls around with a stick. After putting on his golf apparel—tan khakis and an orange knit shirt—he dragged himself out the door and into the garage. The air already felt hot and sticky, and he wished he could change into gym shorts, but they were forbidden at the exclusive slacks-only club. He grabbed his golf bag and threw it into the trunk of his BMW. At least he'd get to drive this beauty over the rolling hills of Arlington on his way to the perfectly manicured lawns of his destination.

He climbed into the convertible, sat there for a minute, and soaked up the exhilaration he felt when he pushed the button that opened the top of his indulgent toy. He traded his Camry in for this six years ago, just before Jamie found out that she was pregnant with Emily. He had hesitated because of the cost, but his benevolent wife talked him into the purchase. She said he deserved a treat for all of his hard work and convinced him that they could afford it. As he backed out of the driveway, he shook his head. Jamie did have a sweet side, but like snow in DC, it rarely made an appearance.

As predicted, the eighteen holes of golf were torturous. Michael came in fourth in his foursome and endured extensive teasing about his awkward swings and stiff putts. He played the role of a good sport and joined in the mockery, making comments like "Just call me hole-in-ten" and "If my law skills matched my golf talent, I'd be typing up board hearings instead of presiding over them." Everyone laughed, thinking Michael enjoyed this banter, but inside he was mortified. Failure was not okay. At least that was what he was raised to believe.

Home was next on the agenda, and it wasn't so he could watch a baseball game. He needed to be there by two to take Emily and Megan to a movie. Sunday afternoons were Jamie's break from the kids. She would shop, work in her garden, or just savor the quietness of the house while the three of them had bonding time. He'd have to talk to her about this. Since both girls were now in school, she had seven hours of space every day, and he had seven years of Sundays with his daughters. Maybe they could switch places. Although he loved Emily and Megan, he had to make time to chill before the volcano in his chest erupted.

The balmy wind swept over his skin and tousled his hair as he cruised along the highway toward the Georgetown exit. He let up on the accelerator when he approached the Mount Pleasant section of DC. He glanced at the clock and exclaimed, "Yes!" It was 12:55, which gave him one hour to stop at that deli and try the roast beef Rufus had raved about on Friday. He leaned forward and gripped the steering wheel in anticipation of this simple indulgence.

A bell rang when Michael entered the long, narrow delicatessen, and a robust man with white hair that matched his apron lifted his head. He was slicing turkey for a customer but took the time to say, "Afternoon, Sir. I'm Sam. Be right with you." He pointed to the clear, clean display case that was filled with a variety of meats, cheeses, and salads. "Enjoy the view."

"Thanks," Michael said, as he walked toward the exhibit of delicacies and inhaled the scents of fresh wholesome food. He scanned the glass case and spotted the roast beef. It was just like Rufus had described, at least ten pounds and pink from bottom to top. Suddenly he was starving. He turned around and saw a couple of empty tables lined against the wall, which were just big enough for two people. Perfect. He'd eat the sandwich right here. Michael loved the idea of relaxing over a meal instead of shoving the food in his mouth at home while Megan and Emily waited for him at the door saying, "Come on, Dad."

"What can I do for you?" Sam asked.

"Can I get a roast beef sandwich on rye, for here?"

"Absolutely. What would you like on it?"

"Lettuce, tomato—sliced thin, and Swiss cheese—also sliced thin, with Russian dressing."

"And how about a sample of macaroni salad, made fresh today?"

"Sounds great."

"Anything to drink?"

Michael recalled Rufus's recipe. "Just water."

A sweet aroma filled the food chapel, and Michael turned toward the scent. The smell of butter, sugar, flour, and chocolate gave him an instant high. A petite woman who had to be in her late sixties pushed the backdoor open and entered the deli from what appeared to be the kitchen. She carried a tray of chocolate chip cookies the size of saucers. Michael couldn't believe he had run into such luck. She placed the tray on top of the counter and covered the cookies with wax paper.

"I knew you were coming, so I made you a special treat— best cookies in town."

"She's not joking. My wife's the finest baker in DC," Sam said.

"DC? Are you kidding me? The nation is more like it." She peered at Michael and shook her tiny finger. "Don't let the secret out, or I'll never get any rest. I'd be in that kitchen 'round the clock. By the way, I'm Becky. And you?"

Michael had to work at suppressing a laugh because of the antics of this elflike woman. "Hi, Becky. I'm Michael, and your secret is safe with me."

Becky looked at Sam. "Better not let men this handsome in the door. I might just run away with this one when you're not looking."

"But you'd be back. Wouldn't take long before you realized you made the biggest mistake of your life." Sam held up his hand toward Michael. "No offense."

Becky giggled as she went back into the kitchen with her ponytail swinging. "Come back again."

With the comedic banter between the deli owners over, Sam began to work on the sandwich. Michael tucked his tongue in his cheek and wondered how this couple—who he guessed had been married for a very long time—still had evident affection for each other. Sadness enveloped his heart at the reminder that the spark of love in his marriage was frozen under a sheet of ice. He tried to think of a way to delete this dreary thought and came up with the perfect solution.

He hesitated, bit his lower lip, then stammered, "Rufus said not to forget the pickle."

Sam laughed heartily. "That old hound Rufus. You know Rufus?"

Michael's eyes widened. He couldn't believe that he had caused such a jovial reaction from Sam. "I played chess with him on Friday at Dupont Circle. He raved about your roast beef and your wife's cookies."

"What a joker! I'll give him two pickles next time he comes in and tell him to put one in the freezer in case I ever forget."

That made two authentic laughs this weekend, one from Megan and one from Sam. Not bad for a novice, Michael thought.

Michael sat at a table and waited for his sandwich. Except for his gentle breathing and occasionally blinking eyes, he was still. He felt like a boy waiting for his loving mother to place a meal in front of him. The aroma of the cookies, the simplicity of the décor, and the genuineness of the owners escorted him to memories of the childhood kitchen where his energetic mother cooked for hours every day. He was from a Greek family where food was valued almost as much as church and hard work. Oregano, basil, olive oil, and garlic—the smells were as familiar to him as mown grass must be to a child raised on a Nebraska farm.

Homemade bread was a staple in their house. Michael loved the yeasty scent of dough rising on Saturday mornings while his mother made enough loaves to last the week. He especially looked forward to the special bread that was prepared for their New Year's Day feast. It was a family tradition to place a quarter in the dough. Whoever discovered this prize was guaranteed good luck for the year. Before dinner was served, Pa would say the names of those sitting around the table in order of age from oldest to youngest with each slice that he cut. Michael, his cousins, and even his aunts and uncles would silently wait to see who would win this Greek version of a four-leaf clover. When the quarter was uncovered, there were shouts of joy and congratulations, accompanied by applause. It had to be better than winning the lottery.

Michael recalled the year—he was nine at the time—when he found the quarter in his piece. In fact, he still had that quarter. It was buried in a red velvet purse the size of a thumb in his desk drawer at home. Sitting in this deli, at this small square table, the excitement he experienced so long ago seemed to be bubbling up inside of him again. It was funny how scents made the past come alive.

He sighed. What culinary creations would be etched in his children's minds? Fast food French fries in the car while being rushed from one activity to another, candy after it was released from its wrapping—did frozen processed dinners heated in the microwave even have a smell? As often as he ate one of these poor imitations of a meal, he couldn't summon it up. This was all part of the upper middle-class world in America. It was what he had worked so vigilantly to achieve; he doubted this was what Pa had in mind when he told him to do well in school so that he would be successful.

Michael's throat swelled when his pleasant memories faded into an image of his father standing over him at the kitchen table. Michael was forced to do three hours of homework every night whether he had any or not. He could still hear himself say, "But I'm done, Pa."

Pa would sternly reply, "One more hour. Read if you're done with your assignments. Then bed."

Michael jumped when Sam slammed a plate on the table.

"Enjoy and save room for one of those cookies," Sam said.

Sitting in front of him was a mountain of food—the perfect detour from the dark road his mind was starting to travel down.

He wasn't sure that he could open his mouth wide enough to take the first bite of the monster-sized sandwich, but it was a problem he didn't mind solving. He gaped at the edible art for several seconds, picked up one half with both hands and bit into it. "Ah," he sighed, and repeated Rufus's words in full chew, "Life is good."

The quick stop at the deli turned into a ninety-minute retreat. Michael chatted with Sam and Becky and took a mental vacation to an imaginary island that he rarely visited. The sandwich, salad, and pickle were as comforting as being wrapped up in a quilt in front of a fire on a cold winter night. His stomach did not need the chocolate chip cookie and piping hot coffee, but how could he resist? When his indulgence was complete, he felt as stuffed as a bear storing up for winter hibernation. He usually hated this sensation, but here at Sam's, he was filled to the brim with contentment.

Michael's retreat ended when he glanced at his watch. It was two thirty, and he told Jamie that he'd be home by two. It was okay. He was just a little late and still had plenty of time to get the girls to the movies. He paid Sam and was instantly back in hustle mode.

Quiet greeted him when he arrived home.

"Hello," he shouted.

No reply.

He peeked into the backyard. It was empty. Nobody was around. The girls must have changed their minds about the movie. Maybe Jamie took them shopping. Except for the golf game, this was turning out to be a pretty good day. After a moment of guilt, he smiled. Michael was getting the peace he needed, and it might make all the difference.

He walked around, listening to foreign sounds, like the refrigerator humming and his feet shuffling on the floor. These gentle noises had to live here all the time, but the clamor of his family had drowned them out. Michael stopped moving. Closing his eyes, he inhaled the still music. He had found a rare prize and stored it in his memory.

Standing in the middle of the foyer, he couldn't decide what to do next. There was an empty spot on his calendar, and he wanted to make the most of it. He probably should go upstairs and tackle the briefcase full of work that was waiting for him, but he didn't feel like it. Maybe he'd hop on his bike and cycle along the Potomac River, although traffic in downtown DC would be heavy with tourists at this hour on a Sunday.

Michael glanced at the basement door. His guitar summoned him to come and play. He reached for the knob. It would be fun to bang out a tune when no one was home. Then again, he probably wouldn't hear his family when they returned. What if they caught him belting out a song like Bruce Springsteen performing at Madison Square Garden? This was his fantasy, and he didn't want it revealed. He was used to hiding his rock star dreams. Pa had refused to let him buy a guitar when he was a teenager. His rigid father told him that it was an instrument for pot-smoking hippies. Despite the veto, Michael saved the money he earned from his paper route and bought that old guitar, now concealed downstairs. Pa never found out, thank God. Michael kept it undercover at a friend's house and went over to practice whenever he could.

Michael stepped back from the door. He'd find time to have a solo jam session soon. Maybe Jamie and the girls would visit her dad in the near future. In fact, he'd make the suggestion. With that, he turned around and climbed the stairs to the bedroom.

Michael changed into his lightest pair of shorts and an old cotton T-shirt that massaged his skin with softness. Unsure what to do next, he meandered into the kitchen. He looked in the refrigerator, even though he was still full from his extravagant lunch. As the cold air met his face, he exclaimed, "Yes!" One Heineken welcomed him. He seized it, went into the living room, arranged the cushions on the couch, and made himself comfortable. He turned on the TV and shouted, "Yes!" again when he saw the Phillies and Mets in a baseball war.

Michael sat glued to the sofa for two hours, thoroughly entertained by the game. Basking in the luxury of the quiet house was like floating down a placid river on a raft. He felt rejuvenated from his afternoon in Never Never Land, but he wasn't Peter Pan and did have to take care of some home business. First, he punched in Jamie's cell phone number. She didn't answer. He figured that she and the girls were in a noisy restaurant and didn't hear the ring, or maybe they went to that movie after all.

He went upstairs, sat at his desk in the corner of the bedroom, and took out his checkbook from the side drawer. Clicking on the computer, he traveled to his bank and looked at the account balance—over fifteen thousand dollars. The payments started: first the mortgage, then the car loans, Visa, Macy's, Time Warner, Verizon, National Grid, Traveler's Insurance Company, American Express, and Discover. Before he was finished, he needed to transfer four thousand dollars from savings into the checking account.

"What the hell? How do we spend so much money?"

He locked his ankles together and gripped the arms of his chair as he pored over the long list of expenses that had been charged last month. A siren was blaring in his head, but it was interrupted by the sound of the garage door opening. Michael jumped up. His lips were pressed together so tightly that a pry bar couldn't open them. He marched down the stairs and greeted his family by shouting, "Why are our charge card balances so high?"

Megan and Emily ran up the stairs without saying a word. He was sure they did not want to witness another one of their parents' feuds, but he had to get to the bottom of the outrageous bills. Jamie ignored his question, put down her packages, moved her sunglasses from her face to the top of her head, and confronted him with narrow eyes.

She hissed like an angry goose then attacked, "Where were you?"

"What do you mean?"

"I mean, where were you?" she asked slower and louder as if he was deaf. "You said you'd be home by two at the latest, and by two thirty I decided to take the girls shopping because you pulled a no-show."

"I didn't pull a no-show. I was just a little late. We had plenty of time to make the movie."

"You could've called," Jamie scolded, folding her arms.

"I did. You didn't answer."

"That was at six, four hours too late."

"If you were so concerned, why didn't you call?"

"I'm not in the mood for your flimsy excuses right now. Just do the right thing and apologize." She stormed off like a jet soaring down a runway. Her departure was swift and dramatic, but it didn't stop her mouth. "Didn't you wonder where we were?"

Part of him wanted to follow his daughters to the second floor, but he trailed after Jamie. He was not through with his credit card inquiry. "No. I figured you went shopping, which I see you did," Michael said, pointing toward the packages in the hall.

"What did you do, and why were you so late?" she asked, her voice dropping a few decibels.

"I was not that late, and if you want a detailed report, Mom, I'll give it to you," he answered, his voice increasing a few decibels. "Played my usual horrible golf game; stopped for a sandwich; got home around two thirty. No one was here, so I committed a sin and watched a baseball game. I was actually in a pretty good mood until I paid our bills for the month, which brings me full circle to my first question. Why the hell are the charge card balances so high?"

"Well, Mr. Money Police, in a nutshell, it's called *life*. There was the first installment for school tuition, school supplies, uniforms, fall clothes for the girls, soccer, Girl Scouts, swimming and gymnastics fees, plus the shoes and clothes that go along with those activities. You must know that groceries and gas are on the rise. You have a coffee-to-go habit, and we eat out quite a bit. The hot water heater went blink-blink a few weeks ago and needed replacing. I know you'd miss those long hot showers. It all adds up, sweetie; it all adds up."

"What about the charges for even more flowers, some kind of skin cream that must make you look twelve based on the price, and music that you had to download for your new and improved iPod? Plus a Droid, Jamie? Did you forget about that stuff? Life necessities, right? You'd die without them."

Jamie huffed out of the room and went into the kitchen. She was guilty, and he had caught her. Michael was not going to let her dodge the indictment with a simple disappearing act. Just as determined, he followed her once again and found her standing by the counter pouring a large glass of water from a pitcher.

"Seriously, you have to close your wallet and lock it up. I checked the Forbes list of the hundred richest people in the US, and I wasn't on it. By the way, did you call the paper about your old job yet? You really need your own money."

"No. I took the first week of both girls being in school to pat myself on the back for seven years on the mother track."

"It must be nice to lounge around all week like a pampered princess, with periodic breaks to go on spending sprees. Send me a postcard from the land of R & R and let me know what it's like. Right now, I have work to do—it's something called *employment*. Someone in the palace needs to keep the gold flowing in." He pointed at Jamie. "You try and relax for both of us."

"Shut up." She picked up the glass of water and threw its contents at him. Michael jumped out of the way. He glared at Jamie long enough to drench her with venom.

"You've officially gone nuts," he said. "Look at yourself, throwing things around like a two-year-old. Grow up and start taking some responsibility around here. Control your spending, pick up after yourself, get the girls to pick up after themselves. Start contributing somehow in some way. You make deadweight—"

"Stop it," she shrieked. "I am so sick of you. Just move out. I want you gone."

"Is that what you really want?"

Jamie nodded. "More than anything."

He moved close to her and cupped her chin with his hand. He looked directly into her eyes and softly said, "This is my house, and I'm not going anywhere."

She showered his lips with spit.

"You bitch." He wiped his mouth with his sleeve, stepped back, then darted up the stairs. He went into their bedroom, slammed the door, picked up a container of pens, and threw them at the closet. Michael paced around trying to calm his rage. It wasn't working, so he decided to make Jamie's wish come true and flee from the coop he once called home.

Jamie sat on the couch, squeezing an oversized pillow. She was in the middle of a raging sea, and this benign object was her life raft. She rocked back and forth, trying to soothe her grief. Typically after a fight with Michael, she would race to wherever her daughters were to reassure them that all was well. She would tell them that Mommy and Daddy just had a silly argument and that all married people occasionally fight. This evening they'd have to deal with the impact. She didn't have the strength to comfort anyone. Tears streamed down her cheeks, but she couldn't let go of her pillow to wipe them away. If she did, she would drown in the turbulent ocean of her life.

It was happening. The closet where she stored all of her anguish and frustration burst open, and a heap of adversity tumbled out.

"Stop it," she whispered. "Stop it."

She tried to stand but couldn't. It was like she had swallowed a cement block, and it kept her anchored to the sofa. A car engine ignited. Michael was leaving. She sat back and inhaled deeply. Upon exhale, sobs and tears erupted, soaking the pillow where she buried her face.

Chapter Eight

Michael roamed around the cemetery where his parents were buried. He wasn't sure what made him drive all the way to Baltimore, but was glad he did. Death appealed to him, and the graveyard reassured him that he would eventually find peace in this refuge. A blanket of stars and a crescent moon provided soft light as he weaved around the tombstones, inhaling the scent of too many flowers and wet worms. Before long, he was standing in front of his father's grave. He inched close to the gray marble rock, squatted, and traced the letters of his mentor's name with his index finger. Emotion tried to push its way out of him in arduous breaths. He yearned to release through tears the sea of pain trapped inside, but couldn't.

He closed his eyes and stepped into the six-year-old body that used to be his. He was running and laughing. His cousins were over, and they were in the middle of a vigorous game of tag. Michael was just about to escape from his predator when he tripped over a crevice in the sidewalk and ripped open his knee. As blood rushed out of him, he screamed. His mother rescued him with hot cloths, iodine, and bandages. Later his father visited him in his room.

The giant of a man told him that he wasn't a baby anymore and to never cry again. It was something weak men did, and he wasn't weak. Michael said okay, and his father slapped his face. His eyes flooded, so his father slapped him again. The stern sergeant told him that he would have to keep doing this until he was strong enough to keep his tears inside. It worked. Michael hadn't cried since that day.

He opened his eyes and stared at his father's name. "Is it okay, Pa? Can I cry now?"

He willed the dam to burst open, but his eyes remained dry. "I guess not."

The bones that lay six feet under still gripped his soul. His father never struck him after that night, but the thirty-minute boot camp had worked. He did whatever he was told. Whether it was doing homework, sawing wood, or becoming a lawyer, he followed orders like an obedient solider. The problem was the shoes his father forced him to wear didn't fit. They choked his feet and gave him blisters, which were sore and infected.

"I need a new pair of shoes, Pa." Michael waited, as crickets sang and a dog howled. Even the damn dog could cry.

He leaned against the memorial and gawked at the night. Except for his body's pulsations, he was as still as the dead. Michael stayed put for a long time, waiting for a sign, but it didn't come. His meditation transformed into impatience, and he rose to leave. He shook his head.

"I need new shoes," he whispered.

Goosebumps shocked his skin. He half grinned.

"Hey, Pa, can you find me a new pair and send them down?"

The goose bumps intensified. Could the gift be on its way? He stroked the top of the stone and patted it one time. He then turned and trudged back to a world that didn't fit, just like the damn shoes.

It was after midnight, and Jamie was still on the couch. She did force herself up at some point to tuck Megan and Emily into bed with a kiss and reassuring words but then returned to her life raft.

The garage door opened and footsteps followed.

"Michael?"

Within a few seconds, the man she used to love was sitting on the couch next to her, elbows on his knees and fingers interlaced. Jamie tried to think of something to say. Something that would fix them. Something that would prevent the inevitable. Eventually she managed, "I can't believe I spit at you."

"Things are crazy, huh?"

"How'd they get this bad?"

"I guess that's what we're trying to figure out in counseling," Michael said.

"We fight all the time."

"I know."

Jamie inhaled deeply. "Please look at me."

Michael sat up and faced her. His eyes conveyed regret, but it wasn't enough. And then they came—the words she promised herself would never travel from her mind to her lips. "We need a break," Jamie said softly. "We're miserable, and the girls are going to be so screwed up."

Michael closed his eyes, and his jaw trembled.

"I'm thinking you can get a hotel room for a week or two. Let things settle down, and then we'll start fresh. We have about a million Hilton Honors points, so the cost won't be an issue," Jamie said.

"No. No way. That's one thing we always agreed on—no divorce. We'll try harder in counseling and work things out."

Jamie took Michael's hand and held it firmly. "You know how I grew up. Always trying to get used to Mom's new boyfriends. Then her awful marriage to that jerk, Gary. Dad trying to make up for everything by being overindulgent. I want to keep Emily and Megan far away from that road. I just need some time to sort things out. I'm gonna go nuts if I don't get some peace. Look at how I behaved tonight. And I'm not crazy about our counselor."

"Me neither. We'll get a new one. I get the feeling that guy gives the same formula to all of his patients."

"Where'd you go tonight?"

"To visit my father."

"At the graveyard?"

"Yup."

"All the way to Baltimore?"

"Yup."

"Why?"

"I needed to say some things to him that I never did."

"Like what?"

"Like the life he ordered for me is all wrong."

"What are you going to do?"

Michael squeezed her hand. "I wish I knew. I'm so sorry things have turned out like this. I can't stand who I am."

"It's not all you. I'm messed up too."

"You?"

She tapped her thumb on his knuckle. "You have no idea."

"What's the matter?"

"I need time to figure that out, and I think you need to do the same. We need to travel solo for a while."

He leaned in. "I hate this. I love you, Jamie. I really do."

She looked down.

"You don't love me anymore?"

Jamie pressed her palm against her heart. She could feel the pain seep out with each beat. "I need to be honest with you and myself. At one time I loved you so much, probably too much. It blinded me from seeing who you are. Such a perfectionist, so intolerant of the tiniest slip-ups. It's hard living with you. So hard that I've gone numb in order to survive."

Michael pressed his face into his fists. He then looked up and turned to Jamie. "I was raised to be a perfectionist. I had to be in order to survive. One grade below ninety, one book on the floor instead of the shelf, one moan on a Sunday if I didn't feel like helping with the chores, and Pa was right there with a penalty to make sure it didn't happen again. I don't know if I can shake the disease he gave me."

At that moment Michael wasn't her husband anymore, and he wasn't the father of her children. He was a friend who was suffering. She touched his shoulder. "I'm sorry. I know you grew up in a penitentiary, but do you see what's happening? You're doing the exact same thing to Meg and Emily, and to me, that your father did to you."

"I have to get control of myself, let go of my past." He sat back. "There is some good news."

"What?"

"If I leave, maybe you'll meet a new man, someone you deserve."

"Oh, Michael. That hasn't even crossed my mind," she lied.

He smiled and patted his chest. "I meant me. There's someone else in here. I just have to find him."

"That could be interesting. How are you going to do that?"

"I wish I knew."

"Hey."

"What?"

"I'm sorry I overreacted when you were a little late this afternoon. I should've called you before I left with the kids. It probably reminded you of your father, to be scolded like that."

"And I should have called you when I looked at my watch and saw the time." He shook his head.

"What?"

"I hoped you wouldn't notice. I used to do the same thing with Pa. It never worked back then either."

"This might be a hard journey," Jamie said.

"At least I know where I'm starting. I'm going to find a good therapist this week. Maybe one with a halo."

"Good luck."

"What are you going to tell the kids?"

"The truth. That we fight too much and need a break. That it's not good for any of us."

Michael covered his face with his hands.

"I won't say anything bad about you. I'll make sure they know we both love them and that we're trying to work things out."

"When can I see them?"

"Come over on Friday. Bring a pizza and visit with the girls. I'll go see a movie with a friend or something."

"If this is how it has to be."

"For now," she said.

She hoped Michael didn't notice the moisture in her eyes. This could be the beginning of the marriage bust. The one thing she never wanted. Could Michael really change after all he had been through, and even if he did, could she trust that it was real? Jamie cleared her throat. "Stay on the couch tonight. Tomorrow I'll take the girls to swim lessons; then we'll grab dinner out. That should give you enough time to pack up some stuff."

"I can't believe this."

She lowered her head.

"Jamie?"

"Yeah?"

He hesitated. "We'll work this out."

Jamie forced a slight nod.

Chapter Nine

Michael woke up on the couch at 4:57. His head throbbed, and he tried to remember if he had a nightmare or if life as he knew it was about to change. The image of Jamie telling him to move out was fuzzy, so maybe it really didn't happen. He rose, wobbled up the stairs and into the bathroom, swallowed three Advils, then stepped into the shower. As he soaped up, the events that led to these flu-like symptoms became clear. He was leaving home. Now, the day needed to begin. Michael felt like going to work about as much as he felt like searching for a hotel to stay in, but he didn't have a choice.

He went into the bedroom with a towel wrapped around his waist. He stared at his sleeping wife then sat next to her on the edge of the bed. She rustled a little then barely opened her eyes.

"What?" Jamie whispered.

"I don't want to move out."

"Michael, just for a couple of weeks. It's settled."

"Look, I have to go into the office for a little while. I'll be home by noon; then we'll talk some more."

Jamie sighed and sat up. She peered at the ceiling then at Michael. "I can't remember when this raging river we call a marriage was last calm. It's going to take more than one or two conversations for it to settle down."

Michael's Adam's apple took a giant step upward in his throat. "When can I come back? I need to know when."

"I already told you. Come home after work on Friday with a pizza. In the meantime, find a wise counselor, and I'll try to do the same."

He narrowed his eyes. "I don't want to, but I have to go to work. It's going to be a hell of a day."

Jamie lay back down and covered her head with the blanket. Michael put on a light gray Armani suit. He glanced at the lump in the bed and bit his lip hard. The self-inflicted pain felt right. Maybe he wanted to make his mouth bleed. Anything to distract him from the grief that was tearing him apart. He plodded to his desk and opened the top drawer. Reaching to the back corner, he felt the velvet pouch that held his lucky quarter. He removed it, placed it between his thumb and forefinger, and rubbed it gently. Perhaps a genie would jump out and make everything all right. He placed the coin back in the small sack and stashed it in his pants pocket. Someplace deep down, hiding under a huge chunk of coal, was an ember of hope that he and Jamie could work things out. He shook his head at the thought. He didn't have a clue how to begin the quest toward marital bliss. This coin was all he had. His eyelids fell as he cleared his throat and left the room.

Michael almost went into his daughters' rooms but stopped. They'd wonder why he was coming in just to say good-bye. He had to keep the routine the same. On his way out, he grabbed a sixteen-ounce bottle of orange juice, a breakfast bar, and a banana that he would try to eat at some point during the day.

The emotional flu symptoms were in high gear by the time he was in his car. Hordes of remorse germs were attacking, and his hands could barely grasp the wheel. The garage door opened, but he didn't remember lifting his finger to push the button. He tried to think of what he needed to accomplish that day but couldn't.

"Come on, Michael. Keep the routine the same. Just go," he whispered.

He followed his own order, inched out of the driveway, and rolled down the street where home used to be.

Michael sat in his brown leather chair reviewing reports, when three staff attorneys and his assistant entered his office for their ten o'clock appointment. His body still ached, but he had to get through this meeting. He swiveled away from his walnut desk, glanced out the picture window, and lifted his eyebrows. When he stood, he offered a closed-lip smile then told his employees to have a seat at the conference table. He joined them, carrying a stack of documents. Michael gazed at their droopy expressions and muttered, "Good morning."

"Good morning," they mumbled.

Michael straightened his tie then delivered the bad news. "I reviewed the briefs you prepared for next week's preliminary hearing, and I'll have to be honest with you: they're Swiss cheese—full of holes. There were sections that made sense and some questions that were answered, but at this point they still need a lot of revision, and more research needs to be done."

He pressed his fingers together. "I made comments on your reports. Make the changes and have them back to me by Wednesday at one. That will give me the afternoon to go over them. Then I'll meet with each of you individually on Thursday. Jim, be here at nine thirty; Marilyn, eleven; and Ted, twelve."

He glanced at his gray-haired assistant, who peered over her bifocals. Her eyes told him to be kind.

Michael creased his forehead. "Got that, Cathleen?"

Cathleen pursed her thin lips then nodded.

Michael observed his staff's confused faces. "Any questions, concerns?"

"My brief is ironclad. I'm not sure where the holes could be," Jim said.

Michael leaned in. "We must have different definitions of *ironclad*. You'll see what holes I'm referring to when you look at my notes. Like I said, there were sections that were very good, but there were also some serious unanswered questions that could result in a lawsuit for our client." Their baffled expressions annoyed him, and he couldn't help adding, "You can figure this out. Everyone here has a law degree, right?"

Cathleen sighed.

If the malice emitted from these eight eyes were daggers, Michael would be dead. They despised him, but he wasn't paid to be popular. On the other hand, his cruel demeanor was destroying his life. The ogre had to start losing some battles to the prince who was hiding somewhere inside him. His marriage was hanging off a cliff, and if this gentle character didn't start making some appearances, his job just might end up next to it. Come on, Prince Michael. It would be a good chuckle moment, but what could he do. It wouldn't be appropriate to say, "And don't forget the pickle." He didn't even want to contemplate what they would interpret that to mean. Tweaking each of their noses and saying "I'm keeping these until all work is complete," certainly would cause some smirks, but not in the way he wanted. Suddenly, the prince came through.

First motivate. "Of course you have law degrees, and an impressive performance record. That's why I know you can produce high-caliber work. The sessions next week will be successful."

He walked over to his desk, opened the top drawer, and pulled out a gag gift that a senior partner had given him when he was appointed to this position. It was a pen that had a judge's bobble head attached to the top. Michael shook it at his staff. "You can do it."

Their sharp glares turned into saucers of surprise. Silence filled the room, followed by genuine chuckles. The light laughs dispersed the tension, and body postures went from rigid to relaxed. As they got up to leave, each one took their reports, and Marilyn said, "Thanks for the input." Michael couldn't remember the last time he'd heard that.

After they left, he leaned on his file cabinet and looked out the window. He laced his fingers together and brought them to his chin. A stream of warmth flowed through him. He closed his eyes, savoring the sensation. This laughter medicine really worked. "One point for Prince Michael, and more to come."

All too soon the phone jolted him. He picked up the receiver and grimaced. His boss wanted to see him immediately.

He hung up then froze. What was Jamie doing right now? Was she feeling sad? He gazed at the floor. Probably not. She was probably sipping coffee while perusing today's deals on Amazon. Michael grabbed his notepad as he headed out of his office. "Must be nice," he grumbled.

The garage door opened, signaling Jamie to get out of bed. She rose and stretched. Frankenstein was finally gone.

After washing up, she put on a faded pair of blue jeans and a comfy T-shirt, and slipped into a pair of sandals. She woke Megan and Emily, fixed them apple cinnamon oatmeal, and got them on the bus by eight. She needed to pick them up at three thirty, take them to swim lessons, and get them dinner. When they got home, she'd tell them that their dad would be staying in a hotel for a little while. That was about all of the future she could handle right now.

Jamie traipsed into the kitchen and poured coffee into a blue stoneware mug that she bought at a pottery shop when she and Michael went hiking in Wyoming. She circled the rim with her finger. They took that trip eight years ago. She couldn't help but smile as she recalled how Michael imitated an agitated bison they had seen in Yellowstone Park. Thank God they were in the car, because the open mockery could have provoked the beast to charge if they were with it on the prairie. She furrowed her eyebrows. What had happened to her husband's silly side?

Jamie sipped her coffee and swayed. The air felt light. She picked up the salt shaker and sprinkled tiny white crystals onto the counter. No one screamed, "Why'd you do that?" She could leave the salt there for three days, and no one would care. Jamie smiled and spun around. This must be how a duck feels when a snapping turtle leaves the pond. She sat on a stool at the island and clasped the oversized mug. The warmth from the coffee seeped into her palms, and she focused on the calm.

When her mini-meditation was over, she glanced at the kitchen doorway. A madman wouldn't be bursting in blaming her for some felony, like the girls leaving their yogurt containers on the coffee table. She sat a while longer trying to figure out what she could do. Stumped, she roamed to the refrigerator and perused her list.

"First things first: that hornets' nest has to go." She peered out the kitchen window. At least twenty hornets buzzed around the nest attached to the outside casing. How should she handle this dangerous project? She glanced at the can of insect killer sitting on the counter. The safest thing to do was to open the window and screen, spray, and then close them quickly before the disturbed insects attacked.

"Okay, my little pests, I hate to ruin your morning, but you are about to be history." She held the can in one hand, raised the window then the screen, and blasted the poison at her target. There was a flurry of insect activity, and Jamie swiftly sealed her house back up for safety. When she looked up, she saw dozens of hornets emerging from the nest to join those already outside. She couldn't figure out how they could all fit in their dwelling, which was the size of an apple. Some of the hornets sensed the venom and fled. Others circled around the nest as if considering their next move. They sensed the toxic substance but weren't quite ready to leave home. Then there were those that darted back and forth in a straight line, knowing they should depart but unsure of where to go. A few of the circlers and darters flew away, determining that uncertainty was better than death. The hornets that remained were lifers, and that life was about to be terminated.

"Go on, little hornets," Jamie said. "You'll find a new and better home. Just go."

But they stayed.

"The poison will kill you. Go on."

The hornets did not respond to her warning. Jamie watched them fall to their death into the alley that separated her home from her neighbor's.

"What a show," she whispered.

She contemplated the creature feature she just witnessed. Why did some hornets flee the instant they suspected danger? Why did some cling until it was almost too late? Why did some hang on until annihilation was inevitable?

"Hmm, if I behaved like a hornet and was aware that I lived in a house that had been sprayed with malice, cruelty, and arrogance, what would I do?"

Jamie roamed around the kitchen with her arms folded. She stopped at the window and peered down at the cowardly hornets who had chosen death over adventure.

"You are a darter, Jamie," she murmured. "You were about to be poisoned, but you had the courage to fly away. The question is, will you return?"

She thought about money. She thought about Megan and Emily having to travel between houses. She thought about working full time while trying to take care of a home and children. Then she thought about spending another forty or fifty years with Michael.

"God, life is hell."

She put her face in her hands and tried to will away the confusion.

Her stomach started to ache. She picked up the phone to call Matilda. They could have lunch and joke around. Matilda would be so jealous of Jamie's possibly single status. She might even persuade Jamie to go away some Saturday night for a wild girl's night out to celebrate. Jamie punched in three numbers then stopped. If she told Matilda, all of their friends would know before nightfall. In fact, everyone in DC would know. Kids might ask Meg and Emily about the split, and she couldn't have that. This was a private matter.

She rubbed her belly, hoping the pain would dissipate. It didn't work. She traipsed to her computer and signed in to Facebook. There was a message from Steve. "What's up?"

That was it. She could tell him about her troubles. Steve didn't know any of her friends. It was safe, and venting would make her feel better. Maybe he'd even offer some good advice. In fact, now that she was separated from Michael, she might just meet Steve for that cup of coffee on Friday. It would be nice to make a new friend.

Jamie typed, "Feeling a little blue. My husband and I separated."

Michael pushed Ctrl+S on his keyboard to save the document he had been working on. He then pushed the pads of his index fingers together and whispered, "Control save." He shook his head and dropped his hands. "You've resorted to hocus pocus to fix the mess you're in."

Michael glanced at the digital clock in the corner of his monitor. It was seven and time to go who knew where. He shut down his computer, grabbed some clothes, which he stored in his office closet, and walked out of the office. As he pushed the down button to call the elevator, he wondered where his body would take him.

About a half hour later, Michael found himself sitting on a bench in Dupont Circle. The park was relatively quiet except for the spraying of the fountain. A few elderly men played chess, but Rufus wasn't around. Michael felt disappointed. He could use a little positive energy, and that guy had plenty to spare.

His growling stomach told him that he needed to eat. It was a good sign. Loss had consumed him all day, and hunger felt so much better. He turned his head when a dog barked. A man and a woman walking a black Irish wolfhound approached. They laughed and talked—a happy couple. "Good luck," Michael said under his breath as they passed by. The commanding presence of the giant dog reminded him of a bear, which reminded him of the trip he and Jamie had taken to Yellowstone a long marriage ago. She was so afraid they would be attacked by a grizzly bear as they wandered along the Storm Point Trail. She insisted on wearing a small gold bell on her belt loop, confident that this would prevent a fatal attack. So instead of savoring the gentle sounds of nature, all Michael heard was *ting-a-ling*, *ting-a-ling*. The memory made him smile.

He and Jamie once had such an incredible love. It started with the hollowing of his insides when he first met her at a party. It seemed to be making room for a strong emotion that he had never experienced. When he asked her to go see *Star Wars* with him, Jamie exclaimed, "I love *Star Wars*!" Michael had actually met a sweet, smart woman who was well versed in the adventures of R2-D2, Han Solo, and Chewbacca.

That love had to be somewhere. They'd find the treasure again. Dusk was quickly turning into night, so Michael stood and slowly walked to his car. When he turned the key to start the engine, the clock on the dash flashed 8:00. If he were home right now, he'd be reading to Megan and Emily. Michael paused before he drove away.

"Mommy, you don't read it right," Emily said, as she cuddled up to Jamie.

Jamie put the paperback copy of *Charlotte's Web* on her lap. "What do you mean?"

Emily sat up straight and squeaked, "'Yahoo!' That's how Daddy makes Wilbur the pig talk."

Jamie laughed. "Daddy squeals like a pig?"

"And he makes Charlotte the spider talk like this. 'I drink them. Drink their blood. I love blood,'" Megan said, trying her best to imitate a Transylvanian vampire.

Jamie never paid attention when Michael read to the girls at night. Instead she loaded the dishwasher, wiped down the tub after her daughters' baths, or did some other mundane chore. Maybe she should have sat with them once in a while. It sounded like Michael's silly side came out during the reading ritual.

She rubbed Megan's and Emily's backs. "I'll work on my acting skills for story time, but right now it's bedtime."

"Can Daddy come over tomorrow to read to us?" Megan asked.

Jamie sighed. "No, honey. I told you. Mommy and Daddy are taking a little break. We're fighting way too much, and it's not good for any of us."

She felt Megan's shoulder blade tense through the cotton of her pajamas. Jamie was eight when her mother explained why Daddy wouldn't be living with them anymore. She recalled the panic that imploded when she heard the news. "I know it's hard, but sometimes married people need time away from each other." She pulled her daughters close. "Daddy loves you, and so do I."

"Will Daddy get nicer in the hotel?" Emily asked.

Jamie shrugged and almost whispered, "Highly doubtful."

Chapter Ten

Jamie felt nauseated and hoped she wouldn't vomit. Her insides were signaling that it was a strong possibility. The booth she chose for her rendezvous with Steve was close to the bathroom just in case. She needed this spot, not only because her stomach might erupt, but it also provided a quick escape route in case she chickened out. Yesterday she had been so excited about this holiday away from her dreary existence, but today anxiety ruled.

She bit her fingertips like a naughty girl who was about to try her first cigarette. When Jamie finally stopped nibbling, she glanced at her hand. "Ugh." Her nails were uneven, and cuticles were sprouting. Why hadn't she treated herself to a manicure?

Jamie practiced smiling and listening with her fingers interlaced. This was awful. Not only did she have to stay seated to conceal her potbelly, she had to think of ways to make her hands go underground. She sighed as she remembered how horrible dating could be. Michael's face popped into her head. Why didn't he turn out to be the prince she had hoped for—the dumb bastard.

"Michael," she whispered. She hadn't even been separated five days and was already meeting another man for coffee at a hotel. Jamie waffled about this date the entire week, but Steve convinced her it was a good idea. He told her it was harmless, and she had the right to have a little fun after all she had been through. It felt good to be nurtured, and she wanted more.

Beads of sweat broke out from every pore on her forehead. Soon Jamie's foundation would melt away, and her sunspots would reveal themselves. What would Steve think when he saw this dowdy housewife and not the glamour girl on her posts? Well, maybe not glamorous, but certainly cute. Maybe her low-cut black sweater would distract him. She scanned the restaurant, and when no one was looking, she shoved her breasts into place. More than one magazine article told her that a voluptuous chest could make up for a lot in a man's eyes. She gazed toward the ceiling. This whole thing was so ridiculous, and her anger at Michael was growing. He was to blame for driving her to this level of insanity.

No matter how weird this meeting was, one thing was clear: she would not have sex with Steve. Just to be sure, Jamie wore graying white briefs and a pink bra that she bought at Target last year. A potential lover would not get his first view of her modeling grandma-style underwear that should have been tossed out months ago. Even if red lace hid beneath her outer layer, Jamie was ninety-nine percent certain she wouldn't take a giant step away from her marriage by sneaking between the sheets with a strange man. She was not a cheater. Although, Steve did have incredible hands, at least in his photos, and it could be a pinch tempting. These garments were her shield against sensual persuasion.

Oh my God. There he is. Oh my God. He's a bum. Jamie hid behind the menu.

Steve had shaggy hair, whiskers, and a crumpled shirt. His rugged style looked so much better on Facebook. The son of a bitch didn't even own an iron, a razor, or a comb. For an instant she pictured how clean and polished Michael always looked. He really was easy on the eyes, but she didn't have time for comparisons right now. If she got up to leave, he'd spot her.

Think, Jamie, think. When he finds me, I'll stand up, say my daughters' school just called, go home, and delete his profile. I promise, God, I'll never do this again. Just get me out of here.

"Hey, Jamie." Steve bent over and kissed her cheek. "You're even prettier in person."

The vomit would be here any minute. "Thanks." She smiled. Why was she always so damned polite? Why didn't she stand up, deliver her planned excuse, and dart out?

A waitress came over and asked if they wanted coffee.

Steve asked, "Do you?"

She was speechless.

"We'll have two coffees and whatever muffins are the best," he said, staring at Jamie.

Steve grinned. He did have nice teeth. She'd give him that. And his green eyes really did sparkle, but the rest of him was so sloppy. She couldn't do sloppy, not after Michael. She'd have a little conversation then say she had an appointment. It was that easy.

"So you have a little time off from the tennis club this morning?" Jamie asked.

"Yup. Not much scheduled this month, but I'll be in the pro shop quite a bit. Then we shut down from November till March."

"Then what?"

"Unemployment. It's great. I get paid to do nothing."

Jamie felt like saying, "So a healthy thirty-five-year-old man takes tax dollars to sit around and do nothing," but refrained. "You don't do anything for four months?"

"I go up north, ski a little, visit with friends, check out the local bands. I'm open. How about you? I know that you're married—well, sort of married—with kids, and don't work, right?"

"That's right. My daughters are both in school now, so I'll be looking for a job soon. And I'm still very married. We just need a little respite."

"Don't you have a Diamond Jim kind of husband? And I think it's so cool that you're meeting with a dude you met on the Internet while he's off slaving away. He's a real pit bull, right?"

Steve had just thrown a heavy ball of reality at her, and it hurt. She lowered her eyes.

"What's wrong?"

"My husband can be difficult, but his job is very demanding, and I'm not with him for his money."

"Jamie, sweetie, it's okay. Lots of women are out there doing the same thing. Don't leave me for a guilt trip. Milk the situation. We could have a lot fun on his dime."

"That's not going to happen." She was relieved when the waitress came over, poured the coffee, and set the blueberry muffins on the table. She needed a second to think.

"How do you know a lot of women do this?"

"I've met them. Lots of lonely ladies out there in cyber-space. You happen to be one of the prettiest. Like, are you wearing color-enhanced contacts, or are your eyes really that blue?" He bit off half of his muffin and swallowed it along with a gulp of coffee.

At that very moment, Jamie swore off men. Muffin crumbs speckled Steve's lips, and she wanted to tell him to use a napkin.

"I mean, you're not just pretty, beautiful is more like it." Steve ogled her face then shifted his gaze to her chest. "Incredible."

Jamie's stomach turned. She managed, "Excuse me," and ran into the ladies room.

The vomit landed in the toilet. She held the rim for a few seconds then stood. She washed her hands with hot water and lots of soap, then rinsed out her mouth several times. Finally, she splashed her face and wiped it dry with a paper towel.

When she turned around, she saw Steve. Jamie froze. She barely heard her own voice say, "What are you doing in here?"

"Wanted to make sure you were okay. Are you?"

Jamie tried to walk around the predator, but he blocked her. She inhaled deeply. "You know, Steve, this is not work-ing for me."

He took a step forward and cupped Jamie's cheek in his hand. "It's normal to be a little nervous."

"You're in the ladies room."

"A little risk isn't a bad thing."

Before she could slap his hand, Steve pressed his lips to hers and plunged his tongue into her mouth. It tasted like a cigarette omelet, and she bit it, but that just stimulated the action. His free hand squeezed her left breast. Jamie thrust him away with the strength of Tarzan, ran out the door, and hurried to their table.

Steve trailed after her. "What's wrong? You were so different on the net."

She glared at him. "Big mistake. It's over."

"Damn. Really? You don't want to put a room on your sugar daddy's credit card just once? We'll order mimosas to help you relax. It'll be a blast, and I mean a blast."

"Oh God." Jamie took a twenty out of her wallet and threw it on the table.

"You're really leaving?"

"Don't contact me again."

"No problem. Hey, have fun with your suit and tie in your ice mansion."

Jamie rushed out of the hotel and walked the streets for a long time. She didn't want Steve to see her get in the van. He probably wasn't a stalker, but how did she know?

When she got home, she fired up the computer and logged onto Facebook. Steve's photo welcomed her. Jamie gasped and turned away. After she caught her breath, she told herself to act fast and think later. She deleted her entire account. It wasn't enough. She ordered a system recovery and trashed her life in cyber-land. All evidence of her fling with Steve would soon be gone along with every file she ever created. She just hoped it would be that easy to erase this whole fiasco from her mind.

After some time spent in shock, reality set in. Jamie glanced at her reflection in the computer monitor. It hurt, so she walked away. Right now she was safe in her house, but that Steve was a real creep. Who knew what he would have done if he got her alone? The bathroom grope was just a prelude. Jamie thought she might vomit again, but her insides were empty. What if he had harmed her? What would Meg and Emily do? She had to stop her stupid games. They were the same games her mother used to play. They weren't fun to watch, and they weren't fun to imitate. Her head started to ache.

Jamie went to the medicine cabinet to get a painkiller but stopped. She deserved the pain. Hanging her head, she slogged into the kitchen and peered out the window. The hornets' nest was still there, but the life inside was gone. That's just how she felt. She had a body, but it was vacant.

It was time to change. Do something meaningful. Jamie leaned against the wall. "Easier said than done," she murmured. When in her life had she felt confident, valuable in some way? Her throat thickened as she tried to think of a time. After a few minutes, she whispered, "College, work." Jamie pulled her smartphone out of her pocket and punched in the number for the newspaper where she used to work, surprised that she still remembered it. Jamie wanted her old job back.

Chapter Eleven

Michael sat at his office desk. He tried to review a document, but the words merged together on the page. It may as well have been written in Chinese. His brain was broken along with his spirit. He flung the report onto the floor and swiveled around to view the world from his window. The reality of his situation was sinking in. He lost his family and was living in a hotel. Jamie told him it was only for a week or two, but Michael knew the truth. It was her way of convincing him to leave. Soon she would have the door locks changed. He didn't blame her. Living with him was like walking on a mine field. She didn't know when he would detonate, and neither did he. At least Jamie could banish him from her life. He couldn't move out of his own body, no matter how much he wanted to.

Tonight he'd go home for a visit, share a pizza with Megan and Emily, read them a bedtime story; then Jamie would ask him if he had figured out why he had such an erratic temperament. He'd say yes and explain that it was because he was walking around in shoes that his father made for him, and they didn't fit. She'd ask if he found a new pair. He'd have to say no, and that he didn't think he would. What was he going to do? Quit his job, ditch his obligations, and begin a journey to find a comfortable pair? While he was on his adventure, there wouldn't be any money. Jamie and the girls could stay in a homeless shelter and get their meals in soup kitchens. Michael closed his eyes and tried to release his grief through tears, but they still wouldn't come. If this pain didn't ignite them, nothing would.

He had to get out of his office. The chocolate and wheat tones of this space were the color of his prison, and he couldn't look at them one more minute. Michael crammed several files into his briefcase, grabbed it, and told Cathleen he was taking off early.

"Are those reports ready for Frank? He's been asking for them."

"They still need work. I'll finish them at home."

"The preliminary is on Monday, and Frank will be by to get the documents before he leaves."

"Tell Frank I've got everything under control," Michael said, even though he didn't.

"If you say so."

"Have a good weekend, Cathleen."

It was three o'clock, and he had more than two hours to kill before his dinner date with the girls. One thing was certain: he wasn't going back to that hotel. It reminded him that he was a bad boy and had been placed in timeout. Suddenly, Dupont Circle popped into his head. He grinned as he stepped onto the elevator and silenced his BlackBerry. Maybe that guy, Rufus, would be available for a chess match.

The crisp air on the sunny September afternoon helped lift Michael's spirit. He walked into Dupont Circle and smiled when he saw Rufus sitting on a stone bench, watching pigeons hop around. Michael took off his tie and stuffed it into his suit jacket pocket. As he approached, Rufus looked up, then stood.

"Hey, it's Michael Stolis, my chess buddy."

"Hey, Rufus, hope you're up for a chess rally with a feeble opponent," Michael replied as they shook hands. He couldn't figure out what it was about this man that settled his nerves. Maybe there was a message hiding under his skin, a message just for him.

"How'd you ever remember my last name?" Michael asked.

Rufus's eyebrows shot up. "I am up for a chess rally, but not with a feeble opponent. I prefer the novice I played last Friday, and I'm good with names. Lots of practice."

"I can't even remember my next door neighbor's name. Where'd you get the practice?"

Rufus reached for his windbreaker, which was about to be disturbed by a gust of wind. He put it on and zippered it. "Drove a bus for the DC Transit Authority for forty years. That's a long time to ride around this town. Found I needed some games to play to make my time on the job a bit more fun. I decided to learn all of my regular riders' names. Don't sound like much of a thrill, but it kept me entertained." Shrugging his shoulders, Rufus continued, "Anytime someone new got on the bus I'd say, 'Good morning and to whom am I greeting?' I got a kick out of seeing the surprised expressions when the patrons encountered this friendly chauffeur. You see, most bus drivers just nod at people when they climb aboard, and some don't even do that. It kind of shocked people when words popped out of my mouth."

"And you'd remember their names just after hearing them one time?" Michael asked, as he sat down on the bench.

Rufus settled in next to him. "There's a trick to it. I'd say, 'Good morning, Mark' or Chris or whoever. I'd introduce myself, tell them to enjoy the ride, and use their name again, then say it silently three times."

Michael nodded once. "I'm impressed. You must have a phenomenal memory."

"My memory's not so hot. At least that's what my teachers told me back in the day," Rufus said, chuckling. "After I rehearsed their names, I'd match something about the passengers to it. Like when Penny first started riding with me; I said there's Penny with her penny-pinchin' nose. Or with Bob, I'd look in my rearview mirror and see his head bobbing up and down, ya know, bob bob bob. Like I said, it was a game to help the time pass, and I found that people appreciated it too. I swear some of the regulars thought of me as their best friend, sitting up front, telling me about their family problems and work issues. I felt like a bartender on wheels."

"It sounds like you had a party bus."

"Oh yeah. Decorated it with lights around the holidays. Sometimes I'd bake cookies and hand them out to the folks when they got on. It was amazing how they responded to this simple gesture. I'd say, 'It's not a million dollars. It's a cookie.'" Rufus shook his head and looked directly at Michael. "Try the name game sometime. You'll see how people brighten up when you say *hi* or *bye* then put their name after it. Now, if you haven't noticed, you soon will: it's dangerous to ask me a question. Might not make it home till Thanksgiving the way I can go on," Rufus said.

He patted Michael firmly on the back, walked over to one of the chess tables, and placed a quarter on it. "Hey, Jonas, you got two more games; then my turn. You've been hogging this table for near an hour."

"Go away, Rufus."

"Two more games, and I'm countin'."

Michael observed this man with a sense of wonder. It was like Rufus had a magic wand and used it to put a spell on him. For the first time since he had been banished from his home, Michael didn't feel sick, and he needed to figure out why.

When Rufus returned, he sat back down and asked, "So what'd you do for fun this week?"

Michael narrowed his eyes. "It was not a fun week."

After some silence, Rufus said, "Come on, one fun thing. There had to be one fun thing."

"I had a great meal last Sunday at Sam's Deli. After that I went home and watched a ball game. That's just about all that I would categorize as fun."

Rufus studied Michael like he was a jigsaw puzzle that was put together all wrong. "Sam's is always fun if you like to eat, which I do, and I love watching a good ball game. So out of one hundred sixty-eight hours in the week, you had roughly four hours of fun."

Michael quickly inspected the park and saw all kinds of fun going on around him, but he wasn't part of it. "That about sizes it up. Not just this week either. I don't have a lot of experience with fun."

"What about that dinner you went to last Friday? Wasn't that fun?"

"Don't bring it up. It was a disaster."

111

"Understood. Your life must—well, it must suck."

Michael frowned, "It really does." It felt good to admit this out loud.

Rufus's eyes deepened with concern.

Michael welcomed the sympathy. There wasn't anyone he could share his anguish with, but Rufus seemed willing to listen, maybe even help. It suddenly occurred to him what was happening. He was making a friend. At this point in his life, he had some acquaintances, who he didn't really care for, but no buds to hang with. Michael smiled. He liked the idea of having a friend.

Rufus sat back and clasped his hands behind his head. "Are you ready for a crash course in fun?"

Michael's smile widened. "Bring it on."

"Here goes. It all has to do with how you view your time on this planet. You see, I pretend. Now, pretending is fun," Rufus said with a nod. "Anyway, I pretend that before I came to earth I had a conversation with Saint Peter or God or Jesus or Buddha—don't matter who—and whoever said, 'You're going to earth for one hundred years, at the most. I'm going to put you in the United States, so you'll have a lot of opportunity. I think I'll make you black, as that may give you a bit of a challenge with some in that country. It'll make you stronger. I'll give you a special talent—up to you to find it. Pay attention, and you'll figure it out. Now go and have fun. It's a real neat place—some problems, but always solutions too. Again, up to you to find them. Remember, you've only got one hundred years, at the very most. When you come back, I'll be waiting, and I'll want to hear all about your trip.'"

Rufus whacked his knees. "And off I go. Michael, I often think about what I'm going to report when I go back home.

Ya know, what kind of fun I had. Did I solve some problems or just sit around and complain about them? Did I ever find that talent? Makes me think about how I live from day to day. Now, what would you say if your time here was up right now and you had to make your life report to God or one of his assistants?"

Michael was silent for several seconds. "Pretty good, Rufus. That's two times in five minutes that I can't think of an answer to one of your questions. Can I have an extension?"

"If you need an extension, you'll have to make some changes with how you spend your time. Nothing's going to surface if it's not coming out now."

"I don't have room for changes. My bag is packed so full with obligations that I can hardly zipper it."

"You'll have to take a few things out and add some new clothes that have a little more pizzazz. Go through your bag and see if you can't find a couple of outfits that just aren't working for you anymore. Toss 'em. If you look hard enough, you'll find something."

"What do you do for fun?"

"There's so much. I take long walks every day. Always something new to see. I couldn't ask for a more vibrant city to wander around. There are the museums, the zoo, the people, the exhibits. It's endless here. Eating is always fun. I like coming down to the circle and chatting with people like you. I enjoy reading, riding my bike, watching a good ball game. I volunteer at the Boys & Girls Club. Always a good feeling to help someone out, especially young people. I could go on, but I think you get the idea."

"You're retired, right? That helps. And what do you do at the Boys & Girls Club?"

"Being retired frees up time, but I made sure to have some fun on that bus every day. At the club, I play chess with the kids, maybe some hoop. Believe it or not, I'm not bad with a basketball. The guys think it's a hoot, seeing this old guy rack up points."

"What's it like there?"

"What you'd expect for a nonprofit. Most of the facilities in DC need repairs. They're understaffed, underequipped. I'll give you the fifty-cent tour of the branch I work at if you want."

"Sure. How'd you get involved?"

"My nephew is the director of the Northwest DC branches, and he asked me to help out."

"That sounds like a big job. When are you there?"

"It's a huge job, but he loves it. Sort of his mission. I'll be at the Westland Middle School for a while. They're starting a new after school program, and we're getting it ready. Gonna focus on music. I'm there all different times." Rufus leaned in. "What's good for you?"

Rufus was really serious about giving him the tour. Next week was tightly scheduled, but he could stop in one evening. Michael took out his BlackBerry. Of course, there was a voicemail and a text message from both Frank and Cathleen, but they could wait. He checked his calendar.

"Monday at five thirty?"

"Sounds good. Your family won't mind?"

Michael smirked, "Not at all. What's the address?"

"Hey, Rufus, your turn at the table, and I got three games in with all that yappin' you're doing," Jonas yelled.

"When you have something to say, you speak it. I don't think you'd understand that, Jonas."

"Always with the comebacks, you are," Jonas said. "Don't play too long. Friday night is upon us, and I want to make some cash for dinner from the newbies? You don't want me to go hungry tonight, do ya, Rufus?"

"Wouldn't want that at all. Give us a few; then you can keep the table until you earn what you need."

With that, Rufus put his hand on Michael's shoulder and looked him straight in the eye. "Let's start the weekend with a little fun. The chess game is on."

They played four games in thirty-five minutes, and Michael didn't come close to winning any of them.

"Man, I can't beat you."

"Of course you can beat me; just keep coming. It'll happen. My chess advice is to add a little more spice to your life. It'll loosen you up, make you less jittery. Once you're more relaxed, the wins will come."

"I'm not jittery."

"Don't tell yourself lies. You're as jittery as an old woman in DC traffic," Rufus said, as he got up from the table. "Hey, Jonas, time for work. The table is yours."

Michael followed Rufus. "What makes you say I'm jittery?"

"The way you turn your head from side to side. The way your eyes dart around the board. The way you tense up before each game. It's all jittery. Your movements need to be fluid when you play this game."

Rufus was right. Michael did all of those things. In fact, he was jiggling the keys in his pocket at that very moment. He stopped, rested his hands on his hips, and asked, "What should I do?"

"Add that fun to your life, and it'll start to happen. Clean out your bag. I know you'll find some clutter. Now, I'll see you on Monday?"

"You bet."

The two men parted in opposite directions. After Michael walked a few yards, he turned to watch Rufus head up Massachusetts Avenue. He wondered if he was going home to his family. Did he even have a family? Except for his nephew, he hadn't mentioned anyone. Maybe Rufus was going to Sam's Deli or the Boys & Girls Club. Wherever it was, Michael felt like following him. He was certain that if he trailed after that man, he'd find shoes that fit.

Michael thought about their conversation and contemplated the concept of *fun*. What was it? Was it simply doing what you liked? Was it laughing out loud at something funny? Did exercise count as fun? No. Exercise was something he did to keep his body fit, his mind clear, and his stress level from exploding. Michael walked to his car, stepped in, and tapped the steering wheel. He stared out the windshield almost forgetting where he was. After a few moments, he shook himself out of his trance.

He reached for his BlackBerry to order the pizza. He fiddled with it then put it back in his jacket pocket. Grinning, he maneuvered his way out of the parking spot and drove to a gourmet grocery store in Georgetown. He strolled through the market and threw green peppers, garlic, spinach, homemade sausage, mushrooms, grated mozzarella cheese, and tomato sauce into his basket. In the bakery section, he ordered four freshly made pizza rounds then took the bag of goodies home to his family.

Chapter Twelve

Michael stood by the door inside the garage with the paper bag in his arms. Should he knock or just go in? He'd have to ask Jamie what the protocol was. Maybe she'd say, "Come home, and we'll work everything out." He closed his eyes, said a prayer, and walked inside.

Megan and Emily ran down the hall shouting, "Daddy." They hugged him around the waist. He put the bag down and squeezed them hard. He hadn't received a greeting like this in a long time.

Emily looked up at him. "Mommy said you moved to a hotel. Can we come over and use the pool?"

Michael's heart sank. Jamie had used the word—*moved.* "Of course you can, but I won't be there long."

"Mommy said if you come home, there won't be any more fighting," Megan said.

Hearing the word *if* hurt worse than stubbing his toe. He needed to change the topic fast. "That's right, and I've got a surprise for you guys. Where's Mom?" Michael picked up the bag, went into the kitchen, and set it on the counter.

The girls ran after him. "What's the surprise?"

"Let me talk to Mom first; then I'll show you."

They followed him into the living room. The TV was blaring as usual, but Jamie wasn't glued to her spot at the computer. She huddled under a blanket on the couch. Her body was there, but it didn't seem like anyone was in it. She stared at the garden through the French doors, oblivious to the fact that he had returned. The girls plopped on the floor and continued to watch some show. Jamie still didn't move.

"Hey, are you okay?"

"Michael," she whispered, glancing up at him.

"I wasn't sure if I should knock or just walk in."

"Don't be silly. Come right in. We're not at the knocking point yet."

These small words were killing him—*yet* and *if*. He was a lawyer and knew exactly where this case was headed. "Anyway, are you okay? You look awful. No offense."

"None taken. I've felt nauseated most of the day. Sit down."

Michael sat on the far end of the couch, stretched his arm over the top, and placed his ankle on his knee. "Sorry, Jaim. Do you need anything?"

She shook her head. "I'll feel better soon. How was your week?"

"Awful. I hate that hotel. When can I come home?"

Jamie sighed. "I don't know. I'm not ready yet. We'll talk when the girls are in bed."

Michael furrowed his eyebrows. "How'd they react when you told them?"

"Emily thinks you're so lucky because you get to live in a hotel, and Megan wants to know if she can go to Banana Splits, that kids program for divorced families."

"Kids, huh?"

"I know. They're so resilient." Jamie sat up straighter. "Did you bring home a pizza? I don't smell it."

"I brought something else. How can you think about pizza with an upset stomach?"

"I meant for the kids."

"Is anything else wrong? I mean more than a bellyache."

"I called my old boss about a job at the paper today, and he almost laughed out loud. Keith said they just had to lay off staff, and that newspapers were becoming dinosaurs. Everyone gets their information from the Internet or twenty-four-hour news, so papers around the country are going under. Then he said, because I had let my skills go stale, I might as well start a new career."

"Ouch. What are you going to do?"

Jamie fiddled with her hair ends. "I'm not past the panic stage yet, but once I can think clearly, I'll pull together a resume and start searching. Not sure what I'll say about the past seven years."

"Something will come up," he said, wondering if it really would.

Michael's BlackBerry beeped. He saw Frank's name on caller ID and pushed the ignore button. "Damn it."

"Who was it?"

"Frank. Third time he's called since I left the office, and it's not even six."

"He's a real thorn in your side, huh?"

"More like a cactus up my ass. One time he e-mailed at midnight and was having a shit fit by seven in the morning 'cause I hadn't gotten back to him."

"Watch your mouth in front of the kids."

"Jamie, look at them. They didn't hear it. They're hypnotized by that screen—wouldn't even notice if you switched the channel. It's like *Poltergeist* is in our own living room."

Jamie almost smiled. "What's the surprise?"

"Get ready for the whine fest." He turned off the TV.

"Dad, why'd you do that?" Megan cried.

Michael winked at Jamie and walked into the kitchen. His family followed him. They sat around the kitchen island and waited.

"Did you bring us a puppy, Daddy?" Emily asked.

"No."

"Thank God," Jamie said.

"But, Mommy, I want a puppy," Emily said.

"No sense arguing. I don't have a puppy in my pocket," Michael said.

"Are we going to Disney World?" Megan asked.

Michael wondered if she'd still be excited when he pulled an onion out of the bag. "Sorry. Nothing that big."

Megan moaned.

"Just tell us, Michael," Jamie said.

He placed the brown sack in the center of the island, and his family peeked inside.

"Dad, those are groceries. Where's the surprise?" Megan asked.

"The surprise is we're going to make our own pizzas tonight. I'm sure we can do much better than Mario's. I bought lots of different things, so you can put whatever you like on it."

"You can make the pizzas. I'm going to finish watching Dora," Megan said, as she slid off the stool.

"Wait for me," Emily said. "Pizza's not really a surprise, Daddy."

"No TV. You watch way too much. If you want to eat these pizzas, you have to help make them," Michael said.

"Your father's right. You two do watch too much TV. I'm helping," Jamie said, as she started taking food out of the bag.

Michael tapped both his ears. "I think there's something wrong with my hearing. Did you just say I was right?"

"Yes. You're right. They watch too much TV," Jamie said, as she walked over to the sink with some vegetables in her hands.

"I feel the stun rays going right through me. You never say I'm right."

"Yes, I do. When you're right, I agree with you. It's just that you're usually wrong."

"I'm not usually wrong. When was the last time I was wrong?"

"I refuse to bring up the hundreds of things that I could, which would lead to a big feud. Now, do you want to keep bickering about the fact that I said you're right, or do you want to get on with the pizza party?"

"I choose the pizza party. Toss me a pepper."

"Good. Em, your job can be to break up the meat and put it in the frying pan; Meg, you can put the sauce and cheese into bowls, so they're easy to scoop out. I'll work on cutting the mushrooms. This is fun. Good idea," Jamie said with a grin.

"Fun? Did you say fun?"

Jamie put the knife down, folded her arms, and looked at him. "Yes, I did. Who would have thought? The Stolis family is having fun."

"I hit a triple. I'm right, then this is fun, and finally, good idea. Blow me over," he said, waving a napkin in the air. He whacked his head with it then fell to the floor. The stunt resulted in giggles from the three ladies in his life. When he gazed up at Jamie, a flicker of light shimmered in her eyes. Maybe that spark would eventually ignite a fire. It was a long shot, but it was all he had.

"You're funny, Daddy," Emily said when he stood.

Michael bent down and kissed the top of her head. "I'm starving. Let's get down to pizza business."

After dinner, stories, and goodnights, it was time for Michael to leave. When he came downstairs, he found Jamie sitting in the window seat of the dining room, with her knees pulled to her chest. He went in, grabbed a chair, and moved it close to her before sitting. He scratched his chin and said, "What's going on?"

"That really was fun tonight."

Okay, she needed to ease into the tough talk. "You think?" Michael said. "We should cook together more. The kids got a kick out it."

"They loved it!" Jamie exclaimed. "Wasn't it neat how Emily made a face with her toppings? She has a creative side."

"She really does." He didn't have the patience for this. He had spent the past week wandering around like a nomad and wanted some clear answers. "Now, what's going on?"

"Nothing's changed since Sunday. I need a few weeks to think about things."

"You said a week or two. Now it's a few?"

"Whatever, it's only been five days."

"I hate not being here. I feel sick all of the time. I can't do my job. I get to that damn hotel room and just sit there. I try to read but can't comprehend a single sentence. I want to come home, Jamie."

Jamie rolled her eyes. "You were unbearable to live with. I mean it. I found at least a million ways to dodge your wrath, and it turned out to be a little dangerous."

"What do you mean *dangerous?*"

She clicked her fingernails before responding. "I don't know. I lost myself, and I don't even know where to start the search to find me again. I can't do it with you here."

"Damn. This sounds like it's going to take a long time."

"It might. Maybe...never mind."

"What? What's *maybe* mean?"

"I don't know."

"It means forever, right?"

"You're badgering, and it's not helping. I just need some time. That's all I know."

"Easy for you. You get to keep the palace, complete with two princesses. I get a pay-per-night room."

Jamie sighed.

"I'm sorry. I know I'm a son of a bitch."

"Oh, Michael, why? Did you find a counselor?"

"I have an appointment with someone I heard on a radio talk show. He sounded pretty good, but I can't get in for three weeks."

"What are you going to do until then?"

"I'm trying to figure it out. I think I've found some answers."

"What are they?"

"For one thing, I'm going to get rid of some of my obligations."

"Like what?"

Michael sat back. "Soccer," popped out of his mouth. "I'm not going to soccer anymore."

"Soccer?" Jamie asked bewildered.

"I hate going."

"Michael, you have to go and support the girls, especially now that we're living apart. I think as far as the kids are concerned we have to keep our routine the same."

"Megan told me she hated going too. Let's see if she wants to cut that activity loose along with her dad. I'll come over tomorrow and hang out with her, and you and Emily can go to soccer. How'd we get involved in it anyway?"

"Well, umm, I think I got a flyer in Megan's backpack when she was in kindergarten. I thought it would be fun."

Michael frowned. "You were wrong. It's not fun. Do you like going?"

"I don't care about soccer, but I like seeing everyone. You know, chatting around, and Emily was so cute last week trying to kick the ball."

He almost raised his voice but stopped himself. There were way too many *if*s, *yet*s, and *maybe*s floating around, and he wanted to tip the scale in his favor. Instead, he quietly said, "She missed it every time. I didn't see a bit of natural talent. Why don't you socialize on your own time, and we'll ditch the soccer gig?"

"It was her first day, Michael. Give her a chance."

"Ask her if she wants to play. The kids need to pick their own activities. How are they ever going to discover what they really like, what they're good at, if they don't have space to explore?"

"I can't believe you. Do you want Megan watching TV all morning?"

Michael inhaled deeply. "No. I'll keep the TV off and see what she does. Now, there's an activity for you."

His gentle manner seemed to defuse Jamie. "We'll ask the girls if they want to quit, and if the answer is yes, I'll go along with it. Just so you know: they'll be the only kids in their class who aren't involved."

"Good. Give them all something to talk about. I bet we'll start a trend. Can't wait to read about it in the paper, and, yes, I still read the paper. 'Arlington Soccer Club Bankrupt.' What will all of the children in DC and Virginia do?"

"We'll talk in the morning and get the girls' input."

"Okay. I guess I should leave, huh?"

Jamie nodded.

Michael bent over and put his head in his hands.

"Are you crying?"

He looked up. "I wish. It might help release some of this grief."

"Why can't you?"

"It wasn't allowed in my house when I was growing up, so I think it's dammed."

"Oh, Michael."

"Anyway, I better go. See you tomorrow around eight."

He walked to the garage, and Jamie trailed after him.

After saying good-bye, Michael, in his car, sat back, stared at the closed door, and whispered, "Hey, Jamie, it's been a long time since we uncorked a bottle of wine and drained it dry. What do you say? We can watch a movie, laugh a little, and I'll stay put on the couch for the night." He turned on the ignition. Maybe next time.

Jamie opened the door when Michael was gone. She imagined that he was in the corner of the garage tinkering with some tools. He wore blue jeans and an old sweatshirt. She could smell his freshness, his clean crisp vitality. She called to him, and he came right over.

"What's up?" he said, concerned.

"I had an awful date with a creep I met on Facebook, and I'm scared to death about what could have happened. What almost happened. I just need you to put your arms around me and tell me I'm safe."

"Sure, baby. It was all a crazy nightmare." With that, he held her close and gently rocked her. She melded into his strength, and her fear drifted away.

"Maybe next time," she whispered.

She walked through the house, making sure all the windows and doors were locked. What if Steve somehow knew where she lived? After checking on Megan and Emily, she went into the kitchen and took a utility knife out of the drawer. From now on, the cell phone and this weapon were going to be her bedside companions.

Jamie meandered into the living room, plopped onto the couch, and observed her dead computer. She flipped through TV channels and found people shouting at each other on so-called news programs. There was a reality show about people racing, or was it fighting, across America. Then there were movies that had been broadcast about a thousand times. She shut the TV off. The quiet spooked her, so she turned it back on then looked inside the small cabinet attached to the coffee table. There, she found a jigsaw puzzle of a Hawaiian beach. Michael bought it for her years ago and said that when she put it together, they'd be ready to take a trip to paradise. The box had never even been opened. Jamie slit the binding with her handy knife then dumped all five thousand pieces onto the table. She went to the refrigerator, grabbed a handful of peanut butter cups, and went back to the couch. After eating a few, she started separating the edge pieces into a pile.

Michael slipped the stupid card into the slot on the door of his hotel room, and the green light flashed. He wanted a normal key to a normal house. The thought of entering that sterile space made his throat tighten. Daily maid service, miniature shampoo bottles, and bleached white towels—all screamed, "You're an upscale vagabond." He froze, unable to confront the dejection that loomed behind that door. Nothing he could do about it. He had earned this sentence. Right in the middle of his self-pity session, a soft sweet voice rescued him.

"Hey, neighbor. I'm Rachel."

Rachel was gorgeous—probably in her late twenties, with long copper hair, evergreen eyes, and what appeared to be an incredible body.

"Hi," Michael managed.

"I saw you a few times this week at those hotel hospitality dinners. Aren't they awful?"

"The worst," he agreed.

She smiled. Her teeth were as white as the hotel bed sheets. Why was he thinking about sheets?

"So are you in DC for business?" she asked.

"I guess you could say that. Long-term business."

"Me too. A few weeks."

"Where are you from?"

"Atlanta. Hey, I'm sick of pay-per-view movies in my room, and it's Friday night. Want to continue this conversation over a drink at the bar?"

Michael hesitated. Was she asking him out on a date? No, he determined. She wanted a little company, just like him. With that, he said, "Sure."

Chapter Thirteen

"Yippee!" Megan yelped, when Jamie told her she didn't have to play soccer. "I really don't have to?"

Jamie cracked an egg into a stainless steel bowl. "No. Daddy told me you don't like it. You should have said something."

"I hate soccer. Thanks, Dad!" Megan shouted, as she squeezed a seed out of an orange slice while sitting at the kitchen island.

Jamie whisked the eggs. "Daddy will be here any minute. You can express your gratitude then."

Emily entered the kitchen and sat next to her sister. "What did Daddy give you?"

"Nothing."

"Why did you scream, 'Thanks, Dad!'?"

Megan smiled teasingly. "Because he said I don't have to play soccer anymore."

"It looks like it's just you and me, Miss Emily. They lose," Jamie said, as she poured the eggs into a cast iron pan.

"It's not fair. Why can't I stay home? I can't even kick that ball it goes so fast," Emily whined.

"Megan has been playing for two years, and she realized that she doesn't like it. You need to give it a chance. And those orange slices aren't toys, ladies. Stop flicking them and eat."

Emily jumped off the stool, folded her arms, and said, "I quit."

Michael walked into the kitchen and smiled. "It looks like you'll be making that long journey to the soccer field all by yourself this morning. What's cookin'? It smells like the best diner in town."

Jamie mixed the eggs with a spatula. "We're encouraging them to give up. I'm not sure it's a good idea." Jamie turned to her daughters. "Your friends will wonder where you are." The bread popped out of the toaster. "Can you butter the toast, Michael?"

"Sure. Bacon too?"

"Yes, Sir. It's keeping warm in the oven."

"Everyone will be so jealous. Everyone hates soccer. Well, Laura and Jessica like it. That's it," Megan said.

"All week I have to go to school," Emily said frowning. "I even have homework, and it's only kindergarten. Then there's Brownies and gymnastics and swim lessons. No soccer. I need a rest."

Michael stopped buttering. "I hear you," he said, giving Emily a high five.

Jamie forcefully set the spatula on the counter. Hands on hips, she examined each of her family members. Mist glazed her eyes. She wanted to walk out the front door and never return. Let Michael stay here, and she'd go to that luxury hotel. There had to be a better life somewhere in the world. She fled from the kitchen, ran up the stairs, went into her room, and closed the door. As she wiped tears away with her wrist, she listened for footsteps, but no one rushed to her rescue. Jamie crawled into bed and pulled the blankets up to her chin. She rolled onto her side and tried to sleep away the throbbing that started in her stomach and traveled to her throat.

"Mom must really like soccer," Emily surmised.

Michael looked toward the space in the kitchen where Jamie stood a few seconds ago. His smile faded. This wasn't about the girls. Jamie was going to miss soccer. Her role as a mother was changing. The shift from a child in tow twenty-four hours a day to having a substantial amount of free time must feel strange. Jamie always talked about going back to the newspaper. She liked writing, interviewing people, and professional banter. She assumed that when the time was right, she could return to her vocation just by asking. The cold rejection by her former boss was probably like being slapped in the face after being kicked in the shin.

Michael turned off the burner, left the kitchen, and started to go upstairs to comfort her. He stopped midway and tried to think of what he would say. Maybe, "Cheer up." That wouldn't work. Maybe, "Keep looking for a job." But her old boss was right. Newspapers were folding, and Jamie had let her skills go stale. Even he knew he shouldn't say that. The "don't forget the pickle" line was out again. Experience warned him that whatever popped out of his mouth would only make things worse. Once when Jamie was feeling blue, he suggested that she take advantage of the babysitting services at their health club and enroll in an aerobics class. He might as well have called her a manatee. He turned around and went back into the kitchen. The girls had left. Michael checked the living room and grimaced. His daughters were already spellbound by the TV. He turned it off.

"Why'd you do that?" Megan asked.

"No TV until tonight."

"What are we going to do?"

"First breakfast, and that means fruit too. Then it's up to you to figure out what to do without TV. I'm going to make a cup of coffee, sit out back, and read a book."

He observed his daughters' confused faces and shook his head. They didn't know how to entertain themselves. Their minds were being anesthetized by that talking box. He fought the urge to say, "Why don't you go upstairs and play with one of the hundreds of toys you've accumulated?" He really did want them to independently tap into their own ingenuity. It had to be hiding somewhere in their brains.

Michael sank into the chaise lounge on the patio and surveyed the garden. The colors of the flowers blended perfectly, and they were impeccably placed. When he lived here by himself, the backyard was a lumpy incline crawling with weeds and scraggly shrubs. Then Jamie came along and transformed the eyesore into a sedate retreat. She didn't just have a green thumb, she was a landscape artist. He'd have to remember to tell her this later. Maybe that would make her feel better.

He opened the new Kevin J. Anderson novel he bought to keep him company in the hotel. Michael figured a story about sea monsters and wizards might do the trick. It didn't work. Even this book couldn't make him forget his problems.

Dropping it onto his lap, he was unnerved by what did distract him: her name was Rachel.

Last night they went to the hotel bar. Rachel had two martinis, and he had two draft beers. During cocktail banter, her sharp red nails grazed his wrist a few times. Once, he didn't pull back. Her skirt lifted with each shimmy she made on the bar stool, and he couldn't help but notice her toned, long legs, which were caressed by sheer black stockings. Michael was not a cheater and really did love Jamie. But it was different now. Jamie didn't love him.

Michael pounded his fists together. An hour of meaningless play was okay, but it was over. He wouldn't take even a small dose of what Rachel was offering. It could be poison. He had his ego boost, now back to the business of renewing his relationship with Jamie. He just hoped things improved soon and that Rachel received a call from her home office telling her to return to Atlanta.

Inhaling deeply, Michael closed his eyes and allowed the sun's heat to melt away his tension. The flower fragrance from the garden added to the calm. As he exhaled, his body loosened, and his hands rested gently on his stomach. Michael never realized, until this moment, how much he enjoyed breathing. Maybe Dr. McCormack was right. Under the right circumstances, focusing on the intake and release of air was relaxing. His jaw dropped, and his upper and lower teeth separated. It felt strange. His teeth must be compressed all the time. He alternated between clenching and releasing his teeth for a minute or so. It felt much better to have a gap between his molars. Michael promised himself that he would practice breathing and keeping his teeth apart. The warmth of the morning permeated him with tranquility. The melody of his gentle puffs deepened the peace massage, and his musing mind stopped.

"Daddy."

Michael startled. "Megan?"

"Can you make us lunch? Mom's tired."

"Lunch? You just had breakfast."

"That was in the morning. I'm hungry."

He looked at his watch—11:55. "Oh my God. I slept for three hours."

"Can you make lunch?"

"Of course."

He followed Megan into the house. His jaw dropped when he entered the living room. At least fifty small stuffed animals had moved in. Various members of the monkey family dangled from the rocking chair in the corner. Bears covered the fireplace hearth. Lions and tigers were scattered around and under the coffee table. Birds were perched on the top of the couch, and giraffes and elephants decorated the floor underneath the television. Emily held a cup of cheerios and pretended to feed the animals.

She noticed Michael and announced, "We made a zoo, Daddy. We just gave them their baths; now it's time for lunch. We're the zookeepers."

"This is amazing. I love your zoo."

"It costs one dollar to get in, but you can go for free because you're the father. Mom too," Megan said.

Michael walked around the animal stations and chatted with the fake creatures. His research study had a positive outcome. His children did have imaginations, and they could entertain themselves. He then saw the puzzle on the coffee table. He picked up the box cover and smiled.

"Mom said, don't touch it. That's her project," Megan said.

"I bought this for your mother before you guys were born."

"It took her a long time to play with it," Emily said.

"Where is Mom?"

"Upstairs," Emily said. "She promised to come down in a little while."

Michael went into the kitchen and made peanut butter and jelly sandwiches, with apple slices on the side. He poured two glasses of milk and called the girls. As they ate, he told them that he was going to check on their mother. He then made the long journey to the bedroom, wondering what disaster he would create.

Michael knocked on the door. No response. He tried again but still did not hear, "Come in." He entered the room and saw a lump in the bed covered with blankets. He rapped on the area that covered Jamie's face. "Anybody home?"

"No."

"Time to come out of your shell, little turtle." Michael sat down and pulled the blankets down to her shoulders. Jamie's hair was disheveled, her eyes were puffy, and her cheeks were red. "You look terrible," he said, immediately regretting his words.

"Go away," Jamie said, as she turned toward the wall.

Michael sat there trying to figure out what to do next. He shouldn't rub her back because he was willing to bet his second chance with this woman, she'd slap his hand. Anything he said could and would be used against him. He silently sighed. Pretend you're in the courtroom trying to convince a judge of something. This is an important case. Win it.

135

Michael looked directly at the back of Jamie's head. "I'm not very good at making people feel better, especially you, but I'm going to try." He took a deep breath. "You've had a couple of rough weeks. You have a lot more free time with the girls at school all day and haven't figured out what to do with it. You always thought that you could waltz back into your old job just by asking, and that assumption was destroyed with one phone call. You just kicked out your husband of ten years and the father of your children, which is pretty big. I know I haven't been the easiest person to live with, but still, my departure has to yank at your security. You probably don't want to depend on me, but you do."

He paused and touched the part of the sheet that clung to the back of her pajamas. "I do promise you, Jamie: it won't be like this forever. Your days will soon be filled with activity that is more adult than kid. Interesting work will eventually find its way to you, and I'm going to change. I know you've heard it before, but I really am."

Jamie squirmed. Michael wasn't sure what this movement meant, but whatever, he hadn't talked to her like this in a long time. He even surprised himself with his sensitive words. His concerns usually involved himself, the world, schedules, house projects, money, work, sports, and their children. Talking about personal feelings was not his forte, and he avoided it as much as he did traffic jams.

Jamie rolled over and sat up. "That was nice of you to say those things, and you nailed it, Dr. Freud."

"I did?"

"You did, but do you really think you can change at the not-so-young age of forty-two? I mean, like you said, you've made that promise before."

Michael gazed at his wife, who looked like she had just emerged from a war zone. A rumpled style suited her. He tried to stop himself from smiling, but it was hard. She was adorable. "I had another conversation yesterday with that guy Rufus—you know, the chess whiz from Dupont Circle. He's making me see things differently, asking me some tough questions like, 'What do you do for fun?' and 'Why are you so jittery?' I don't like who I am any more than you do. The good news is, the outer Michael is not the inner Michael, and I'm going to try and find him."

Jamie ran her fingers through her hair then dropped her hands onto her lap. She hesitated then said, "I'm going to observe your journey for a while. I need to see it, not just hear about it."

"Understood. I'll prove it to you. I have an appointment with a counselor, but do you think we should get someone for us too?"

"I need some downtime. Then we'll talk about it."

"Agreed. Can I do anything for you?"

"Just give me some space." She paused. "Can I help you? Get better, I mean."

Michael's eyes narrowed. "Really?"

Jamie nodded.

"Okay. I spent some time resting on the patio this morning and realized how beautiful your flower garden is, and the scent is so soothing. You really have a gift, you know, for landscaping."

Jamie sat back and placed her hands on her head. "This is way too much. Who are you? My husband would never talk about floral splendor."

"I have the same question, Jamie. Who am I? I don't have a clue." He cleared his throat. "Anyway, as I was resting out back, I noticed that my teeth were clenched. They are most of the time. I tried putting a space between them, and it instantly loosened up my entire body. Do you keep your teeth together or apart?"

Jamie looked at him like he was crazy but set her mouth as if she was working around the house or taking a walk. "Apart, definitely apart."

"I knew it. I knew you were a teeth-apart person. I bet Rufus is too. I'll have to ask him."

"I don't know if that's a good idea—asking that question to people you don't know very well."

"It's a weird question, huh?"

"Not for us," she said. "But for strangers, yes."

"What you can do every now and then is ask me if my teeth are together or apart. I'm going to work on keeping them apart. I figure that will take some of my jitteriness away."

"I can do that. I mean, when we see each other."

Michael grinned. "Thanks. Do you feel any better?"

Jamie nodded. "I do. Good job."

"Really?"

Jamie smiled. "Really."

He had hit a homerun. "Hey."

"What?"

"Why is there a knife on the nightstand?"

Jamie's eyes widened. She looked at the knife then back at Michael. She lightly touched her mouth then said, "I'm so embarrassed."

"What's going on?"

"It's so stupid. I got scared last night, being all alone. That knife and my 9-1-1 ready phone took the fright away."

Michael pursed his lips. It seemed like a silly reason. He'd gone away on business trips before, and she never mentioned being scared. Jamie was depressed, but she would never consider taking her own life, or would she?

He stared at the knife. "Seriously, are you all right?"

"What are you thinking? That I'm suicidal?"

Michael looked at her with grave eyes. "It happens, Jamie. You know that."

She threw her hands in the air and huffed. "I had a nightmare about some creep coming into my room, and it was so real. I couldn't get it out of my head, so I got the knife and my phone. It's that simple. Do you really think I'd cut myself up and let Meg and Em find me in the morning? I'm not that far gone."

"Of course you're not," he said half-heartedly then pointed at her. "And you do still need me for things like bad dreams."

Jamie smiled, "Or a knife and a cell phone."

"Not throwing out any bones today?"

"Not yet."

He squeezed her knee, and she didn't flinch. This was progress, so he went one step further. "I don't want to push you, but I would love to give my old friend Jamie a hug, and I could really use one too."

The anguish in Jamie's face dissolved. "I'd like that."

Michael's heart fluttered.

They moved toward each other. He placed one hand on Jamie's upper back and the other around her waist then pulled her in. She gripped his neck and drew him closer. Jamie's head fell onto his shoulder, and he rested his ear against her hair. It was so soft, just like always. His lips tingled, and he longed to kiss the strands of gold that were massaging his face. Instead, he stroked her collarbone with his thumb. She softly sighed. His eyes closed as he settled into this gift.

"Mommy," Emily yelled.

The sounds of footsteps on the stairs killed the embrace. Michael pounced up and headed for the door. Jamie went into the bathroom while Michael followed his daughters back into the living room.

Megan muttered something.

"What?" Michael asked. The tingling sensation intensified, and it made him dizzy. He adjusted the bulge in his shorts. It throbbed. Damn, how he wanted to make love to that woman upstairs.

Megan said something else. He still didn't hear it.

"Dad!" she exclaimed.

He shook himself out of his stupor and sat on the couch, being careful not to disturb the bird sanctuary that his daughters had designed. "I'm sorry, Meg. Say it again."

"Is Mom coming down?" Megan asked, exasperated.

"In a few. She's taking a shower." Michael thought about her naked body lathered in suds with pellets of water beating the froth down her breasts and legs. He swallowed hard.

"Good," Emily said. "She's being pretty lazy today."

Megan complained, "I'm tired of the house. Can we go somewhere, Dad?"

"Sure. Why don't we go for a bike ride?"

"Do we have bikes?" Megan asked excitedly.

"I think so. Don't you?"

"If we do, I never saw them. I don't even know how to ride a bike."

Michael shook his head. Of course they didn't have bikes. He forced the lustful images out of his brain. He had to focus on his daughters.

Megan folded her arms and looked at him sternly. "Dad, do you remember buying me a bike or teaching me how to ride one?"

"I guess not. Don't know why we haven't though."

He sat up straight, pretended he was gripping bike handles, and bobbed slightly. "It's so much fun. I love how the breeze hits your face as you cruise along, and the speed you generate is awesome. I used to ride everywhere from the time I was ten until I went to college." He rubbed his hands together. "That's what we can do. We'll go bike shopping. By tomorrow afternoon you'll be ready for the Tour de France."

"The tour what?"

"Not important. You'll be a skilled cyclist by bedtime on Sunday."

"A new bike and it's not even my birthday. Yippee!" Megan exclaimed.

"Dad?" Emily said.

"What sweetheart?"

"Did you get nice in the hotel?"

Every muscle in his body drooped. He took her hand and looked directly into her eyes. "It's making me try a lot harder. I'm sorry I'm such a grouch."

"It's okay. Mom says to just ignore you when you growl like a bear."

"Good advice. I'm really gonna try to keep that bear in his cave."

Emily giggled.

Jamie walked in. "Look at all the animals!"

"We made a zoo, Mommy, and you get to go for free," Emily announced.

"I do? I love the zoo."

"Jamie, we never taught the kids how to ride a bike."

"They don't even have bikes."

"I know. How did we let that happen?"

"I guess we never thought about it. They're really not that old."

Michael rubbed his hands together. "We're going out to buy a couple of bikes, and tomorrow we'll learn how to spin them."

"Great. I just need to eat something, and I'm set to go," Jamie said.

"While you eat, I'll get the address for the shop off the net, and map it out."

Jamie snickered. "Just Google the directions. In fact, you don't even have to do that. Just get the address. Shirley will find it."

"Who's Shirley?"

"The GPS lady."

"We have a GPS?"

"Yes, and don't worry about the cost. I got one free just for opening a new checking account."

"Do you need a new checking account?"

"No, but I got a free GPS. I'll close it out soon and will still have my new toy. Plus, I'll never get lost again with Shirley in the front seat with me."

"You named the GPS?"

"Of course. It's rude to call her *the lady*. And Michael, no one uses maps anymore."

"I do. I like maps. You know, trying to find the best route, maybe some interesting back roads, shortcuts."

"You can do that on the computer."

"I know, but there's something about shaking the map out, and I like the challenge of folding it back up."

Jamie arched her eyebrows. "Let's just try Shirley."

"Whatever." Michael glanced at the coffee table. "Hey, you finally started that puzzle."

"Yeah. Do you believe it? I spent two hours on it last night."

"No computer?"

"It crashed. Sort of glad it did. I liked doing something different."

"Do you need a new one?"

"I'll reload Windows soon, but I need a little break."

"Good for you. You were getting addicted to that time bandit, but you're going to need one for your job hunt, and that's a dinosaur," he said, pointing to the hard drive tower. "After bike shopping, I'll buy you a laptop."

Jamie walked over to him and placed her hand on his forehead. "You don't feel sick, but you're acting so different." She stepped back and examined his face. "Did you have sex in that hotel room last night?"

"What? Are you kidding?"

Jamie glimpsed at the girls, busy with their zoo, then continued. "You're wearing that I-just-had-great-sex look," she whispered.

"You remember?"

"Who is she?"

"Stop it."

"Come on, spill. Didn't take you long to find a replacement."

He waved his hand. "If you must know, you don't always need a woman for great sex."

"Oh!" Jamie laughed out loud.

"I'm glad you think it's funny."

Jamie pinched his chin. "I'm going to eat."

When she was gone, Michael bit his lower lip. All he did was have two drinks with Rachel and Jamie detected he did something a married man shouldn't, even a separated married man.

As the family traveled along the streets of DC, they were guided by the latest addition to the clan, Shirley.

"I hate Shirley's voice," Michael complained. "She sounds like an evil alien. Turn her down."

"I'll lower the volume a little, but we don't want to miss something," Jamie said.

Michael swung into the donut shop to get a coffee. "Nothing to eat and no reward card."

"Recalculate. Turn right on G Street NW in one tenth of a mile then turn right on Pennsylvania Avenue NW," said the robotic voice of Shirley.

"What's she talking about?"

"The donut shop isn't part of the directions. She's a little confused. Shirley will figure it out."

Michael saw at least six cars in the express drive-through lane, so he parked the van in front of the store and was gone and back in two minutes. When he turned the key, Shirley said, "Route recalculation. Turn right onto G Street NW in one tenth of a mile. Approaching G Street."

"I'm not an idiot. I know how to get out of a damn parking lot," Michael said.

"She doesn't know that you know. Be patient with her. She can be very helpful. You'll see."

After Michael turned toward his destination, Shirley delivered the next instruction detailing the street, direction, and number of miles. Every so often she reiterated this step with updated information.

"Shut up," Michael growled at the machine. He looked at Jamie. "And another thing about maps, they're quiet."

"You don't know what might happen, Michael," Jamie asserted. "Maybe you'll start thinking about something else, and you'll miss a turn. She doesn't think you're stupid, just human." She picked up Shirley. "Let me show you a great feature. Say we wanted to stop for Chinese food. All I have to do is put in the city name, and it will list every Chinese restaurant with directions of how to get there. See, you can do it for any place in the world."

"How does all of that information fit in there, and what if a restaurant closes?"

Jamie put Shirley back in her stand. "It's all figured out by satellites. The military's been using them for years. I'm not sure exactly how it works. Probably something to do with physics."

"What if there's a solar storm and the signals get all mixed up? I've read that can happen. Shirley could bring us to a tower of horror."

"You read way too much sci-fi. And the weather channel didn't mention anything about a solar storm."

Shirley directed a few exits off of roundabouts, some bear lefts and veer rights, and Michael complied until he spotted a traffic jam. There had to be an escape route. He was in the left lane and needed to quickly get in the right lane to turn out of the congestion. As he tried to make the maneuver, Shirley demanded, "Stay in the left lane."

This distracted him; another car cut him off. He slammed on the breaks; cars backed up behind him, and in the end the van was among the standstill vehicles.

Shirley kept shouting instructions.

"Shut that bitch up," Michael fumed.

Jamie grabbed Shirley and turned her off. "She was just doing her job, and I think there's a way to set this up so it actually avoids traffic jams."

"Can we watch the van TV since we're stuck here?" Megan asked.

Michael gripped the steering wheel as tightly as a child holding onto the safety bar of a roller coaster.

Jamie turned to her children. She put her forefinger to her mouth as a warning to stop talking.

Swerving back to face Michael, she said, "I hate to ask you this, but I promised. Are your teeth clenched or are they apart?"

Michael showed Jamie his teeth and seethed, "Clenched."

Chapter Fourteen

"Relax, Mike. You're as a tight as a rubber band about to snap."

"Shut the hell up, Adam," Michael whispered, as he walked to the sand trap to try and wedge his way out of another last place finish. After three attempts, the golf ball bounced onto the green, and his chuckling colleagues applauded.

"What I'll do to get out of yard work," Michael joked, as he glanced toward the remote hole marked by a teasing flag. A small pond separated them, but to him it might as well have been the Atlantic Ocean.

Michael selected a three-fairway wood from his bag and aligned his stance squarely to the target. He placed his hands in neutral position on the synthetic grip and prayed that the ball would find the sweet spot of the club head.

Just as he was about to swing, Adam shouted, "Stop right there."

Michael loosened his grasp and sighed. "What?"

The wiry, snow-haired senior partner approached him with one hand flailing. "The club can feel your tension. Ease up on your grip and let your body flow in a single fluid motion." Adam demonstrated the perfect swing.

If Michael heard him spout these directions one more time, he'd—well, he'd quit. He smirked. Why wait? "Too bad this is the last day that I'll have this game to get me out of mundane chores."

"What?" Adam said.

"That's right. Who will be the new champ of last place? My bet is on you Alex, although Nick is certainly in the running."

"You're not quitting," Adam said. "You just need to focus." He took Michael's turn at the tee and drove the ball onto the putting green. "See. It can be done. I'm still committed to getting your score down ten points by the end of the season."

"Not going to happen," Michael said, straight-faced.

"Why are you quitting? Even if you hate golf, it gets you out of the house every Sunday," Nick said.

"Bigger and better mountains to climb. The Philadelphia Marathon is coming up, and I need to ramp up my training. Next spring, I think I'll try sculling."

Adam leaned on his club. "You're really handing in your resignation?"

Michael's insides glowed as he nodded. He ambled back to the tee and whacked the ball long, high, and straight over the pond and onto the green.

After slaps on the back, pleas to stay, and best wishes, Michael drove away. Rufus was right. He did have clutter in his bag, and it was liberating to get rid of incidentals like golf and soccer. He bounced in his seat as he waved good-bye to the chemical green lawn, and his broad smile stayed put all the way to the bike shop.

Michael inspected the cycle inventory of the sporting goods store while he waited to pick up the bikes he bought for Megan and Emily. The fumes from the rubber tires were intoxicating, and he felt lightheaded, almost giddy. He grasped the handlebars on one of the hybrid models, put his left foot on the pedal, and swung his right leg over the seat. Before he knew it, he was weaving around the shop. After a few laps, Michael clicked his tongue and hopped off.

He kept his grip on the bike as he reminisced about the rides he and Jamie used to take along the Potomac River. They'd begin their trek at Roosevelt Island early on a Saturday morning and finish at the same spot four hours later. They would rest on one of the benches to people-watch and admire the cherry trees that lined the river. The best part, though, was how the sun's rays polished the dark water, making it sparkle. It was like gazing at an August night sky jam-packed with stars. An ice cream cone or café lunch was their reward, and more times than not, they had a beer on the patio when they got home. Michael lowered his eyes as he thought about this less complex period of his marriage.

He eventually became bored with these casual jaunts and yearned for longer, faster, and more challenging outings. He envied the strong athletes flying around DC on their lightweight racers while he pedaled about on his comfortable but slow touring hybrid. One day he took the plunge and purchased a carbon fiber cycle for four thousand dollars plus change. He tried to talk Jamie into taking the leap to more aggressive riding, but she wanted nothing to do with it. She said that humans were not meant to maneuver their bodies into the position that these contraptions required. "It makes my neck hurt just looking at those Lance Armstrong wannabes," she declared. So Jamie started riding alone.

What he'd give to cruise along the river with his wife again. Jamie gave her bike away four or five years ago when maternal obligations consumed her life. She didn't have time to ride anymore and thought someone else might enjoy it.

A salesman cleared his throat. "Sir?"

Michael snapped out of his trance. "Yeah?"

"Your bikes are loaded and ready to go."

Michael pointed at two of the hybrid bicycles. "How long would it take to have these fit for a five-foot-six woman and a six-one man?"

The clerk inspected them. "They're perfect just as they are. If there's a problem, you can bring 'em in to be adjusted anytime."

"You just made another sale. Let's see if we can squeeze them into the back of the van."

Michael honked the horn as he drove up the short driveway of his home. He hoped Jamie would like his gift. Last year for her birthday, he bought her top-of-the-line Mizuno running shoes because she said she might train for a 5 K. He knew he was in trouble when she unwrapped the gift and laughed at the shoebox. "What did you hide in here?" she asked. Her eyes turned into slits when she removed the top and saw sneakers. She was quiet, but when he pressed her to tell him what was wrong, she said, "Sneakers for my birthday, Michael? Really?" He called her unappreciative, and she accused him of buying things for her that he wanted, like a heart monitor one Christmas. Perhaps he was a gift klutz, but wasn't it the thought that counted?

Jamie was hard to shop for anyway. She lost jewelry and perfume made her break out in hives. Chocolate sabotaged her diet, and how could you buy flowers for the garden queen? Suddenly, he regretted buying the bike. It might make things worse, not better.

The front door slammed followed by the excited squeals of Emily and Megan. Michael got out of the van and turned to see his daughters dash up the driveway.

"Can I go first?" Megan asked.

"No, me," retorted her sister.

"Don't bicker. You have two parents, which means you both can go first," Michael said, pleased that his girls were eager to begin their training. "Where's Mom?"

"Hey," Jamie said as she entered the cramped garage from the side door. She wore black leggings and a sporty striped shirt. Her hair was pulled back into a ponytail, and her face looked as fresh as a pink rose. He forgot about the gift fiascos when he saw this sweet vision. Sighing, he wished it was just the two of them getting ready to take a ride down their bygone days along the Potomac.

Michael silenced that thought. This day was for his daughters. "Can you drive the girls to the park 'n' ride in the BMW, and I'll meet you there? The brick sidewalk here is too uneven for biking."

"Good idea," Jamie said.

Michael ran into the house, changed out of his golf clothes, which he would donate to Goodwill, and threw on sweats. He rushed out the door, excited to start his cycling seminar.

When he entered the parking lot, his daughters greeted him with waves and jumps. He stepped out of the van and removed the bikes from the back. Emily chose silver and Megan picked red. Their eyes sparkled as they seized their shiny new toys.

"And we can't forget Mom," Michael said. He pulled out a midnight blue hybrid bicycle and nervously brought it over to Jamie.

Her jaw dropped and her eyes widened. "I get one too?"

"I thought you'd have fun with it. Remember how we used to ride along the bike path? I figured with the girls in school, you might enjoy some morning jaunts."

Jamie took the bike but gazed at Michael. "I can't believe you did this. Thank you." She smoothed one hand over the seat and softly said, "Of course I remember those rides by the river. They were...they were the best." She mounted her new toy and pedaled around in circles shouting, "Yee ha!"

Megan and Emily yelled, "Go, Mommy," but Michael didn't see their reaction because he couldn't take his eyes off his wife. He wanted to join in the fun, so he pulled out his bike and rode next to her.

Jamie stopped pedaling. "You got one too?"

"Couldn't resist. Wanna race?"

Jamie tilted her head as he continued to cycle around. "Wait a minute. What about your racer?"

"This will be better for family outings. And you're right. It feels good to ride sitting straight up."

"So you're giving up your carbon fiber speed machine?"

Michael stopped abruptly. He looked at Jamie with the seriousness of a police officer about to write a ticket. "Not on your life."

Jamie brushed the back of her hand across her forehead. "Phew! Now for that race." In an instant, she was darting across the parking lot like a filly competing in the Kentucky Derby. Michael followed her but adjusted his pace so Jamie could win. When she triumphed, she turned to him, and stuck out her tongue.

He returned the gesture then said, "Wait till next time."

They laughed and talked as they casually rode back toward their daughters. When their ride was over, Megan asked, "What about us?"

"Who are you two young ladies, and what do you want?" Jamie joked.

"Mom," Megan snapped.

"I'm kidding. I'm excited about my new bike too!" She rolled her eyes at Michael.

He shook his finger. "No fun for you, Mrs. Stolis."

"How do you ride it, Mom? Am I gonna fall?" Emily said.

Jamie stood her bike up with the kickstand and walked over. She squatted, placed one hand on Emily's shoulder, and gently said, "You might, but it won't hurt too much. The fun is well worth a shaky start. Michael, why don't you work with Meg, and I'll teach Emily."

"Aye-aye."

He removed two helmets from the van, placed them on his daughters' heads, and fastened them tightly. Michael held Megan's shoulders firmly and told her to put her feet on the pedals. He guided her slowly up and down the parking lot, so she could get used to balancing and steering. Jamie did the same with Emily, who wanted more speed with each lap. As the afternoon progressed, so did the girls' riding skills. Jamie and Michael began to let go for a few seconds. The seconds

153

turned into minutes, and by the end of their lesson, Megan and Emily were officially cyclists.

"I'm starving," Michael said.

"Stay for dinner. We'll stop and get Chinese on the way home while you try to find a spot for the bikes," Jamie said.

"Yes!" Michael exclaimed, raising his fist in the air.

Jamie smiled wide and looked at him long enough to make him shudder.

Michael couldn't find space in the garage for the bikes, so he locked them up out back. The project of making room for them would give him an excuse to come over one night during the week. It was the best weekend he'd had with his family in ages, and he didn't want to lose the momentum. If he could maintain this harmony, he'd soon be checking out of that hotel and whistling his way back home.

While visions of reconciliation danced in his head, he remembered he had a date with Rachel. His body stiffened as he tried to figure out what to do about it. He plopped onto the couch in the living room and thought about what a mistake it had been to have dinner with Rachel the night before. He should have brushed her off when she knocked on his door, but his ego loved the attention, and she provided an escape from his loneliness. After they ate, she offered to buy him a drink. He refused, but she persisted. By the time he swallowed his last drop of coffee, her pestering, exaggerated southern drawl and frequent hair tossing grated on his nerves. Still, he had trouble saying no when she repeatedly begged him to go to some brew pub tonight. He had agreed just to shut her up. Thank God they had exchanged cell phone numbers. He'd get out of his mistake, and that would be it. He punched in her number.

Jamie brought the Chinese food into the kitchen. As she started unpacking the white cartons, she noticed Michael speaking quietly in the other room. She stopped and placed one hand on her hip. When he was on phone, it usually concerned work or bills, and his voice boomed with frustration. Something was up. She crept into the hall and almost gasped when Michael said, "I know we had a date, but I'm going to eat with my family instead."

Jamie covered her mouth with her hands and tiptoed a little closer. A few unintelligible whispers then, "Not sure when I'll be back."

Jamie scurried back into the kitchen. She hoped Michael would stop in the bathroom before coming in, so she had some time to get over her shock. Mr. "I want to come home" was having an affair. It didn't take him very long. She pressed her lips together. No wonder he was in a better mood this weekend—the slime.

"I had so much fun this afternoon, and I can't believe how quickly our daughters learned how to ride," Michael said as he walked in.

Jamie subtly examined his face. It was light and happy. He was getting sex, and it wasn't self-induced.

"And we didn't fight once this weekend. I think that must be the first time in over a year," Michael said jovially.

Her jaw was quivering, but she managed, "Amazing what a little time apart will do. How are your teeth?"

"What?"

"Are they clenched? Remember, I'm supposed to ask."

"Ya know, they're not."

"Good."

"Do you mind if I stop by on Tuesday to make room in the garage for the bikes; then I'll take you and the girls out for burgers."

"Why not tomorrow?"

"I'm going on a tour of the Boys & Girls Club."

"The Boys & Girls Club?"

Michael picked up a carton and twirled lo mein noodles onto a fork. "Yup. Rufus volunteers there. He's going to show me around."

"Wait till we sit down to eat," Jamie said, grabbing the carton out of his hand. "It doesn't seem like a place you'd go."

"Maybe it is and maybe it isn't. By the way, when did you get so fussy about table manners? I'm the anal one, remember?"

"So I'm a slob?" she said sharply.

"No," Michael said, shaking his head. "I was kidding. Poking fun at myself. What's wrong?"

"I think you know." Jamie opened a cabinet door and grabbed four plates.

"I don't have a clue. We had such a good time today."

She slammed the plastic dishes on the island and shouted, "Come on, ladies. Dinner's getting cold."

She glared at Michael. "One good weekend doesn't erase at least five years in hell."

"Jamie!"

She pointed at the stool, "Sit down and eat."

He frowned but didn't argue.

Jamie pushed noodles around on her plate. The Boys & Girls Club. How'd he come up with that excuse? And was it really Rufus who was giving him life advice or some sweetie pie? At least he was original with his cover.

Emily and Megan chattered like monkeys at dinner, so Jamie didn't have to speak to her unfaithful husband. She felt sick inside and wanted him to leave.

"When are you going to move our bikes, Dad?" Megan asked.

Jamie didn't give Michael a chance to answer. "Come by Tuesday, but I can't stay. I have a PTA meeting," she lied. "You said you'd take Meg and Emily out for dinner."

"Sure," he said quietly without looking at her.

After Michael left, and the girls were asleep, Jamie went into the backyard. The cool autumn air strengthened her spirit, so she stood still while it seeped into her skin. After a few minutes, she sat in the lounge chair and inhaled deeply. Michael was right about the aroma of the flower garden. It soothed her. She sipped cabernet and allowed her mind to take a nap.

When she felt rested, she reflected on the unusual weekend. On Friday morning she met Steve the Snake, and in the afternoon her old boss told her that she was washed up as a journalist. When her mood was just about to go from depressed to catatonic, Michael jovially walked in and initiated a pizza-making party. He announced that he would no longer attend soccer games, and on Saturday the girls jumped right on his bandwagon. After she broke down, he came to her rescue with kind words and a comforting hug. Michael also informed her that he was going to work on self-actualization, which was beyond uncharacteristic. Then they bought their daughters bicycles, and on Sunday he surprised her with the same present.

At some point, he revealed that he quit golf, which he had been reluctantly but dutifully playing since they met.

All of these changes in such a short time. What was going on with him? Jamie guessed the wakeup call of an imminent divorce jogged his more humane side. She was actually beginning to think they might be able to work things out. That was until she eavesdropped on his private phone conversation.

The minute it was marginally legal, he jumped into bed with another woman. Sure, she had coffee with the Internet predator, but it was nothing compared to getting naked with someone. She tossed her head back. What did she expect? Their love life was as boring as a G-rated movie, and she avoided sex as much as she did the South Beach Diet. Michael was quite feral between the sheets, and the abstinence must have been torture for the poor bastard.

In the early days of their relationship, they could spend the entire weekend sex hopping between the bed, shower, couch, floor—anywhere the urge struck. Jamie grinned. How did they ever summon up all of that energy? Her heartbeat quickened. She put her hand over her thumping chest and said, "Stop it." Memories of Michael's sexual enthusiasm weren't supposed to excite her. She gulped her wine and gazed at the empty glass. She needed a refill.

Jamie returned with a full goblet and imagined that Michael was resting in the empty chair next to her. They would continue the conversation they started in the bedroom on Saturday and end with that fleeting embrace. The difference was their daughters were asleep, so they would not be interrupted. The light intoxication and sentimental memories made her want to call Michael. In her best Madonna voice, she said, "Leave that bitch who's nuzzling up to you and come home for some real magic." Jamie cackled, but the mischievous laugh quickly turned into a scowl.

She put down her glass and folded her arms. Michael was a handsome, successful man, and women noticed these traits. Temptation had knocked at his door, and he invited it in. Prior to Friday night, she would have welcomed the new woman into their lives as a way to keep her husband away. Now she was experiencing pangs of jealously for a man that she wished she could banish with hornet poison just one week ago. He was going to leave their marriage, evolve into a teddy bear, give his best to someone else, and she'd be left with the Steves of the world.

Jamie went into the house and placed one hand on the phone. Maybe Michael really was working. She'd be able to tell, if he sounded agitated. Would she confront him if she heard a woman's voice in the background? She resisted the impulse. It would be a pathetic act of desperation. Jamie closed her eyes and put her fingers on her temples. God, she wished her brain would shut up. It felt like a pinball was in her head, bouncing from one feeling to another.

A barely audible voice suddenly said, "Be still." Jamie stopped breathing.

"Who said that?" She looked around the dim kitchen. No one was there. Jamie lightly touched her lips. The words came from her own mouth. She said it again, only louder. "Be still." Somewhere, buried deep inside her, lived a wise woman, and she was trying to get out.

Jamie hugged herself. All of the answers you need will come to you. Just give it time.

Wow. That woman really was wise. Jamie roamed into the living room and glanced at the laptop sitting on her desk.

It would be so easy to turn it on and play for a little while. After all, it was brand new. She shifted her gaze to the puzzle then back to the computer. Grinning, she sat on the couch, picked up a turquoise piece, and searched the ocean scene to see where it would fit.

Michael entered the hotel room and sneezed. The scent of cheap deodorizer was overwhelming, so he slid the window open. He gaped at the brown bedspread covered with sun-flowers. The sight made his stomach turn. He ripped it off, threw it across the room, kicked it into the closet, and pulled the folding doors shut. The textured walls of this rectangular room were closing in on him, and he bit his knuckles to stop himself from screaming.

The entire weekend had gone so smoothly; then Jamie morphed into Wifezilla. He paced around the room. Was she manic, or did she hear him talking to Rachel? She couldn't have. He whispered during their brief conversation while Jamie buzzed around the kitchen. He had to get some straight answers from her. Exactly how long was he going to be in exile? Why was she so temperamental? And why did she really have a knife on the nightstand? A grown woman doesn't sleep with a dagger because of a bad dream. Michael rubbed his face then crashed onto the couch that sat against the wall, next to the bed. Tomorrow he'd arrange a meeting with Jamie. They needed to have a good long conversation when the kids weren't around. Why wait until tomorrow? He popped up and reached for the phone on the desk. He picked up the receiver then slammed it back down. She'd only reject him—maybe even hang up on him. He pounded his fist into his palm then stormed past the kitchenette toward the bathroom to take a long hot shower.

Pure crisp air greeted Michael when he stepped back into the room, wrapped in a hotel robe. He inhaled the freshness that replaced the stale scent, stared at the bed, which was covered with a tan velour blanket, and longed to crawl into it. If he slept, he wouldn't have to think, but his full briefcase on the chair nixed that idea. He had to finish preparing for the hearing tomorrow. Getting fired was not something he wanted to add to his dismal plate.

It was seven thirty, and Michael's stomach growled, reminding him he hadn't eaten. Jamie's hostility had given him instant indigestion at dinner, so he barely touched his *moo shu* pork. He picked up the phone to order a sandwich from room service but was interrupted by a knock on the door. "Who is it?"

"Rachel."

"Shit," he whispered.

"Open the door."

"I'll catch you later in the week. I have a lot of work to do."

"Come on. I have something for you."

He sighed, put on his sweat pants and a fleece, then opened the door. Standing before him was a voluptuous goddess. Rachel wore black jeans a size too small for her curvaceous ass and a plum knit shirt that clung to her full breasts. It was cut low, revealing a trace of her black lace bra. She carried a bottle of red wine and brown tote bag that smelled like Italian food.

"Hey there." She slipped by Michael, brushing her body against him as she passed. Swaying to a small oak table in front of the couch, she set her goodies down then rubbed her bare arms. "It's cold in here," she said with a shiver. Rachel walked over to the window and closed it.

Michael didn't budge. His blood was simmering, and that was a problem. Impulse told him to throw her on the

161

bed and go wild. He slapped his savage thoughts and managed, "What are you doing?"

Rachel tugged at her shirt hem. "We had some fun the past couple of nights, and I wanted to bring the party to your room. You mentioned on the phone that you were having takeout Chinese for dinner, and I thought, poor you."

Her drawl slowed. "So I decided to surprise you and ordered lasagna, crusty bread, and salad from one of the best Italian restaurants in DC. Picked up a vintage bottle of pinot noir too."

Rachel seductively took out the items from the bag. Each move she made accentuated the curve of her hip or the swell of her breasts.

Her provocative dance enticed him, so he let it continue for a minute. After this alluring peek inside *Penthouse* magazine, he knew he had to close it up.

"Rachel, I can't have dinner with you. I'm married," he said flatly.

"Oh come on. Help me eat this food. Besides, you're separated."

"We're just taking a little break. We are still very married," Michael said, as he leaned on the door.

Rachel stopped unpacking and moved toward him. She took his hand and guided him to the table. Her fingers were so delicate, and the tips of her red nails poked his knuckles. He imagined what it would feel like to have those nails scratch other parts of his body. All of the sudden the room was hot.

"Sit down," Rachel said, as she poured him a glass of wine. She served the food. They ate. They drank. They laughed. Michael was playing a dangerous game, but with each sip of alcohol his resolve weakened. All of his life, he had played by the rules, and it felt good to break one.

At the end of their meal, Rachel rose and stepped behind him. She massaged his shoulders and neck. Her breasts caressed his head, and he nestled into the lush embrace. Michael wanted more. Rachel was an oasis in his desert, and he was going to dive into it. So he stood, grabbed her, and pushed her against the wall.

She clutched his face with her palms and kissed him like he hadn't been kissed in years. The swirling tongues, the groping lips, the biting teeth. She tasted sweet and moist. Seduced away from his common sense, he groped her rear then rubbed it hard. He grinded Rachel with his hips. When their mouths parted, Michael turned her around and nailed her to the bed with his body. He plowed his hands up her shirt and squeezed her breasts again and again. Rachel swung her limbs around him and chewed passionately on his ear. He wanted to bury himself inside her. Forget everything. His mouth found its way to the crest of her breasts, and he sucked on the flesh. Rachel's nails were under his shirt tearing at his back. In between pants, she sighed, "I love you. I love you so much."

Michael deflated.

"What's wrong?" Rachel said breathlessly.

Michael lay motionless on top of her then rolled over onto his back. After a few seconds, he sat up and put his hands on his knees. Rachel hugged him from behind. She kissed his cheek and said it again. "I love you, Michael. I've never met anyone like you."

Michael gently pushed her away, stood up, and looked down at her. "I'm so sorry, Rachel. We're not on the same page."

"You love me too, right?"

He almost laughed out loud but determined that this situation could be more frightening than funny. "Look, I'm not the best at beating around the bush so…" He paused. "I'll tell you pretty directly what happened. I was momentarily arrested by your incredible body, my loneliness, the wine, and impulsion. But it's over now. I don't love you, and you don't love me. We just met, and now we need to say good-bye."

"You can't mean that," Rachel sobbed.

Michael turned away from her, threw his hands up, and mouthed *shit*. Rachel's arms circled his waist, and she nibbled on his back. "Stop it, Rachel. I mean it." He released himself from her, walked to the door, and opened it. "I'm really sorry about all of this, but you need to go."

Rachel took off her shirt and started to unclasp her bra. Michael ran over, picked her up, set her in the hall, shut the door, and bolted it. The knocking started; then the banging. A woman who could've passed for a *Sports Illustrated* swimsuit model was standing outside his room in a black lace bra begging to come in and attack him. And he was separated from Jamie. Under different circumstances this might be a good thing, but that lady was crazy—over-the-top nuts.

She whimpered, "Please let me in."

Soon someone would notice this scene, and Michael did not want to be around to answer any questions. Without wasting a second, he grabbed his belongings, stuffed them into his suitcase, and escaped out the window. Luckily, his car was just a few yards away in the parking lot. He hopped inside and was on the highway within minutes.

As he drove off to find a new home away from home, he glanced in the rearview mirror. "Holy shit." He couldn't believe what almost happened. "Sorry, Rachel," he murmured. She responded with a beep on his cell phone.

Chapter Fifteen

Michael sat at his office desk and yawned as he reviewed the materials for the preliminary hearing. It was seven, and he had three hours of restless sleep. When he finally settled into a Hilton close to home, he worked into the wee hours of the morning. Rachel called several times, but it wasn't a problem. He just shut the phone off. The scary part was when he turned it back on, there were almost a hundred missed calls, and his text message box was full. That woman was insane, and Michael could kick himself for allowing lust to conquer wisdom.

He startled when his office phone rang then sighed with relief when he saw that it was Jamie.

"Hey, sweetheart." Wow. He hadn't used this term to address his wife in ages.

"Hi, Michael. My cell phone is dead even after I charged it. Do you know what's going on?"

"Sure do. I was bombarded with crank calls last night. It was crazy, so I called Verizon and had them change our numbers. Check your e-mail. Instructions on how to re-activate should be there."

"What kind of crank calls?"

"Vulgar. I'm not repeating any of it."

"I wonder who it was."

"Some weirdo, but it's all taken care of."

"Why'd you change my number too? It's going to be a pain getting the new one out to everyone."

"Just in case whoever it was started harassing you. Maybe it was some kind of piracy invasion into our account. Just send out an e-mail to everyone on your list."

"I thought piracy only happened on the Internet."

"I don't know, Jamie. I just thought it would be the best thing to do, and it's done. Okay?" Michael hoped he had kept his voice even.

"I guess."

"Jamie?"

"Yeah."

Dead silence.

"Michael?"

Words were stuck in his throat, but he managed, "I'm sorry."

"For what?"

"Everything. I'm such an ass."

Dead silence.

"Jamie?"

"Not really. You're just uptight."

"Well, whatever. I'm sorry."

"I'll see you tomorrow when you come over to put the bikes away, right?"

"You bet, and I'm taking Meg and Emily out to dinner. Do you still have that PTA meeting?"

"Yup."

"Can we talk after—seriously talk?"

"We'll both be tired. Can it wait till the weekend?"

"I'm worried about you, me, the girls—everything. I want to get things settled. Can you get a babysitter for Saturday night? We'll have an uninterrupted talk someplace."

"I'll try."

"Try hard. It's important."

"Okay. See you tomorrow."

Michael hung up and stared at the phone. He closed his eyes and whispered, "I love you, sweetie." It was so true. He loved Jamie more than anything. She was who he wanted in the hotel last night, but she didn't want him, so he took who was available. Jamie's dismissal of their marriage hurt so much, but he couldn't do stupid things just to make the pain go away. Thank God Rachel said, "I love you." That sentiment stopped him cold. He tapped his pencil on his chin. Would he have cheated on Jamie if Rachel hadn't muttered those words? He tossed his pencil on the desk. No. Eventually visions of pregnancy and disease would have appeared, and that would have ended the ardent make-out session instantly.

At eight Michael squeezed drops into his eyes to get rid of the red streaks and guzzled his mug of lukewarm black coffee. He put on his suit jacket and headed down the hall to deliver the case he had haphazardly pulled together. After four hours of PowerPoint slides, Excel spreadsheet reviews, and hundreds of questions, the group of executives agreed to Michael's proposal for a large company resolution between employees and employers. This was always his mission: keep both the bosses and the workers satisfied and prosperous. Although he should have felt pleased, frustration ruled. He spent hours redoing his staff's best efforts, and he didn't know how much longer he could work the number of hours his job required for success.

As soon as the session ended, Michael headed straight for the cafeteria. A hunger headache was sneaking in. When he reached the door of the conference room, Frank slapped his back.

"Great job, Michael. Your team came up with excellent solutions. Now, I need to see you in my office."

Michael followed Frank, although his stomach strongly objected. He hadn't eaten in five hours, and all he could think about was a tuna sandwich on rye with a pile of potato chips on the side. He felt like a weary knight after a grueling battle and hoped Frank wouldn't keep him too long, or worse yet, hand him a monumental assignment.

Michael entered the office and inhaled the leather scent expelled by the executive furniture. He couldn't decide where to sit. A couch was placed against the oak paneled wall; the conference table for eight was at the far end of the room; and Frank's desk was placed in front of a picture window that offered a view of the Capitol Mall. His decision was made for him when Frank took his king's seat behind the desk.

Three mahogany guest chairs were arranged in a semicircle in front of Frank's work station. Michael chose the one in the middle. He straightened up to meet his beefy, bald superior's narrow eyes. Michael lowered his gaze to Frank's mouth. The corners dipped down toward his chin and seemed permanently fixed in that position. Frank mentioned a few weeks ago that he was about to celebrate his fifty-sixth birthday. Michael had guessed that his boss was in his mid-sixties. Frown lines traveled across Frank's forehead, and his jowls jiggled whenever he talked. A shiver ran down Michael's spine. Looking at Frank was like peering into a crystal ball at his own future. Something told him to get up and run for his life, but instead he said, "What's up?"

"Your team does outstanding work. You consistently find a way to bring the company and employee together."

"That's what I'm paid to do."

"Well, you certainly earn your paycheck. You have exceptional problem-solving skills, and your attention to detail is invaluable, but I didn't call you in here just to shower you with praise. We're both far too busy for that."

Michael observed Frank's desk: the phone was in the corner; the blotter was perfectly placed in the center, with two Post-it notes on the side panel and a one-inch binder on top. He felt like blurting out, "This is not the desk of a busy man," but wisely controlled his impulse.

"I have a team in Saint Paul working on a big case. There's a lot of tension within a large retail store. Formal complaints from employees have been submitted to human resources, and management is nervous about a lawsuit. The budget is tight, but they want to keep their workers content. You know the story. Anyway, our group out there is green and would benefit from your expertise. I need you to go to Saint Paul next week and teach them how to get things resolved."

"I don't think so, Frank. I have a lot on my plate and training is not my thing. Get someone else to go."

"That's an unacceptable answer," Frank said. "You're the best one for the job. We'll cover for you here. You'll fly out on Saturday. That will give you time to brief the case and meet with the team before Monday's session. You'll be home for dinner on Friday, and there will be many people who are better off because of your efforts. I'll have Sarah make the flight and hotel arrangements. Here are some reports on the issues." Frank handed him a briefcase full of legal documents.

Michael's mouth froze, which was a good thing. It prevented him from calling Frank a pompous, controlling ass.

"Oh, and Michael."

"What?"

"Get a haircut. You're not going to Saint Paul to audition for a rock band. And are you losing weight? Your suit looked baggy when you presented today."

Michael waited a few long seconds. He stood, looked down at Frank, and purposefully said, "Probably dropped a few pounds 'cause of my marathon training. The haircut may have to wait till after Saint Paul. No time."

Frank stood and put his hands on his hips. "Make the time. A polished appearance is part of the deal around here."

Michael left the office without saying a word. He leaned against the wall in the vestibule and ran his fingers through his hair. "Jealous, Frank?" The bastard would kill for a little hair and to pull his belt in a notch. After taking several deep breaths, Michael traipsed toward his office with his teeth clenched.

"How was the hearing?" Cathleen asked.

Michael went into his den without answering and slammed the door. He hated this place, and that was a big problem. Rufus said, "For every problem, there's a solution." He'd love to prove that statement true. He threw the briefcase onto his desk and paced back and forth. "Twenty more years until retirement, and counting."

Running away from this penitentiary might help, so Michael fled his office and ran down the twelve flights of stairs. As he opened the door to the outside, he hoped Jamie was actively seeking a job. Maybe she'd land a position at a lucrative public relations firm, and he could quit. "Keep dreaming," he muttered.

Jamie stood with open arms in the midst of sun rays streaming into the living room through the French doors. She prayed the light would give her the inspiration she needed to pursue the rest of her life. After her motivational encounter with solar power, she went into the alcove and sat in front of her laptop. This was the first time she used a computer since her awful encounter with Steve. The taste of that vile man's tongue filled her mouth, and she swallowed some coffee to make it disappear. Fortunately, she had brewed a dark roast. Steve had most likely moved on to some other lonely, rich woman, and it was time to delete him from her brain. She had to get down to the business of her future.

Jamie's mind craved stimulation, and her wallet wanted its own money. Michael kept it nicely padded, but he also controlled it. Sure he played Santa Claus this weekend, treating her to an HP Notebook and a Trek hybrid, but next week he'd reprimand her because of a ninety-nine-cent music download on the credit card bill. She pursed her lips. It was time to create a dazzling résumé that would jumpstart a new career.

Opening a vita template on Microsoft Word, she chose a design that was in sync with her personality and appropriate for the communications field. She succinctly stated her educational background, which included graduating summa cum laude from Boston University. She listed her professional experience as a news reporter for the *Arlington Sun*, a public relations assistant for Time Warner, and an internship at the *Boston Globe* during her senior year of college. Jamie radiated with pride as she added her honors, a Hearst Journalism Scholarship and a Peabody Award she received for an investigative series she wrote on tobacco and alcohol. She was the individual who accomplished all these things, and a seven-year break to care for children didn't make her stale. She'd have to make a lunch date with her former editor just to tell him.

Now to recent professional activities. Jamie hit her head with her palm as she tried to think of something of significance to add. She placed her fingers on the keyboard, but they didn't move. Ogling the screen, she willed an idea to pop onto it. Suddenly, her fingers danced along the letters.

Life Experience: June 2004–September 2012: Mother

Responsibilities: conflict resolution, event planning and organization, customer service, training and instruction, public relations

Skills Acquired: multitasking, attention to detail, time management, interview techniques

She smirked at the truth in this description but was certain an employer would feed the résumé to the paper shredder the instant it was perused. Parenting expertise did not matter when it came time to reenter the job market. Maybe her former boss was right. No. You're not stale. You're dead. Jamie was beginning to feel as cranky as a colicky infant. She rocked her chair up and down on its back legs.

She felt privileged to have had the opportunity to stay at home with her daughters and treasured the many special moments they shared, but what was the price? Jamie couldn't help but speculate about where she would be if she hadn't abandoned her vocation. Maybe she'd be working for the *Washington Post* or *Time* magazine. She stopped rocking. She had not made the least bit of effort to stay connected to her career. Now that Jamie wanted it back, it was out of reach. An either/or decision had to be made: staying home and caring for her precious babies or going back to work after a too-short maternity leave. Babies won, but looking back there were other options. She could have worked part time and gotten someone to come in to watch the girls. She knew women who did this, and their children appeared well adjusted. She could have done freelance work, entered writing contests, or even worked on a memoir about being raised by a blond bobble head. Writing was deleted from her world the second Megan was born.

Jamie had a brief interlude with hope when she started this project, but it was over. The possibility that she would be able to reenter a struggling publishing industry was probably less than one percent. On the home front, Michael had left home and was having an affair with some hottie, who was probably smart too. Even if Jamie did decide she wanted him back, there was a good chance that the new world he was discovering was far more appealing than reconciliation with an overweight deadbeat.

Who could his mistress be? She thought about his colleagues. "Ah-ha!" It's that female lawyer who always cozies up to him at office parties. She couldn't think of her name. Then it came to her. "Sherry. That's it. Sherry." Jamie sprang to her feet and circled around the living room. She recalled the last work-related gathering, when Sherry came on to Michael right in front of her. Jamie imitated her rival and gushed, "Ohhh, you must thank your lucky stars every night being married to such a handsome man." Sherry had squeezed Michael's arm and gazed at him like he was a teen idol. Jamie grinned when she thought about the vamp's shocked face when Michael shrugged her away.

"Let's see," Jamie said, as she tapped her cheek. Sherry was in her early thirties, had a sleek French hairstyle, and a body that sizzled. How could Michael not be tempted by this woman, even if he was in the best of marriages, and their marriage was almost as dead as her career.

She imagined Sherry waltzing into her husband's office, wearing too-tight professional clothes. She offered him sympathy when Michael told her that his marriage was crumbling. An understanding ear led to a hug; then kissing and groping started. Consumed with desire, they fled to the hotel where Michael was staying, and he hammered her. It was that simple. While Jamie was home putting together a puzzle of Hawaii, wearing flannel pajama pants, Michael was having a wild fling with Sherry, who most likely wore a leopard pushup bra and matching thong.

Jamie dropped onto the couch. Her marriage was really over. It was what she wanted for so long. Now she wasn't so sure. Michael had a great income, but could it support two households if they ended up divorced? This wasn't a game anymore. She had to find a job. "An employment agency!" she exclaimed. Racing back to her computer, she did a Google search and made an appointment with a top-notch firm for the next day.

The job problem might be on its way to resolution but not her family issues. Jamie needed comfort, so she went to the vegetable bin in the refrigerator, seized the bag of peanut butter cups, and headed to the living room to work on her puzzle. She walked a few feet then stopped. The wise woman was back. *Will that candy make you happier if you eat it or if you put it back?*

"Hmm," Jamie said.

She held the bag up and looked at it. What would happen if she ate them? All of the hydrogenated oil and sugar would clog up her arteries, she'd gain more weight, and she'd feel sad again five minutes after she devoured the treats.

What would happen if she put them back? She'd keep her blood flowing, maybe lose weight, but she wouldn't get a five-minute break from distress, and she really needed a five-minute break from distress. The flimsy plastic felt cold on her fingertips. Jamie shivered. A minute passed, or was it ten minutes? Whatever, it was long enough for beads of sweat the size of pencil points to form on her forehead. Her throat felt heavy, like it had been plastered with cement. She couldn't swallow. Jamie darted to the kitchen sink, set the peanut butter cups on the counter, and filled a glass with water. She gulped and gulped until the glass was empty; then she breathed in and out. For the love of God, she was having an anxiety attack over candy.

Jamie set the glass down and reached for the peanut butter cups. The wise woman said, *Don't.*

Tears welled in Jamie's eyes. "I need them," she whispered.

No you don't, the wise woman said.

Jamie stepped back. A thousand stars twinkled inside her. It was as if the wise woman waved a wand and glitter flew all over the place. Jamie closed her eyes and savored the sensation. When she opened them, the bag of candy was still there, calling her. Her soul told her mind to tell her mouth to say, "No thank you." Jamie tried, but the words wouldn't come. Why was it so hard to say, "No thank you"? After all, wasn't she an amalgamation of the soul, body, and mind, and they were all capable of saying no. An outside force controlled her. Those damned morsels of sugar, peanut butter, and chocolate owned her.

"How?" she murmured.

With eyes wide open, she shook her head. Isolation, fear. Those same feelings she had when her mother left when she was a child. The chocolate soothed her then, and it soothed her now. She stared at the candy. "All those years ago, you promised to stop the pain," Jamie said. "But it always came back."

She grabbed a dish towel and wiped her tears away. Jamie tossed it on the stovetop and reached for a peanut butter cup. She slowly removed the orange and gold wrapper, scrunched it up, and threw it on the counter. Jamie sniffed her craving buster, and for the first time ever, it made her sick. She unwrapped the rest of the peanut butter cups and stuffed each one into the garbage disposal. She turned on the faucet and flicked the switch that pulverized her edible crutches. When the homicide was complete, she smiled. Jamie had just done something wonderful for her neglected soul, and the wise woman so deep inside her said, *Thank you.*

Jamie scooped up the wrappers and threw them in the basket. She slowly walked upstairs, went into the bathroom, shed her pajamas, and got on the scale. "Ugh." She had gained three more pounds. Stepping off the truth meter, she closed her eyes and huffed. As she reached for the door, Jamie turned and stepped back on the scales. She peered at the digital number that flashed at her. "You created that weight. It's up to you to get rid of it."

Thrusting her shoulders back, she ambled into the bedroom. She put on underclothes, which would soon be too big, blue jeans that had a couple of dime-sized holes around one knee, and a purple T-shirt. Humidity seeped into the house from the open window, so she pulled her hair back into a ponytail. The garden was summoning her. This sanctuary of peace would cradle her as she stepped into a new beginning.

Jamie surveyed the backyard. Weeding and digging were definitely on today's agenda. The summer annuals were ready to be pulled. Soon her outdoor arrangement would be abundant with an assortment of vanilla-, raspberry-, and lemon-colored mums, pumpkins, corn stalks, and a sprinkling of oriental kale, to accent with their pink and green leaves. She loved having kids and their parents over on Halloween, and it wasn't too soon to start decorating. A gourd hunt on the patio was the highlight of this event, but bobbing for apples was also a big hit. She always started a fire in the pit, lit the outdoor torches, and played spooky music. The chaos of this night drove Michael nuts. This year he wouldn't be around, so she could have fun without worrying about him having a tantrum.

Jamie put on mud gloves, retrieved a spade from the shed, dug into the earth, and removed the petunias and zinnias. Pulling the weeds, she smiled. It felt good to get rid of the old and make room for the new. She smoothed the soil with a hoe then inspected the plot. Where could she put the mums, so it would look a little different from last year? It would be nice to have a bigger yard, so she could experiment more, but this patch would have to do. A few decorative rocks might add depth, she thought.

Scanning the garden, she realized that it was time to extract the white alyssum, which always made Jamie a touch sad. Subtle and delicate, this had to be her favorite annual. Gazing at these blossoms on a hot summer day was like being greeted by a blanket of snow. Flicking away the melancholy, she continued her work. Sweat poured out of her as she burrowed and yanked.

In the midst of the labor, she pulled her cell phone out of her pocket and exclaimed, "Yikes!" when she saw that it was two. The hours that passed seemed more like minutes. Jamie watered the area with the hose. Before shutting it off, she put her lips on the water stream and sucked in the cold liquid. It felt good, so she sprayed her face and giggled.

Jamie placed the tools back in the shed then went inside to shower. As she scrubbed the dirt off her skin, she decided to make a large salad for lunch. For dinner, she'd mix up stew beef and vegetables with bouillon and put it in the Crock-Pot. Just thinking about healthy food made her feel thinner. When her cleansing was done, she wrapped herself in a large towel and went into the bedroom with a spring in her step. She smiled. Just like the home she had prepared for new flowers to grow, she had planted a seed in her core today for a new Jamie to blossom.

Chapter Sixteen

At five Michael trudged to his car with the new assignment tucked under his arm. His tired body wanted to crash on a bed, even a hotel bed, but rest would have to wait. He had told Rufus he'd meet him at the Boys & Girls Club at five thirty, and it was too late to cancel. He'd take the tour, make some nice comments, go back to his room, get a solid night's sleep, and tackle his work after a revitalizing run in the morning.

Michael climbed up the concrete steps of the brick middle school building where the club was housed. The structure had to be at least one hundred years old, but looked clean, like it had just been power washed. He searched for windows. There weren't any, at least not in front. He opened the heavy metal door. Battleship-gray walls and outdated vinyl tile greeted him. The smell of mold and sewer filled the dingy foyer, and he didn't even want to think about what was causing the stench. He couldn't imagine having to come to this dungeon each day to teach or learn. Michael compared it to the building where he worked and frowned at the contrast. Shaking his head, he said, "The future of America."

A cheery woman, who looked like a college student, welcomed him and told him where he could find Rufus. Michael walked down the corridor, which begged for a new coat of paint. As disgust stirred, he heard something heavenly. In the back corner at the end of the hall, acoustic guitars were singing. Sure, the melody was out of tune, but it was music. It reminded him of when he first began playing, and his heart quickened. He hurried toward the sound, peeked into the room, and saw Rufus sitting on a folding metal chair surrounded by three boys, who must've been twelve or thirteen years old. A tall, slim man, probably in his forties, wearing tan Dockers and a sky-blue polo shirt, stood near them with his arms folded. The serious expressions on the kids' faces conveyed that they were doing their best to make "Hey Jude" sound like something Lennon and McCartney would be proud of. When they finished, Michael clapped loudly, startling the performers.

"Hey, Michael," Rufus said as he stood. "Glad you made it."

"Of course," Michael said, shaking Rufus's hand. He then turned his attention to the boys. "You guys are awesome."

The boys sat straight up and beamed at the compliment.

Rufus pointed at each of them. "This is Jaquel, Joseph, and Zamier."

They nodded and said, "Hey."

Rufus lifted his head, signaling them to stand.

Joseph, a gangly young African American with corn rows adorning his head, offered Michael his hand.

Michael shook it firmly. "Nice to meet you." As soon as they made contact, a surge of energy shot through him.

When Michael released the grip, he gazed into Joseph's chocolate eyes a few seconds longer than might be considered appropriate. A strange feeling whirled inside him. As Michael greeted Jaquel and Zamier, his heart beat faster.

"And this is my nephew, Luke," Rufus said proudly.

Michael gazed at Rufus then back at Luke. "Except for a few years, you two are identical."

"Best gift I ever gave him," Rufus said, chuckling.

Luke extended his hand. "Hey, Michael." He had a strong, smooth voice that matched his confident handshake. "My uncle wanted me to give you the grand tour of our newest facility, and I'm not sure why. All we have so far is a game room and a homework room." He held his hands out. "And this: the beginning of a music program."

The boys sat back down and plucked on the guitars. The urge to join them was overwhelming, and Michael turned his head, hoping it would weaken his desire.

Rufus shot a finger at him. "He'd be a perfect volunteer to help get things going."

Michael's eyes widened. He didn't have time for volunteer work. Maybe he'd write a check, but that was it. Then again—a music program?

Rufus smiled. "So what do you think of our music studio? Impressed?"

Michael pinched his bottom lip. "With the music and r' kids, but man—the facility."

Luke nodded. "Not pretty, huh? And this is an imr ment. The district began work on the school facili' provement plan awhile back, but we're still a lot of) dollars away from completion."

8

"At least there are windows in this classroom," Michael said. "I felt like I was walking into a cave when I first entered this place. And it's so humid in here. And what smells so bad?"

Luke laughed. "It's awful, isn't it? The lighting in this building is poor throughout. The smell could be due to a faulty waste system that needs to be replaced. Believe it or not, the inspection stated that nothing about the plumbing in this school meets ADA code requirements."

Michael could actually feel his blood pressure rise. "You've got to be kidding."

Luke put his hands on his hips. "I wish I were. The drainage in this building is also poor. That, combined with inadequate plumbing, gives you this unique smell."

Rufus chimed in. "Tell him about the humidity."

"They added eighteen A/C units a couple of years ago. This classroom, along with many others, didn't get one."

"No central air in a DC school?" Michael said, eyes widening.

"I knew that would get you," Rufus said.

"Some of the newer schools have it, and, really, there is progress," Luke said. "You should have seen this building before the renovations began. You would have never believed that it was an educational institution just three miles away from the White House."

"Still don't," Michael said.

"Many inner city schools are in worse shape than this," Rufus informed. "Just do an Internet search if you really want to be shocked."

Michael grimaced.

"Enough with the negative," Luke said. "This is all we've ιt, and we're going to make the best of it. The public schools and the Boys & Girls Club are partnering to make a difference in kids' lives."

Luke jabbed Joseph in the arm. "Bottom line is the students who go here really need a quality after school program, and that's our mission. Keep these clowns here instead of making mischief in the streets. Right?"

The guys chuckled.

"Besides, didn't you notice the paint, wood, and tools over there?" Rufus asked, pointing to a far corner of the room. "We're here to work this evening. Gonna turn this dungeon into a grand music emporium."

"A music emporium?" Michael said.

"You bet. The guys want to start a band, and they need someplace inspirational to practice. A few weeks from now this lifeless edifice will extract creativity from these young artists."

Michael froze then gazed at the boys. His throat tightened, and he had trouble swallowing.

"I'll show you around and tell you about my vision for the facility," Luke said. "Don't worry about volunteer work. We have a long list of college students we're scheduling." Luke lifted his chin toward Rufus. "You have to be careful of that guy. Before you know it, you'll have a brush in your hand and paint stains on your suit."

Michael peered at Rufus then sat in a chair close to Joseph. "Where'd you learn to play?"

Joseph shrugged. "Taught myself."

Michael acknowledged the other adolescents, asked the same question, and got the same answer. He shuffled some outdated song books that were spread out on a scratched maple school desk. "With these?"

Joseph nodded.

"No one comes in to give you lessons?"

"We are looking for volunteer music teachers. Do you know anyone?" Luke asked.

Michael glanced at Rufus, who had a smirk on his face. "I can come in one night a week." He rubbed his eyes with his fingertips. "Used to be pretty skilled with a guitar. How are Wednesdays at five thirty?"

Chapter Seventeen

"Hey, Michael. We've got all of your paperwork processed. You are officially a volunteer for the Boys & Girls Club of America," Luke said, as he rose from his desk.

Michael smiled and shook Luke's hand. "Great!"

"One problem."

"What's that?" Michael asked.

"Fifteen kids signed up for lessons, and you're our only guitar teacher so far. We're doing our best to get more."

"Wow. Fifteen kids?"

Luke clapped his hands. "Yeah. It's fantastic to have that kind of interest in a new program, and I don't want to lose any of them. For right now though, we're going to have to put ten on hold. We'll walk down to the music room and do a drawing to see who gets the first lesson."

Michael's expression turned serious. "Hate to disappoint anyone. There are three guitars, right?"

"Yes, Sir."

"Let's see what we can do."

The two men walked into the freshly painted room. Three walls were pale green and one bright white. The renovation had added about a hundred pounds of vitality to the area. Outdated maple desks were pushed to the back of the room, and several folding chairs were arranged in a semicircle. A few mismatched drums sat in a far corner, along with a couple of tambourines and one amplifier. Three acoustic guitars stood in their stands ready for action, and fifteen adolescents gathered around, staring at Michael.

They were all black: some with Afros, some with corn rows, some with straightened course hair, and some with shaved heads. They dressed like typical teenagers: the guys wore baggy jeans and hoodies; and the girls, far too little, with lots of ear piercings. Michael felt nervous, even more so than when he had tried to comfort Jamie on the previous Saturday. Was he anxious because he was surrounded by black kids in a high crime area of DC, or would he feel just as uncomfortable if a group of white kids were standing in front of him? He knew he wasn't a racist. So why did he feel funny being the only white person in the room? In fact, with his olive skin, he was probably darker than some of the attendees. It had to be a culture clash—an uncertainty about how to connect when there wasn't a common thread around to attach them. But he was mistaken. There was a link that would bind them, a powerful link—music. They were all here for music.

Michael picked up a guitar by the neck, and his apprehension dissipated. He was actually going to play for people instead of the four walls of his basement. He sat on a metal chair and placed the instrument on his lap. His left fingers found the G chord, and his right fingers found a pick on the adjacent table. The B. B. King in him had arrived, and he banged out a tune that might have landed him a spot in the blues master's band. He may have played a little too long and a little too hard, but it felt so damn good. When he was through, a thunderous round of applause raged into his ears. They loved his performance, and their eager faces told him they wanted more. He had them in his palm.

Full of adrenaline, Michael put the guitar back in the stand, sprang up, and addressed his audience. "Who wants to learn to play like that?"

Fifteen hands shot up.

"Here's the deal. We got fifteen of you and three of them," he said, pointing to the guitars. "That means we're gonna have to share." An instant lesson plan sprouted from his mouth. "For tonight, we work in groups of three. When you're not playing, you watch and listen. Got it?"

All heads nodded.

"By the end of our session, you'll have three chords to practice. Imperative that you master them before we move on."

He picked up a guitar. "They're called C, D, G." He strummed each one. "And there are a lot of songs you can play with those chords." Michael paused. "I'm going to post a practice sign-up sheet on the door before I leave. We'll have guitar one, guitar two, and guitar three. You'll need at least two hours of practice each week to make any progress whatsoever, and that's the minimum." Michael slapped his thigh then boomed, "Let me emphasize: at least two hours a week. The more you play, the more people are going to want to listen to you. So if you say you're gonna be here, be here. Sign in and sign out. Too many no-shows, and you're out. Got it?"

They all nodded.

"By the way, I'll know instantly if you practiced one hour instead of two, so don't even think of trying that one." He held up his hand and flexed his fingers. "You should have calluses on your fingertips the next time we meet, from the friction of the strings. Great guitarists' fingers are as tough as steel."

"I forgot one important thing: my name. It's Michael. What are yours?" He pointed to one of the students, and shouts of identity began. When they were finished, Michael said, "I'll probably have to ask you to repeat it every week because I suck at remembering names."

They all laughed.

Luke walked over from a corner in the room. He looked at Michael with enthusiastic eyes. "I'm here to help."

"Let's get these kids..." He paused. "These *musicians* into their groups."

The music began.

After two hours, everyone had a chance to practice the chords, and the class ended. Michael announced that the lessons would resume in two weeks because of his business trip. By then they should be ready to move to the next step.

Luke interrupted, "Show up next Wednesday even though Michael can't be here. I want to hear your progress."

The students headed toward the sign-up sheets. Luke and Michael high-fived.

"You are a phenomenal teacher!" Luke exclaimed. "Any experience?"

"No. Unless spouting at hearings counts. I'm a lawyer."

"Well, it must. Because you instantly engaged those kids. Not an easy thing to do."

"The guitar helped."

Luke nodded. "Your playing made me want to sign up for lessons. Ever think about becoming a music teacher, playing in a band?"

Michael's chest tightened. After a few seconds, he said, "Played in band when I was a teenager. Never even thought about being a music teacher."

Luke's eyebrows arched. "You are one now. Can't tell you how glad I am to have you on board." He lifted his head toward the kids, who were signing up for practice spots. "You're going to make a big difference in those lives. I can tell."

Michael creased his forehead. He liked the idea of teaching. In fact, he liked teaching. The past two hours were two of the best he'd ever had. Helping the kids get their fingers in the correct position on the fret, seeing them smile when the changes in chords created a tune, the way they laughed at some of his comments, the way they listened to him. He also liked the idea of making a difference in someone's life. Wow. He liked giving, helping.

"Thanks," he finally said.

Luke nodded. "I'm going to work on getting more volunteers, and will make some calls to get more equipment. We have some grants in the works, but I'm still looking for a program director for this facility, so things are going slow."

"A program director?"

"Yeah. Not an easy position to fill. We need a dynamic, intelligent person, and dynamic, intelligent people don't work for the salary we offer."

"I see. Do you think the position will be vacant long?"

"Possibly, but I don't hire until I get the right candidate. Better to have no one than the wrong one, if you know what I mean."

"I hear you loud and clear."

"Anyway, Michael, thanks again. I have to catch the train to Morrisey, so I better move."

"Morrisey?"

"Small town in Virginia. That's where I live with my wife and kids."

"Small town living. Never done that. Do you like it?"

"It's home. A great place to raise kids."

"You better run. Don't want to make you miss your train."

Luke waved. "See you in two weeks?"

"You bet."

What was it about Rufus and his nephew? Michael detected an intensity from Luke that Rufus didn't have, but the guy was running programs for the DC Boys & Girls Clubs, commuted back and forth from Virginia, and had a family. Even with all of that going on, Luke seemed happy. He hadn't complained once, had a positive vision for his organization, and made Michael feel welcome.

Michael scanned the room. All of the kids were gone except for one, Joseph. He held a guitar and was doing his best to make his fingers go from chord C to chord G without stopping the flow of sound. Michael walked over and sat in a chair across from him.

"This is hard," Joseph said, with a pained expression.

"Most worthwhile things are, but you'll get it," Michael encouraged.

"How long did it take you to play good?"

"A few months. Then it got easier and a lot more fun. You're Joseph, right?"

"Yup. Do you need to go?"

"Not really. How about you? I don't want your mom to worry."

"She's working."

"Did you finish your homework?"

"Don't got none."

"It's 'I don't have any.' And yes, you do."

"What?"

"First part. When you're in school, you need to use standard English. You're not going to get very far in life if you don't."

Joseph scowled. "You sound like a teacher."

"Not a bad thing, and it's true. You'll never get a good job or make good money unless you learn the language of success, and it's not that hard."

"How do you know how hard it is?"

"My parents spoke Greek and poor English. When I started school, it was like walking into a foreign country. I had no idea what anyone was saying, but I had to learn the code."

Joseph crinkled his nose. "You didn't speak English?"

"Some, but not enough to understand much. I didn't fit in."

"You learned it?"

"Yes, Sir," Michael smiled. He liked this kid; felt a connection with him.

"Did you go to college?"

"Yes."

"Are you rich?"

"Yes."

"Wow."

Michael smiled again. "What grade are you in?"

"Eighth."

"Eighth graders always have homework. Is that your backpack?"

"Yeah."

"Go get it."

Joseph reluctantly retrieved it.

"What do you have for homework?"

"Some math. Stupid DBQ for history."

"I love document-based questions; math, not so much. Let's pull over a couple of desks and take a look."

"For real? This is Guitar Club."

"I just made a new rule. In order to be in Guitar Club, you have to have at least Cs on your report card. I'll check 'em every quarter."

"You can do that?"

"Sure. I'm the boss of Guitar Club. If you're having a problem with some subject, you better let me know ahead of time, and we'll work something out. Come on. Let's get your homework done. I can tell that you're going to be an awesome musician, and I don't want to lose you."

"For real?"

Michael smiled again. "For real."

The sun's light was leaving the sky, and it would be dark in a few minutes. Michael unlocked his car with the push of a button but didn't get in right away. He stared at the decrepit building, which blended with the twilight hour. Michael narrowed his eyes. The building spoke to him. It said, "Help me."

Michael's gaze deepened. At his office he had the finest of everything, from furnishings to windows to lighting. The most valuable item in that school would have been tossed out as garbage. It fact, that chipped pressboard teacher's desk in the classroom would never have even gotten near his firm. Regardless, there was something special in there. Something priceless, and it called him. The longer he lingered, the louder the voice became. Soon it was clear. He found his treasure. Shoes that fit were in that building.

A waterfall of energy cascaded over him. Michael closed his eyes and allowed the phenomenon to settle into his bones. When he opened them, the building faded into the night. Frowning, he got into his car. He found his shoes. Now he had to figure out how he was going to put them on and take them home.

Chapter Eighteen

A late-September breeze zipped through Dupont Circle, delivering the message that autumn had arrived. Michael caught himself humming as he observed the park dwellers, who wore nylon jackets and sweatshirts. He cut out early again this Friday, but no one seemed to notice—not even Frank. As long as he kept meeting deadlines and presenting his cases with clarity and precision, he could afford to play hooky once in a while.

Rufus strolled into the circle from the north shortly after three thirty. He sported a royal blue windbreaker, khaki pants, and black basketball shoes. The leaves on the trees rustled in the wind, and Rufus stopped before wandering over to the chess tables. He gazed at the foliage as if it were some kind of miracle.

Michael walked over. "Hey, Rufus. What's up?"

Rufus pointed to the chattering green leaves. "In a few weeks, there'll be a big spray of yellow, red, and orange shading us. The color shift is about to begin. Feel it."

Michael closed his eyes. The vibrant wind bathed his face, and he delighted in nature's massage. It was the perfect compensation for the crazy week he just had. Rufus was the first to finish the seasonal cocktail and asked Michael if he wanted to get a cup of coffee.

The two men hurried across the busy street and entered a café nestled between a bookshop and a pub. It had a wide front window that provided a postcard view of Dupont Circle. The scents of cinnamon and freshly ground coffee dominated the air, helping to free Michael's mind from his work and family headaches. The display case featured an array of desserts, and Michael ogled them. Rufus ordered French-pressed Colombian brew and two slices of apple pie, heated, with vanilla ice cream.

"I think you're my new best friend," Michael said, as he shifted his eyes from the desserts to Rufus.

"Why?"

"Ordering that pie. It's calling me."

"Better ask the waitress to cut you a slice. I just got myself two pieces, a la mode, to boot," Rufus said, chuckling.

"You probably could eat both."

"Wouldn't be a problem."

He paid for the decadent snack under Michael's futile protest, and they sat at one of the booths that lined the wall. When Rufus took off his jacket, it was like watching an Ivy League athlete making himself comfortable at the campus union. No one would have ever guessed he was seventy years old. At some point, he'd ask Rufus where he found the fountain of youth, but somehow he already knew. It was called simple, relaxed living, something Michael never learned about in his twenty-plus years in school.

Rufus took a bite of the pie, sipped his coffee, and leaned back. "There's something about eating that makes conversations so much better. I wonder what that is. Anyway, I'm going to ask you the same question I did last week. Only this time I want a better answer. What have you been doing for fun?"

Michael wanted to say that except for the guitar lesson it was the worst week of his life. Jamie had been so curt since Sunday, and she refused to meet with him. He felt like divulging his troubles to this kind man, but didn't. No one knew he and Jamie were separated, and he'd keep it that way as long as possible. Not speaking about it somehow made it seem less real.

So he tried to muster up some fun talk. "I initiated a make-your-own-pizza party with my daughters. I sat on my patio and inadvertently napped for three hours on Saturday morning. I bought the family bikes; then Jamie and I taught the girls how to ride. I cleared some junk out of the suitcase. Golf and soccer are no longer part of my life. Loved the session I had at the Boys & Girls Club. What made you tell Luke I wanted to volunteer?"

Rufus set down his fork. "You told me you wanted to."

"No, I didn't."

"Yes, you did. You said that your life was crowded with junk and that you wanted to get rid of it—start making room for fun and important things. To me, that's the same as saying I want to volunteer."

"Unbelievable. Have you ever thought about going into politics?"

"Can't stand long meetings, bullshit, and wasting money, so crossed that off my list long ago."

Michael sat back. "First, if you ever decide to run for president, you'd win with that slogan."

"Maybe I'll sell the line to our neighbor down the street," Rufus said, shifting his eyes in the direction of the White House. "So what happened at that club? Luke said fifteen kids showed up."

"That's right, and only three guitars. I had to think quick."

"What'd you do?"

Michael told Rufus the details, and his voice grew more enthusiastic with each word. When he was through, he was nearly jumping in his seat like on overexcited toddler.

"You found your calling!" Rufus exclaimed, throwing his hands into the air.

Michael froze. "What do you mean?"

"Your whole demeanor changed when you told me about the music, the kids, how you engaged them, helped Joseph with his homework. You went from gloom to elation in seconds. Fireworks going off in your eyes. Do you feel it?"

Michael nodded. "I do."

"What are you gonna do about it? A fine day when you realize what you were put on this earth to do."

"I'm going to keep volunteering."

"Won't be enough. You're gonna want more."

"I don't have time for more."

"What do you do for a living?"

"I'm a managing attorney at a national labor relations firm."

"Do you like your job?"

Michael paused and swirled a forkful of pie in the melting ice cream. "No. I mean, it's important work, bringing employees and employers together, but the effort is life consuming. I don't mind the research or helping to solve problems, but I hate managing people—trying to get them to do their best, fixing all of their mistakes. And to be honest with you, I'm terrible at it."

"What made you decide to be a lawyer?"

Michael tapped his spoon on the edge of his coffee cup, set it down, and stared at the ceiling. When he lowered his head, he directed his gaze toward Rufus. "I didn't have anything to do with the decision. My father pounded it into me. Becoming a doctor or an engineer—those were also options, but I wasn't into math and science."

Rufus leaned forward, "Did you and your father get along?"

Michael furrowed his eyebrows. "Does a knight get along with his king? It was that kind of relationship."

"Tell me about your dad."

"He was from Greece, grew up in a small farming village, and spent the first twenty-five years of his life picking olives from his family's trees. When he married my mother, they came to the States, Maryland—hoping for a prosperous life, like so many others. They were penniless and lived with relatives who came before them."

Michael took a sip of coffee. "My father borrowed some tools and began peddling for work as a carpenter. His business started slowly, but he soon earned a reputation for reliability, fairness, and craftsmanship. He saved his money and was able to buy a house just before I was born. It was a three-family dwelling in a working-class neighborhood."

"He sounds like a pioneer."

Michael nodded. "And an entrepreneur. We lived on the first floor and rented out the others for additional income. Pa wasn't educated, and his English wasn't very good, so carpentry was all he had. He'd ride the bus or walk to whatever job he could find every morning but Sunday, and he'd be home at nightfall for dinner. Always made sure I was busy with some kind of work. As long as I followed his orders, I was fine, but I didn't dare defy him."

Rufus looked at Michael soberly. "So you becoming a lawyer was your father's dream because he wanted you to have a better, richer life. Makes sense. Is he alive to enjoy it? What about your mother? Did she push you in that direction too?"

"Pa died about ten years ago, shortly after Jamie and I were married, and my mother died a few years later. He did live to see me graduate from law school." Michael shook his head slightly. "Rufus, he was waiting to be seated hours before the ceremony started. I don't think a more satisfied man ever lived. After the graduation, we went back to the hotel and toasted with warm Metaxa—best shots I ever did with my dear old dad. As far as my mother goes, she stayed in the background—cooked and cleaned, made sure we went to church. My parents never talked much, and my mother always seemed sad. It was an arranged marriage, and I don't think either one of them was thrilled with the setup."

"I've heard about those kinds of marriages. It's funny how people endured so much not so long ago, and now divorce is more common than staying together. Too many glitches and it's over. Anyway, now that you achieved your father's dream, what's yours?"

Michael breathed in deeply then slowly exhaled. "Never paid too much attention to dreams. I've always done what I was told. Whether it was being a good student, getting a haircut, or flying off to Saint Paul to train a bunch of neophytes.

The command is given, and I respond. No wonder I'm so miserable."

"Saint Paul?"

"Yeah. I have to go there tomorrow for a week on business, and am not looking forward to it."

Rufus nodded. "Well, I think you have a dream of your own." Rufus waited. "Oh come on, Michael. Be a kid again. What did you pretend when you were young?"

The waitress came over and poured them another cup of coffee. Rufus thanked her and ordered two more slices of pie.

"I can't believe you just did that. You're really having another piece?"

"Yeah, why not? Neither one of us needs to lose weight. Can you think of a good reason why we shouldn't?"

"Not one. Anyway, you go first, while I think of my dream. It sounds like you were an awesome bus driver, but did you ever want to try something else?"

Rufus nodded. "I was fascinated with airplanes when I was a kid. But I just didn't want to be a pilot. I wanted to know about the engine, the mechanics of flying. I had model airplanes and took them apart and put them back together. Borrowed books from the library about flying and read them cover to cover, from picture books when I was a boy to texts when I was in middle school. If I were young today, I'd be an aeronautical engineer."

"Why didn't you go for it?"

"Remember, I grew up poor and black in the nineteen fifties. Unless you were a real fighter, you were kept down. I didn't care much for school anyway, and I wasn't prepared for college. No one around to give me a real push." Rufus wiped his mouth with a napkin. "But I tell you, Michael, many times when I was driving that bus, I imagined wings popped out from the sides and scooted me into the air." He pointed at Michael. "Your turn."

"It sucks that you couldn't pursue your dream just because of your skin color."

"We're not going there. I'm done with the anger. Accept my life as it is." Rufus looked at Michael with serious eyes. "What concerns me is things haven't changed much since the fifties."

"Sure they have. The civil rights movement was huge, and we've elected our first African American president."

"And high school graduation rates for black boys are about the same."

"It doesn't seem possible."

"You have to go deep into the cities to find the problem, and who wants to do that? It'd be like taking a vacation in Bagdad. Urban war zones. You got a peek at the situation this past week in that school. Aren't the conditions deplorable?"

"Awful."

"I went to middle school there, and the place still has many of the same parts."

"I can't believe I've lived in DC for twenty years and wasn't aware of all this. I mean, a little, but I didn't know how bad it really was."

Rufus's voice rose ever so slightly, and there was a tenseness in his face that Michael had never seen before. "Now, your dream. What is it?"

"This is big for you, and I get it," Michael said. "You're one smart guy, and you should've been that engineer. For heaven's sake, look at how you put together a roast beef sandwich, analyze a chess board, and notice the minute summer starts turning into fall. *Meticulous* could be your middle name."

Rufus's voice evened out. "It's not going to happen at this point. That's why I go down to the club as much as I can. Draw out the smarts in those kids. Get 'em on the right track. Lord knows, there are enough wrong tracks circling around." Rufus turned away and looked toward the ceiling. Within seconds, he faced Michael again and cleared his throat. "Now, the dream, Michael—the dream."

Michael hesitated. Rufus was not the carefree man he appeared to be. Anguish, frustration, grief were hidden behind his pleasant demeanor. This man had a story to tell, but he had buried it a long time ago and didn't want to dig it up. Although Michael was curious, he wasn't going to push.

So Michael straightened up and relayed his dream. "I wanted to be a musician, a big rock star. I wanted to push Bruce Springsteen off the charts. That's it. That's what I wanted."

"Woo-ee! A rock star? That's how you got so good at the guitar. Ever act on it? Ya know, join a band?"

Michael nodded. "When I was twelve, I told my father I wanted a guitar for my birthday. He forbade it. Said it was nonsense and would interfere with my studies. Told me to get it right out of my head. I couldn't. I watched people play on television and wanted to jump right into the set, so I started a paper route. I saved every dime, and when I had enough, I bought myself a beautiful guitar. I worked two years for that instrument—a real beauty." Michael smiled and ate a big chunk of pie.

"What did your father say?" Rufus asked, leaning in. "Did he let you keep it?"

Michael swallowed the pie and took a swig of coffee. "He never knew about it. I kept it at my friend Max's house and learned to play in his basement. I told my parents I was going over there to study, but we played music the entire time. Then I stayed up late to get my homework done."

"Did he ever find out?"

"Never. I lived at home during college, but always found someone who lived on campus or in an apartment to store my hidden treasure. Whenever I could, I escaped to a practice room, wrote music, and sang. During law school, I finally got to live with my guitar."

"Then what happened?"

"I got a job, and it consumed me. If I wasn't working, I was golfing or socializing with my superiors to get ahead. I was really driven at that point. Put my guitar aside. When I bought my house, it came with me. At first, I played at night. Then I met Jamie and fell hard. Between her and everything else, music faded away. Jamie and I got married, and I didn't feel as comfortable playing with her around. I was programmed to keep the guitar concealed, so I put it in the basement."

"Where is it now?"

Michael rolled his eyes and chuckled. "Still in the basement."

"That's a good story, Michael. You go down to that basement tonight and get that guitar. Knock Springsteen off the charts. He's still there, ya know."

"I know."

"Do you think your guitar is still playable?"

Michael nodded. "Every now and then, I sneak down and play." He stopped talking for a moment. Did he just reveal his secret? After clearing his throat, he said, "Needs to be refurbished, but it's okay."

"Bring it back to life."

Michael shrugged. "Maybe I will."

"No *maybe*s. Just do it."

"Yes, Sir," Michael said, smiling.

Rufus sat back and dusted his hands. "How about I set up a meeting between you and Luke? He can tell you about some of the jobs at the club."

Michael's jaw dropped. "Are you kidding?"

"No. You hate your job, and you love the club."

"I'm sure the salary for a recreation leader at the Boys & Girls Club wouldn't even pay for my groceries, not to mention the hundreds of other expenses I have."

"Not a rec leader. Something in management: writing grants, reviewing vendor contracts, program development. Just think what someone like you could do with that music endeavor."

There it was again—a tingling that covered his skin from head to toe. Was this what a calling felt like? "Are there positions like that available right now?"

"I know of one. It's hard to fill because the pay is low and the credentials are high."

"I think Luke told me about it. How low is *low*?"

"Probably around fifty thousand a year. If they could get someone like you, they'd come up with a little more."

Michael choked on his coffee and had to wipe his chin with a napkin. "Are you kidding?"

"Big pay cut?"

"Huge. I could never do it."

"Start thinking about how you spend your money. Make some adjustments."

"It's all tied up."

"Does that fancy car you drive make you happy? Do your kids like all of those activities they're in? You could cut some fat to answer the call."

Michael quietly said, "It's impossible."

"Such an ugly word, *impossible*," Rufus said.

When they arrived back at the circle, all the chess tables were full, and people gathered around to watch the games in action. The benches were crowded with mostly males waiting for their turn to play. Michael and Rufus took a seat with some fellows, and they started talking about which team would take the World Series. Naturally, Rufus had his opinion, and so did Michael. When the sports talk ended, Rufus announced that they were in the company of an accomplished musician and spoke about how Michael sang, played guitar, and wrote songs.

"Rufus!" Michael exclaimed, embarrassed at the description of a talent that departed his life long ago.

"Don't be shy. I'm just telling them about your gift. Be proud."

One of the guys shouted, "Sing us a song."

"Are you kidding?"

"Why not? Let's get a song going."

"Be my guest," Michael said.

"Sing," said another, as Rufus sat back grinning.

Michael crossed his hands. "No way. I'm not going to sing at Dupont Circle."

"*Why not* is right," piped in Rufus, as he got up and looked around. "Where's the sign that says no singing at Dupont Circle? Did they pass a law downtown that says a red siren will go off at the first bling of a musical note?"

Michael shot Rufus an astonished stare.

"It'll be fun," Rufus said.

Michael shifted his gaze between Rufus and the energetic crew. "Okay, but I'm going to need some drums with a three-four beat. Rufus, get on it."

Rufus rhythmically banged his hands on the bench.

Michael pointed to some of the guys. "You three, I need some snapping and clapping. Make sure you stay with the rhythm of the drums." Michael demonstrated then signaled them to join in.

"You are a rock star," Rufus bellowed while drumming in perfect rhythm with the clappers and snappers. An audience gathered to watch the show. Michael belted out his own version of "Pink Cadillac," keeping tempo with his newly formed band. When the performance ended, onlookers applauded, and the entertainers bowed in appreciation. Michael bent over in a hearty laugh. All four men joined him as the spectators jovially requested an encore.

Rufus spoke through the merriment, "Springsteen ain't got nothing on you, Stolis. You were born to sing." At that, Michael took another bow.

Chapter Nineteen

Michael approached the room in the back corner of the basement, slowing his pace with each step. He had actually told Jamie that he was going into the cellar to get something. No more sneaking around in order to play his guitar. Melancholy feelings intensified as he confronted the dream that he had put to rest so long ago—the dream he never was allowed to pursue. He pulled on the ceiling light string, and a dull glow filled the area. He faced the friend he had discarded along with his spirit, unlatched the buckles on the case, and pulled out his guitar. It certainly needed some work, and it was about time he took care of that.

Michael grabbed a cloth from an old black lacquer shelf, sat down, and placed his back against the cold concrete wall. He put the guitar on his lap and stroked its neck, inadvertently causing a spider to scurry along in search of a new dwelling. Dusting his treasure, Michael said, "I'm sorry I've ignored you for so long."

The guitar seemed to say, "I've been cooped up in this prison for an eternity. Play me, and we'll bring some harmony into both of our lives."

Michael nodded. Sure, the tuning pegs needed to be replaced and the nut at the top of the neck needed to be re-glued, but that wasn't a problem. He'd make a trip to the music shop when he returned from Saint Paul. After being refurbished, this relic would resonate with acoustic beauty.

Regardless of its current condition, Michael played the re-prise from a song he had written about a fly trapped between a window and a screen.

"Let me see...how does that go...," he muttered.

He plucked the strings and fiddled with some chords. "Maybe..."

There's no way out, no way out.
I see freedom from this trap but there's no way out.
It's making me crazy, but there's no way out.

Up and down, banging all around.
Searchin' for some air.
I'm dying in here, but there's no way out, no way out.
It's hell in here.
I'm sick and tired but there's no way out.
Just rest awhile 'cause there's no way out, no way out.

As always, it felt so good to release his emotions through song. The edginess that plagued him weakened. "See what you do for me, amigo." He stood with his guitar, walked to a corner cabinet, and began searching for his songbooks.

Jamie tossed a blanket over the girls, who snuggled on the couch. They were freshly bathed, zipped up in their pajamas, and smelled like talcum powder. After inhaling their freshness, Jamie clicked on the DVD they had chosen for their Friday night movie.

"Did Dad leave already?" Megan asked.

"No. He went to get something from the cellar."

"That was right after stories. What's taking him so long?"

"Not sure. You two watch the movie, and I'll check on Dad."

Megan and Emily nodded.

Michael had disappeared into the basement an hour ago, and Jamie also wondered what he was doing. He only visited that part of the house when there was a need for some obscure item, and the trip lasted five minutes. Maybe he was hurt or something.

Jamie crept down the stairs and shivered when she reached the bottom step. It was cold and damp, so she rubbed her hands together to warm herself. She looked around but couldn't see Michael. A couple of lights had already been turned on, but it was still so gloomy. Before moving forward, she scanned the area. She did not want to walk through a spider web. Just the thought of its inhabitant's legs running along her body made her shudder.

The back door creaked when she pushed on it. Michael's shadow jumped. She closed her eyes and took a step back. She didn't want to talk to him. He was heading to Saint Paul, or wherever, with another woman tomorrow and had told her it was business. Who went away on business on Saturday? She couldn't believe Michael expected her to believe that blatant lie. Now that she knew he was okay, she'd run back upstairs.

Michael appeared from behind the door and greeted her with a tender smile. Jamie was amazed by the softness in his face. She hadn't seen him this tranquil in—well, ever. He must really be enamored with his new girlfriend.

He placed the music notebook on the cabinet. "Come here. I want to show you something."

Jamie took another step back. "I have to go upstairs. Just wanted to make sure you were all right." She was curious and wanted to ask him what he was doing but couldn't stand to be in his presence, the lying cheat.

Michael walked toward her and reached for her hand. Jamie folded her arms.

He looked at her with disappointed eyes. "What is wrong? I've asked you that a hundred times. Tell me."

"We're separated, Michael. Separated people don't hold hands," she said sharply.

His face crinkled like a raisin. "We hugged last week, and we were separated. What happened?"

"Nothing. Okay? Nothing. I need time without you around. What don't you get about that?"

He let out a long sigh then changed the subject. "Can you at least tell me how your job hunt is going?"

Jamie lowered her eyes.

"Nothing?"

"Let's see," Jamie said, "What were some of the better jobs...bank teller, hotel reservationist, car rental agent."

"That's it? With your qualifications?"

Jamie's shoulders stiffened. "Not any more. I killed my career." She positioned her fingers like a gun. "Pow."

Michael offered his hand again, but she turned away. He grabbed her by the forearms and spun her around. When she looked up at him, their faces were inches apart, and she scratched him with her eyes.

"I am not going away for a week until I get some straight answers. There are two little girls upstairs who happen to be mine." Michael's voice rose. "I'm not sure you're up to taking care of them. Emotions that turn on a dime, slamming dishes around like you did when we were making pizza tonight, a knife by your bed." His fingers pressed firmly into her arms. "I'm worried sick about you."

"Screw you, Michael."

She shook herself away from him and tried to escape, but he caught her by the shirt and pulled her into the dingy room.

Her heart went wild, and it took all her restraint not to punch him in the face, stomach—anywhere.

Michael held her wrist. "What is wrong?"

She dragged out each word, each syllable, purposefully in an even tone. "I heard you on the phone with your lover on Sunday. You liar. You lying son of a bitch."

Michael let go of her and wiped his face with his hand. He forced a swallow. She caught him. Jamie put her hands in her pants pocket and waited for a response.

He looked straight at her. "I don't have a lover."

"I want all of the cards on the table. What's going on?"

"Nothing."

"Michael, I heard your phone conversation Sunday night before dinner. Spill." She couldn't believe she was asking him about this. It wasn't planned, and it made her sound like she cared.

He stepped back. "Okay. I'm going to tell you everything."

Jamie nodded expressionless.

"It was nothing. So nothing that I didn't want you to find out about it."

Jamie tilted her head. "I'm very curious about *nothing*."

"Here goes. There was a woman at the hotel in the room next to me, and she was interested in, ya know, me."

"The hotel? It's not Sherry?"

"Who?"

"That Sherry lawyer from your office. The one who always flirts with you at parties. It's not her?"

"No. Are you crazy, Jamie? Where do you come up with these things?"

"I'm not crazy. Sherry's gorgeous, and we're separated."

"It's not Sherry, believe me. Her flirtations are not just for me. She'd come on to Homer Simpson if he worked in our office. Besides, she's plastic. It would be like having sex with a mannequin. Every time she goes on a vacation, she comes back with some alteration: bigger breasts, a flatter stomach, rounder butt, smaller nose. She's not real."

"So you notice?"

"I heard some of the guys talking about it."

"Okay, Saint Michael. Now, tell me all about your new neighbor."

Michael started pacing. "All right, and I'm flattered that you care."

"Don't care. Just want to know."

Michael told Jamie all about his little tryst, and when he was through, he moved toward her. "I am so sorry. It meant nothing, and she was such a wacko. I hate being single so much."

Listening to Michael detail his escapade was like being hit with a powerful ocean wave. Jamie was jealous and furious at herself for feeling that way. Although Michael didn't spell it out, she surmised this bitch, Rachel, was hot, and Michael wanted her in an animal kind of way. Jamie remembered when he wanted her like that.

"You're so quiet. How mad are you?" Michael inquired softly.

Jamie rubbed her temples then shook her head. "I'm not mad. Our marriage is a mess. Something like this was bound

214

to happen. I had a little cyber-fling, and that was a disaster too."

"You what?"

"What did you think I was doing on the computer all of the time? Playing solitaire?" She mimicked Michael and sarcastically said, "I'm glad you care."

"Damn right I care. The Internet is crawling with predators. You didn't give him any personal information, did you? And how do you have a cyber-fling anyway?"

"It's so stupid. He knows nothing about me. I did a system recovery on my computer after I met him, so he's history. It really didn't crash."

"You *met* him?" Michael shouted.

"Shhh."

He repeated in his loudest hushed voice, "You met him?"

Jamie folded her arms. "Don't worry; it was brief and not half as exciting as your encounter with the psycho."

She didn't know how much she should tell him. Michael's hands were trembling, and it looked like he was about to have a stroke. Jamie rolled her eyes. The real Michael Stolis had returned. "I'm not telling you a thing unless you calm down. I did something stupid at a vulnerable time, learned from it, and moved on. Just like you."

"Yeah, but I didn't meet Rachel on the Internet."

"Hotel, Internet, a bar, a PTA meeting—what difference does it make? We both considered cheating, and that's a real problem."

"Is there someone you're interested in at the PTA?"

Jamie screwed up her face. "Don't be ridiculous."

Michael took a few deep breaths. "I'm calm now."

"You're not going to blow a cork when I tell you about it?"

"Nope."

"Promise?"

"Yup."

Jamie told the Steve story, and when she was finished, Michael's face was crimson.

"He grabbed your breast? He stuck his tongue in your mouth?"

She pointed at him and seethed, "You promised you'd stay calm, and look at yourself. You're an irate devil."

"Jamie, he almost raped you."

"Were you listening to me? A tongue wedge and a nano-second grope aren't even close to rape. I had worse moments when I was a teenager on those awful field trip buses."

"You weren't scared?"

"I have to admit, the whole fiasco freaked me out. That's why I got the knife. I was afraid he followed me and might break in during the night, but he didn't."

Michael kicked the corner cabinet. "This makes me sick."

"It's over. Control yourself, or I'm going upstairs."

He inhaled deeply.

They exchanged glances. "Are you calming down?" Jamie asked.

He nodded. "I guess. I'm glad you're okay."

"I'm fine, Michael. Seriously, I think you need meds."

He shook his head. "I hate it that I drove you into that situation."

Jamie winced. Michael's neck veins looked like they were going to burst, and his jaw quivered. He was trying so hard to control his rage. She had to do something to make him feel better. "You know what?"

"What?"

She rubbed his upper arm. "I'm glad we confessed our little sins. We really messed up, didn't we?"

Michael nodded then closed his eyes.

"What were you doing down here anyway?"

He looked in the direction of his guitar.

"I remember that," Jamie said, glad to take their conversation away from infidelity. "You used to play once in a while when we first dated. As I recall, you were pretty good."

Michael walked over and ran his thumb across the strings. "I'm gonna have this baby refurbished and bring music back into my life."

"You are? Play something right now."

"It sounds tinny. Wait till it's fixed up."

"What made you think of your guitar?"

"Rufus and the Boys & Girls Club."

"You really went to the Boys & Girls Club?"

"Yeah. I told you."

"I thought…never mind. What happened?"

"I offered to give guitar lessons to some of the kids," Michael said proudly.

Jamie was stunned. She couldn't imagine Michael being patient enough to teach anyone anything, and he didn't have a civic cell in his entire body—or did he? "You liked it?"

"Yeah, I did." He paused. "Hey, have you figured out what you're going to do about a job? I'm not concerned about money, but it might be good for you to get out, find something you enjoy."

"I'm taking the teller position at the bank."

Michael frowned. "Really?"

"It's the best I can do right now. The hours are perfect—nine to two, Monday through Friday—so I don't have to worry about daycare for Meg and Emily, except for vacations. I can even walk to the branch."

"I don't see you at a bank."

Jamie shrugged. "They have classes. Maybe I can work my way up."

"When do you start?"

Jamie half smiled. "My training starts on Monday."

"Really?"

Jamie nodded.

"I'll call you Monday night from Saint Paul to see how it went."

"Do you feel like going?"

"Put it this way. I'd rather go into Emily's kindergarten class this week and teach shoe tying and nose blowing."

Jamie laughed. "That bad."

Michael nodded.

"One more thing."

"What?" Michael asked.

"I'm glad we came clean tonight."

"Me too. Let's promise not to get mixed up with anyone until we figure us out."

"Agreed."

Michael walked over to Jamie. He cradled her cheeks tenderly and stroked them with his thumbs.

Jamie sighed. Michael's hands were so strong and nurturing. He lifted her face and gazed at her with his complicated mocha eyes. In an instant, she was hypnotized, and he could have taken her anywhere—to his lips, to his heart, to his bed. At that moment, he owned her. He let her go, which was a good thing. She wasn't ready for this. Then he wrapped his arms around her and pulled her close. He set his chin on top of her head.

"I'm glad you're okay," he said.

Jamie melded into his chest. "Me too."

Chapter Twenty

Jamie noticed a few red leaves spattered among the green as she strolled along Dumbarton Street. She smiled. Autumn was her favorite season, and it had just begun. A welcome wind pushed the heavy summer air away along with its sluggish mood. Invigorated, Jamie inhaled the freshness.

Gloom threatened to strike, however, as she climbed the steps to her home and pulled the key from her pocket. Megan and Emily were spending the day at Busch Gardens with Matilda's family then would go back to their house for a sleepover. The girls were requesting more and more time with friends. Megan had a core group of school pals, and Emily had found her niche as a social butterfly. Jamie was glad they were well liked by other kids, and it did give her more alone time. But more alone time was the last thing she needed.

Checking her smartphone, she walked into the house. It was nine thirty, which meant Michael was about to land in Saint Paul. She rolled her eyes as she thought about the fling with

Sherry she had concocted. It was such a relief not to worry about that anymore. Time to move on. She'd begin her career as a bank teller on Monday, and although it wasn't her dream job, at least she'd get out every day, meet new people, and earn a little money.

Jamie hung her sporty utility jacket on a hook in the hall and placed her baseball cap on the one next to it. Her hair fell to her shoulders, and she shook it out. She stepped into the living room and plopped onto the couch. *Now what?* She was an off-duty mother for about thirty hours and should make the most of it.

I could hop on my bike and get reacquainted with my butt muscles. She quickly nixed that idea. Bike paths would be mobbed at this hour on a gorgeous morning. Her puzzle lay unfinished on the table. She picked up a piece then tossed it back. It was too nice a day to sit inside. Her garden stared at her. That's it. She still needed to buy some mums and cornstalks. *I should get it done before the bank job starts.* Jamie shifted her gaze to her cargo pants. *Maybe I'll go shopping for career clothes too.*

She grabbed her keys, threw on a jacket, and swung her tapestry bag over one shoulder. In the van, she looked at the GPS. "Where do you want to go shopping, Shirley?"

Shirley seemed to say, "Someplace different."

"Sounds good." Glancing in the mirror, Jamie adjusted the collar of her polo shirt, lifted Shirley out of the stand, and pulled up a map of the DC area. Route 66 had a good reputation for road trips, so she selected it.

"East or west?" Shirley asked.

Jamie touched west. Route 66 west was all the direction she needed.

She zipped out of DC. Tapping her thumbs on the steering wheel, Jamie figured she'd head two or three hours west before turning around. If a store appealed to her along the way, she'd take a break. If not, she'd just cruise along. After Arlington, she veered onto Route 29 for a more scenic view. Jamie drove past horses nibbling on grass in meadows, barns sitting high on hills, ponds basking in the sun's light, and once she had to stop because a turkey was crossing the road. She and Michael used to take this trip when they went for hikes or canoe outings in the Blue Ridge Mountains. She'd forgotten how beautiful it was. A conglomeration of hazy, periwinkle peaks appeared in the distance. They provided a striking backdrop for her adventure and called her to come and play. Maybe next fall they'd rent a cabin in Shenandoah National Park and bring Megan and Emily. Except for crowded beaches and city parks, the girls had never experienced the joys of nature. If her marriage worked out, she'd talk to Michael about it. If not, she'd take them on her own.

Jamie's stomach growled, but she was getting used to the noise. A chocolate chip cookie, a potato chip, ice cream—nothing decadent had gone into her mouth since she killed her peanut butter cups on Monday. The first three pounds were gone. Only fifteen more to her goal. Regardless of her diet, she needed to eat, but she would make sure to choose something nutritious.

Within minutes, Jamie saw a black-and-white painted sign, Welcome to Warrenton. "Thank you," she said with a nod. After passing some fast-food restaurants along a busy road, she drove into a quaint village. The world seemed to quiet down. She had a strange feeling that she'd been there before, but couldn't place where or when. Maybe she and Michael had stopped here to eat on the way home from a hike. Shrugging, she parked. She couldn't help but smile when she stepped out of the van. It looked like a scene from a Norman Rockwell painting. A loud chime erupted from the white courthouse, complete with pillars and a steeple, signaling the eleven o'clock hour. Jamie contentedly strolled along the tree-lined, brick street as a peculiar sense of wonder fluttered inside.

She meandered into a coffee shop that resembled an eclectic living room, with mismatched couches, stuffed chairs, and Formica tables. The scones and muffins smelled wonderful, but she chose a toasted whole grain bagel with a touch of peanut butter and a cup of coffee. She sat at a small round table near a window and watched people stroll by while she ate. Feeling better, now that her belly was full, Jamie began her self-guided tour of the town.

She passed a knitting shop, a toddler's gym, an athletic store, and finally, a florist. Jamie stopped under the maroon-and-white awning to view the display in the front window. A thick garland of autumn leaves framed the glass, while cornucopias stood on marble pedestals of various heights. These seasonal baskets were filled with dried flowers and surrounded by small pumpkins. She admired the living picture but thought some greenery would add a splash of serenity to the colorful scene. In any case, she liked novel stores, and this one fit the bill. Maybe she'd find some trinkets inside to accentuate her garden. Clutching the strap of her shoulder bag, she entered the shop.

Hanging spider plants adorned the ceiling, and vases bursting with vivid flowers stood on platforms. Baskets sporting unique arrangements were scattered on the quarry tile floor, and floral accessories were strewn over shelves. Jamie wandered over to an oak mantelpiece and picked up a hair comb with a red silk gardenia attached. Holding it above her ear, she looked into a gold-framed mirror and murmured, "A Polynesian blonde." She imagined Michael's dumbfounded face when he walked into the kitchen and saw her wearing this hairpiece along with a sexy Bohemian sundress. Jamie wiggled her hips then set the hairpiece down. "Silly girl," she whispered.

Water flowed from a wall fountain. It made Jamie feel like she was near a stream that was in no rush to go anywhere. She inhaled the scents of roses, greenery, and soil—earth's glory. As she browsed, a woman with short, funky black hair, probably in her early sixties, scurried in from the back room. She had thin lips and a long narrow nose that had a ski-jump tip. Jamie admired the woman's blue motif tunic, tan stretch denims, red leather hip belt, and black heels. In fact, Jamie felt shabby in her presence and suddenly wished she'd been born with a higher fashion IQ.

"Hi. I'm Pam. I'll be in back if you need anything. Busier than a short order cook on a Sunday morning." She held up both hands. "I've got a bitch of a bride on my tail who wants her flowers before the wedding, not after. Three hours to make that happen." As she hurried away, Pam said, "Make yourself some tea. It's on the table in the corner." She pointed at Jamie. "And that's an order."

"Well, okay," Jamie said.

She fixed two cups of chamomile tea and roamed into the back room. Every variety of yellow flower that existed on the planet covered a full-length wall counter. A waist-high table, with glass vases and bouquets on top, was in the center, and white boxes were piled on a shelf in a corner.

Jamie set a mug of tea down on the counter where Pam was putting together a centerpiece. "Drink this. It'll help you relax. Do you need help?"

"Why, thank you," Pam said with a surprised grin. "How are you at flower arranging?" Pam pointed with her eyes to a bouquet on the table. "I need six more just like that one."

"I'm on it," Jamie said.

After several minutes of piercing daffodils, daisies, and yellow lilies into a bouquet, Jamie lifted it up. "How's this?"

Pam set a lily down, walked over to Jamie, and poked her gently in the arm. "Are you an angel?"

"No. Just a good witch," Jamie said, with a twitch of her nose. "You're hired."

Jamie began work on the next bouquet. "Why all the yellow?"

"Bridella wants a sunshine wedding," Pam said in a mocking tone. "When I opened this shop, I made a commitment to originality. Advertised: theme weddings with innovative designs. Regretted it ever since. Next Saturday it's "Fly Me to the Fuckin' Moon," minus the *fuck*—or was it minus the *moon?*"

"Hydrangea for the night sky, baby's breath for the stars, and yellow roses in the center if it's the moon," Jamie said, as she picked up a daisy. "Replace the roses with a picture of the groom if it's the fuck."

Pam laughed as she put her hands on her hips. "You are an angel and a good witch."

"Really, I'm just a mom with a day off, and I landed here."

"I'm glad you did," Pam said, as she put a completed centerpiece in a long cardboard box on the floor.

Jamie had to stop herself from giggling as she chatted with Pam. The animated merchant was undeniably funny. She was about five feet three with a pear shape. Her attractiveness came from confidence and flair, not common Hollywood beauty. She hustled around on her high heels like they were sneakers and didn't let her multicolored bead bracelets and ringed fingers interfere with her breakneck flower arranging. Whenever the bell rang, signaling a customer had entered the shop, she'd fly out to the front and make a snide comment, like, "Must've forgotten to put the Keep Out sign up. You can look around, but don't bother me—busy, busy." Patrons would laugh or tell her to go to hell. It was evident people enjoyed her wit and stopped in just to get a dose of it. Pam didn't hesitate to swear when the conversation called for it and treated Jamie like a friend she'd known for years.

"Why the rush job on this wedding?"

"My assistant quit on Wednesday, and I was out of town for a funeral on Thursday and Friday. I don't want to take advantage of you, but will anyway. Can you help me deliver all of this around three? First stop, the bride's house, then the church, then the reception hall, then I'm buying you one heck of a dinner and putting a little cash in your pocket. Seriously, if you have time, I'd be forever grateful."

"I have until one o'clock tomorrow, and I'd love to help." Jamie grinned. She really did love the plan. She looked toward the ceiling. When was the last time she loved a plan?

Jamie twirled fettuccini onto her fork and dipped it in fra diavolo sauce. "Perfect."

"Not too spicy?" Pam asked.

"Not for me. I use habanero peppers to make my sauce at home."

"Ouch. You must have an iron tongue." Pam filled their wine glasses with pinot noir.

"My father used to grow them in his garden. The inside of my mouth desensitized when I was about twelve," Jamie said, as she looked around. "It's so cute in here, and Italian's my favorite."

Pam sat back and patted her lips with a red cloth napkin. "Me too. Homemade pasta, locally grown vegetables, and organic vino from Virginia wineries only. Now drink up. Remember, you're staying at the hotel two doors down, so no worries about driving."

"What about you?"

"I have a cape four blocks from here, so I'm safe." Pam winked. "Your father grew vegetables?"

Jamie nodded. "He had the biggest backyard garden I've ever seen. One part for veggies; the other for flowers. Even three peach trees and a berry patch."

"So that's where you get your green thumb."

"I used to help him with everything from tilling in the spring to raking in the fall. It's the only place I ever felt..." Jamie shifted her eyes to the side. "I loved helping him, and he taught me everything I know about plant life."

Pam pointed at Jamie. "Avoider."

Jamie jiggled her head. "What?"

"You're an avoider. Any time the conversation gets a touch deep, maybe a touch hurtful, you change it." Pam snapped her fingers. "Like that. You're good at it too. If I hadn't been one myself, I never would've guessed."

Jamie turned a shrimp over on her plate.

"You were about to say, 'It's the only place I ever felt...' What?"

"Are you a counselor?"

"Hell no. Just nosy. Now complete the sentence."

"Home. The only place I ever felt at home."

"You're one of us."

"What do you mean?"

"An emotional survivor. You've been through something big, maybe a few things, but you've managed to behave according to life's rules in spite of it."

Jamie scratched the nape of her neck.

"I'm right, aren't I?"

"You too?"

"See. You're avoiding again. Anyway, adopted at birth, an only child. My parents died in a car accident when I was eleven. Raised by an aunt and uncle, who never considered me a 'real' family member; left the day after my eighteenth birthday. Married four times, looking for someone to love me. Divorced four times, when they didn't. Got a PhD in physics, so I didn't have to think about my orphan status, and it worked out pretty good. Taught at the University of Virginia for twenty years, discovered flowers in the process, found Warrenton, quit my job, opened my shop, and that's my story," Pam said, slapping her hand on the table.

"My God. You've been divorced four times?"

"I hate being married; 'cause when you're married, you have to be tolerant, and I'm not." She sat back. "Harry used to reprimand me for turning the corner of my page down in a book instead of using a paperclip to mark where I left off. Jack always said something dumb right at the best part of *ER*. Fred was addicted to Fox News, and Ben constantly complained about knuckle pain. Whoever heard of knuckle pain? I could go on for hours, but we had a long day, and God knows, at least I need my beauty sleep. Before we change the topic, though, tell me one little thing your husband does that makes you want to superglue his toes together at night." Pam looked at Jamie with wide eyes and a mischievous grin.

Jamie burst out laughing. She held her sides and tried to breathe. Pam broke out in laughs too. Finally, Jamie inhaled and managed, "I'm separated."

"You are? What did the son of a bitch do?"

227

Jamie held up her hand. "Don't make me laugh again. My lungs can't take it."

Pam poured a little more wine for each of them. "Having fun?"

Jamie's whole face smiled.

"So, what'd he do?"

"He's cranky, anal, impatient, a perfectionist, prone to temper tantrums. Other than that, he's not a bad guy."

"That'd do it for me. Besides those whoppers, one little thing he does that really bugs you. I like hearing about quirks that drive people nuts."

"There are so many. Like making fun of me for voting on *American Idol*, or how he says he has to get up and run every morning, like it's a job. Then there's how he cuts across five lanes on the highway to get to the toll booth with the shortest line. If he beats the other cars, he gets this smug look on his face like he just won the Indy 500."

Pam shook her finger. "See what I mean. It's the little things."

"I'm glad you're into flowers. You'd make a terrible marriage counselor."

"The worst. Do you think you'll get a divorce?"

"I'm not sure," Jamie said sincerely. "I promised myself after my parents split up that I never would, and even though Michael can be a bear, he loves me and our daughters, incredibly."

Pam flicked her hand. "Chill awhile and you'll figure it out. You didn't like your parents being divorced?"

"My mother was crazy, and my father spoiled me. He felt guilty because I had to live with the wacko most of the time. Dad meant well, but I never learned how to be truly independent. He took care of everything." Jamie whispered, as if it were a shameful secret, "He even paid my rent after I graduated from college. Wanted me to have someplace nice." She resumed her normal volume. "Anyway, he married my step-mother when I was fifteen. She was nice but came with two of her own kids, and I never felt like I belonged."

"How was your mother crazy?"

Jamie sipped her wine then winced. "An insecure narcissist—borderline personality. She had an addiction to men, had to have them swoon over her. She became frantic when she didn't have someone calling her, courting her. When I was fourteen, she started treating me like a girlfriend, telling me about her relationship issues, wanting to borrow my clothes, so I moved in with my father. She threw a fit because she didn't get child support anymore. Blamed me for her destitute life. Called me a selfish, ungrateful brat. There's more, but I don't want to ruin a perfectly good day."

"I feel for you, honey. Where is she now?"

Jamie looked Pam straight in the eye. "Dead. Committed suicide when I was nineteen. Took a knife and slit her wrist."

Pam took Jamie's hand and squeezed it. "You didn't find her, did you?"

Jamie barely nodded.

"It's okay. We can stop."

Jamie felt her voice drift away. "I found her during spring break. She invited me over for dinner, and…well…She was on the couch waiting for me." Jamie blinked then looked up at Pam. "It was a gift she gave me that I'll never forget. Revenge for abandoning her." Jamie leaned in. "I never told anyone but Michael this: I had to fake tears at her funeral. I was relieved she was gone."

Pam nodded, "I get it. Really do. Does Michael get it?"

"Totally."

"He's an emotional survivor too?"

"Oh yeah."

"We tend to find one another. How'd you deal with it all?"

"My father nurtured me through the whole ordeal. Carol, my stepmom too. Michael took care of any residual scars when we met. He made me feel so loved, and he listened to me. Really understood my history."

"So they're basically good men, your dad and husband."

Jamie nodded. "Thanks, Pam."

"For what?"

"For getting me to talk, really talk. It's been awhile. And for not being shocked when I told you about my mother."

"It's life. Whoever said it's a bowl of cherries forgot to mention the pits. We all have hurdles. The trick is to get over them and keep running."

The waiter came over. "Would you two ladies like dessert, coffee?"

Pam said, "Two coffees, two forks, and the chocolate molten cake."

Jamie held up both hands. "I can't. I'm on a diet."

"So am I, but we're going off it for five minutes."

"We are?"

"Five minutes out of twenty-four hours can't hurt. Anyway, we burned a ton of calories with all that flower lugging today. And we should celebrate."

"Celebrate what?"

"Making a new friend. Not often you run into someone you can share your deepest, darkest side with."

Jamie nearly smiled. *The last time for me...Michael.* "Okay then. Bring on the cake!"

Jamie sat in a booth in the hotel breakfast area, reading the local newspaper. Yesterday's clothes felt grubby, but not in a bad way. It added to the adventurous ambience of her twenty-four-hour getaway. Skimming an article about Warrenton's green initiative, she wondered why Michael complained so much about staying alone in a hotel. Jamie liked it. No chores and the service was great. She stirred her coffee but didn't drink it. Her parched mouth called for ice water after last night's wine indulgence. A closed-lip smile formed on her face. Jamie had such a good time with Pam and would definitely visit again.

She turned to the classifieds. Pam's ad for an assistant was the first thing she saw. God, how she'd like to take that job. A seventy-five-minute commute, twelve dollars an hour, some evenings and weekends made it an impossible dream. She scanned the real estate section and was surprised at how reasonable house prices were. One jumped out at her—a converted barn. A home for horses was now a home for people. Jamie couldn't picture it and was happy to see that an open house would begin at eleven. She had time to take a quick peek if she hustled.

The driveway leading to the barn was long and wide. Simple grasses, wild plants, and white horse fencing surrounded it. A circular island with polished jade beach pebbles, manicured bushes, and mums broke up the pavement and served as a prelude to the barn. Nestled comfortably in the woodlands to the rear sat a large cedar structure with windows of different shapes and sizes. It summoned Jamie to come in and stay awhile. Mesmerized, Jamie haphazardly parked the van and stepped out. The scents of meadow and snappish air welcomed her, and she stood still just to breathe it in.

She tentatively climbed the four steps to the entrance and turned when she reached the country porch. The expansive fields of green dipped and rose, forming an uneven carpet to the foothills of the Blue Ridge Mountains. Jamie touched the wood railing and listened. Instead of zooming vehicles, a brook's babbling and a woodpecker's tapping filled her ears.

"Wow!" Jamie exclaimed, entering the house. Rough-hewn exposed beams and columns adorned a spacious room. Exposed-brick walls, built-in bookshelves, and a stone fireplace declared, "You're home."

"Hello. I'm Rita."

Jamie gazed down at a professionally dressed, pint-sized woman with curly blond hair and pink-framed, rectangular glasses. Words were stuck Jamie's throat, but she eventually managed, "I love this house...barn...whatever."

"Isn't it beautiful? Three thousand square feet, four bedrooms, two full baths. You have to see the country kitchen— and windows all over the place with incredible views. Are you actively looking for a home or just browsing?"

"Unfortunately, just browsing. I was curious to see what a converted barn looked like."

"You found a gem. The owners used top quality materials to renovate, yet managed to keep a hangar feel to the place."

"Why are they selling?" Jamie asked.

"Job relocation. Sign in and feel free to explore."

The wide plank floors occasionally squeaked as Jamie toured around. It sounded like the barn was alive, like a friend saying *welcome*. In the kitchen, she ran her fingers along an ax mark in an uneven elm mantle above the potbelly stove. A farmer must have found a piece of wood outside, polished it, and nailed it to the wall. Although she discovered ceiling cracks here and there, it didn't bother her. Like people, it just needed a little work.

She stepped outside onto a redwood deck. A small yard bordered the woods, but to the left was a plot of flat land the size of an Olympic swimming pool. Jamie sat on the deck's edge, put her feet on the ground, and closed her eyes. Corn stalks, tomato plants, pumpkins, squash, zucchini, and carrot ferns in full bloom filled the space. Her father was picking ears of corn and tossing them into a basket while a young Jamie stood next to him chewing on a green bean. He told her how to snap off the ear, so it wouldn't damage the stalk.

Jamie opened her eyes and suddenly missed her dad incredibly. She hugged herself then removed her smartphone from her pocket.

"Hey, Dad."

"Jamie!"

She smiled. "I miss you."

"Aren't you the sweetest thing. When are you coming for a visit? Wilmington's not on the other side of the world, ya know."

Jamie made an instant plan. "How's the weekend after next?"

"Perfect. Gives me plenty of time to shop, cook, bake—the works."

"Don't you dare go overboard. How's Carol?"

"Don't order your father around. Carol's just fine, and will be thrilled you're coming. Michael and the kids too?"

"Probably just me and the kids. Michael's really busy with work."

"Tell him jambalaya's on the menu."

Jamie laughed. "That might entice him."

She shook her head as they chatted. Her father must have been born with an extra generosity gene. Giving gushed out of him, which is probably why he married her very needy mother. After Jamie hung up, she strolled into the field. Mother Nature swept her away with vibrant air, chirping birds, and color. Black-eyed Susans, weeping willows, cardinals flying above, purple mountains against the topaz sky— all blended together to create a symphonic, living portrait. She had found paradise, and it was for sale.

Paradise—Jamie always thought it involved a handsome prince and a castle, but she was wrong. Fresh air, plenty of land for a garden, a quaint town just down the road, and a comfy barn to call home—this was her new definition of paradise. She strolled farther into the meadow and turned around a few times with arms outstretched. When she stopped, her eyes met a chipmunk's who was sitting on a tree stump rubbing his paws together. Jamie giggled. She viewed the land again then glanced at her phone. Like Cinderella, who had to leave the ball just when she was falling in love, Jamie had to do the same. She ambled back to the barn with her head held high. She wanted to capture this vision in a mind photo and pull it out whenever she needed an escape from the real world.

On her way out, she took a fact sheet, thanked the realtor, then climbed into the van, and slowly drove down the driveway. Pam's business card lay on the passenger seat. Jamie had promised to keep in touch through e-mail and offered to help with weddings if Pam was ever in a bind. On Route 29, Jamie glanced in the rearview mirror. The Blue Ridge Mountains began to fade away. Her gaze lowered to the road ahead. She had finally found home. If only she could figure out a way to move in.

Chapter Twenty-One

There is a God, Michael thought. This mysterious spirit had blessed him with a free day before traveling home from Saint Paul. After five days of meetings, lectures, negotiations, paperwork, and more paperwork, a resolution was achieved. It was Thursday, and his services were no longer needed. Michael considered having a debriefing with the staff to discuss the mechanics of the compromise but decided against it. Stealing time made him feel like a teenager abandoning a day of school. For once, no one was around to tell him it wasn't a good idea.

Michael jogged through the hotel parking lot, wearing his running shoes, denim jeans, and a midnight-blue fleece. The sun was just peeking over the horizon and the chill of the night air left remnants of frost on the car windshield. Michael started his rental vehicle to get the heat and day moving then reviewed the map that would lead him to his destination. He drove to a park about two hours north of Saint Paul, which was reportedly full of streams, waterfalls, hiking trails, and even a lake. It had been years since he communed with nature. A sense of excitement rose as he anticipated the peace it always brought him.

He pulled into an empty dirt lot and parked. The scent of pine trees and crisp air greeted him. Invigorated by a brisk breeze, he inhaled deeply and stretched up as far as he could. Michael grabbed his backpack from the passenger seat and walked to the trailhead. Peering down the path, he saw the white bark of birch trees, golden coin-shaped leaves on the aspens, and evergreens that soared into the brilliant blue sky. Mossy grass lined the trail, and hundreds of bushes sprouted from the ground.

Michael hiked a few feet into the forest then turned back and looked at his car. He really wasn't sure where he was going or what kind of creatures lurked in these woods. Although apprehensive, he continued his adventure. The nervousness dissipated as he ambled further down the dirt road. The breeze stroked his face, and fresh air streamed into his lungs.

Each step took Michael farther away from reality. Pins and needles prickled his skin as a bundle of energy swirled inside him. He did not question the reason for the power surge. Although curious, it was something to savor, not analyze.

After a few hours, he stopped at a lake that resembled a liquid emerald. Michael sat on a mound of dirt, placed his back against a boulder, and inhaled the magnificent sight. Then, he closed his eyes. His muscles loosened. Whines, tiresome conversations, technical gadgets, arrogance, material possessions, complaints, and obligations erupted from him and dove into the lake. He imagined the bomb of excess creating a splash that touched the sky. When the spray from the blast dispersed, it showered Michael with an orchestra of music. This symphony gradually turned into an acoustic melody from the strings of a guitar. The soothing sound encouraged Michael to rest. He fell asleep as tranquility stitched his soul.

Struggling with gravity, he narrowly opened his eyes. Ripples spread across the water, maybe from the fabricated explosion. Intrigued, Michael roamed to the lake's edge. He picked up a stone and skimmed it over the body of water, creating circles of movement. He longed to be one with this glimpse of heaven.

As his gaze deepened, his body froze. His father's face glazed the lake's surface. Michael reached toward it and whispered, "Pa." The image radiated love. It shot through Michael like an arrow of acceptance. The instant the tip pierced him, the strum of the guitar heightened into a concert of strings. His father smiled. Tears streamed down Michael's cheeks. "It's okay. Cry," his father said softly. "Then, come play."

Michael ran into the lake. When it deepened, he swam. Although fully clothed, he felt as boundless as a dolphin gliding through the ocean. His movements were synchronized with the orchestra that continued to play. He didn't tire. In fact, he had the stamina of an Olympic athlete, and it wasn't only his body. His mind was open and free.

He stretched to take another stroke, but his fingers touched sand. Michael had reached the end of his voyage, but the music still played. The sun warmed his back, and he turned, so it could heat his face. When he glanced to the side, he saw Rufus wearing his usual neat casual apparel, and his signature smile.

"Rufus, what are you doing here?"

"I wanted to show you something."

"How'd you get to Minnesota?"

Rufus chuckled. "Oh, Michael, you're not in Minnesota anymore."

Michael followed Rufus's gentle steps. Was this his Land of Oz? Was he going to meet a wizard, and was Rufus the good witch of the forest? Everything felt so strange. His clothes were soaked, but they didn't feel heavy or uncomfortable. The temperature couldn't have changed, but he felt warm as he walked, his shoes spitting out water.

Rufus stopped and turned. "Stop thinking. Be open, like when you were swimming."

"Okay," Michael said.

They walked for some time, but Michael couldn't determine how far. Back home he always knew the exact number of miles he ran and how long it took him, but it didn't matter here. He enjoyed the smells of nature, the beauty of the land, and the sound of the exquisite orchestra. From the strum of a guitar to the pluck of a bass, every instrument knew its part and when to sing.

They approached a clearing. A wide path led to a stunning piece of architecture that blended with nature's brilliance. The stone building was three stories high, and pillars extended across the front. In the middle, several steps led to grand oak doors with gold-plated handles.

Michael and Rufus walked up the stairs and opened the heavy doors. They were welcomed by the orchestra playing in a grand ballroom. Chandeliers hung from the ceiling, sculptures stood on pedestals, and paintings adorned the walls. Michael squinted, focusing on the orchestra. He couldn't believe what he saw. His twin conducted the ensemble made up of more than one hundred adolescents.

"See what you did, Michael," Rufus said.

"I didn't do this."

"Well, not yet. Come on. There's more."

The two men strolled down a long hallway into a complex of enclosed cubicles. "Go ahead," Rufus said. "Peek in the windows."

Michael gingerly approached a booth and peered in. Five young men played in a band: two on electric guitars, the others on the drums, bass guitar, and piano. Michael turned to Rufus. "I can't hear them."

"The rooms are soundproof. That way lots of different things can go on at the same time. You insisted on it. 'Let the kids explore the kind of music that speaks to them' were your words."

"When did I say that?"

"Look in the window over there."

Michael jogged to it. Inside was a recording studio complete with mixers, microphones, headsets, and even video recording equipment.

"Wow," Michael said.

"I agree. What you did was incredible."

"How?"

Rufus grinned.

In an instant, Emily and Megan were tugging on Michael's jacket. "My babies. I miss you," he said, as he bent down to hug them. "Where's Mom?"

Emily and Megan were silent.

Michael's bliss shifted to worry. He stood and looked directly at Rufus. "Where's Jamie?"

Rufus frowned. "You've got to find her."

"Where?" Michael shouted.

The sound of his own voice jolted him, and he opened his eyes. The lake sparkled. He sat on the patch of dirt with his back against the boulder. "Whoa," he whispered.

Michael rubbed his thighs. His pants were dry. He lifted his hands to his cheeks and felt moisture. Did he really cry? He tasted the substance. It was salty but different from the sweat that dripped into his mouth when he ran, and it felt like some kind of emotion had been released. He scanned the land then closed his eyes. His body ignited as he recalled every detail of the dream.

Walking to the water's edge, he wondered if he was dreaming again. No image of his father; no compulsion to jump into the cold water, but the free feeling he had while swimming remained.

Michael kicked the ground. It couldn't have just been a dream. He had dreamed thousands of times, but this illusion had power. He gazed across the lake. It was a message. His father told him to cry and play. He had been released from the harness of stringent obligations that had imprisoned him up until this moment.

Michael bent down, scooped up some water, and splashed it on his face. He then reached for the clear plastic bottle that hung from his belt loop and filled it with the divine substance. Sealing it, he promised to cherish the memory. Michael remained in the vortex for several minutes. When it was time to journey back through the woods, he thanked his father for the visit and for providing him with the blessing of Rufus to help him find a gentler life. Michael then turned to leave. Before taking a step, he looked back and whispered, "I love you, Pa."

Chapter Twenty-Two

Michael landed in Dulles Airport early on Friday and was pacing around Dupont Circle by one thirty. The mystical experience he had in the woods was taking up a lot of space in his head and he couldn't wait for Rufus to show up. Maybe it would help Michael understand what it all meant. Wandering over to the chess tables, he thought about striking up a game with one of the regulars, but wouldn't be able to concentrate. Instead, he sat on a bench and stared at the clouds.

Tapping his knee, Michael wondered how Jamie was doing at teller training school. He had called earlier in the week, and asked how she liked the banking business. "Eh," was all that she told him. He was supposed to be home by six—but no pizza party. Jamie was cooking something, which surprised him. Michael figured she'd be exhausted after her first week of work.

He smiled when he heard the laughter of children. A few yards away, a mother and her sons were engrossed in a game of pop the bubbles. Michael had seen bottles of this liquid toy on a shelf in the garage. Jamie must have amused his daughters with this same pastime. He hardly ever engaged in things like this when he was a boy, and he hadn't done it with his own children. His father in the lake was right. It was time to start playing.

Before long, someone whistling "Pink Cadillac" interrupted Michael's musings. He jumped up and greeted Rufus with a high five.

Rufus stepped back and eyeballed Michael. "Where's your suit?"

Michael glanced at his faded blue jeans, mint green T-shirt, and denim jacket.

"What'd you do? Quit your job to start a career as a street musician?"

"Don't tempt me. This is my second day on holiday from the stuffed shirt look, and I like it."

"You'd miss the executive costume," Rufus said, checking his watch. "Why so early?"

"I caught a seven o'clock flight out of Saint Paul this morning. Got into DC at noon and didn't feel like going to the office. Much prefer watching the sport of bubble popping," Michael said, as he sat back down and pointed to the action a few yards away.

Rufus laughed, walked toward the jovial activity, and poked a large clear orb too high for the boys to reach. "Couldn't let that one fly away," Rufus said playfully. The boys clapped and giggled. He waved at the mom then took a seat next to Michael.

"How was your trip?"

"Surprisingly, not bad. Negotiations went quickly, and we finished up on Wednesday. That gave me a full day on

Thursday to explore. I ended up taking an amazing hike in a forest north of the Twin Cities."

"A hike in a forest? Never done that."

"You've got to be kidding."

"No. Lived my entire life in DC. My dad died when I was three, so Mom was the sole provider. She worked a couple of jobs just to keep food on the table and a roof over our heads. We never had extra cash for travel of any kind. I got used to staying put."

"Your mom must have been a busy lady."

"She certainly was. Raised two, three kids. Even though she worked, she had plenty of energy left over to keep us in line. Made sure we got to church every Sunday. Homework had to be done, and we had chores from the time we were small."

"'Two, three kids.' What's that mean?"

Rufus folded his arms. "Long story, and I'm not going there today."

Long stories never stopped Rufus, and Michael wondered what was different about this one. After some awkward silence, he said, "Sounds like your mom was like my dad."

"They must've gone to the same child-rearin' school. I was lucky though. My granddad lived with us. He evened things out with his lightheartedness."

"Didn't you tell me that your grandfather taught you how to play chess?"

"Yes, he did. One of the best memories I own. Now, tell me about nature, Michael. Teach me something."

"It's great, peaceful."

"More than that."

"I'm not used to gushing about trees and bushes."

"Give it a whirl."

Michael grinned. "Here goes. The mountains, the ocean are my favorites." He hesitated for a few seconds.

"I'm listening. Tell me why."

"Hard to describe. I guess, besides their magnificence, they're where God lives, for me anyway. When I'm in the mountains or a forest, I sense an incredible energy—like I'm safe, cared for. The sounds of a stream flowing over rocks, birds chattering, and leaves rustling are symphonic. Even I can unwind in the gentleness of the woods. But when I stand before the ocean, I feel God's power and strength. The mountains are still, but the ocean is vigorous, and its roar is thunderous. I feel like a grain of sand in its presence. No matter how important I think I am, when I'm face to face with the sea, all arrogance washes away. In the early morning, when hardly anyone's there, the crashing of waves makes me so aware of its force. Nothing else seems important."

Rufus sat back, shaking his head. "I have to get to both of those places."

"You've never been to the ocean either?"

"Not first thing in the morning."

"Believe me. It's a different place without the crowds."

"Do you go often?"

"To the ocean, once or twice a year. The mountains, hardly ever. My walk in the woods yesterday made me realize that I have to go more. I'll take you on hike in the Appalachians one of these days."

"Really?"

"Maybe even next weekend, if the weather's good."

"Will your wife mind?"

Michael shook his head and frowned. "Not at all. Hey, have you been over to the club?"

"Sure. Painting every day, and I helped out with your music program last Wednesday."

"Did all fifteen kids come back? And it's not my program."

"Yes, plus five more. It's popular. A lot of buzz about your guitar playing."

"Twenty kids? That's too many, Rufus. There's not enough equipment or room, and I'm only one guy."

Rufus shot a finger at Michael. "What are you going to do about it?"

"I haven't a clue. Did Luke get more volunteers?"

"A couple of college students showed up, but Luke said they didn't have your command with the kids. And a few more guitars were floating around. More donations may come in next week. By the way, I can tell the kids have been practicing. They're becoming friends, and I noticed some calloused fingers. That Joseph even wrote a song."

"He did?"

"And it wasn't bad. Give that child something meaningful, and good comes out of him. No one pays much attention to him at home. I don't want to lose him to the streets."

"What do you mean?"

"Gangs, drugs, dropping out of school. All part of urban warfare. He's twelve now, and this music thing is speaking to him. You could save a life if you keep him coming back."

Michael wrinkled his forehead. "That's a tall order, Rufus."

"Have you thought any more about taking that job at the club?"

"Of course not. It's too much of a pay cut. Absolutely impossible."

"There you go again with that ugly word. Do you think Lewis and Clark said 'impossible' when they decided to explore the West? What about the Wright brothers when they wanted to invent a flying machine? Do you think Barack Obama said 'impossible' when he decided to run for president?"

Michael gaped at Rufus. He didn't know how to respond but decided blunt was the best approach. He cleared his throat. "Those people did great things, and I wish I could follow in their footsteps, but it's not going to happen. We, my family, could never survive on that salary, ever. I'll help out at the club with guitar lessons, but that's it. Wish I could do more, really do."

"How do you feel right now?"

"I don't know. Why?"

"How did it feel to say no to a job you are meant to do?" Rufus smiled. "Just say yes. I'm going to talk to Luke about the job."

"That's crazy," Michael said, as he looked away.

"Just do it."

Michael rolled his eyes but gave it a try. "The job sounds good. Give me Luke's card, and I'll call him." A rush of energy ran through his body. He inhaled deeply.

"Feel a little different than when you said 'no way'?"

"Look Rufus, I really appreciate your urging me to follow this calling, if that's what it is. To be honest, there's a part of me that would love to leave my job and try something meaningful, but my personal life is a wreck. I can't change anything right now."

246

Rufus furrowed his eyebrows. "What do you mean?"

"Jamie kicked me out a few weeks ago, and she's not sure she wants me back. I've been staying at a hotel," Michael's voice cracked. "My marriage is a mess. I'm a mess."

Rufus put his hand on Michael's shoulder and squeezed it. "I'm sorry to hear that, not surprised, but sorry."

"What do you mean 'not surprised'?"

"The day we met, right here, you and your wife were full of hostility. You ignored her, and she looked miserable. I figured you guys were on your way to a divorce or a homicide. What went wrong?"

Michael rubbed his forehead. "A slow death. I have a bad temper. Jamie has some bad habits. It's not working. And the girls. They see it all."

"Do you still love her?"

"Yes. She's not so sure about me."

"You've got to win her back."

Michael startled. Rufus sounded just like he did in the forest dream.

"Something wrong?" Rufus said.

"Just not sure how to go about doing that. I've been nicer lately, but I'm still uptight, anxious. Jamie knows it and doesn't trust I'll be able to contain my anger."

"Do you think you can?"

"I'd like to say yes, but I've said it before, then boom— I'm in full explosion mode."

"Maybe if you left that job."

Michael held up his hand. "You're not helping, Rufus. A lot of your advice has been great, but that is one suggestion I'm going to ignore. Are you married? Have a family?"

"No. I was married a long time ago, but my wife passed, and I never met anyone quite as special. Got my sister, brother-in-law, a niece, my nephew, and their kids—makes for a nice family."

"I'm sorry about your wife. How long has it been?"

"Whew...let me see, almost thirty years."

"What happened?"

Rufus leaned back and crossed his arms. His gaze drifted from Michael to the sky.

"I was twenty-three, driving my bus, picking up this one and that one. After my runs, I'd go out for a beer, date different women, hang with the guys. Well, one day my Angela gets on the bus and stops my heart." Rufus sighed. "She had the purest smile and these twinkling eyes. Her skin was the color of cinnamon and smooth as silk. She wore her hair pulled back, and it accentuated her sweet face."

"She sounds beautiful," Michael said.

"Indeed she was," Rufus said. "Angela was in nursing school, doing a clinic at GW, right on my route. I'd see her every day. She'd sit up front, and we'd chat about this and that. One day I gathered up my courage and asked her to have coffee with me, and, to my surprise, she said, 'What's taken you so long to ask?' Thought I'd jump up and down in my seat."

Rufus stopped for a long second, grinned, and shook his head. "That woman had the most contagious, easy laugh, like a child." He glanced at Michael. "You know by now, I can go on with my tales. Just let me know when you have to be on your way."

"I'm in no rush. Keep going," Michael said affectionately.

"One thing led to another, and we fell in love, got married. I drove the bus while she finished nursing school. She told me I could go to college when she graduated. Told her I wasn't sure I wanted to. Didn't really care for school—way too hyper for all that sittin' and studying. She kept pushing though." Rufus shook his head. "If Angela lived, she'd be a doctor, and I'd probably be an aeronautical engineer. Well, she got her degree, and a job followed. We were still young so decided to enjoy the two incomes before I went to school."

Michael smirked. "I understand completely."

"So we had quite the time. Shows, movies, dining out—the works. Then one Saturday morning, she was sitting at the kitchen table, reading the paper. I was heading to the gym to play some hoop with the guys. I gave her a passionate kiss, and told her how much I loved her. She called me a sentimental fool then kissed me again. When I returned, she was dead on the floor. An aneurism killed her instantly. Doctors said there was nothing I could've done, even if I had been home."

Michael patted Rufus on the back. "That's terrible."

Rufus stretched out his legs and clasped his fingers behind his head. He turned and looked at Michael's concerned face. "None of that. The sadness is over. Only beautiful memories left, and I have many. Plus, I'll find my Angela again. I just know it."

"I'm sorry. Really sorry. How long did it take you to get to this point? I mean, happy again," Michael said softly.

"For about a year, I moped around like a puppy dog locked up in a cage. My heart was dead. I didn't want to live—really didn't. Wished God would take me—prayed for it. But he didn't. I kept working, but that was it. Work and home, home and work. I lost a lot of weight, couldn't fit anything in my stomach 'cause the pain consumed my insides. But time goes forward, and one day, I decided I was tired of the constant ache. God wouldn't take me, so I chose to live again. Angela wouldn't want me sulking around my whole life. I could hear her say, 'Come on, Rufus. Get going.' So I started smiling at people, asking their names, talking to neighbors, and I started to feel better."

"Did you feel like you were wearing a mask? My old counselor wanted me to act nice, but I couldn't pull it off."

Rufus chuckled. "At first, it was like wearing a mask and acting in a movie. I went through the motions, but my outside didn't match my inside. Still carried a lot of sorrow. After a while, the grief faded, and joy replaced it. Even without Angela, I was able to be happy again—really happy. I think if you act a certain way, eventually it changes who you are."

"Did you ever meet anyone else?"

"Eventually, I dated some more but was very careful not to go too fast. Call someone I met, and we'd go to a movie. Then call a week later and make arrangements for a bite to eat. Maybe phone her to go see an exhibit at a museum. Ya know, just for company."

Rufus looked at Michael seriously. "I'm no love doctor, but the women I dated didn't like casual courtin'."

Michael grinned. "I hear you."

"It's true. By the third or fourth date, they wanted more attention. That's when I'd walk."

"You were a heartbreaker, Rufus."

"I guess I was." He lowered his eyes. "Not proud of it. Just didn't fall in love. Finally, I stopped dating. Way too much trouble. But, if someone hit me like Angela did, that'd be a different story. I've heard it happens. And I'm blessed, Michael. I know what true love is. Some people never experience it. Although it was for just a speck of my life, I had it.

How about you? You said you love Jamie, but do you love her from the heart?"

Michael nodded. "She's the only woman who ever stopped my heart, like Angela did to you. Jamie made me feel things I never felt before, brought out a lighter side in me that I didn't know existed. Yes. I love her, from the heart, like you say."

"How often do you tell her?"

"When I lived at home, I didn't even say hello when I walked in the door. I told her I loved her before I left home." Michael sighed. "Our life is so stressful, so filled with work pressures, the kids' needs, house stuff, my exercise regimen. The tension caused us to argue—a lot."

Rufus shook his head. "It's not good. You find a treasure then stomp on it. Is it dead?"

"What do you mean 'dead'?"

"If she could, would she have you sign the divorce papers today? Probably scared 'cause she has the children and finances to think about, but if a load of money were to fall in her lap, would she be gone?"

"About a month ago, the answer would have been yes. But, things are getting better since I started filling some of the prescriptions you've been writing. I think we're on the mend."

"Does she think you're on the mend?"

"I think so."

"You got to ask her, son. She's your wife. Talk to the woman. As I recall, she's beautiful. I'm sure other men notice. Believe me, you weren't the first to be captivated by Jamie, and you won't be the last. How would you like another man to come into her life and melt her insides like marshmallows in hot chocolate?"

Michael sat back and frowned. Jamie's Internet date popped into his head. Rufus was right. It wouldn't be long before someone decent jogged into her life, and Jamie must be lonely.

Rufus continued. "Don't you think she'd like to feel her heart dance again?"

Michael turned away. "All right, Rufus. Enough."

"No, it's not enough. You've got to tackle this with vigor. You're a smart man, and smart men can figure things out. If you love her from the heart, you gotta let her know and start courting her back into your life."

"You think?"

"I know. No chess this week. You have more important matters to attend to." Rufus smirked. "And I'd beat you anyway."

"You are so arrogant."

Rufus shook his head. "Just realistic."

Michael smiled. "I'm not very good at courting. What should I do?"

"I don't need to tell you everything. You know the answer. Now scoot."

"Will you be at the club on Wednesday?"

Rufus stood, did a little two-step, and snapped his fingers. "Wouldn't miss it. And, Michael, you're a good man. Let the goodness come through."

"You think?"

"I know. Now get out of here and lasso your wife back. Too much time's been wasted."

Chapter Twenty-Three

I love you, Jamie, Michael thought as he leaned against his car. The awful story about Rufus discovering his wife dead on the floor was stuck in Michael's head. One minute here, the next gone. He imagined going home tonight and finding Jamie that way. She had been missing from his dream in the forest. Did that mean something tragic was going to happen?

Stop it. He couldn't walk around worrying about something that couldn't be predicted. And that dream he had in the woods was just that. He would not let it control his actions or his emotions. It was actually silly. His father in the lake telling him to play, his imaginary twin conducting an orchestra, the feeling of complete serenity—all wishful thinking from somewhere deep in his psyche. Clenching his teeth, he wondered why he had let himself get so swept up in a fantasy.

What he did have to worry about was the reality of his present situation. Jamie hadn't given him any indication that she'd be putting out the welcome mat. Her face was growing fuzzy, like she was fading out of his life. He had to win her back, just like Rufus said. Maybe he should stop and buy her a gift. Picking just the right one, however, was more frightening than figuring out what he was going to do with twenty kids at the club on Wednesday.

Michael ventured into a nearby gift shop and picked up a trinket. Now what? He looked up and down the street. His favorite music store was only a few blocks away, and it had been ages since he'd stopped in. A visit might be just what he needed to distract him from thoughts of dead wives, hallucinations, and volunteering.

Michael did a double take when he saw the sign, Strings and Things. The cramped shop he remembered had turned into a music emporium. Hundreds of string instruments dominated half of the space, drums had a room of their own, and brass instruments lined one wall. A young woman with a ponytail and wire-rimmed glasses serenaded customers with tunes from her folk guitar in a cozy cafe attached to the store. Michael walked past a portable piano and shelves filled with music sheets. He spotted a shiny, red electric guitar, picked it up, and shivered when his fingers made contact with its neck.

A middle-aged man wearing a navy sweat suit and red Keds approached. The top of his bald head reached Michael's shoulders, and he sounded like he had laryngitis when he asked, "Do you need any help?"

"I'll take them all," Michael said, keeping his attention focused on the instruments.

"That's what I thought thirty years ago when I walked through a music palace, and look where it got me."

"You own this place?"

"Sure do," the man said, as he patted his chest.

"I used to come in here quite a bit when I went to law school, but it's a different place now."

"When I first opened this store, it was a narrow closet. Eventually, I summoned up some business. Things got better, so I bought out neighboring buildings, knocked them down, added on, and this is the result."

"You're the original owner? Pete?"

"That's me, Pete. Do you need help or just browsing?"

"I can't believe you're Pete. You've lost so much weight."

"It's called cancer."

Michael's jaw dropped and all he could think of to say was, "I'm sorry."

"Me too. Not just about the cancer, but for springing it on you like that. I'm so used to having it. Just spill when people ask me about my weight, bald head, and barely there voice."

"You're in treatment?"

"Yup. Coming to an end soon. Let's hope it worked."

"What kind?"

"Chemo."

"I meant what kind of cancer."

"Throat. My own fault for smoking all those damn cigarettes, plus some other stuff. Damaged my insides, not to mention the big hole it put in my wallet."

"You don't smoke anymore, right? Does it hurt to talk?"

"Can't even stand the smell of those homicidal bastards. Marlboro and I had a long affair, but a tumor broke us up. Don't worry about the voice. It hurts more to hear it than use it. Now, anything I can help you with? And your name?"

"I'm Michael," he said, trying not to laugh at Pete's dry sense of humor. "Do you have any used equipment?"

"Sure do. I'll show you the room. Used stuff, but in good condition. Nothing like bringing a dead instrument back to life."

Michael followed the slight man who walked swiftly through the store to a separate area filled with a variety of musical artifacts.

"Probably not good for business, but I'll tell you a little secret." Pete put his finger to his lips. "The stuff in here is way better than some of that crap out there. These beauties have the richness of history built into them." He signaled Michael with a wave of his hand to follow him to a folk guitar in the corner. "Rumor has it Woody Guthrie wrote some tunes on this prize, but it's not for sale."

"Can I strum it?"

"Go for it."

Michael squatted and ran his thumb over the strings, then did it again.

"Feel the magic? A little different than that young babe you were handling on the floor?"

Michael stood and nodded.

"So, you need something used?" Pete asked.

"I'm teaching guitar at the Northwest Boys & Girls Club. We have a lot of interest, but not much equipment," Michael whispered.

"You're a guitar teacher?"

"Just volunteering. I'm a lawyer by day."

"Stop whispering."

"I'm whispering?"

"Happens all the time," Pete chuckled. "People start imitating my tone without even knowing it. Anyway, you've come to the right place. Looking to get rid of some stuff in the basement. I've been hoarding all kinds of musical paraphernalia for a decade."

"Are you serious?"

"Damn serious. All those treasures down there gathering dust. It's a shame. Let's go shopping." Pete's eyes widened. "Best kind of shopping. Everything's free."

Michael stared at Pete like he was his fairy godfather. "Free?"

Pete patted Michael's arm. "The expression on your face is all the payment I need. It'll be good to get those rusty gems singing again. What day are you at the club?"

"Wednesday evenings."

"Works for me. Wednesdays are slow here, and I have good help. Can you get here early?"

"Slow down. What are you talking about?"

"I'm gonna need help getting the equipment over to the club."

"How early?"

"Seven o'clock sharp."

"In the morning?"

"Of course, the morning. We have a lot of work to do. Let's go down and start labeling the gear we want."

"I work. I can't take the day off."

Pete laughed. "Like they're gonna miss you."

"Actually, they will, in a big way."

"You're kidding yourself. No one's that important."

Pete paced slowly, rubbing his chin. "What kind of space you got?"

"The size of a classroom."

"And you said twenty kids?"

"That's right."

"Ain't gonna work. Put your lawyer skills to good use and call one of the hotshots at the club. Get us another room, maybe two."

"I can't. I'm just a volunteer."

"Seriously, I was downstairs yesterday and promised myself to donate most of the stuff. Then you walked in. Meant to be. So make a phone call and get us more space. The kids are going to flip when they see what Santa Pete brings 'em."

Michael hesitated. "I'll try."

"Trying isn't good enough. Just do it. You can give your lessons in one room, and I'll teach the kids how to refurbish in another. They've got to be part of the rejuvenation process."

Michael shrugged. "I like the idea. We'll have more space on Wednesday," he said, hoping he could make it happen.

"Got a card?" Pete asked.

"What?"

"A business card. In case something comes up, like a chemo attack of vomiting."

"Sure," Michael said, as he reached for his wallet.

Pete glanced at it. "Stolis is your last name?"

"That's what it says."

"Any relation to Jamie?"

"She's my wife. How do you know Jamie?"

"Your wife?"

"Unless there's another Jamie Stolis around. Do you know her?"

"Can't say. I'll ruin the surprise." Pete clamped his hand over his mouth.

"What surprise?"

"Shoot my damn mouth."

"Come on. Tell me."

Pete moved in close to Michael. He looked to his left then his right. "Promise you won't tell her I let the cat out of the bag?"

Michael traced an X over his heart.

Pete sighed. "Your wife came in early Saturday morning with your old guitar. She begged me to have it fixed up by this afternoon. Couldn't say no to such a sweet thing. So it's home waiting for you, and it's better than new."

Michael felt like he had just been injected with a shot of love. He stood immobile as it penetrated into his veins.

"Sorry I ruined the surprise."

"You didn't ruin anything," Michael said slowly.

"You've got a beauty of a guitar, and a wife."

"I know."

"Do you have a few minutes to check out the inventory?"

Michael nodded, but was still too surprised to move.

"Come on, slowpoke," Pete shouted.

Michael swallowed hard and walked to the door where Pete was waiting. He checked his watch. Only forty more minutes and he'd be home.

Jamie settled into the comfort of the couch as she took a sip of tea. Thank God, bank teller training school was over. Going to class every day this week was too much for her attention span. Or maybe the material just didn't interest her. On Monday she'd start working with customers, and hopefully it would be more stimulating.

"When's dinner?" Megan asked, as she hopped into the living room.

"As soon as Daddy gets home."

"Why is he so late?"

Jamie looked at the clock on the digital cable box. "He's not late. He'll be here in fifteen or twenty minutes."

"I'm hungry, Mom."

"Me too. We'll eat when Dad gets here, but give him a minute when he first walks in the door."

"Mom, I'm hungry now, and why can't we have pizza?"

Jamie frowned at her daughter.

"Mom. Why aren't you answering me?"

"Because you're whining. Stop it right now," Jamie said firmly.

Megan pouted and folded her arms.

Jamie's eyes narrowed as she contemplated what to do about Megan's bratty behavior. If only she could send that royalty attitude down an incinerator, just like Willie Wonka did with Veruca Salt. After indulging her daughters for years, Jamie was making a concerted effort to pull back.

Jamie mimicked Megan by standing up, folding her arms, and pouting.

Megan stepped back. "What are you doing?"

"I'm showing you what you look like. Not pretty is it? Stop sulking and wait patiently for your father."

"Can you call to see if he's on his way?"

"No. Just wait."

Megan's lower lip quivered. "When's Dad going to start living with us again?"

"Oh, Meg." Like a kick in the shin, Jamie recalled the anguish she felt when her parents split up. Dad hugging her good-bye, the For Sale sign hanging in front of the house, deciding which parent she wanted to live with—these were the exact experiences she wanted to protect her children from. Jamie wished she could say, "Everything will be all right," but that would be dishonest. Instead, she took Megan's hand and brought her to the couch. They sat down, and Jamie hugged her. "I don't know, Honey. We need to work things out. It might take a while."

"Why did you and Dad fight so much?"

"That's what we're trying to figure out."

"Do you think you will?"

Jamie rested her chin on the top of Megan's head and sighed. "I hope so," she whispered.

The door opened. Megan jumped up, and Emily scurried down the stairs. "Daddy!" both girls shouted.

Jamie stood and glanced down at her outfit. The new V-neck shirtdress was a touch wrinkled but still had a vogue flare, especially with the beaded fashion belt that wrapped her waist. She slid into two-inch heels and was ready to greet Michael. It had to be an insecurity issue, but she wanted to look nice when he arrived, so she didn't change after she got home from work. It bothered her that Michael was so turned on by that other woman, Rachel. Even though they were separated, and Jamie wasn't sure about reconciliation, she still wanted Michael to be attracted to her.

When she saw him, her insides did a somersault. She felt like hugging him, even kissing him. What was wrong with her? She had to get control of her emotions. And where were these emotions coming from anyway? Think of something bad, quick. Kenny Chesney popped into her head.

Jamie had joined his fan club just so she could get in on the concert presale when the country music star came to DC. She ordered the tickets online the second they were offered. On the big night, Michael complained the whole time because people were standing. He must have been the only person in the arena who sat instead of bopping to the music. Then he made her leave at the encore, so they could beat the traffic. Good. That loathing feeling was back.

"Hey, working girl. What smells so good?" His gaze scanned her body. "You look beautiful."

Jamie's heart sighed. The Kenny Chesney memory wasn't strong enough.

"Thanks. Chicken stir-fry for dinner. How was your trip?"

"Not bad. I can't believe you cooked after your first week on the job."

"Trying to eat healthier. I'm sick of the take-out diet."

"Whoa! Is that really you talking?"

She fiddled with her dress. "The one and only."

"What's in the bag, Dad?" Emily asked.

"Presents for everybody. Let's go into the kitchen."

Michael set the bag on the island. "So do you like your job? What'd you do?"

Jamie sat on a stool. "Learned about financial math, customer service strategies, and banking sales concepts."

"What about the presents?" Megan asked.

"Two minutes," Michael said. "Do you like it?"

Jamie chuckled. "No."

"What are you going to do?"

"The same thing most Americans do. Get up and go to work anyway. I did like getting out, and I can't wait to see a paycheck with my name on it."

"Are you still looking for a communications job?"

"No. But I will soon. This is fine until something better comes along."

"Is it two minutes yet?" Emily asked.

Michael picked her up and put her on a stool. Megan leaned against the counter, and Michael tousled her hair. "First, you two." He pulled out a colored soap bubble three-pack complete with a launch gun.

"Colored bubbles!" Megan exclaimed.

"Orange, green, and purple. And this gun thing is supposed to blow out hundreds at a time."

"Can we try it?" Emily asked.

"If it's okay with Mom, I'll take you guys to a park tomorrow, and we'll blast 'em."

"You and colored bubbles? I have to see this," Jamie said.

"The more the merrier. But, I thought I'd take the girls for the day. That way you can work in the garden. You must've mentioned not being able to get to it about ten times this week."

"Thanks, Michael. But I'm keeping one of those bottles so I can play too when you get home. Maybe we'll barbecue."

"It's a plan." Michael pulled out a square white box and handed it to Jamie. "Your turn."

She glanced at Michael, pulled off the top, and rummaged through the tissue paper. "How pretty!" she said, as she took out a hot plate in a black iron stand. Hand painted on a ceramic tile was a basket of sky-blue asters sitting on a rocking chair, with a hazy meadow in the background.

"I saw it and had to buy it. It was like looking at a picture of you, so delicate and pretty," he said, with his hands in his pockets.

Jamie lowered her face into her palm. A tear tried to escape from the corner of her eye, but she forced it back. "This is so sweet."

"You like it?" Michael said, grinning.

"I love my present! And the words that came with it." She thought Michael was going to lean over the island counter and kiss her, but he didn't. He just looked at her like she was an angel. Her heartbeat accelerated. Kenny Chesney, Kenny Chesney, Kenny Chesney. It wasn't working.

"I'm glad you're here," he said.

"What?"

"I'm just glad you're here. That's all."

"What are you talking about? Where else would I be?"

"Can we give Daddy his present now?" Megan asked.

"I get one too?" Michael said.

"Before or after dinner?"

"Before," the girls shouted, and ran into the living room.

Jamie couldn't wait to see the expression on his face when he saw his refurbished guitar. Just as she was about to move, Michael walked around the island and stepped into her personal space. He picked up a napkin and wiped a tear off her cheek.

Darn. It must have fallen out, Jamie mused.

"You liked my present?"

She nodded and inched back. "And this," Jamie said, holding her hands out.

"What?"

"A happy family. I never had one."

"And you so deserve one."

"Come on. I want to show you your present." She shimmied around him.

"Oh my God!" Michael exclaimed when he spotted his guitar. He picked it up, sat on the couch, and strummed it. The richness of its sound resonated.

"Mommy took it to the man at the guitar store, and he made it all better," Emily said.

Michael looked at Jamie as if she had given him a precious jewel. He fiddled with the tuners and strings, and tried a few chords. "Perfect," he whispered. "Ready for a song?"

All three of them just stared.

Smiling, he belted out a verse from "The Bear Went Over the Mountain." Emily and Megan moved closer to him, mesmerized.

"Sing more, Daddy," Emily murmured.

He sang two more verses, then set the instrument down and hugged his daughters. "Thank you. My guitar is back!" Michael smiled at Jamie, gratitude flooding his eyes.

"Can you play 'Puff the Magic Dragon'?" Megan asked.

"It's one of my favorites," Michael said. He picked up his guitar and played like he had never thrust it aside.

Jamie leaned against the wall. Her husband really did have a beautiful voice. Michael looked so content as he strummed and sang; the girls standing close were hypnotized by the magical music. Right this second, she really did have a happy family. Of course, it wouldn't last. Happy moments never did. Just like a balloon floating through the sky on a hot summer day, it would burst. As much as she wanted to jump into the fun, fear stopped her. If Jamie anticipated the explosion, it wouldn't be so hurtful when it arrived. So she quietly sat in the rocking chair and observed the merriment from a distance, as if it were someone else's life. She gripped the handles and thought, how nice.

Chapter Twenty-Four

Like long bike rides on desolate roads, a haunting Coldplay song, or a bagful of crispy French fries—all good things must come to an end. And so it was with Michael's holiday from his job. The hike in the forest, his visit to Strings and Things, and the lighthearted weekend spent with his family were over. He rubbed his eyes then returned to the business of reviewing John's best attempt at solving a dispute between employees and employers at an ice cream factory.

Workers were disgruntled because the company was ending its two free pints per week policy, decreasing its contribution to the 401(k) plan, and increasing the employees' contribution to their healthcare plan. Michael squeezed his pen as he wrote "Really???" next to John's solution, which included replacing the ice cream giveaway with a weekly raffle. The money saved could be put toward medical and retirement benefits. Michael rolled his eyes and scribbled, "Buyback plan!! Reduce ice cream giveaway to once a month!! Think!!!" He then tossed the proposal on the floor. He shook his head. Would John really bring up a raffle at a mediation session? It wasn't like Michael expected his staff to develop a world peace treaty. He just wanted them to use common sense.

Michael's patience was growing as thin as the paper on his desk, and his throbbing blood vessels were about to burst, so he switched gears. He swiveled his chair around to confront the e-mails that had been piling up since Thursday. Hundreds of bold black messages stared at him: some with red flags next to the address, some with *urgent* in the subject line, and one from Frank: "WHERE ARE YOU???" Michael squeezed the mouse. Impulse told him to delete it all, so he popped up and headed for the door before he did something he would regret. *Take a walk. Release the stress. Breathe. Start your Monday over.*

Michael stopped when he touched the doorknob. By now the place would be swarming with empty heads in search of their brains. If he emerged, they'd attack with questions, itineraries, and tales of mishaps that occurred in his absence. He'd explode.

The click-clack of his assistant's heels approached. He wasn't ready for the volumes of information she'd deliver. Panicking, he dashed back to his desk, scooted under it, and pulled the chair in to seal his hiding place.

Cathleen knocked on the door.

Michael froze.

She opened it. "Michael, are you here?"

Does it look like I'm here? Go away.

Cathleen entered and placed something on his desk. She tapped her nails on a file cabinet. "I wonder where he is. I didn't see him come in, and I didn't see him leave."

Michael saw her legs. She had stopped right in front of his chair.

"He has to be here."

His pulse accelerated. *What if she finds me? What will I say?*

He heard her pacing around. Michael closed his eyes, bit his lower lip, and prayed for her departure.

"I wonder where he is," she muttered again. Her step quickened, and she left the office. "Has anyone seen Michael?"

He pushed the chair back and emerged from his hiding place. Cathleen was not at her desk, so he darted out the door, around the corner, and into the men's room. Secure in a stall, he closed his eyes and visualized that sparkling Minnesota lake. He inhaled and exhaled deeply. His heartbeat slowed, and his shoulders dropped. The thunderstorm had subsided, but his internal radar warned that more were approaching. *Keep them contained; lock them up.* He shifted from one foot to the other then strolled back to his office. Cathleen moved toward him from the opposite direction.

"Where have you been? I have a suitcase full of information that needs to be reviewed."

"I got here a little before seven."

"I just checked your office, and you weren't there."

"I was in the men's room."

"I didn't see you leave."

"I guess you weren't looking."

She wrinkled her forehead. "Anyway, Frank wants to see you in his office at ten. That gives you a half hour to prepare. Then we really have to meet."

"Prepare what?"

"Prepare to see Frank. He didn't tell me what he wanted. I figured you knew."

269

"No clue," Michael said, as he walked toward his office. He stopped and turned around. "By the way, how was your week? Sounds like it was hectic."

Cathleen looked at him with a stunned smile. "Busy as usual. Thanks for asking. How about you? How was Saint Paul?"

"Not bad. Glad to be home though." He nodded and continued on his way.

Michael closed the door and slouched in his chair. Did he really hide under his desk? Had he crossed the bridge into insanity? When his cell phone rang, he answered it immediately.

"Michael Stolis."

"Hey, Henry here. Pete told me to give you a call."

"Pete?"

"From Strings and Things."

"Of course. Sorry. I'm a little distracted."

"No problem. I can't remember names, and I'm always distracted."

"What can I do for you?"

"Pete told me you're starting a music program at the Northwest Boys & Girls Club. I'd like to help."

"It's not my program. I just volunteer to give guitar lessons. Do you want a number to call?"

"If need be. Anyway, I'm in a band and have some instruments we don't use any more. I'd be happy to donate them to your program."

"It's not my program, but we could use some instruments. What's the name of your band?"

"Koffee Kake."

"Wow. You guys are huge around here."

"We keep busy. I can meet you at Pete's on Wednesday morning with some pretty good gear, just a little outdated. I got a van to help cart it over to the club. We'll probably need a few trips, between my stuff and Pete's."

"I have to find out about space," Michael said.

"Pete says you're working on it. Good thing, 'cause we're gonna need it."

"I'll call the director to see what he can do."

"I'll help with lessons too."

Michael rubbed his forehead. "Let me get back to you about procedures. I had to fill out some papers, and the club did a security check before I started."

"No problem. Save my number on your cell and let me know what I need to do. Glad you're starting this program. I grew up in DC, and there wasn't anything like this going on."

"It's not my program."

"See you on Wednesday."

"Holy shit!" He had to get hold of Luke and let him know about this. Michael hoped he hadn't overstepped his bounds.

Luke wasn't overwhelmed or angry. He was ecstatic. An additional room had already been secured. Luke said something about making the club a center for music. Koffee Kake was his favorite DC band, and he couldn't believe that the lead guitarist wanted to volunteer. He promised to clear his Wednesday and would meet Michael at Pete's early that morning.

Michael tightened his lips as he grabbed a notepad for his meeting with Frank. This music endeavor had so much energy, and it felt a touch dangerous. His body was here, but his mind had checked into his volunteer job. Loads of work surrounded him, and he wasn't motivated to do any of it. Clicking his tongue, he decided to enjoy Wednesday, regroup, then get back into the swing of his paid position.

As Michael strode down the hall, his employees shouted questions at him. Some scurried next to him, detailing problems that occurred in his absence. The volume of their chatter intensified, but Michael remained stone-faced and silent. He couldn't deal with these pesky squirrels right now. He opened the door to Frank's office and slipped in, shutting out the noise.

"Good morning, Michael," Sarah said. "How was your trip?"

"Not bad. The accommodations could have been better."

"We're tightening up the budget. No more luxury business retreats."

"For Frank, too?"

"Excuse me?"

"Didn't think Frank was up to basic lodging. Anyway, can you let him know I'm here?"

She glared at him, waited a moment, then buzzed her boss.

Michael entered the office and sat in the chair across from Frank's desk.

Frank took off his bifocals, pushed some papers aside, and sat back. "Where have you been?"

Michael leaned forward and looked directly at Frank. "Guess."

"For heaven's sake, Michael. I know you were in Saint Paul, but there are inventions like e-mail and cell phones. You haven't responded to anything since Wednesday."

"I was busy, and you said you'd take care of everything."

"There were some problems I needed to talk to you about." Frank's voice rose. "And you were not reachable by e-mail, phone, pager—nothing."

Michael's mouth went dry. "You caught me. I checked out, but I'm back. Do you want to hear about the smooth dealings in Saint Paul, or do you want answers to those urgent questions?"

Frank stood, put on his suit jacket, then slid one hand over his bald head. "I don't like your attitude."

Michael watched the senior partner pace around the executive suite. Maybe Frank would say, "You're fired," but it didn't come. Michael's eyes widened as Frank sat on the couch and said, "What's up with you?"

Michael inhaled deeply. "I'll be honest. The demands of this job have been getting to me. The negotiations in Saint Paul went quickly, so I took a little vacation. Went hiking on Thursday then spent an overdue weekend with my family, without interruptions."

Frank stood. "Let's get a cup of coffee."

"Thanks, Frank, but I'm swamped and need to get back to work. I'm fine now. What did you want?"

Frank leaned on the conference table. "You're a valuable employee. That's why I tolerate your cockiness some of the time—actually, all of the time. Don't take advantage of that. Next time you need to check out, let me know. There's an e-mail waiting for you about the mediation session with the electronics firm on Wednesday. Look it over and get back to me with your game plan before you leave today."

"Greg's handling it, so I'll forward the e-mail to him. I need Wednesday off."

Frank's ears turned red. "No way. This is big. Greg can't handle it."

Michael's voice tightened. "He's been working on it, and he'll do fine. No other option."

Frank sprang forward, threw his hands up, and boomed, "He can't handle it."

Michael stood and seethed, "Then he should be fired. I'm so damned sick of doing the work of ten people."

Frank slammed his fist into his palm. "You could see seven figures with your bonus this year. That means you do the work of a hundred people if I say so."

"I cannot be here on Wednesday. It's impossible. Greg will be prepared. I'll see to it," Michael said deliberately.

Frank shook his finger. "If he screws this up, it's your fault."

"Understood."

"You better get moving."

Michael hurried to the door.

"We need to go out for a drink and talk about your attitude. Get things straight," Frank said.

"Sure. Next week?"

"E-mail me, and we'll pick a day. Things need to change." Frank cleared his throat. "And get that haircut."

Michael raced through the swarm of bees buzzing questions at him. The vibrant red exit sign at the end of the hall seemed miles away, and he hoped to reach it before a scream erupted from his mouth. The thunderstorm roared and lightning flashed. He had to stop the disturbance, find some composure. As he dashed down the stairs, the rage attacked his throat, his head, his chest. His breaths transformed into pants. A tornado of angst whirled through his body, and perspiration oozed out of his pores. Outside, he tried to run away from the assault, but it was faster than he was. Still, he ran and ran. After several minutes he wavered near a marble bench. The storm weakened, and the aftermath left him sweating and breathless. He looked toward the sky. That damn dust devil hadn't been killed in the Minnesota forest. The hike, the weekend with his family—it was all so wonderful. Now, the tyrant had returned. Michael tried to summon the feeling he had while he swam in that magical lake. He shut his eyes tight, but it wouldn't come.

What triggered his nemesis this time? Was it being in his office, work demands, his fading motivation to do his job, or Frank's command over his life? The conflict between how he lived and how he wanted to live was causing him to implode. Little things like refusing to get a haircut and taking a day off were just small protests to subdue his internal call to leave the world he had created and step into the new one that begged him to enter. Trying to figure out how to make this happen was like trying to open a soda can when the pop top had been torn off. It was a hopeless battle.

Michael felt lightheaded, so he sat on the bench. He was trapped in a prison cell covered with dollar bills. The gold bricks on his back and the diamond ball chained around his ankle were so heavy. He couldn't walk away. He stared blankly at the cars and busses that zoomed by.

After a long shudder, his lips pressed into a thin line. *Get a hold of yourself.* He had to prepare Greg for the hearing, meet with Cathleen, and answer his staff's questions. In fact, he'd have a meeting later in the day and apologize for running away from them. His BlackBerry beeped—a text from Jamie. "Just making sure you're coming over for dinner."

"I'll be there at six," he typed.

Michael didn't have time tonight, but he couldn't cancel. He had to keep the momentum of the weekend going. Friday night they sang songs while he played his guitar. Saturday he spent an outrageously silly day with his daughters. They drained four bottles of bubbles and imitated ducks by a park pond. On Sunday, they went for an early-morning bike ride along the Potomac River; then he brought them to Sam's for brunch. Jamie even agreed to let her father watch the girls on Saturday, so he could take her on a surprise trip—someplace they could relax and talk without interruptions. A reconciliation might be on the horizon. Then again, how could he go back home when his pet monster still lurked inside him?

When he got back to the office, he'd call Greg and tell him that they needed to have a night meeting. They had so much to go over before the mediation session. Michael released an explosive exhale. All this, so he could take Wednesday off for a volunteer job. He shook his head. He really was crazy.

The scent of Italian food and the sound of quiet greeted Michael when he entered the house. He glanced at the calendar on his watch to confirm the date. Yes. It really was Monday. Megan and Emily had swim class after school, which usually meant a microwave creation for dinner. This was clearly not the case tonight.

As he passed the dining room, he saw a candle glowing in the middle of a floral centerpiece on the table, draped in gold linen. Cloth ivory napkins were rolled into their matching holders and placed on top of the fine china they had received as a wedding gift from Jamie's dad. He barely recognized these elegant dishes and couldn't remember the last time they had been used.

When Michael walked into the kitchen, Jamie jumped. Although she didn't notice, the tomato sauce she was stirring splattered, garnishing her pretty pale blue blouse, which he had never seen before.

"Where are the kids? What about swim lessons?" Michael asked, after he made himself comfortable on a stool.

"Swim lessons were canceled—a clogged drain in the pool. The girls are upstairs doing who knows what," Jamie said, as she poured two glasses of merlot.

"Did the TV break?" Michael asked.

"No. Decided to continue the TV-off-until-seven rule that you started a couple of weeks ago."

"That's good," he said halfheartedly. Jamie was coming alive, and he knew why. Michael the Monster had moved out.

She smiled, gave Michael his wine, then clinked it with hers before she took a seat across from him.

"What's this all about?" Michael asked.

Jamie shrugged her shoulders. "I'm trying to seduce you."

He almost fell off his stool. "Really?"

"Would a seduction work?" she asked.

"It already has."

Jamie giggled. "Seriously, I needed a distraction, so when swim lessons were canceled, I cooked away my frustration. I hate my job."

Michael frowned. "You are such a tease. And you hate your job? Already?"

"Don't worry. I don't have to like it." She sipped her wine then set it down. "And I'm glad my seduction would have worked."

"First of all, of course your seduction would have worked. You got me all excited."

"Good."

"What is going on with you?"

"Okay," Jamie said blowing out a long stream of air. "I'm jealous. I thought about you with Rachel all day at the bank when I was supposed to be counting money. My drawer was five dollars short."

"You were five dollars short? Did you get in trouble?"

"A little reprimand. I can't let it happen again—like HSBC can't handle a five-dollar loss."

"This job isn't for you."

Jamie shrugged.

"And Rachel. Please don't be jealous of her. I don't even like saying her name."

"I just wish I looked like her."

"Oh come on. You didn't even see her, and you are way prettier. Let's delete Rachel and that Internet guy from our thoughts—write them off as big mistakes."

"All right," Jamie said reluctantly.

"So, no seduction?"

"Not yet, but I'm glad it would've worked. How was your day?"

"My day sounds about as good as yours. That seduction would have really helped."

Jamie walked over to the stove, stirred the sauce, then leaned against the kitchen counter. "What happened at work?"

"I had a run-in with Frank. He thinks he owns me, and I guess he does. On top of that I have to train Greg on how to mediate a session Wednesday, which he already should know how to do. In fact, I have to meet him at eight tonight because we have so much to go over. I shouldn't even be drinking this wine. Did I mention the truckload of e-mails I have

278

to respond to after I meet with Greg?" He paused. "I'm complaining, aren't I?"

"That's okay, and one glass of wine won't hurt. It'll help you relax." Jamie's eyes narrowed. "Did you get angry?"

"What do you mean?"

"Did you lose it, blow up at Frank?"

She was testing him. If he admitted to having a panic attack, he'd be back at square one, just when she was talking about a seduction. Jamie didn't need to hear about today's events. He just had a setback. "No," he said.

"You didn't?"

Except for hiding under my desk, shouting at Frank, and running away from my staff. "I didn't."

"Good for you, Michael. That's real progress. Are you hungry?"

"Famished. Let's eat whatever you're wearing on your shirt."

"Huh?" Jamie looked down and saw the red speckles that decorated her blouse. "Oops. Nice touch. Don't you think?"

"Love it."

"On the menu tonight is ravioli filled with ricotta, portabella mushrooms, and red pepper, tossed salad, and crusty French bread. We'll end with tiramisu from El Docci's, and I might even break out the cappuccino machine."

"Sounds delicious. Do the girls like all that?"

"Who cares?" Jamie said, grinning.

Michael half smiled.

Jamie left the kitchen. "Time to wash up ladies," she called. "Five minutes until dinner."

He watched her until she was out of sight then dropped his head. He had blatantly lied because he didn't have a choice. She would flip out if she knew how he behaved today. Michael tugged at his belt loop. He had to figure out a way to poison that tyrant inside him.

The next thing he knew, Megan and Emily had their arms around him. They told him that they skipped swim lessons and were going to have a special dinner just because it was Monday.

In the midst of his daughters' excitement, Michael's eyes met Jamie's. They said, *I don't believe you.* Maybe she would forget about this little lie, just like he hoped she would forget about Rachel. He silently winced. *Highly doubtful.*

"Come on. Let's eat," Jamie said.

Michael picked up the basket of bread and headed to the dining room without looking back.

Chapter Twenty-Five

The crescent moon faded away as the sun's rays brightened the morning sky. Michael drove down G Street NW, singing along with John Mayer, who played on Sirius XM. Wednesday had finally arrived, and he couldn't wait for a day of work and play with his new friends. Feeling generous, he stopped at a bagel shop and bought a baker's dozen, a couple of tubs of cream cheese, six oversized blueberry muffins, and a box of coffee to go.

The scent of warm yeast filled the car as he waited at a traffic light. The delicious fumes mellowed his bustling mind. He reached into the brown bag and snatched a bagel covered with sesame seeds. As he bit into it, crumbs fell onto his blue jeans, the seat, and floor. He didn't even care.

Michael pulled into the parking lot next to Strings and Things, grabbed his goodies, and walked into the shop. Pete and a tall man stood with arms folded, examining about a hundred pieces of gear. They turned when the door opened.

"What'd ya bring us?" Pete asked.

Michael hesitated for a second as he adjusted his ears to Pete's raspy voice. "Figured we'd need some energy to get us started. Bagels, muffins, and caffeine ought to do it."

"Great. I'm starving. Put it on the counter, and we'll dig in before the work starts."

Michael set up the breakfast quickly and headed back over to the inventory.

"This is Henry, lead guitarist and singer for the famous Koffee Kake. You two talked earlier this week," Pete said.

"Hey, Henry," Michael said, as he looked up to meet the slim giant's eyes. He shook Henry's hand.

Before either of them could get a word out, Pete chimed in, "Besides being an ace musician, he's my partner."

Michael's head snapped back.

"Why ya got to shock people like that all the time?" Henry said, annoyed.

"Proud of you is all. Do gays bother you, Michael?"

"Not at all."

"Your eyes grew an inch when I told you we were part-ners. Is it because we're a biracial couple?"

"Absolutely not."

"What's up then?"

"It's the height thing...I mean, the difference. Henry's at least a foot taller than you. I just can't imagine...never mind. What do you have here?" Michael asked, refocusing the con-versation on the instruments.

"At first the height difference caused some problems, but we worked it out. You see..."

"Never mind, Pete. I don't need to know," Michael said, putting one hand up.

"Just tell him to shut up," Henry interrupted, shaking his head. "Sometimes it works."

Pete lifted his index finger. "But not always. You got lucky this time. Let's get some carbs in us; then we'll argue about what we're going to load up first."

"So this is where our music program begins," Luke said, as he walked in the door. He wore old gray corduroys, a flannel button-down shirt, and beat up sneakers.

"Luke!" Michael exclaimed, then made introductions. "Where's Rufus?"

"At the club, continuing with the renovation. He's been putting in ten-hour days since I told him about our good luck."

The men chowed down and guzzled coffee while Henry kept them entertained with sidesplitting jokes. The gang debated which of the gems would be chauffeured to the club first. After fervent campaigning for their favorite pieces, they had enough paraphernalia for a trip to the instruments' new home.

Michael gasped when he walked into the club carrying a bass guitar and a microphone stand. Rufus faced a wall, holding a baby food jar of purple paint in one hand and a toy paintbrush in the other. He dabbed dots onto the shirt of a man who had been created with colorful oils and acrylics. Happy people banging on bongos, blowing horns, shaking tambourines, and dancing in a park covered the rest of the wall. They were set against a sky-blue canvas decorated with trees and birds.

A vibrant chill shot through Michael. It was the same surge he had experienced in the forest when he had the vision of Rufus standing at that spectacular building. The message was so clear.

He was home. After forty-two years of running through life with shin splints and a dry spirit, he had finally finished the marathon. Closing his eyes, he tried to swallow but couldn't. The lump in his throat was too large. In spite of the intense emotion, he did manage to conjure up a quick prayer. *Let me stay.*

Luke's strong voice jolted him away from his whimsical wish. "Holy shit, Uncle Rufus! How did you manage this?"

Rufus turned, set the painting tools down, and walked toward Luke. When he reached his nephew, he hugged him then grabbed his shoulders. "We did it."

Rufus then walked over to Michael and surprised him with the same hug. The warm energy from this man rushed into him. Michael tentatively returned the gesture. Except for Jamie and the girls, this kind of unguarded physical expression was rare, but it felt so right. When Rufus pulled back, he looked at Michael and sincerely said, "Thank you."

Michael could not think of anything to say. Even if he could, the lump in his throat was as big as a plum, and words could not plow through it.

"Ya see, Michael, I've had this dream of making a fun place where kids in the city could come and hang out. Keep 'em safe, keep 'em laughing, keep 'em learning. It's not a new dream, but an awful big one. A place where kids' eyes sparkle when they walk in. You, the music, the camaraderie made that happen here." Rufus held up his hands. "And now we're growing it."

Michael nodded slightly.

"Those guitar lessons you started got the kids talking, and the word spread like wildfire. A glorious blaze." Rufus gently shook Michael's shoulders. "We've landed on Mars!"

Michael was dumfounded. Sure, it was all great, but Rufus was acting like he had just discovered a car that operated on water. His enthusiasm seemed a little over the top, but then again Rufus was an over-the-top kind of guy. For him eating one of Sam's roast beef sandwiches was just as exciting as dining at the Eiffel Tower.

Henry and Pete stepped into the room, carrying parts of a drum set. As they set the pieces down, Pete said, "This is fantastic. I'm moving in."

Henry introduced himself to Rufus. "You did all of this?"

"Hell no. Mostly supervised. The art teacher here asked kids to help out—even let them use class time to work with me. Some super talent inside this building. Recruited kids from the shop classes to build partitions and paint 'em. I had so much help. They're all coming to celebrate tonight, so we better get going."

"I'm on it," Pete said as he headed out the door.

Rufus looked at Michael. "Guess who else is coming to the party?"

"Who?" Michael asked, relieved that his emotional throat tumor had receded.

"Sam. He's bringing loads of food. Said it was the least he could do for a loyal customer like me."

"I'm speechless, Rufus. That's great."

"It is. The kids are gonna be blown away when they walk in. Better get to work."

"Yes, Sir," Michael said.

"Come on, guys," Rufus hollered over to Luke and Henry, who were studying the wall painting.

Luke saluted, and both men walked off to get more equipment.

Michael tagged behind, slowed down by his curiosity. Why was Rufus—or Luke, for that matter—so devoted to this endeavor? Actually, *devoted* was too weak a word. They were driven.

"Come on, slowpoke," Pete said, as he walked by, carrying two electric guitars.

Michael smiled and sprang into a jog.

Sam joined the party at four. By then, both classrooms had been transformed into music studios. He pushed a cart loaded with sub platters, salads, chips, and, of course, jars of pickles. Sam picked up the largest container and handed it to Rufus, who was resting in a chair. "This one is all yours."

Rufus stood, patted Sam on the back, and took the pickles. "They should last about a week."

Sam chuckled. "This place is amazing. You told me you were making progress, but I had no idea."

Sam was right. Four drum stations with partitions were in one room, along with three keyboards. Several headphones hung on the walls, so people could practice at the same time without disturbing each other. The other room was full of strings—bass guitars, electric guitars, folk guitars, and a couple of ukuleles. Odds and ends—like amplifiers, microphones, and tambourines—were also scattered about. Pete had even set up a table for equipment repairs. Michael felt like he was floating through a dream and barely noticed Sam's loud exclamation, "You did great, kid!"

"Hey, Sam. I had a lot of help." Maybe for today, Michael would pretend this really was his program.

"Don't be so modest. Rufus raves about your efforts. Do you have a minute? I need some help loading up the drinks and desserts."

"Sure. Did Becky bake her chocolate chip cookies?"

"Enough for an army."

"Great," Michael said, as the two men headed down the hall.

Sam cleared his throat a few times as they loaded the cart with treats.

"What's up?" Michael finally asked.

Sam didn't answer, but Michael noticed a concerned expression on his face.

"Something wrong?"

"Not with me."

Michael straightened up. "With who?"

"You."

"What?"

"Rufus told me you and your wife are separated."

Michael lowered his eyes. People were starting to find out about his marriage split, which made it all too real.

"How are you holding up?"

"I'm doing okay. Jamie and I are trying to work things out."

"Becky and I went through a rough patch when our kids were small. Not an easy time."

"You can say that again." He paused. "You and Becky?"

Sam put a cooler on the cart. "You see, I worked for the government—transportation department. It was a desk job, and I'm the type of guy who needs to move around. Sitting in that cubicle all day drove me nuts—made me crabby."

Michael furrowed his eyebrows. "What'd you do?"

"I quit my job."

"Just like that—you quit?"

"Becky and I always wanted our own business, but for some reason figured we couldn't afford to make it happen. We both loved to cook and dreamed about opening a deli."

"How'd you do it?"

"When things got really bad with Becky, and I couldn't stand walking into that office one more day, I went to the bank and applied for a loan. It wasn't easy, but I got it. Tended bar for awhile to earn the cash we needed to pay the bills. Sold our house, bought the place on Connecticut Avenue, and that was the beginning of our life—the good part anyway."

"Where'd you live?"

"Above the store. It worked out well with the family. We could go downstairs at night or early in the morning and get things ready for business without worrying about daycare."

"It couldn't have been easy—bartending, kids, starting a business."

"I ran like an efficient machine. Never been so pumped about anything. I hardly needed sleep. Maybe that's how you get when you finally start living your dream."

Michael looked down at his shoes. "Did it make a difference with Becky?"

"You have no idea. We became a team, and as hard as it was to get it going, the deli is quite profitable now. The best thing is: I can say I saw that castle in the sky and moved in. Didn't turn my back on it. Owning a deli doesn't sound like much, but it was to me. Even if it failed, at least I tried."

Michael wished he had Sam's courage. He felt like a coward—afraid to take control of his own destiny.

"Anyway, Michael, I hope you and your wife work out whatever is wrong."

Michael smiled. "Thanks, Sam. Keep rooting for me."

"You bet. Where are you staying?"

"A Hilton, close to home."

"Isn't it expensive?"

"Now that I've used up my hotel points it is, but I can manage."

"We have a room next to our flat. Used to rent it out when things were tight. You're welcome to it. Just pay your own electric bill, and it's yours till you head home."

"That's nice of you, Sam."

"I mean it. It's small, but there's a fridge, stove, and a private bath. Very clean, too."

Michael considered it. Jamie needed time, and his monster came back in full force on Monday. He couldn't go home while it was still alive. "I might take you up on it, but I'll pay rent."

"Stop by tomorrow, and we'll talk. I'll make us both one of my famous roast beef sandwiches."

"Thanks."

Sam grabbed the cart handle and said, "Let's get these goodies inside."

Folding chairs covered with orchid linens held mounds of food. Sam had prepared a feast fit for the president. When the kids started coming into the strings room, their excited voices were the day's big payoff. Each and every one of them looked around as if they had been transported to a palace.

Michael scanned the faces. He soon spotted Joseph piling meat and cheese onto a sub roll at the buffet table.

"Hey, Joseph. Good eats, huh?"

Joseph seemed hypnotized by the cuisine. "This is awesome."

"Well, enjoy. Have you been practicing?"

Joseph looked at Michael with a wide grin. "Yup. Hey, I got an eighty-eight on that DBQ you helped me with."

"An eighty-eight? That's great. And I can't wait to hear you play."

Joseph beamed as he grabbed a bag of chips.

About thirty kids, a few volunteers, and Michael's gang soon filled the room. Luke stepped up to a microphone. He welcomed everyone, gushed about the project, and explained the strict rules for participation. He thanked Sam for providing the food and then introduced the people who made it possible. They included Rufus, Pete, Henry, and, of course, Michael. As the men stood together, everyone cheered. Rufus gripped Michael's shoulder. If only time could stop. If only he could live in this moment for the rest of his life.

Chapter Twenty-Six

Megan and Emily were on their way to school. That gave Jamie one hour of think time before she had to leave for the bank. Today she had to focus on counting money, not Michael, Warrenton, flowers, and the Halloween party she was planning. Yesterday her drawer was twenty dollars short, and her supervisor was getting annoyed. All daydreaming had to be reserved for after hours.

She lumbered upstairs to the bedroom to finish getting dressed. Her feet ached from standing in teller position all week, so she slipped on a comfortable pair of black Sketchers to match her gray tweed slacks. Jamie traipsed into the bathroom, applied light makeup, and glared at her reflection. "A bank teller?" she mused. Nothing wrong with it, but she wasn't used to being in one spot all day. She waitressed through college, hustled as a reporter, chased her daughters around as a mother, and gardened as a hobby. She never realized how motor driven she was, and her right-sided brain begged her to find a more creative job.

When Jamie was through primping, she plodded downstairs into the kitchen and stared at the refrigerator. She could really use a handful of peanut butter cups to quell her gloomy mood. The candy had been devoured by the garbage disposal, but cookies hid in the cupboard. She grabbed a bag of Oreos and checked the calorie count: fifty morsels of energy each. A few wouldn't hurt.

Yes, they will, the wise woman said.

"Shut up," Jamie said. "Five little cookies; then I'll stop." She put the craving busters on a plate, poured herself a cup of coffee, and trudged into the living room.

Jamie startled and almost dropped her snack. A strange woman sat at the computer, mesmerized by the screen. Orange candy wrappers covered the floor, and the intruder stuffed peanut butter cups into her mouth. The figure looked horrible with her unkempt hair, baggy red T-shirt, and faded plaid pajama pants. Jamie gasped. Her twin had come to pay a visit.

Jamie's throat tightened. "Go away. It's over."

Tears spilled from the figment's eyes.

"You poor thing," Jamie muttered.

Then, like a willowy ghost, the illusion dissolved.

Jamie placed her coffee and cookies on top of her half-finished puzzle. She crept over to the computer and stared at the blank monitor. Several weeks ago she lived in this imaginary world, and it would be so easy to return. Jamie pushed the chair tightly against the table. It was not going to happen.

"Don't come back," Jamie said.

She scowled at the cookies. Reaching her goal weight wasn't the biggest reason for sticking to her diet. Keeping a promise to herself was what mattered. So what if she didn't like her job and her marriage was in limbo. A sugar binge wouldn't fix anything. Next week she'd look for work with a florist. At least she'd be surrounded by flowers. Then again, the bank had opportunities for advancement and benefits. If she and Michael divorced, she'd need that. Even if they didn't, a position with growth potential was important. She nodded firmly. The bank provided her with a path to independence, and that's where she would stay.

Now for the business of her husband. He was taking her on a mystery trip this Saturday, and she had to mentally prepare. Jamie opened the doors to the patio. A brisk, warm wind swept across her face. Her freshly shampooed hair flew back, and her black peasant blouse rustled as she sat down in the lounge chair.

Closing her eyes, she made a conscious decision to let her feelings flow. She smiled softly. The butterflies inside fluttered. She was falling in love. What surprised her most was the object of her adoration was Michael.

Jamie often fantasized that someone would come along and take her away from her dismal life. In her dreams, she had finally left Michael, bought a house of her own, and had a meaningful job. Wherever she went, she imagined various men as the perfect partner—at a cafe while she sipped on a vanilla latte; when a single dad sat next to her at a PTA meeting; on the bike path, when a mysterious man joined her to rest on a bench. She had so much love to give, and these imaginary adventures helped release it. Now, it was all coming true, and she didn't even have to leave home. Jamie shook her head. Could Michael be changing? Could a villain turn into a hero?

All of his demeaning comments and uncalled-for tantrums sat on the many shelves in her mind. It was hard to pretend that they didn't exist. Living with him had been like walking around the rim of a volcano, never knowing when lava would spit out. She winced. Was a month enough to erase all those years of malice? And how could she be sure his old ways wouldn't creep back in? On the other hand, he had strong values, was a great provider, cared deeply for their children, and genuinely loved her.

Jamie closed her eyes and imagined that she lived on an island. Spiky plants grew wildly, and poisonous snakes slithered around. Although it was her home, she dreamed of escaping from the pricks and venomous bites. An ocean surrounded her. If she tried to swim away, she would drown.

One day, as she walked along the beach, a message flew into her hand. It said all of the evil had disappeared, and she was free to enjoy the pleasures of paradise without fear. An occasional storm might occur, but it wouldn't last long. Although intrigued, Jamie didn't know if she could trust this impromptu note. She strolled awhile and hoped for the best because she was still stranded. Then, to her surprise, she came upon a large, sturdy rowboat providing her with the means to flee. She looked at the promissory note, then the vessel, and finally at the beautiful landscape. Could the serpents and thistles really be gone? What a lovely place to live if they had truly been banished. Jamie turned toward the sea. Hurricanes brewed and sharks prowled in the dark water. Looking back and forth, she decided to walk away from the vessel, but would remember where it was. She sat in the sand and rubbed her palms on its grainy texture. The complex, mysterious island provided her with comfort and security. Now that the malice was gone, she could begin an exploration, but she still had the rowboat if she needed it.

Jamie opened her eyes. Her fingers brushed the fiber of the chair. Yes, she loved Michael, but thorns grew back and snakes hid under rocks. She went inside and stopped abruptly in the hallway. Michael lied to her the other night about his interaction with Frank. She could tell because his eyelids lowered ever so slightly whenever he tried to evade one of her inquiries. He had a blow up with his boss and didn't confess to it. She looked at the clock. Grabbing her lunch sack, she decided that was the sign that told her she needed more time. Michael wouldn't be pleased, but he'd have to understand. Honesty had to accompany him if he returned.

Chapter Twenty-Seven

Michael observed Jamie from the corner of his eye. She sat up straight as she viewed the scenery from the car's passenger window. Except for trying to guess where they were going and relaying how her father reacted to the news of their separation, she had been silent for most of the ride. Michael was relieved Norm didn't hate him. He even told Jamie he'd watch the kids anytime, so they could work out the rough patch common in all marriages. After providing a few clues about their outing, Michael was also quiet. With the clutter of home, children, and work left behind, they didn't have much to talk about. At least they weren't bickering or, worse yet, screaming at each other. Their healing journey was launched when he successfully comforted her a few weeks ago. He hoped it would continue, but a big pile of trash still divided them, and he wished a garbage truck would come along and take it to a junkyard in another galaxy.

Jamie's hands looked lonely resting on her lap, but he didn't have the nerve to take one into his. So much history lived in those hands. They had prepared wonderful meals, soothed his children, tousled his hair, tended a garden, threw objects at him, and caressed his body. He wanted to embrace her hand, run his thumb along its knuckles, feel the space between its fingers. It was right next to him, but it may as well have been back in DC. Jamie might welcome his touch. Then again, she might pull away. Predicting her reactions lately was like trying to guess what card the dealer held during a game of blackjack. He couldn't make himself place the twenty-dollar chip on the table, so he put Jamie in control.

Michael moved his head from side to side. "Man, my neck is sore. I must've slept funny."

Jamie snapped out of her trance.

Michael's heartbeat quickened when she reached over. She was going to massage his fabricated sore area like she used to a lifetime ago. Jamie stalled shortly before she reached his shoulder and faked a stretch. She glanced at him with hesitant eyes and picked up her pocketbook. "I've got some Tylenol."

"Thanks," Michael muttered. He frowned as he watched Jamie fumble through her purse, searching for medicine he did not need. This courting thing was not going to be easy.

As they drove into town, Jamie realized their destination.

"The ocean!" she exclaimed.

"Up for a beach walk?"

"This is perfect."

Ocean City seemed quiet on the mid-October morning. Only a few vehicles buzzed along the three-lane boulevard. The high-rise hotels had vacancy lights on, waterslide parks were closed, and the miniature golf establishments were empty.

Michael pulled into the parking lot of lodging that soared to the sky. Pungent salt air and the sound of crashing waves greeted them as they got out of the car. Michael grabbed their totes and strolled to the entrance, keeping time with the rhythm of the surf.

Jamie hit his arm. "You're taking me to a hotel?"

"Yeah," he said opening the door.

"We're separated."

"I heard ex-sex is phenomenal."

She hit his arm again.

"Seriously, I got us an oceanfront room. We can relax and talk. I don't want people listening to us in a restaurant. Then we'll take a walk, maybe get a bite to eat, and I'll drop you off at your father's later. We don't have to stay all night."

"You are so sly."

Michael was still holding the door open. "I said we don't have to spend the night. Do you want to come in?"

"Well, okay. After all, you are my husband. We've been in hotel rooms before."

A few guests milled around the lobby, as Jamie stopped to take in the vivid colors of sea creatures in a saltwater aquarium. Michael checked in then turned and studied his wife. Her peach fleece top complimented her gentle features. She could have passed for a college student in her khaki pants and sneakers, with her hair pulled loosely into a ponytail. She certainly didn't resemble a thirty-nine-year-old mother of two who had been overlooked and mistreated by an insensitive husband. Michael moved toward her with his bag draped on his shoulder and his hands in his pockets. He bit his lower lip, hesitated, then said, "You look so pretty."

Jamie blushed. "Thanks."

Michael lifted her daypack. "Let's get settled; then we'll take that walk."

Michael slipped the key card into the slot on the door, and a green light blinked, signaling them to enter a world of pristine splendor. He let Jamie pass by him and waited for her reaction. She walked through the foyer and into the living area of the suite. It was painted pale blue, and pictures of ocean scenes decorated the walls. The carpet, beige and plush, contributed to the calm ambience. A bottle of red wine, two glasses, and a gold box of chocolates adorned a bar that was angled in the corner with two welcoming stools. A round, glass dining table surrounded by four wicker chairs was placed at the far end of the romantic room. In its center stood a vase of yellow roses with a sprinkling of baby's breath. Jamie walked over and inhaled.

She turned to Michael, her light turquoise eyes sparkling. "Wow!" She sank into an oversized, paisley pastel couch. "You brought me to paradise."

"And the tour has just begun. Keep going," Michael said, happy that the airy atmosphere was breaking up their shared nervousness.

Jamie passed through the fully equipped galley kitchen. She scanned the white cabinets and tile floor, creatively designed with cream and topaz hues. The next stop was the bathroom. Michael watched her step in and grinned when he heard, "Wow!" again. His-and-hers vanities complete with lighted mirrors and cushioned benches spanned one wall. Red rose petals, votive candles, and vases holding various flowers added to the ambience. A Jacuzzi big enough for at least four people was the highlight. Although Michael was standing right in the doorway, Jamie yelled, "Come here."

Michael stopped himself from laughing out loud at her childlike excitement and gladly followed her command.

"Look at this," she bellowed. "I could live in this room. There's even a bottle holder."

"We just need champagne to go with it."

She slipped past him, and continued her tour. A king-sized bed with a lilac comforter at least two inches thick, was the main attraction of this large but simple room, which also held a light oak desk, two easy chairs, and an ivory cabinet, where the TV must have been hiding.

"The best part is right here," Michael said as he opened the French doors, revealing a balcony with a spectacular view of the ocean.

After standing still for a minute, Jamie turned to him. She looked as vibrant as the sun that was emitting its rays onto the wild glistening water.

"Come on," she said, stepping onto the deck. They both leaned over the railing and gazed at the beach, speckled with only a few people meandering around. The sparseness—so different from the crowded beach in summer—made it look like a place they had never visited before. They lost track of time, entertained by the music of crashing waves and chatty seagulls. The gentle wind caused wisps of Jamie's hair to escape from its confines and dance about, glazing Michael's ear.

Jamie inched toward him. Michael welcomed this invitation to warmth and wrapped his arm around her shoulder. She nestled in and gently rubbed his chest. Michael closed his eyes and rested his cheek on her head. His wife was finally in his embrace, and he never wanted to let her go. Jamie softened into his body, and he could tell she felt the same. They swayed for several minutes.

Eventually she broke the spell. "What made you think of this?"

"We needed to go someplace where we could really relax. Try and figure out our marriage."

"Let's keep it light for a while."

"Okay, but at some point…"

"I know. Right now I'm just enjoying no kids, no house-work, no job, no boredom. I feel fifteen years younger." She put her arms around Michael's waist and hugged him. "Let's pretend we just met."

"I'll order a plate of shrimp from room service, put it on your lap, say hello, and watch your knees jerk them onto the floor," Michael chuckled.

Jamie nudged him with her hip. "You surprised me. I couldn't believe anyone would come on to me the way I looked that night. A bulky sweater, corduroys, and damp hair aren't exactly man bait."

"You were the prettiest woman at that pretentious party. Like spotting a deer in a forest of wolves."

"Normally I would have dressed up a little. And I only went because Paula practically forced me. My plan was to go with her, so she didn't have to walk in by herself, nibble on the hors d'oeuvres, then go home and read. I felt like going to a party that night about as much as I did the dentist."

Michael gingerly pulled her ponytail. "Are you glad you went?"

"Yes. No matter what, yes. We had some great times. I just wish we took better care of us, our incredible love."

"What do you think we could have done differently?"
Jamie faced the ocean and leaned into Michael. "Ditched DC, moved here, bought a little hot dog stand. You could've

brought your guitar to the boardwalk and watched your case fill up with cash while you serenaded tourists by the sea."

"Can we still?" He laughed, as he rubbed Jamie's shoulder.

"Do you think we'd ever really take the plunge? Give it all up for an easier life?"

"No. I have a feeling the intrigue would fade when one of the kids got sick and the medical bill for a simple cure came in at over a thousand bucks. That's a lot of hot dog sales and dollar bills in my guitar case."

"Like my dad always said, 'Money can't make you happy, but it can sure make you miserable if you don't have enough.'"

"Yeah, I can recall some pretty tough conversations between my parents over bills and not enough food. I can even remember my mother yelling at me to stop running down the street because it would wear out the soles of my shoes. Money was so tight for them."

"Meg and Emily will never know what that's like. You get an A-plus for being an exceptional provider."

"Thanks," Michael said, pleased she recognized what he considered to be a valuable asset. "It's actually unbelievable, quite a change from how I grew up. I don't know how good it is for the girls to have everything handed to them though. They have joined the ranks of the entitled generation, and it bothers me."

"We'll have to work on that," Jamie said. "But I don't feel like drawing the blueprint for a solution right now."

"Agreed."

This was an opportunity to go to a deeper level of conversation, but his sentiments were stuck in his throat. Jamie always rejected him when the topic of love came up, but she seemed open right now. He inhaled, hoping it would calm him. The vision of Rufus finding his wife dead on the floor surfaced. She went instantly and without warning. He had to let Jamie know how strong his feelings were for her. Life was uncertain, and a multitude of tragedies happened every day. He then recalled Rufus's words, "She's your wife. Talk to the woman." Michael needed a minute more to summon up some courage.

"What if we could give it all up? Start our life over. What would you be?" he asked.

"A farmer."

"A farmer?"

Jamie nodded. "Surprised?"

"Yes. Are you serious?"

"Absolutely. I'd want acres of land to grow all kinds of vegetables, and fruit trees too. Maybe even wheat. I'd have a tractor, a reaper, and horses."

"Come to think of it, you would be a good farmer," Michael said. "Your thumb is so green it makes the Wicked Witch of the West look pale."

"Lots of experience too. My father taught me so much about gardening."

"When did you come up with the farmer idea?"

Jamie told him about her trip to Warrenton. "Amazing how much I discovered about me in twenty-four hours."

"Are you going to do anything about it?"

"You mean becoming a farmer?"

"Yeah."

"I'll quit my job, sell our house, move to Warrenton, buy the barn, work for Pam, and spend my Saturdays at the farmer's market. Sound a little far-fetched?"

"I guess it does."

"What about you? A rock-and-roll star, right?"

"Used to be."

Jamie's eyes widened. "It's not anymore?"

"Nope."

"What then?"

"A middle-school music teacher."

"Oh come on."

"I'm serious. I love teaching guitar at the club. The kids are awesome."

"You don't have the patience to teach kids."

"You're wrong. I don't have the patience to teach adults who are supposed to know what they're doing. Kids—especially twelve, thirteen years old—are different. They're so open. I'm really having a great time in that rundown school building on Wednesday nights."

"Are you going to do anything about it?"

"Sell everything we own, quit my megabucks job, get a teaching certificate, and try to find a job for fifty thousand dollars a year."

Jamie frowned. "I guess you'll never be a teacher, and I'll never be a farmer."

Michael closed his eyes for a long moment then turned to Jamie. He placed his hands on her waist. "I want to tell you how sorry I am for my behavior over the years. I have this ogre inside me that's so easily agitated, and you've taken the brunt of its outbursts. I'm starting to figure out ways to tame it. I can't believe what you've put up with."

Jamie clutched his arms and narrowed her eyes. "Is it enough, Michael? These changes you talk about."

Michael wanted to say yes, but couldn't. He'd be lying, so he tried to explain it instead. "These changes started when I met Rufus. He's taught me so much in such a short time.

And it all feels right. It's like I've been on the wrong path all my life. Rufus came along and said, 'Wrong way. Try the road around the corner.' I took his advice, and for the first time ever, I feel—I don't know—in sync with who I am."

Jamie released herself from Michael. She leaned on the railing and asked, "Back to the 'I'm sorry' thing. Apologizing is a big deal, so thank you. I'm actually starting to like you—a little." She paused. "What have you done that's worked the best?"

Michael folded his arms. "A combination of things. You know, giving up golf, deleting the dreary and unnecessary things. Having some fun. Even taking time to rest and do nothing. Music, exercise."

"But it's still there, right? That ogre?"

Michael nodded. "But I'm going to keep working on getting rid of it. I can't let it destroy us—our family." He cupped Jamie's face in his hands. "I love you. I have from the second I laid eyes on you. With all that we've been through, the love has always stayed."

Jamie didn't say a word. A few seconds passed. Her silence stung him. She smiled tentatively and stepped away from him. She looked toward the ocean then back at Michael. "That's nice of you to say."

Michael's voice cracked. "Well, it's true. What about you?"

Jamie folded her arms. "I still don't know what I feel. I'm certainly intrigued by your changes, but a month ago I wanted to poison you with a can of hornet spray. A month ago you barely spoke to me, except to complain. A month ago we were both on the verge of having flings."

"Wait a minute. You wanted to poison me?"

Jamie plopped into a cushioned chair, and Michael took a seat in the one next to her.

"We had a hornets' nest on the eave in the kitchen window. I killed the inhabitants with the push of a button, and I wished it would be that easy to get rid of you. Of course, I wouldn't have done anything that crazy, so stop looking so freaked. Really, I'd never risk going to jail for you, but the fantasy was a little fun." She then lifted her finger and said, "Psss," as she directed it toward Michael, while grinning mischievously.

"You are evil."

"You have no idea how bad I can be," she said.

"I guess I can't blame you for wanting to blast me away with insect killer, but things are different now."

"Are they Michael? If you moved back in tomorrow, would you leave your tantrums at the hotel for good, or would they be hiding in your suitcase ready to pounce out as soon as something agitated you?"

"I can't promise you that the new me would be like living with a Buddhist monk, but the things I'm doing really are helping."

Jamie looked up. "I need more time. You need more time."

Michael leaned in. "But do you still love me?"

Jamie took his willing hand while shaking her head. "I don't know. The years with you have been hard. I couldn't leave because of the girls and money, but it finally got so bad none of that mattered. I just wanted you gone. I can't do a one-eighty this quickly." She paused. "The first time I fell in love with you, I jumped in so quickly and never got to know who you really were. How can I explain this? I guess...meeting you was like getting on a jet to Hawaii—fast, fun, and full of exotic anticipation. Then the plane crashed and fell into a desert. I never made it to my dream. It's going to be hard to get back on that plane again."

She looked at him with kind eyes. "I do love the man you are becoming. I really do, but the next time I tell you I love you, I want it to come from my head as well as my heart. I want to make it to Hawaii."

Michael squeezed Jamie's hand then brought it to his mouth and kissed it. "You take all the time you need. The plane is not taking off without you. I'll just have to court you on board."

"That might be fun. What are you going to do to court me?"

"Surprises, surprises," Michael said, as he didn't have a clue.

Jamie gently whacked Michael's back. "Let's stop the serious discussion. I want to try out that whirlpool. What are you going to do?"

"I'll be dreaming of being naked in that tub with you."

"That might be interesting." Jamie giggled.

"For real?"

"Put your tongue back in your mouth. Not yet."

Michael watched Jamie go inside, grab her backpack, slide into the bathroom, and close the door. When she was gone, he stared at the ocean. He wished he had received a better response to his romantic confession, but at least she didn't ban him forever. He did ache for her, however, and wanted to move the falling in love process along. What could he do to get her head and heart in sync?

Michael walked back into the hotel room, picked up his BlackBerry, and punched in Jamie's number.

Jamie's cell phone rang as she prepared her bath. She rummaged through her backpack and found it.

"No, you can't come in."

"Excuse me. Is this Jamie Merrill?"

"That was my name before you married me, silly."

"I'm Michael Stolis. We met at that party on Friday. I happen to be in Ocean City. You mentioned that you were heading over there too."

"Are you stalking me?"

"Yes. Anyway, since we're both here, I wondered if you'd like to go for a walk on the beach; then I'd love to take you out to dinner later. Are you available?"

"I have a few things to do, but could meet you in the lobby of the Sand Piper Hotel in an hour." She gazed at the luxurious tub filling with hot water. "Make it an hour and a half."

"Great. I'll be waiting."

Jamie clicked the off button on her phone.

She smiled then looked in the mirror. She had work to do for her big date. A shampoo, blow-dry, a touch of makeup, and something sexy to wear. She dumped her duffel of clothes onto the floor and sorted through them. A lacy bra and panties fell out, but that was it. She tapped her chin. *Do I own any sexy clothes? Maybe in the back of my closet.* She just might pay a visit to her old friend, Victoria's Secret, when she got home.

Jamie started to unfasten her jeans. She ran her thumb along the roomy top. Giving up junk food and walking every day worked. Her waistline had shrunk. It was hard, but she had kept the promise she made to herself. She patted her flattening belly and shook her head at the endless war she, and so many women, had to fight between slim and chocolate. Sherry, from Michael's office, might have the right idea with plastic surgery. Maybe Jamie could call her to see where she bought that incredible body. A little trim and some suctioning was all she needed. She examined her rear and added *lift* to the list. When the house needed repair, it was done without question. The same rule should apply to the body. The wise woman inside laughed. "Okay," Jamie murmured. Healthy eating and exercise were also successful strategies, and didn't involve anesthesia and knives. She whispered, "Acceptance. Accept who you are." After all she had a date with a handsome lawyer who was smitten with her regardless of her hip fat.

She poured a capful of jasmine bubble bath into the tub and turned on the jets. When the soap erupted into mounds of white froth, she gathered a handful of red rose petals and sprinkled them on top. She shed her final garment and immersed herself in the fragrant spa. Jamie closed her eyes as the swirling warm water soothed her skin, and the vision of Michael telling her that he loved her appeared. She put her hand on her heart and felt its beat accelerate. This romantic instrument still genuinely loved that man, but her head had put an iron fence of protection around it. She wasn't sure if she'd ever develop the trust to break it open. Heaps of bubbles gathered around her cheeks, ears, and hair, calming her confusion. Soon all thinking was put on hold as she dissolved into another universe.

Michael smiled when he saw Jamie enter the lobby. She resembled a daisy, with her buttercup zip-up sweatshirt and vanilla corduroys. He really did enjoy looking at her, and it was going to be difficult to resist going to the next step of touch. He needed to remember they were playing a game of first date, and he had to behave.

"Shall we?" he asked. "The dolphins want us to come out and play."

"Are they close to shore?" Jamie asked.

"I saw them swim up the coast about a half hour ago." Michael could tell that she was nervous. *Time. She asked for time. Give her that gift.*

The couple walked out the atrium door, across the deck, and down the wooden steps that led to the beach. They kicked off their sandals, and Michael jogged close to the surf. He jutted toward and away from the white foam of the waves, teasing the ocean to try and catch him. Jamie joined the game and shouted above the crashing surf, "I bet you get wet first."

"I bet you're wrong," Michael said as he splashed water in her direction. Jamie coyly approached, taunting him to try again. He eventually succeeded, dampening her freshly dried hair. Jamie laughed and retaliated, spraying his windbreaker with droplets from the sea.

When water tag was over, Michael took Jamie's hand, and they walked along the shore with the sun on their backs and the breeze dusting their faces. The comfort of familiarity warmed him. He remembered how it felt when they frolicked on the beach before they were married, but it was richer now. Back then they danced on the sea's crest, but over the years they had discovered the treasures and horrors buried deep within its core. He gazed at the complex body of water. It was a vision of hope. The prescription for healing an ailing relationship had been written; the first few doses of medicine, swallowed. The energy swelling inside caused him to hold Jamie's hand a little tighter as they trekked through the sand.

Chapter Twenty-Eight

Lounging in an oversized recliner, skimming an article in *The Oprah Magazine* about the positive side of procrastination, café au lait by her side, and the background music of a roaring ocean—what Jamie would give to live in this refuge for a month. She set the magazine on her lap and peeked at Michael. He was stretched out on the bed, engrossed in his book. Relaxing was the perfect coda to their beach walk, which really was like a first date. It had been so long since she and Michael held hands, talked without interruption, laughed about nothing, and quietly reflected. Jamie grinned as he scanned his pages with his lower lip protruding. He looked so peaceful, and she was glad. He needed this respite.

Jamie did wish, he would show a little more interest in her as a woman. They were nestled in romance, but Michael was perfectly content to read away the afternoon. She glanced at her sweatshirt zipper. Maybe she should pull it down a bit. Her outer layer was sporty, but her undergarments were trimmed with black lace. She should have been more encouraging when he declared his love for her. Made it clear that sex didn't have to mean reconciliation. At some point Jamie would tell him about Pam's diet rule: five minutes of indulgence out of twenty-four hours was okay. Maybe they could have a sex rule: one hour out of seven days.

Michael put his book on the nightstand. "Are you getting hungry?"

"Starving."

"What do you think about spending the night?"

Jamie licked a drop of whipped cream from the café au lait. *Finally.*

"Don't worry. I'll sleep on the couch."

He could do that knowing she'd be naked in bed? Maybe he needed a clue. "I don't have pajamas with me."

"Just wear a T-shirt."

She frowned. Their marriage really was in bad shape.

"I'm so relaxed and don't feel like driving back to your dad's. Plus I thought..."

Jamie perked up. *Here we go!*

"We could have drinks with dinner—talk a little more without the kids around."

Talk a little more?

"You're so quiet. What do you think?"

Jamie sprang up. "I'll call Dad. Let's walk to that blues bar down the street. Get stinkin' drunk."

Michael clapped his hands together. "I'm in."

She walked over to the bed, took his hand, and tried to pull him up. "Come on."

He grabbed her around the waist and flung her on the bed.

314

"Whoa!" She hadn't expected to be manhandled like that.

"On second thought, let's call room service."

Her breath caught in her throat.

"I just want to hold you for a while. Touch you. You can still have your time."

"Deal," Jamie whispered.

Michael wrapped her up with his arms and legs. His sandalwood scent and heavy breathing engulfed her. He slipped his hand under her sweatshirt and kneaded the small of her back.

"Ohhh."

"Remember when I discovered this spot," Michael said.

"Shhh. My mind's taking a nap."

His hand roamed to her chest. He pressed. "But your heart's still awake."

"Oh God."

Jamie cradled his face and pulled it close to hers. She gazed into his mocha eyes, so deep and loving. Her mouth found his, and she lightly stroked it. Michael ran his tongue gently over her bottom lip. Then soft kisses. Her skin ignited. His hands meandered around her waist, hips, and stomach. Except for her pounding heart, she lay motionless, allowing Michael to travel in any direction he chose. His tongue entered her mouth, and he kissed her passionately as if he wanted to swallow her. Jamie released her hesitant mind and welcomed this luscious gift. Michael nuzzled his face in the nape of her neck. He rolled on top her and pushed his hips into hers. His groans, his desire, captivated her.

Jamie massaged his shoulders as she held him tightly. Her insides hollowed, making room for the love that had eluded her for so many years. She wanted to feel his skin, every inch of it, so she reached beneath his shirt and rubbed his back—up and down, over and over.

Michael moaned, "I love you, baby." They undressed each other, stopping now and then to touch, stare, and kiss. Soon they were naked, exposed. He caressed her, held her, made love to her. He released his soul, and she gave all of her love, all of herself. He gasped. She dug her nails into him and bit his neck. He sighed. Then the calm. The deep breathing, the sultry skin, the racing hearts. They slipped under the blankets. He spooned her and kissed her hair. "I love you," he whispered. She still couldn't say it, but he had to know. How could he not? They closed their eyes.

Twilight transformed into dawn as the crest of the sun appeared on the ocean's horizon. The sky radiated with violet, red, pink, peach, and yellow, painting a portrait only nature could create. Long rays of white soon formed a path along the dark water—a carpet of enlightenment. A new day had arrived. Michael leaned on the deck railing, mesmerized by the animated canvas. Just like the light he saw last night, it represented a beginning.

His meditation was interrupted by Jamie's voice. "Beautiful."

He turned to face her. She sat curled up on the lounge chair, wearing a plush hotel robe, hair tousled and cheeks flushed. Jamie stood and squeezed his forearm. "It looks like Hawaii. At least the Hawaii in my puzzle."

"I wish we could stay forever."

Jamie leaned her head on his shoulder. "But we can't."

Michael's throat tightened.

Jamie let out a long sigh. "Should we make a plan? Probably a good time to figure out the next step for us."

They adjusted the deck chairs side by side then sat down, legs touching.

Jamie smiled. "This was the best first date ever. I never thought we would make love like that again in our lives."

"I know. When I pulled you onto the bed, I figured you'd pounce up and start lecturing me about time and trust."

"So I surprised you?"

"Yes, and I don't want it to end."

Jamie lowered her eyes. "It has to."

Those words were like a boulder being hurled into his chest. "So we'll eat breakfast, pick up the kids, and return to our shitty lives."

"Michael," she said deliberately.

"How would you describe our existence? We hate our jobs, we love each other, but can't live together. We've found our dreams, but can't pursue them. It's moments like this that make the phrase *life sucks* so popular."

Jamie looked at him like she was scolding Megan or Emily. "Don't be so negative. We have so much to be thankful for."

But he wasn't a child and wasn't going to take her silly advice. "Save it for your gratitude journal." Michael stormed into the bedroom and started packing his duffel.

Jamie followed him. "What are you doing?"

"I have to get out of here. I can't stand the feeling of hope."

"Stop it," Jamie said firmly.

She had gone from elated to dismal in a matter of minutes, but he didn't care. He was tired of her waffling and just wanted to escape.

"We're supposed to be making a plan."

"You want my plan. Well, here it is." Michael's voice rose, but he didn't care. "Sam, the guy who owns that deli, has a room I can stay in for a while. So I'm going to drop you off at your dad's, go to my new home, and decorate a little."

Jamie pointed to a chair. "Sit down."

"Why should I?"

"Because I said so."

"Go to hell."

"Do you really mean that?" she said sharply. "Do you want to work on our marriage or leave it right here? For some strange reason, I want to work on it, but I need a partner, so sit down." Then, as quietly as a fairy, she said, "I understand your frustration."

He sunk into the chair. "You said it has to end."

Jamie sat on the edge of the bed. "Last week Emily wanted to get out the Play-Doh, and I said, 'No. It's too messy.' Then I remembered you weren't coming home, so I changed my mind. We had a ball. Little pieces of red, blue, green, and yellow all over the kitchen. Every few minutes, I'd tense up because I envisioned you walking in and ripping our heads off with your mouth, like you do when anything is out of order, a little chaotic."

Michael didn't want to hear this so turned away.

"I can breathe in my own house now, and I want it to continue. Yesterday you said the ogre was still inside you. I don't want to live with him again." She stopped for a few seconds just to inhale. "And I know you lied the other day about some outburst you must've had at work. For the sake of peace, I still don't want to hear the details, but you have to find a way to poison your monster, Michael."

318

Jamie was right. He couldn't stand living with himself either. At least she could run away. He looked straight at her. "The only time the ogre left was during that dream I told you about in the forest. And he wasn't around last night. That's for sure. He shrinks when I run, play guitar, and when I'm at the club. And thanks for ignoring my work incident. I'd like to do the same."

"Oh, Michael. I do love you, but I can't live with a time bomb. Have you seen that counselor yet?"

"You love me?"

"I can't help it. I don't want to lose you to that ogre. He's more threatening than Rachel and Sherry combined."

"My appointment is this Thursday. I'm going to take it so seriously this time. Do everything he says. Maybe even take meds."

"You've always been so opposed to meds."

"If I had cancer, I'd do whatever it took to get rid of it. Maybe I need a pill to kill that damn monster."

Jamie pointed at him. "You start counseling. We'll see how it goes." She leaned forward. "But I don't want you living in a room above a deli."

"No choice, and it'll only be for a little while. I'm going to beat this disease. Then we'll start over."

Jamie held out her arms.

Michael collapsed into her. She stroked his head and back. After she softly kissed his ear, they lay on the bed. He cradled her around the waist. Except for gentle breathing, they remained still until it was time to check out.

Chapter Twenty-Nine

Moving involved one stop at home and one stop at the hotel. Then to the room: a twelve-by-fourteen-foot box. It took Michael less than an hour to unpack. He brought clothes, toiletries, his computer, printer, and three essentials—a framed picture of his family, his guitar, and his lucky quarter. Tomorrow he'd go grocery shopping for orange juice, power bars, and fruit, maybe some potato chips for moments like this.

After rummaging through the cabinets, he sat on the forest green couch and stared at a nineteen-inch TV. It had to be an antique, with its dials and bulging back. Sam had revealed that he was a master handyman and didn't purchase anything new before the old had died a certain death. That included the old-fashioned icebox, gas stove with the black iron burners, and the cot in the corner. Although outdated, the apartment looked as though a maid had just polished every inch of it. A wide window offered a view of the street.

He glanced at his watch then looked toward the ceiling. Last night he was holding Jamie in bed. At this very moment, she was probably reading a story to Emily and Megan. She had to miss him. Her body couldn't fake the strong emotion it released when they made love. Michael took his BlackBerry out of his pocket. He punched a few numbers then stopped. She asked for time, and he promised to give it to her.

He fired up his laptop and opened his work e-mail. Four messages from Frank shot out at him. He clicked on the first one. "You got lucky on Wednesday. Greg did a good job. Hopefully your vacations are over." Michael shook his head. *One day off was considered a vacation?* "Stop by my office tomorrow at 10:00 to discuss the Bradley case."

"Screw you."

Frank annoyed him more every day, but he had to be fair. Michael was the one who was changing. His boss had started the firm in his late twenties and turned it into a lucrative mega-corporation. He had high expectations, and up until a few weeks ago, Michael delivered. When Frank said twirl, Michael spun like a blue-ribbon show poodle. Now he didn't want to listen to his trainer anymore. *Get over it,* he thought. *You can't change the script in the middle of the performance.* Michael opened the Bradley file. Just as he was about to begin reading, his BlackBerry beeped.

"Hey, Michael."

"Luke."

"Just wanted to thank you again for your involvement in the music program, update you on a couple of things."

"Like I said before, everything fell into place. What's going on?"

"Researching grants, developing an iron-clad volunteer list, if there is such a thing. I have a meeting with the board tomorrow. Going to request additional funds and a salary increase for the program director position."

Michael straightened up. "What kind of increase?"

"Ten thousand a year. That'd bring the annual up to sixty thousand dollars, plus benefits. Any interest?"

Michael slouched. "Yes, but it's not enough."

"That's what I figured. Thought I'd give it a try. Wish we had enough cash to lure you in, but can I count on you to continue with guitar lessons?"

"Sure. Thanks for thinking of me. Anything else I can do? I mean besides lessons."

"If you feel like researching some grants, go for it, but don't feel obligated. The program development position has been vacant for over a month, and we really could use some help. I decided to give drum lessons on Wednesdays, so we can touch base then."

"Great."

Michael clicked off his phone and threw his head back. His dream job had just appeared, and he turned it down. He tapped his fingers on the coffee table. Someone would be hired soon, and whoever it was would mess up his program.

Michael stared at the wall for a while then returned his attention to the Bradley file, but couldn't focus. The print was small and hard to read. He switched it to fourteen-point Courier font. He read the same paragraph three times, but nothing sank in. This lack of motivation was really becoming a problem. Maybe a diversion would help.

He wondered what kind of grants were available so Googled "Inner City Music Funding." Hundreds of sites popped up. The BMI Foundation had a "request for a proposal" that sounded perfect. So did Disney. He tightened his lips. There had to be way to break free from a life when the real deal came along.

Michael nodded off around midnight but didn't sleep long. Jamie, his job, the grants, this room, taking medication—all made too much noise in his head. It was like trying to nap in Grand Central Station. He checked the wall clock—4:00. At least he made some headway with the Bradley case. He jotted one more note on a yellow pad of paper and had to admit it was a damn good strategy.

Now for a steamy shower. He stepped into the stall. Hot pellets of water beat down on his face, chest, and back. The scent of sage shampoo eased his congested mind, so he stayed a few minutes longer. He wrapped a towel around his waist and ambled back into the room to get dressed. The lumpy mattress on his cot greeted him. Buying a new bed would go on his list of questions for Sam.

Michael sat on one of two chairs at the Formica table. It was a few minutes before five, and he was set to go. He should be out running, but just didn't feel like it. Rufus always woke up early and went to the market behind his apartment building for breakfast. Today he'd have company. Michael grabbed his briefcase, lumbered down three flights of stairs, and got into his car.

"That's strange," Michael said to the grocer.

"Sure is," the middle-aged woman said. "Rufus comes in every day—five o'clock sharp. Sits at his table in the back, reads the *Post* page by page, drinks two cups of coffee, and orders an egg, bacon, and cheese on a toasted bagel."

"Probably just a little late. It's only five fifteen."

She took off her glasses. "Rufus is never late. And he lets me know if he's going to visit his sister in Philly. Do me a favor. Run around to his apartment building. It's on the other side of the alley. Make sure he's okay."

"Sure. What's your phone number?" Michael jotted it down on a piece of scrap paper.

"Bring him back, and breakfast is on the house."

Michael ran toward the narrow alley. Every cell in his body told him something had happened to Rufus. What if he didn't answer his door? Michael would call Luke, who had to have a key to Rufus's apartment. Luke was most likely still in Virginia. He'd try a neighbor. If worse came to worse, he'd break in.

Michael felt like he was entering a chimney as he darted into the dark, dingy alley that smelled like cigarette smoke and day-old beer. His heart flooded with dread as he scanned the space. Then he spotted a person sprawled out on the ground. Michael leaped toward the body.

"Rufus," he whispered. His friend lay unconscious, his shirt stained with blood.

"Rufus!" he shouted.

No response. Michael thought he might vomit but ignored the nausea. He had to act fast and react later. Michael called 9-1-1. He touched Rufus's lower neck and felt a faint pulse.

"An ambulance is on the way," the dispatcher said.

"Should I start CPR?" He turned on his speakerphone and put it on the ground.

"He has a pulse?"

Michael nodded. "I mean, yes, hardly there."

"He's breathing?"

"Shallow."

"Find his pulse on his wrist."

"Got it."

"If you lose it, start pumping."

"It's gone."

"Begin CPR."

The operator spouted instructions, but Michael didn't need them.

"Thirty compressions, two seconds apart, two breaths of air."

Michael pumped and pumped. He shouted, "Rufus... Rufus...Rufus..."

This gentle man's face was covered with cuts and bruises. His mouth hung open, lifeless. Sweat dripped from Michael's pores. He kept shouting, pumping. Michael had to save Rufus. Finally, the sirens were in earshot. *Thank God.* Michael tilted Rufus's neck, breathed air into him, then pumped again. An EMS crew arrived before he reached thirty.

Michael jumped up. A woman took Rufus's pulse, and a man placed an oxygen mask over his face. Two police officers rushed in, followed by paramedics pushing a gurney. They carefully, but swiftly, lifted Rufus onto it and carried him off.

"Are you related to the victim?" an attendant asked.

"A friend."

"We're bringing him to George Washington University Hospital."

"Will he be okay?" Michael asked through his constricted throat.

A tall police officer interrupted. "Did you find the victim?"

Michael nodded, his breathing labored.

"Did you witness the assault?"

"No."

"Anyone close by when you arrived?"

"No." Michael felt hot all over. "Just smelled cigarette smoke—beer."

"Do you know his name? Who we should contact?"

"Rufus Williams." Michael picked up his BlackBerry. "I have his nephew's phone number."

"Sir, you need to come down to the station to make a statement. The investigators will be here soon."

"Sure." He pointed down the alley. "My car is parked on the street." He took a deep breath. "I was going to meet Rufus for breakfast, and he didn't show, and I went to look for him, and this." Michael's knees quivered. Suddenly everything looked blurry.

Michael felt dizzy, so dizzy.

"Huh?" Michael murmured when he opened his eyes. He was lying on a cot, a young man with a blue shirt was taking his pulse, and a siren filled his ears.

"What happened?" Michael whispered.

The attendant half smiled. "You fainted, Sir. We're bringing you to the hospital."

Michael tried to sit up.

"Lie back."

"Rufus?"

"Your friend is at GW. Have you ever fainted before?"

"No."

"Have you been drinking water?"

"Yes."

"When was the last time you ate?"

"Yesterday." Michael fiddled with his tie, which had been loosened, and realized he had skipped dinner the previous day. "Around two. I'm feeling better now. How's Rufus?"

"A doctor at the hospital will examine you, and I'll have someone find out about Rufus. Just rest, Sir."

The doctor told Michael that his fainting was most likely caused by stress on top of an empty stomach. He had to stay in the emergency room stall until a nurse brought him orange juice and a bagel with cream cheese. Even though he finished his meal like a good patient, he still wasn't free to go. Someone had to come and get him, and that someone was Jamie. Michael sat on the hospital bed with his fingers interlaced and tried to think of who he'd call if he didn't have Jamie. Maybe a work associate, but most of them didn't like him. He lowered his eyes. Things really did have to change.

A nurse walked into the treatment room. "Your wife is here. I need to check your vitals one more time; then I'll bring her in for instructions."

"How's Rufus?"

"He's in surgery. That means he's alive and in excellent hands," she said with a reassuring smile. "You're a real hero. Temperature, ninety-eight-four; pulse rate, seventy; blood pressure's a little high, but normal for the situation. I'll go get your wife."

Jamie walked in and squeezed Michael's hand. "Are you okay?"

He nodded, and the nurse said, "Good to go. A police officer is waiting to ask you questions. I'll have an attendant bring you to the security office."

Michael signed the release papers, and they walked down the corridor. He barely noticed the shuffling shoes, machines rolling, and sterile smell. Michael had to find out about Rufus. The vague reports were driving him crazy.

"What happened?" Jamie asked.

"I'll tell you all about it after I talk to the police."

"What were you doing walking around DC at five in the morning?"

Michael raked his hair back with his fingers. "I'll tell you everything. Just be patient, and thanks for coming."

"I don't like any of this, and of course I'd come."

"The officer is right in here," the attendant said, nodding at a closed door.

Jamie and Michael walked into a vestibule that smelled like burnt coffee. A stocky policeman with a Charlie Chaplin mustache emerged from a room down a short hallway. He pointed to an orange plastic couch and looked at Jamie. "You can have a seat while I ask your husband a few questions."

Jamie peered at the couch. "I forgot my lipstick in the car. Be right back."

Michael smiled at her then mouthed, "Lipstick?"

She barely shrugged, and he thought she just might laugh.

"Let me get this straight," the officer said from behind a pressboard desk in a windowless office the size of a big closet. The serious man reiterated each detail. "Anything else at all?"

Michael shook his head. His eyelids felt heavy, and his head was starting to ache. He shifted his hips in the folding chair and took off his suit jacket. "Can you check on Rufus's condition?"

The officer's cell beeped. He said, "Uh-huh" and "Got it" several times then turned to Michael. "The investigators figure the assault took place approximately ten o'clock last night."

Michael perked up. "What happened?"

"Hard to say. Most likely started as a robbery. Rufus went to Jan's Market often?"

"Yes."

"Went out to get a bite to eat and met up with some thugs. Not unusual in DC, or any big city. The medical examination indicates resistance wounds. Rufus fought back."

Michael's jaw tensed. "Do you think you'll find who did it?"

"We'll do our best. The night streets are full of hoodlums. Check the crime report on the Net some time." The officer tossed his pen on the desk. "I have enough for now. Thank you, Mr. Stolis. And good job with the rescue." He stood and offered Michael his hand.

Michael popped up and shook it. "Where can I find out about Rufus?"

"Go to the sixth floor waiting area. Your friend's nephew is there. I'm sure he has all of the details."

Jamie was standing with arms folded when he walked into the vestibule. "Let's get you home," she said.

"I'm not leaving until I find out how Rufus is. Do you have any painkillers?"

She furrowed her eyebrows. "What's wrong?"

"I have a little headache."

Jamie searched through her pocketbook as they walked out. "Should we find a nurse? I don't want you to faint again."

"I'm fine. Sitting in that sweatbox of an office brought it on."

Jamie handed him two Advils. "The nurse said you should rest. Are you sure you're okay?"

He swallowed the pills dry. "Just shaken up. It's Rufus who's in real trouble." He gave Jamie a synopsis of what happened.

"It's awful," Jamie said, fingering the cuff of his shirtsleeve as they waited for the elevator.

After Michael pushed the six button on the empty elevator, Jamie hugged him hard. "I freaked when the hospital called."

Michael caved into her embrace. "Thank God for you."

They let go of each other when a ding informed them they had reached their destination.

"What time is it? What about your job—the kids? I have to call Cathleen," Michael said, as they turned the corner and headed down the hall, bustling with doctors and nurses.

"It's nine thirty. I dropped the girls off at Matilda's. She brought them to school. I took the day off, and I called Cathleen."

"Was she upset when you told her I wouldn't be in?"

"Of course not. She was concerned and said she'd let Frank know."

"I'll call her later. That woman from the market, too."

"What woman?"

"The lady who told me to go look for Rufus. I don't know if anyone told her what happened."

A few people were scattered in the large waiting room with chairs, couches, and tables. A plasma TV murmured, but no one listened. Luke stood, gazing out a window.

Michael and Jamie ambled over.

Luke turned to Michael. "Uncle Rufus," he choked.

Michael's chin dropped. "He didn't..."

Luke wiped the wet streaks off his cheeks with his palms. "Made it through surgery."

Luke grasped Michael's shoulders. "You saved my uncle's life."

Jamie sniffled. Michael touched her back and introduced them. She clasped Luke's hands. "I'm so sorry."

"What did the doctor say?" Michael asked.

331

"Rufus was beat up bad, lots of cuts and bruises, a few broken ribs. Stabbed in the stomach. Fortunately the blade missed arteries, so he didn't bleed to death. You found him in the nick of time and did all the right stuff."

"Good thing I decided to meet him for breakfast today. I hope I didn't break his ribs with the CPR."

"You had no choice. He was about to die. Besides, the doctor said there's extensive bruising on his sides. Most likely struck with a bat."

Michael pressed on his stomach. "It makes me sick."

"Come on," Jamie said. "Let's sit down." She escorted the men to a section in the corner with three blue club chairs surrounding a coffee table. "You two rest. I'm going to get you a water bottle and an energy bar from the cafeteria, Michael. Luke, what can I get you?"

"Coffee would be wonderful."

"Do you want help?" Michael asked.

"Just rest."

Luke glanced at his watch. "I have about an hour before my parents get here. My mom's a wreck."

"I bet, but Rufus is going to make it, right?"

Luke shrugged. "He's in stable condition. My guess is yes, with a painful recovery."

"He was a mess when I found him."

"I haven't seen him yet. Not looking forward to it. But Ruf's a fighter. If the White House awarded Purple Hearts for people who fought the war in the streets, he'd have one."

Michael furrowed his eyebrows. "What do you mean?"

"My uncle is an easygoing, self-assured man, but took a rough route to get there. He grew up poor and black in the fifties. That squelched a lot of his dreams. He attended schools

332

that were more about controlling behavior than learning. No one ever took the time to notice his brilliance."

Michael nodded.

"Did he ever tell you about his brother?"

"I didn't know he had one."

"Shot and killed at the age of ten. Right in front of his house, broad daylight. Rufus watched from the window. He was only eight years old."

Michael flinched.

"Luke, my namesake, was playing outside after school, and a bullet found him—a fifteen-year-old assailant. Rufus shrieked. My grandmother was working, but my great-grandfather and my mother came running. You can just imagine the rest."

A bitter taste filled Michael's mouth. "I can't believe he witnessed that."

Luke's neck muscles tightened. "It's the horror story of my family. My mother got out of the city as soon as she could, hated living in an urban war zone. Moved to a peaceful suburb of Philadelphia with my dad. But Rufus stayed to fight the battle."

"Is that what he's doing?"

"It's exactly what he's doing, in a quiet, positive way. He's a youth leader at his church, puts in tons of hours at the club, and recruits people like you and me."

Michael shifted his gaze down then looked directly at Luke. "Is that what he did?"

"Don't worry. You weren't manipulated into your obvious passion for the music program. You were just introduced to a building and some kids by my uncle. You took it from there. He did the same thing to me, despite my mother's strong objection. The kind of devotion we have comes from the soul, not suggestion."

Michael paused. "How did he know?"

"That man has an astute eye for people and situations. I don't think he realizes how extraordinary his senses are."

"I know," Michael said, as he scratched the back of his neck. "Do you think it's helped—all the work he's done?"

"I'm certain of it, and so is the research."

"What does it say?"

Luke leaned forward. "Juvenile violence peaks between the hours of three and six. If we, as a society, provide positive, stimulating alternatives to gangs, drugs, and mischief, hostility will decrease."

"Has it been proven?"

"Yes. Youth involved with quality after school programs get higher standardized test scores, have better work habits, and not as many behavior problems. But we have a long way to go. We need more adult mentors—like you."

Michael picked up a magazine from the coffee table and rolled it up. "Still a lot of chaos out there, huh?"

"More gangs in the cities of America than horses in Kentucky."

"Why the cities?" Michael asked.

"That's where the poverty is. Parents of kids in the suburbs are able to afford activities like hockey, music lessons, gymnastics—the works. Children who grow up poor don't have those options. They often turn to gangs both as protection and a place to find acceptance and understanding— a place to belong. You are providing that with the music program."

Michael said softly, "I like it too."

"Glad to hear it." Luke sat back. "And my uncle's not just good at reading people. When he recovers, have him give you some tips on the stock market."

Michael tossed the magazine back on the table. "He's good with stocks?"

"A genius. Made a mint."

"You're kidding? He lives so modestly."

"Just his choice. Thinks most stuff sold in stores is a bunch of junk."

Michael chuckled. "Sounds like Rufus."

"He donates most of his profits to the church and the club."

Michael said tenderly, "He's one in a million."

Jamie walked in with a tray of coffee, water bottles, bananas, and a few granola bars. After about thirty minutes, Luke checked his watch. "Look, my parents and wife will be here soon. My mother will be hysterical. I don't want you to have to witness that after all you've been through today. Would you like a quiet moment with Rufus before they get here?"

"Can I?"

"Let me check."

Luke returned after a few minutes. "The doctor said you can see him."

Michael walked into the room and crept toward the bed. He bit his lower lip. Rufus was covered with white gauze and blankets. His face was swollen and bruised. He resembled a prizefighter who lost after twenty rounds. Michael turned away but forced himself to look back at his battered friend. He needed to share his pain. If it were possible, he'd trade places with Rufus.

Tubes connected to machines ran from Rufus's nose, hand, and heart. Machines designed to sustain a life after a person tried to take it. Michael stared blankly at this man that he... well, loved. He rubbed his stomach as if that would stop the curdling. In fact, the longer Michael gazed at Rufus, the sicker he felt. The noisy breathing, the beeping of the heart monitor, the silence of this spirited man shouted at him to do something, but he was helpless. Nothing could be done. Michael hesitated. Or could he do something? Maybe Rufus was talking to him right now. If his mentor could speak, what would he say? Michael looked at his friend's closed eyes then lowered his head. There really was a war going on in his home city, in his home country, and he never paid attention until now.

When Michael looked up, he managed, "You have to hang on. We've got that music studio to build, like the one in Minnesota. Your life is so not over." He paused. "And neither is mine."

Michael was silent for a moment then cleared his throat. "Just so you know: you're my best friend, my only friend." He nodded. "I need you."

Michael reached to touch Rufus's hand, but didn't want to hurt him, so stopped within an inch of it. The beeping of the heart monitor seemed louder. He closed his eyes. *Beep... beep...beep*. It grew and grew until it blasted in Michael's ears. When he opened his eyes, the green lines and dots on the screen were the first thing he saw. The heart was all that mattered. Michael put one hand over his, and the pulse radiated into his fingers. He knew what he had to do.

He wandered to the window near Rufus's bed and stared at the night sky. It was clear, and stars illuminated the darkness. He made a wish on all of them that his friend would recover then stood silently. Before departing, he said, "Please be okay, Rufus." He put his hands in his pockets and left the room.

Jamie waited outside the door. "How is he?"

"Beat up."

She closed her eyes for a few seconds. "His family's here."

"I'll call Luke later."

They walked by the waiting room and heard the cries of grief. It had to be Rufus's sister. Now, she had to deal with another brother victimized in the combat occurring right in the center of the nation's capital. Jamie sighed as they waited for the elevator.

Michael examined the row houses as he and Jamie walked toward his car in the Adams Morgan neighborhood. Rufus's attacker could be inside one of them, eating a sandwich or playing a video game. Two young men passed by. Maybe they did it. Michael had checked the DC crime map on his BlackBerry earlier in the day. Last week alone over three hundred assaults, thefts, robberies, and shootings had been reported. He shivered. His hometown was not safe.

"You should come home tonight," Jamie said, when they got to his car.

"I can't."

"Why not?"

He looked down. "It'll hurt too much to go back to the room tomorrow."

Jamie frowned.

"I've been hotel hopping for over a month. I need to settle in someplace."

"Start in a few days. The nightmares after a trauma can be horrible."

"I can handle a nightmare."

Jamie's voice cracked. "I can't."

Michael studied her troubled face. "Today brought back your mother, didn't it? You know, finding her."

Jamie squeezed her eyes shut and nodded.

Michael rubbed her shoulder. "It still haunts you."

She folded her arms. "It seems like yesterday."

"Oh, Babe. Do you think about it often?"

"Yes. Flashes of her on the couch with blood everywhere."

Jamie tugged at Michael's suit lapel, and he pulled her close. "What you've been through. You haven't had it easy, ever."

"You either." She stroked his neck. "Your father demanding so much, and slapping you. Now working in a place you don't belong."

"I guess it's life. We all have something. I wonder how often Rufus sees flashes of his brother being shot."

"Stay tonight, not as my husband, but as my friend."

Michael kissed her forehead. "Hop in, and I'll drive you to the van."

"I can walk. It's only up the block."

"A block can be a life away. I don't trust the world right now."

Jamie approached the passenger door. "Do you think I'm weak, needing you to stay tonight?"

"Just the opposite. I needed you too but wasn't strong enough to admit it."

Chapter Thirty

The phone on Michael's desk had been silent all morning. He willed it to ring as he fiddled with the cord. Luke didn't call last night to let him know how Rufus was doing. The hospital reported stable condition, but Michael needed more. He picked up the receiver then put it back down. It was only eight thirty. Maybe Luke was sleeping after what had to have been a long night with his family.

Michael turned to his computer and opened the Bradley file. The issues involved the same ones he'd read hundreds of times: employees complaining that employers were unfair, and employers protesting that employees expected too much. He added a few notes to his yellow pad of paper then clicked on his personal financial folder. Not bad, he thought.

The phone rang.

"How is he?"

"He's going to make it," Luke said.

"Thank God."

"The broken ribs are his biggest problem. I guess complications include possible lung puncture from the fractures and pneumonia from fluid buildup. They have him on a ventilator to monitor lung function. It's quite painful too, but he's getting morphine through his IV."

"What about the stab wound?"

"All stitched up."

"How's your mom?"

"Okay. She's comparing the assault to her other brother's shooting. That woman has a passionate hate for city streets. She wants to meet you. Say thank you. Rufus wants to see you too."

"He's conscious?"

"Yup. The medication is making him drowsy, so he's in and out of sleep."

"I'm so relieved."

"Thanks to you, he's alive."

"And an exceptional medical team," Michael said.

"Can you stop by the hospital later?"

"As soon as I'm through with work."

"I'll tell him to expect you. Around six?"

"Or earlier."

"Thanks again, Michael."

"And one more thing…"

Frank sat at the head of the conference table. "How's your friend?"

Michael tried to stop the tapping of his foot, but his nerves wouldn't let him. "He's going to make it."

"Glad to hear it. Cathleen said you saved his life."

"I guess I did. Just in time."

"Ready for work?"

Michael cleared his throat and folded his hands on the table. "First, I need to apologize for slacking off lately. I've had a lot going on."

"You aren't yourself lately—at all. What's up?"

"I've been unfair to you and the firm. It needs to end."

"I'm glad to hear you say that. The past few..."

Michael held up his hand. "I agree with everything you're about to say. I've lost my edge. I'm leaving early way too often. I'm paid far too much to be acting so irresponsibly."

"You're right. What are you going to do about it?"

Michael's hands felt clammy, and his heartbeat accelerated. In spite of his nervousness, he looked directly at Frank. "I had my glory days with this firm, and I appreciate all you've done for me, but it's over. I've tried, but I can't muster up the energy I need to do this job any longer. I'm resigning."

Frank sprang up from his chair. "What?"

Michael reached into his suit jacket pocket and pulled out a white envelope. "Here's my letter of resignation—one month's notice. When I leave, everything will be in order."

Frank tossed the envelope on the table. His face puckered into the mug of a pissed off eel. "You're spawning your own firm, aren't you?"

Michael shifted in his seat. "The firm's wallet is safe. I'm not opening a legal boutique across the street."

Frank wasn't listening. His cheeks puffed into fat plums, and he shouted, "You ungrateful son of a bitch."

Michael stood. "Save your heart attack for something real. I'm not taking a long list of clients with me." He let out a quick breath. "I've accepted a position in program development with the Boys & Girls Club of America."

"The Boys & Girls Club? You're kidding?"

"I'm serious."

"They can't pay very much."

"My salary is crashing."

Frank sat down. He picked up a pen and rapped it on his palm. "Do you need help, Michael?"

"Help?"

"This is a crazy decision. You've been with this firm a long time and have a stellar performance record. If you need to take a leave to get some counseling, it's yours." He set the pen on the table. "We all have times like this."

Michael tried to suppress a smile. "Thanks, Frank, but I'm fine. In fact, I'm better than I've ever been."

"If you're serious about quitting, what can I do to change your mind?"

"Nothing."

"The firm's annual bonus meeting is next week. All of your cases this year have been resolved through mediation, no lawsuits. I think I can get you five hundred thousand. Of course, that's on top of your salary."

"Whoa."

"Money talks."

"It talks, but I'm not listening." He offered Frank his hand.

Frank ignored it. "This wasn't a ploy to get a bigger bonus?"

"No." Michael's heart pounded. He had just quit his job and refused half a million dollars.

"What does Jamie think?"

342

"I haven't told her yet."

Frank's eyes widened. "I wish you'd get some counseling."

"I'm fine." Michael put out his hand again. "Thanks for everything."

Frank ignored it again. "We'll have to meet quite a bit to get things in order."

Was his *former* boss ever going to shut up? Maybe if he changed the subject. Michael pointed to a framed picture on Frank's desk. "Your kids are turning into adults."

"I know."

"Good looking trio, Frank."

"Thanks. Two in college, and the youngest is a senior in high school. Don't see them much anymore. They're mostly with their mother and stepfather. Living in South Carolina now."

"I see."

"You could've had your kids' picture on that desk one day, but you're throwing the opportunity away." Frank shook his head. "The Boys Club."

Michael looked at the picture again and imagined Jamie married to someone else, only seeing Megan and Emily once in a while. "I'm happy with my choice." He extended his hand yet again. "Thanks, Frank."

Frank stood and shook it this time. "Let's meet on Wednesday at one to discuss you're exit plan."

"Sure."

Michael stepped into the corridor. Thousands of pins and needles prickled his skin, just like in the forest, only more peculiar. He stopped. Something strange was happening inside him. Pinching his chin, he realized what it was. For the first time in years, he left Frank's office without anger. A smile slowly formed on his face.

Michael put his hands in his pockets and strolled through the hall. Greg stepped out of his cubicle and asked a question.

"I'll e-mail you a document that should help. Did you see the ball game last night?" Michael asked.

Greg looked confused. "What?"

"The baseball game. Couldn't believe the Phillies came through in the ninth inning."

"Baseball?"

"It's a game with a bat and a little white ball."

"I know."

"Who are you rooting for in the Series?"

"The Phillies."

"Me too. I'll get you that document as soon as I get back to my office."

Michael continued walking. This was the first time he could remember having a casual conversation with one of his employees. They were all probably good people, but he never took the time to notice. He passed the exit door and headed toward the elevators. For some reason, Michael didn't feel like sprinting down the stairs.

The revolving door spun him into the outside world. A marble bench on the other side of the street invited him to sit for a while, so he did. The prison he used to call *work* stared at him. His eyes flickered, and his throat thickened. Michael lightly touched the puff beneath his eyes, then his lashes and his lids. They were wet. A single tear dripped down his cheek. Could he be crying? Did he just break the spell his father cast on him? He tasted the tear, now on his finger. Less salty than sweat, just like in his dream, his vision. He willed more to fall, but they didn't. Just a little leak—but a beginning.

He closed his damp eyes and allowed his mind to travel to a faraway land. Luke Skywalker held a laser gun and chased Darth Vader. With a push of a button, light beamed, and his enemy vanished. When the battle ceased, Michael entered the brightness and stepped into Luke Skywalker's body. He flashed a vivid smile as he welcomed the new world.

There's a solution to every problem. It's up to you to find it. Rufus's farfetched philosophy was true. Michael had just proved it by resigning. Now, he had to address an even bigger issue. He had to find Jamie and bring her home.

Michael wiggled his toes. He looked down. His leather shoes weren't choking his feet. In fact, they felt like slippers. He looked toward the heavens and thought about his visit to his father's grave. He had asked for a new pair of shoes, and here they were. "Thanks, Pa," he whispered.

Chapter Thirty-One

Yesterday Michael sensed decay and death when he walked into the hospital; today, hope and healing. His outlook had changed the instant he took charge of his fate—a new day, a new beginning. Luke met him on the sixth floor and escorted him to Rufus's room. A nurse stopped them.

"Immediate family only."

"He is," Luke said.

The nurse eyeballed Michael then Luke. "Are you sure?"

"Yes. He's the man who saved my uncle's life."

"That would make you family," she smiled. "Don't stay too long. He really needs his rest. And one at a time."

"Go ahead. He'll be glad to see you," Luke said.

Rufus lay in a semi-reclined position with a blanket pulled up to his waist. His eyes resembled two rotten peaches with slits in the middle. An intravenous bag hung above the bed, and the monitor still recorded his heart's activity. A tube extended from under the blanket. The bloody pus in the drainage bag made bile rise in Michael's throat, and he turned away. At least the ventilator had been removed.

Except for croupy breathing, Rufus was quiet. Michael touched the bedrail. He couldn't tell if Rufus was sleeping. Michael certainly hoped so. The pain had to be intense. Luke had told him violence was a product of fear. Michael pressed his lips together. Thousands of frightened people must be roaming around. The consequence of this particular beating reinforced his decision to take the job at the club. Music had the power to engage and restore. He couldn't wait to plant this seed in the middle of DC and watch it grow.

"Hero," Rufus whispered.

Michael's heart sank. This vibrant verbose man could hardly get one word out. "Don't talk. I know it'll be hard, but you shouldn't."

Rufus curled four of his fingers down, leaving the middle one to stand on its own.

"Don't make me laugh."

Rufus half smiled.

"Are the meds helping the pain?"

Rufus nodded.

"Just listen." Michael held up his palm. "Promise?"

Rufus nodded.

"I quit my job, and I'm taking the one at the club."

Rufus's eye slits widened.

"I'm joining your army. Gonna fight the war, and we're gonna win."

A tear rolled out of Rufus's eye.

"Luke?"

"Luke knows. I start in one month, and I need a good general. You have to recover, and soon."

"Happy?"

"Shh. Very."

"Jamie?"

"She's thrilled," Michael lied. He actually had no idea how she'd react. "You need to rest. In a couple of weeks, we'll be making a ton of plans."

Rufus inhaled. "Thank…"

"Anytime. And no need to thank me again. I saved your life, and you saved mine. We're even."

Rufus nodded.

"I'll be by tomorrow. Now sleep."

The clutter in the hallway had disappeared, and the scent of lemon furniture polish filled the air. Michael scratched his head and wandered into the kitchen. The countertops glistened and the hardwood floors' gleam had returned. He shrugged, poured two glasses of wine, and headed into the living room. Jamie sat on the couch working on her jigsaw puzzle. She looked up and smiled.

"Where are the girls?" Michael asked.

"Upstairs. Megan's doing her homework, and Emily's building a castle with Legos."

Michael handed Jamie her wine. "It's weird not hearing the TV, and the house is spotless."

"Doesn't it look great? I finally hired a cleaning service now that I'm working. One stress factor busted."

Michael sat down. "You hired a cleaning service?"

"Is that a problem? You've been bugging me to do it for years. How's Rufus?"

The image of Rufus lying in the hospital bed appeared. Michael swallowed hard.

"Is he okay?"

Michael's jaw quivered.

"Are you okay?"

Like a raging river that burst through a dam, Michael's tear ducts erupted. He covered his face with his hands. Jamie pulled him into her arms and gently rocked. He wept into the nape of her neck. It felt right to release the emotion that had been bottled up for years. He didn't even try to stop. Eventually his sobs relaxed into gentle huffs, and he encircled Jamie's waist as she stroked him.

"You cried," Jamie murmured.

"Do you believe it?"

"No. What happened?"

"It's been an eventful day."

"Rufus?"

"He looks horrible. Tubes running out of him. His face is swollen and bruised. He can barely speak."

"That poor man."

Michael sat up. "It makes me sick."

"Does Luke know what happened?"

"Rufus mentioned something about a sandwich and a game. Luke figured he was watching a baseball game on TV, got hungry, and went to the market to buy a sandwich. Someone, or a gang, probably tried to rob him. Rufus resisted, so they beat and stabbed him. It's not right. People have to fear walking to the corner store when they're hungry."

"It's awful and wrong, but that's how it is. You have to be so careful."

Michael cleared his throat and sat up straighter. "It doesn't have to be. There's a lot more good in the world than bad. If the good banded together, things might change."

"I've never heard you talk like that, so altruistic. And the crying?"

Michael took a deep breath.

Jamie pulled back. "Something's different about you."

"Yup."

"What?"

"Do you promise to be open? Think outside of the box."

"What is going on?"

"I resigned today."

Jamie furrowed her eyebrows. "Resigned to do what?"

"Not like that." He paused. "I quit my job."

"No, you didn't."

"Yes, I did. And don't worry about the money. I have it all figured out."

"You quit your job? Don't worry about money?" she said.

"Calm down. It's a good thing."

Jamie stood up and flung out her hands. "Are you crazy?"

"Sit down. We have a lot to talk about."

Jamie walked toward the French doors then turned around. "You are crazy. Call Frank and get it back."

"No. Let me explain."

"I'm going to see Frank tomorrow. Tell him you had a breakdown." She sighed. "How are we going to live?"

"I understand your panic, but it's the best thing that's ever happened to us."

Jamie shook her head.

"Sit down and give me fifteen minutes."

She glared at him, but sat.

"Money first. I checked our accounts, and we have enough to pay our expenses for at least a year."

"Then what? Move in with my dad? Did you even consider discussing this with me first?"

"Shhh. I'm going to trade my BMW in for a Ford Focus. One mega bill gone."

"A Ford? You?"

"Yeah. They're reasonably priced and get great gas mileage. We'll all have to learn to live with less. No more impulse spending. It'll be a lean Christmas."

"A lean Christmas?"

"It'll be good for the girls. Reverse the spoiling. We'll have to sell the house."

"Sell the house?"

"You sound like a parrot. Please listen to plan A. If you don't like it, I have a plan B and C. Again, we'll sell the house. We can buy that barn in Warrenton with the equity. You can take the job with the florist in town, if you want. I'll work for the Boys & Girls Club—take the train to work. The public school system in Warrenton is excellent; their green initiative is something out of the future; it's close to the—"

"Warrenton? The barn? Pam's?"

"Yeah. I did some arranging, not to exclude you, but I needed to build a case. I thought you might have an issue with my resignation."

Jamie could barely speak. "How did you know?"

"You mentioned your trip to Virginia when we were in Ocean City. Then I found Pam's business card in the van with *dream job* written on it; the flyer for the barn too. You wrote *home sweet home* on that one."

"What arranging did you do?" Jamie asked softly.

"We have an appointment to see the barn on Saturday. I called Pam, and she still needs an assistant."

Jamie looked at him as if he were Santa Claus. "This is impossible. I have to be in a dream."

"It's not impossible, but you are in a dream. A dream about to come true."

"What did Pam say?"

"Something like, 'Quit your job at the bank. HSBC won't sink without you.' She's 'up to her elbows in lilies, orchids, and roses. Help!' She wants to 'see your ass in the store by ten on Friday.'"

"The barn? How can we afford two mortgages?"

"We can't. We need to sell this house to get the money for the barn. We should be able to pay cash. Isn't that something?"

Jamie's eyes widened.

"So, here's what we're going to do. If we decide to buy the barn on Saturday—by the way, the realtor said she'd show us other houses too—"

"I don't want another house."

"I'm fine with that. The pictures on the barn's website are amazing. The real estate market is bad right now, so we could get a good deal. We'll make a deposit—tell the sellers we can close in three months. We'll list this house below market value and pray. Do you want to hear plan B?"

Jamie smiled broadly. "I love plan A. Is it really possible?"

"Absolutely. I got this house dirt cheap, put twenty-five percent down, and have been putting extra on the principal every month. We'll even have money left over for a riding mower and, of course, a tractor."

Tears streamed out of Jamie's eyes.

"You're going to be a farmer," Michael said.

"You just gave me my dream."

Jamie's face looked like a fairy flew by and dusted it with gold. Only Michael did it. He had found his wife. "And you so deserve it."

"How'd you quit?"

Michael told her every detail. "I felt like an elephant in a circus show marching around with all the other animals." He twirled his finger. "Frank was the ringmaster and cracked his whip anytime a creature wavered. I stuck my toe out once and liked it. Didn't even mind the crack of the whip. The links of the chain loosened, and this morning I broke them. The elephant walked away."

"I'm overwhelmed. You should have talked to me first."

"For once in my life, I needed to chart my own course. Trust me. I would have trudged around in that circle if leaving meant destitution for you and the girls."

"What made you do it?"

"Rufus's heartbeat on the monitor." Michael took Jamie's hand. "Our heart keeps us alive, and we need to move with its rhythm. I wasn't and neither were you. We had plenty of glitz surrounding us, but inside we were dead."

"You're so right."

"I read an article written by a nurse about the five biggest regrets people have when they're about to die. Guess number one."

"Just tell me."

"It wasn't that they never remodeled their kitchen, took a trip to New Zealand, owned a two-carat diamond ring, or had an elaborate spread under the Christmas tree. People didn't follow their dreams. They were sad before they died because their dreams were going with them."

Jamie squeezed Michael's hand. "Like me pursuing a career in banking when I want to be a farmer."

"Exactly. Why not be that farmer?" Michael felt passion flood his voice. It was if he had just discovered the Holy Grail. "What do you feel like when you're in your garden?"

"Like love is pouring out of me. The earth graciously accepts it and returns my gift with beauty."

"You never told me that."

"You never asked."

"We've known each other twelve years, and we still have so much to learn. By the way, as new as it is for me, that's how I feel when I teach, like love is pouring out of me. The kids graciously accept it and return my gift with music."

Jamie looked toward the ceiling. "Do you think it will be difficult, this dream-chasing thing? I don't know too much about being a farmer."

"It'll be challenging. You'll start with Pam and a small patch of vegetables. See where it goes. I'm researching grants to build a music studio. Maybe dream chasing is like climbing a mountain. You know, finding the trail, stepping onto it. At first you're energetic and it's easy. Then you trip over a root, face a huge boulder, or a steep incline. So you stand up after the fall, find your way around the boulder, and trudge up the vertical. Eventually, you're on top of the mountain with an expansive view of the world."

"So we'll take our dream climb, and the peak will be a deep view of ourselves, our potential."

Michael slapped his thigh. "You've got it!"

Jamie put her palms together. "I'm going to be a farmer." She hesitated. "Is it gone?"

"The ogre?"

Jamie nodded.

Michael made a tight fist and opened it. His hand fell. "Feels gone, but I'm still keeping my appointments with the counselor."

"You're afraid it might come back?"

"That...and I want to learn how to handle anger. It'll scare me if I feel it coming on, and I'm sure it will at some point. Tripping over roots is not pleasant."

Jamie hugged him hard, then pulled back. "How am I going to work for Pam? It'll be a while before we move."

"Call her. She's flexible. Put the kids on the bus in the morning, and I'll be home by 3:30 to get them. I can work here in the late afternoons. You'll probably have to be at the shop some weekends, which won't be a problem."

"You'd do that?"

"Of course. After all you've done. For heaven's sake, you gave up a career for our daughters and roomed with a grizzly bear for years. But all of this doesn't necessarily mean I have to move back in. I'm not trying to buy you."

"You're moving back. I'm not turning away a man who just offered to buy me a tractor. Besides, when I married you, I promised 'for better or worse.' I stayed for the *worse*. I'm not leaving just as the *better* is about to start."

Emily and Megan skipped into the room.

"You guys are hugging," Megan said.

"Is that okay with you?" Jamie said.

"Is Daddy coming home?"

Jamie gazed at her family. "We're all coming home. Our life is about to begin."

One Year Later

The granite staircase sprawled across the center of the vestibule. It split at the halfway point, veering to the left and right, up to the second floor. Michael envisioned a king swathed in a purple velvet robe and a jeweled crown parading down it. The brass railings needed polishing, as did the quarry floor tile, but it wasn't a problem. All part of the renovation plan.

Rufus kicked the bottom step. "I like granite. Strong and solid, from the core of the earth."

Michael ran his hand along a mahogany strip of wall molding. "Constructed before we figured out cheap and easy ways to put a structure together."

"Do you think it'll work?" Rufus asked.

"It might just be perfect. Walking distance to a high school and middle school, on a bus route, plenty of space and the price is right."

"Luke said the district is willing to bargain, too. They can't wait to get rid of this dinosaur, or should I say, dragon of a school."

Michael walked up a couple of steps then leaned on the railing. "It does have a castle feel to it. What do you think?"

"Wait here." Rufus headed down one hallway, then another. When he returned, he said, "We can put the recording studio in the back, the auditorium is perfect for performances, lots of classrooms for practice, lounges and offices. Upstairs—a jam area, group lessons. What else?"

"A radio station and a multi-media center."

"Plenty of room."

"And the cafeteria for eating, of course," Michael said.

"Did you work out a deal?"

"Pizza Hut and China Express are interested in the food court idea as long as they can have a delivery service too. The rent money should cover electric and heating costs, especially if we invest in new windows."

"Buy it," Rufus said.

"That's all I needed to hear."

"Do you have the money?"

"The capital fund raising campaign brought in a couple million. Rock stars, corporations, philanthropists. The support has been incredible. And we won some hefty grants."

Rufus put his hands on his hips and flashed his infectious smile. "Do you believe it?"

"No. This time last year I had just moved into the room above the deli and you were almost dead in the hospital."

Rufus pointed to a scar on his cheek. "The doctors put me back together quite nicely, wouldn't you say?"

"It adds to your character."

Rufus nodded. "And it gives me a story. Gets better every time I tell it."

Michael shook his head. "All this because I decided to stop at Dupont Circle and play a game of chess."

Rufus pointed to his scar again. "And I'm so glad you did."

Luke walked in through the front door along with two representatives from the school district and a realtor. "I'm ready for the grand tour."

"A table's set up in the office. We'll talk first, then explore," Rufus said. He slapped Michael on the back. "Ready to put your dream to work."

A smile flashed on Michael's face. "Never been so pumped. We'll celebrate with a barbecue at the barn after the hike on Sunday."

"Who's going again?"

"You, Luke's family, Jamie, the kids and Pam."

"Ohh."

"What?"

"Pam, with all her yappin' and opinions. Last time we got together she badgered me about buying an iPod for my walks. Why would I want music in my ears when I got the sounds of the world to keep me company?"

Michael chuckled. "You're calling her verbose? And you're just pissed because she beat you at chess."

Rufus's eyes widened. "Am not."

"I think you're smitten. Why don't you ask her to a movie?"

Rufus's jaw dropped.

"You'd never have to worry about Pam being clingy. She likes her space, just like you."

"That woman's been married four times."

"Come on, Rufus. They're waiting for us," Michael said pointing toward the office. "And she doesn't ever want to get married again. Isn't that a plus?"

Michael took a few steps.

Rufus remained still. "What's gotten into you?"

Michael turned on his heels. "Jamie says you light up like the Vegas Strip when Pam walks into the room and Pam's eyes explode like a sparkler when she sees you."

"I think we better get to that meeting," Rufus said in a high voice.

"I'm on my way. You're the one frozen in place."

Rufus exhaled. "I suppose a movie wouldn't hurt. Just for the company."

Michael smiled. "It wouldn't hurt at all."

Silk flowers, hair combs, glue and nail polish covered the knotty pine kitchen table at the barn. Pam filed Jamie's nails into perfect arcs. Setting the buffer down, Pam asked, "What color?"

"Pick red, Mommy," Emily said as she sat on her knees squeezing a line of glue onto the edge of a hair comb.

"No, purple with glitter," Megan said holding up the bottle.

Jamie gazed at the splashes of red on her black Bohemian sundress. "Red wins. Sorry Meg."

"Don't worry. I'll paint your nails any color you want later," Pam said.

"Me too?" Emily asked as she placed a silk lily on the hair comb.

"Of course," Pam said. "First, we'll go to the shop and help Erin close, then dinner at the diner. After that, my house for brownie sundaes and a makeup party."

"Yippee!" both girls exclaimed.

Jamie smiled. "Thanks so much for taking them for the night."

"Are you kidding? I should thank you for letting me steal these two smurfs. We're going to have a blast. Right ladies?"

"I can't wait," Megan said as she placed the floral hair combs into a white boot box.

"Then tomorrow the farmers' market. Do you think people will buy my hair combs?" Emily asked.

"I'm sure you'll sell out, just like your mom's fra diavolo sauce does every week," Pam said as she screwed the nail polish cover on and reached for the sealer. She looked at Jamie. "Did you put the jars in my truck?"

"Boxed up and ready for market," Jamie said. "But that's it for the year. The plum tomato plants have finally stopped sprouting fruit."

"Can you buy some at the grocery store? That way you could sell all winter."

"Are you serious?"

"Sorry Farmer Stolis." Pam sat back and looked at Jamie with teacher eyes. "Now don't touch anything for twenty minutes. You don't want to smudge the polish."

Jamie held her hands out and gazed at them. "Stunning."

Pam slid a hair comb, with a red gardenia attached, into Jamie's hair. "Now stand up, but watch those nails."

Jamie stood, twirled around then curtsied.

"You look beautiful Mom," Megan said.

Jamie shimmied in place.

"Are you and Daddy going to kiss?" Emily asked.

"Lots and lots," Jamie said beaming.

"Yuck," Megan said.

Pam chuckled. "Come on ladies. Let's clean up." She stood and fluffed up Jamie's hair. "You really are gorgeous. What time is Michael coming home?"

"Around 6:30. He's probably finishing up with his counselor right now, then he'll hop on the train."

"He still sees the counselor?"

"Twice a month. He says it helps. Doesn't ever want that ogre to grow back."

"Good for him. And he's really adjusted to the commute, hasn't he?"

"Actually loves it, Pam. He sits on that train and unwinds with a novel—catching up on a ton of reading."

"Does he have an e-reader?"

"Michael and an e-reader?"

"I guess not." Pam rolled her eyes. "Anyway, don't rush to the farmers' market tomorrow morning. The girls and I have it covered." Pam kissed Jamie's forehead. "Have a wonderful anniversary."

The makeup Jamie applied was perfectly balanced, somewhere between glamorous and sweet. The texture of her knee-length dress caused it to cling to her body in all the right places and a tease of cleavage lingered at the edge of the scooped neckline. She wore open-toed shoes with two-inch heels that accentuated the shape of her legs, yet also allowed her to walk without too much effort. Staring at herself in the mirror, she wondered what Michael would think. The farmer was gone for the night—an exotic starlet had taken her place.

She studied herself further, but her self-love session was interrupted by the slam of the front door and Michael's voice.

"Hey guys."

Jaime suddenly felt as apprehensive as a child entering
a dark cave. Would Michael even recognize her? Would he
think she was being silly?

"Where is everybody?" he shouted.

"I'll be down in a minute," Jaime said as she searched the
closet for a jacket or shawl to cover her bare arms and back.
Though she knew after one potent martini, the jacket would
be history.

"Where are the kids?"

"With Pam." She faced the mirror and whispered, "Just
go for it chicken shit. You are a knockout. Now move your
ass and make that man's fantasies seem as dull as the life you
left behind one year ago. You are one hot bitch."

The lecture Jaime gave herself was just what she needed
to step into the role of diva. She opened the bedroom door
and sashayed down the stairs with the confidence of a model
right off the cover of *Vogue Magazine*. She caught Michael's
gaze and promenaded toward him until they were nearly
touching.

Jaime couldn't remember the last time her husband was
speechless, but words seemed to be trapped in his throat.
Michael's eyes were on fire and his lips parted. A speck of
a smile formed on Jamie's face as she released her feminine
energy in his direction. She continued the eye lock, lingering
in the luxury of being a woman who blew thru this man like
a tropical storm. Jaime continued her seduction by taking a
step back, just so Michael could have a better view.

Michael inhaled deeply. He took Jaime's hand and pulled her close. When he leaned in for a kiss, Jamie tilted her neck. As tempted as she was to jump into the main course of the evening, she didn't want to abandon the appetizer.

"Slow your pace running man. We have the whole night."

"The kids are staying at Pam's?" Michael asked as his fingers traveled up and down her back.

"Uh huh. Martinis, brie and candles are waiting for us in the kitchen."

"They can keep waiting," Michael said.

"Oh no they can't. I want my date night." She turned and fell back into the comfort of Michael's body.

"You are so damn beautiful," he said.

Jamie closed her eyes. She had always thought fairy tales were fantasies—a temporary escape from the pain of reality. Snuggled in her husband's arms she changed her mind. After all, she was standing in the great room of her dream home with the man she loved. She had reached the happily ever after part of her story and this enchanted evening was the perfect way to celebrate.

"Happy Anniversary," she whispered.

Acknowledgements

While relaxing with my husband, Keith, on a park bench in Dupont Circle, DC, I witnessed a compelling interaction between two men playing blitz chess. I turned to Keith and said, "Wouldn't that be a great start for a novel?"

And so my journey began. Four years later that idea has been transformed into *A Stop in the Park,* and there are so many to thank for helping me weave my dream into reality.

Susanne Poulette, my dear friend and writing partner, I will always treasure our weekly get-togethers when we shared and critiqued each other's stories. Your creative input, laughs and nods of approval are on every page of this book.

Kim Lamparelli and Carol Bromley, my early readers, who accepted the brave assignment of reviewing my first draft. Your insight, respect, compliments and suggestions are so appreciated.

Robin Ringler, my independent editor and owner of East Line Books and Literary Center. You are an amazing talent.

Your dedication and devotion, not only to *A Stop in the Park*, but to the literary community in the Capitol Region of New York State are invaluable. I am so happy to be part of the East Line family.

The New York State Writers Institute provides aspiring writers an incredible resource. The craft workshops that I refer to as "literary boot camp" are well worth the muscle cramps. I learned so much from all of the esteemed authors I had the privilege of studying with and listening to.

To my consultative team at CreateSpace for your attention and guidance.

To those who went above and beyond with their encouragement and support: Karen Domski, Jane Figueroa, Sharon Groves, Cindy Marra, Jim Panagopoulos, Marilyn Panagopoulos, Janice Prichett, Phil Seward, Frosine Stolis, Jimmy Stolis (thanks for the use of your name—perfect), Nancy Smith, Dennis Sullivan, Margaret Sullivan, Sue Ullman, Pat Worley, my Facebook friends for all of the thumbs up and comments when they were needed the most, my online community of writing friends, and East Line Writers.

To my sons, Max and Greg Morehouse, for taking on the role of parent during this project and supporting me every step of the way.

To my husband, best friend and love, Keith. It's not easy being married to someone who's writing a novel, but you made it seem like a breeze. You listened, respected the hours I needed to follow my dream, offered your honest opinions and shared champagne with me when the occasion called for it. This book would not have been written without your attentive ear and temperate words.